Penguin

The Stories of F

Frank Sargeson was born in Hamilton, New Zealand, in 1903. In 1926 he qualified as a solicitor, though he did not follow that profession. In the same year he went to Europe, 'a walker instead of goggled motorist'. He returned to New Zealand in 1928 and since 1932 has lived at Takapuna in Auckland. Though he has worked for brief periods as a market gardener, milkman, pantryman and freelance journalist, he has devoted the bulk of his time to writing the stories and novels for which he is highly acclaimed.

Frank Sargeson's works include *I Saw in my Dream, Memoirs of a Peon, The Hangover, Joy of the Worm, Man of England Now, Sunset Village*, and *Once is Enough, More than Enough* and *Never Enough!*, the three volumes of his autobiography (published in one volume as *Sargeson* by Penguins).

Frank Sargeson

The Stories of
Frank Sargeson

Penguin Books

Penguin Books (N.Z.) Ltd, 182-190 Wairau Road,
Auckland 10, New Zealand
Penguin Books Ltd, Harmondsworth,
Middlesex, England
Penguin Books, 625 Madison Avenue,
New York, New York 10022, U.S.A.
Penguin Books Australia Ltd, Ringwood,
Victoria, Australia
Penguin Books Canada Ltd, 2801 John Street,
Markham, Ontario, Canada L3R 1B4

First published as *Collected Stories* by Blackwood & Janet Paul 1964
Reprinted 1966
Reprinted by Longman Paul Limited 1969
Reprinted with additional stories as *The Stories of Frank Sargeson*
by Longman Paul Limited 1973, 1974, 1975, 1978, 1980
Published in Penguin Books 1982,
Reprinted 1982

Printed in Hong Kong by Wah Cheong Printing Press Ltd

CONTENTS

Conversation with my Uncle   9
Cats by the Tail   11
A Piece of Yellow Soap   12
Chaucerian   14
The Last War   16
In the Midst of Life   18
White Man's Burden   20
Good Samaritan   23
A Good Boy   26
I've Lost my Pal   30
They Gave her a Rise   35
A Pair of Socks   39
An Affair of the Heart   43
Cow-pats   52
In the Department   54
Three Men   58
An Attempt at an Explanation   62
A Great Day   68
Last Adventure   76
Miss Briggs   83
Toothache   85
Tod   87
Boy   89

Contents

A Hen and some Eggs   *page* 92
Sale Day   95
The Making of a New Zealander   99
An Englishwoman Abroad   106
A Man and his Wife   112
Old Man's Story   117
Big Ben   125
Park Seat   130
Two Worlds   131
A Man of Good Will   135
That Summer   145
'Gods Live in Woods'   228
Letter to a Friend   235
Showers   240
The Hole that Jack Dug   243
The Undertaker's Story   251
The Colonel's Daughter   262
Just Trespassing, Thanks   272
City and Suburban   284
Beau   292
Charity Begins at Home   300
A Final Cure   308
An International Occasion   321
Making Father Pay   342
BIBLIOGRAPHY OF FRANK SARGESON'S IMAGINATIVE
   WRITING   347
COMMENTARY   356
SELECT LIST OF WRITING ABOUT FRANK SARGESON   357

6

PUBLISHER'S NOTE

We wish to thank Mrs Jean Bartlett for her help with the bibliography.

CONVERSATION WITH MY UNCLE

My uncle wears a hard knocker. His wife put him up to it. She says it's the thing for a man in his position, and my uncle's position is pretty good. He's a partner in one of those big firms. He grumbles a bit but who doesn't grumble a bit? I admit that these days his trousers are a bit shiny but people don't look at his trousers. They look at his hard knocker.

It's difficult to have a talk with my uncle. You can walk under his nose in the street and he won't see you, and if you sit next to him on a tramcar he'll find out you're there just as soon as you tell him. It chills you a bit if you're a sensitive person. It's because he's got a lot to occupy his mind. He's often told me that. You see he's on the City Council and one of those Boards, the sort you get paid for being on. Once he stood for Parliament but he didn't get in.

It's very difficult to have a talk with my uncle. It doesn't interest him to listen to what you've got to say any more than it interests him to look into people's faces in the street. But he likes to get going himself. He loves the sound of his own voice and he's all the time waiting for you to finish so that he can get going himself. I know we're all like that a bit, but all of us aren't as commonplace as my uncle. Oh Lord! I hope not. He never reads a book—well, just a murder story now and then.

I've tried talking about lots of things with my uncle but it's too difficult. Once I asked him, suppose he went to a picnic and there was only one banana each, would he try to get two bananas for himself, or three or more? He said he never went to picnics. Now you might think my uncle was trying to be funny. He wasn't. He can't suppose. So I said, say anyone went to a picnic they wouldn't try to monopolise the bananas, would they? Not if they were decent? He said, no, of course not. Then I asked him, what about the social picnic? Social picnic? He repeated the words. He didn't understand and I had to leave it at that. He was so puzzled I felt sorry for him.

Once or twice I've tried talking to my uncle about risky subjects. Just out of devilment. He's an ascetic, my uncle is. He eats only a few mouthfuls of food a day. He's very thin, very cold to shake hands with. His wife says his hard knocker is the thing for a man in his position. I say it's the thing for a man with his asceticism too. He dislikes me when I bring up a risky subject. He says, Change the subject. A decent man doesn't let his mind dwell on those things. He looks very serious, very responsible.

Oh Lord! it's a good job everybody isn't like my uncle. We don't want a world full of dead men walking about in hard knockers.

CATS BY THE TAIL

The other day the boy next door held my cat up by the tail. I thought I'd take his attention off the cat, so I asked him what he liked best in all the world. He told me, cake. I asked him didn't he like holding cats up by the tail? He said he did. He's a dear little chap. He said, 'Will you give me a piece of cake? Will you? Will you? Why won't you give me a piece of cake? Why won't you? Why won't you give me a piece of cake?'

Now I'd always thought Wordsworth was wrong in that bit about the child being father of the man. But I'm not so sure. I've gone about asking people, don't they like cake better than anything else in all the world? And don't they like holding cats up by the tail? They were all quite nice people. They all said, what nonsense! None of them said he liked holding up cats by the tail, and they all mentioned lots of things they liked better than cake. Yet the strange thing was I got the idea that whatever they said they liked was only another form of cake. And something about them told me that none of them had properly grown out of holding cats up by the tail. Well, just between you and me have *you* never felt you'd like to hold a cat up by the tail? And never felt you'd like to be let loose in a cake-shop window with the blinds down?

It all seems to me pretty serious. How are we going to run a League of Nations if we can't take our minds off cake, and holding cats up by the tail? If you asked me I'd say that lots of people must say their prayers like that. 'Will You give me a piece of cake? Will You? Will You? Why won't You give me a piece of cake? Why won't You? Why won't You give me a piece of cake?'

A PIECE OF YELLOW SOAP

She is dead now, that woman who used to hold a great piece of yellow washing soap in her hand as she stood at her kitchen door. I was a milkman in those days. The woman owed a bill to the firm I worked for, and each Saturday I was expected to collect a sum that would pay for the week's milk, and pay something off the amount overdue. Well, I never collected anything at all. It was because of that piece of yellow soap.

I shall never forget those Saturday mornings. The woman had two advantages over me. She used to stand at the top of the steps and I used to stand at the bottom; and she always came out holding a piece of yellow soap. We used to argue. I would always start off by being very firm. Didn't my living depend on my getting money out of the people I served? But out of this woman I never got a penny. The more I argued the tighter the woman would curl her fingers on to the soap; and her fingers, just out of the washtub, were always bloodless and shrunken. I knew what they must have felt like to her. I didn't like getting my own fingers bloodless and shrunken. My eyes would get fixed on her fingers and the soap, and after a few minutes I would lose all power to look the woman in the face. I would mumble something to myself and take myself off.

I have often wondered whether the woman knew anything about the power her piece of yellow soap had over me, whether she used it as effectively on other tradesmen as she used it on me. I can't help feeling that she did know.

Sometimes I used to pass her along the street, out of working hours. She acknowledged me only by staring at me, her eyes like pieces of rock.

She had a way too of feeling inside her handbag as she passed me, and I always had the queer feeling that she carried there a piece of soap. It was her talisman, powerful to work wonders, to create round her a circle through which the more desperate harshnesses of the world could never penetrate.

Well, she is dead now, that woman. If she has passed into Heaven I can't help wondering whether she passed in holding tight to a piece of yellow washing soap. I'm not sure that I believe in Heaven or God myself, but if God is a Person of Sensibility I don't doubt that when He looked at that piece of yellow washing soap He felt ashamed of Himself.

CHAUCERIAN

When I was a young man I used to go to the Unitarian Church. In those days it was the thing for quite a number of young men to go to the Unitarian Church. It was their way of letting people know they had grown up and had independent minds. These days I think it is the thing for young men who want to let people know that they have grown up and have independent minds to join the Communist Party.

Well, I went to the Unitarian Church. As far as I could make out about a dozen other people went there too. Sometimes there were less. There was something wrong somewhere. I couldn't make out just what it was.

Then one lunch hour I went for a walk in Freeman's Bay. In case you don't know I'd better say that Freeman's Bay is that part of Auckland over beyond Hobson Street. It's a very interesting place. Any New Zealand poet who hasn't absolutely dedicated herself to kauri trees and bell-birds couldn't do better than go and live there.

As I was saying, I went for a walk one lunch hour in Freeman's Bay and I saw a big navvy with bowyangs tied round his trouser-legs. He was striding along hand in hand with his little girl, and the little girl had to run to keep up with him; and the next moment they both disappeared into the bar of a pub. I was shocked. You wouldn't blame me for that if you knew how strict my parents were. I didn't know a thing for all that I was letting people know that I had grown up and had an independent mind by going to the Unitarian Church. From where I stood I

14

could see inside that bar and I saw the barman pump up some beer and put it in front of the navvy. The little girl had a rag doll under her arm, and after she had stood on her toes and tried to look over the bar she came out to the door and tried to make the rag doll sit on the door-knob.

Now I admit that in those days I didn't know a thing. My parents had been too strict. But I had read a few books, and I was fond of reading Chaucer's Canterbury Tales. Well, as I stood there watching the little girl trying to make her rag doll sit on the door-knob all my confusion about myself and about the Unitarian Church suddenly left me. I got the idea that what I was looking at was about as near as I'd ever get to the Canterbury Tales outside the covers of a book. I'm not quite clear about how I got inside that bar but I did get in. And I drank two half-handles with the navvy. Sure enough he told me things that might have come out of the Canterbury Tales. And he called me mate. The little girl showed me her doll. It was called Humpty Dumpty and could have done with a dry clean.

Well, it all happened a long time ago; and it's a long story. The navvy and his wife were looking for a boarder.

As I say it all happened a long time ago. The little girl is grown up now, and she's got a mind that's a good deal more independent than mine is. A moment ago she looked over my shoulder and said, 'You big silly, what do you want to write about that for?'

I'm glad I didn't marry that Mabel Tittering who was so good at playing Winking at the only Unitarian Church social I ever went to.

THE LAST WAR

When the last war began I was in Standard IV. We used to write compositions on the war. We weren't bothered over the retreat from Mons, we said it was strategy. All except one boy. He said the Germans were getting the best of it, and we made his life a misery for weeks afterwards. Some of our teachers told us that we were born just at the right time. Such a lot of young men were being killed, and there'd be great careers waiting for all of us.

When the last war ended I was at the High School. We got the news of the armistice on our annual sports day. We all hated having to leave off our sports to go and take part in a demonstration held outside the Post Office. The mayor made a speech, and it bored us to death.

A man from our town came home from the last war without his legs. My mother wasn't satisfied until she made him come to tea. He came, and he answered all our questions; and except for answering our questions he didn't have anything to say. We asked him how many Huns he killed, and what it was like in the trenches. For tea we had cold boiled chicken, with lovely pieces of jelly sticking to it, and fruit salad and cream, and cake with filling nearly an inch thick. Of course we had had things like that for tea right through the war. My mother kept on pressing our hero to eat. Do have some more fruit salad, she said. Oh, *won't* you!

That was how the last war affected us children. We wrote compositions about it, and believed there'd be great

16

careers waiting for all of us; the armistice interfered with our annual sports day, and the man who came home without his legs came to tea. We also got a thrill of pleasure out of reading about the German atrocities; and once, towards the end of the last war we were badly frightened. There was a chance of our father's having to go. He was near the age limit, but he had to fill in a paper saying whether he'd be willing to go or not. We never said anything to each other but we were frightened. We were frightened too that our father would say on the paper that he wasn't willing to go. That was a worse fear. We were frightened in case we should find out that our father was frightened.

Of course the grown-ups were affected by the last war in lots of different ways. A lot of them, I know, actually did go to the war. But my uncles who were farmers were simply made. They gave a certain amount of money and land to the patriotic fund, and in 1920 they sold out and retired.

IN THE MIDST OF LIFE

Frances is my cousin. She housekeeps for her father, my uncle Joe. There are just the two of them living in the house together, Frances and my uncle Joe.

Frances will soon be thirty-five. She's just beginning to get that spinsterish look. She's very unhappy. She hates housekeeping for uncle Joe. Every morning uncle Joe takes her a cup of tea in bed. Sometimes she pretends she's not awake and the cup of tea gets cold. I've known uncle Joe make as many as three fresh pots of tea because of that. He doesn't mind. You see, he's frightened that Frances will clear out and leave him. She's all he's got.

I've noticed that Frances is very particular about her friends—well, if you can call them friends. They have to be the right sort of people, who're sure to say and do only the right sort of thing. Once uncle Joe got friendly with a barmaid. He was lonely no doubt. He took her home to play bridge and Frances wouldn't speak to her. Afterwards there was a row and uncle Joe had to climb down. Frances threatened to clear out, and uncle Joe said, 'Don't do that Frances, you're all I've got.' Evidently he wasn't certain about the barmaid.

Once Frances told me how things stood with her. She said she never had any life at all. I told her I'd noticed plenty of life going on all around. She told me that was nonsense. I said, didn't she think the trouble might be with herself? She told me I was an unsympathetic wretch.

Oh Lord, I don't know what to do about Frances. I've asked her why she doesn't get married, and she's asked me who'd marry her? Who would, indeed! But for the life of me I can't see that it's anyone's fault but her own. You see, she reads only Ethel M. Dell and romances about Wagner and things like that. And she believes them! I mean she's preposterous enough to connect them with life right here in New Zealand in the year 1936. Once she got properly on my nerves and I asked why she didn't try seducing the milkman or something like that? She told me I had a disgusting mind. Well, I don't know. There's a thing of W. H. Davies:

> *It's better that a woman had*
> *A love-child at her breast,*
> *Than live a heartless, selfish maid . . .*

It's only imaginatively true, I know. But I believe it's the imaginative truth that's the truest truth. Only of course you don't want to have an imagination like Ethel M. Dell.

Anyhow, I think I'll give up going to see Frances and uncle Joe. It's too much like going into a cemetery.

WHITE MAN'S BURDEN

It was a long road, that road up North, but I'd been told I'd find a pub there. I did. You may know the sort of pub. It sometimes has a notice up, FREE BEER HERE TOMORROW.

I found I knew the barman and I felt bucked when I saw him. When you're on the road and you see someone you know you feel that way. You can't explain it. I asked him how he was, and he said that he was a ball of muscle. I said it was a hole of a place. Oh boy, but it's a quiet dump, he said. All Dagoes. Do I have some long serves!

We talked and he pumped some air into a benzine lamp and it fizzed and lit up bright enough to blind you. Then I couldn't see out the window but I didn't mind that. The mudflats had looked too fat and juicy, and the hills had looked starved. Why, coming along the road I'd watched a cocky ploughing, and he was turning up yellow clay. If you ask me there's a hell of a lot too much of this land of hope and plenty like that.

I asked Bill if there weren't any *pakehas* and he said there were a few. I can't describe what they're like, he said, except they wouldn't wake up if . . . It was a good crack, but there's a law against putting such things in print.

We heard a car pull up and Bill said it would be only his third or fourth serve that day.

They came in, about six Maoris. They were the fleshy sort, their trousers held up by leather belts that finished with only about half an inch of leather to spare. They asked for hard stuff. They asked me to have some too, and

20

I did. They asked Bill what about him, but he said no. He told me he was keeping strictly off the hops. If you once went on the bust in a place like this it was good-bye McGinnis, he said.

A lot more Maoris came in and a few white chaps. Gosh, Bill was right. They were rough, rougher than the Maoris. Bill said that one of the Maoris wrote the best hand he'd ever seen. I noticed he spoke nicely too. He told me that at one time he was going to be a parson. They all started on hard stuff and went on to beer later. There wasn't a radio, but Bill put an H.M.V. portable on the counter and a pile of records, and they took turns in putting the records on. Puddin' Head Jones was popular, then someone wanted Clara Butt to sing Daddy, but Bill couldn't find the record so for a joke he put on Gipsy Smith singing one of those Blood and Fire hymns.

Talk, there was plenty of talk. You may know the sort of talk. And plenty of cigarettes too. They were all chain smokers. Sometimes they crooned with a crooner and did fox-trots.

Then a woman looked in the door. She gave me a nod. Then she caught Bill's eye and I caught her giving me another nod—a reverse one. Bill winked. He said that I was O.K. When the woman went I asked Bill how he knew I was O.K.

Well, you are, aren't you?

I suppose I am, I said.

A man's got to think first of his living.

I told him that was true enough, but a man had the feeling it was the devil's gospel all the same.

There was a young Maori who came and talked to me. He told me he made money ploughing for whoever would give him any ploughing to do. Then he'd go to town and blow his money in, usually at the races. He told me it made him sick to look at a race. When he'd put his money on he went and stood behind the tote. He liked the talkies too, he said. Joan Crawford was the best actress. If it showed her in bed you always got a better kick out of seeing her in bed

than you did out of seeing anyone else in bed. Well, I told
him that so far as I was concerned Joan Crawford was just
a gangster's girl. Then he asked me if I had a sweetheart.
He said he had a sweetheart. She lived in town, a *pakeha*
girl. She was very good and very young, he said, but too
dear.

While Bill went and had his supper the woman came
and looked after the bar. She was a titian blonde and the
lipstick she was using didn't match. She told me the Maoris
were good customers, and when they'd spent all their
money they didn't want you to let them go on drinking on
credit like the Europeans do. And another thing, they *did*
have a sense of refinement. Why, some evenings when a
few *pakehas* she could name were down it wasn't safe for
her to put her head outside the front door.

Before Bill came back about half a dozen Maoris had
shouted her, and each time she had less than half a glass
beer and the other half she put in out of a bottle that didn't
have a label. Bill told me afterwards that it was squash.
Oh, she was keen enough on the hops he said, but she was
like that. Never missed a chance of making a bit.

I slept out in a shed that night but it was hard to get to
sleep because the row in the bar came across the yard. At
any rate I had Maoris on the brain. You see I was brought
up in the South and never saw many Maoris. But I've seen
the press photos of the Arawas turning out for Lord what's
his name, and the pictures in the Art Gallery. And once I
read a couple of books by a man called Elsdon Best.

Gosh, there's a great day coming for Abyssinia when
civilisation gets properly going there.

22

GOOD SAMARITAN

To-day I met my pal Jones and he said he was all to blazes. Well, let's have a drink, I said, and we went and sat in a pub.

Jones isn't much to look at but he's about the most good-natured man I know. He'd do anything to help you. And he's very touchy. You have to be careful what you say to him. To-day he was upset I could see, so I waited for him to give me the works. Well, he said that last night he was cutting across the rubbish dump down by the station and he saw a man lying behind an oil-drum. The man had on the dungarees that ships' firemen wear. He was lying doubled up and retching something awful. Dry retching.

Drunk, I said.

Jones said yes, it looked like it. I didn't do anything, he said. I walked up and down and then I walked away.

I felt uncomfortable when Jones told me that. And at the same time I felt pleased that it was Jones who saw the drunken fireman and not me.

I didn't know if he was drunk, Jones went on. Someone might have bashed him.

And you didn't do anything?

I walked up and down and then I walked away.

Forget it, I said.

I can't, Jones said. He might have passed out.

He didn't. I've just read the paper.

But Jones shook his head.

Say I'd spoken to him, he said. There were people parking their cars. They might have seen me speak to him.

What of it?

They might have seen me walking away. And he might have passed out even if he was just drunk. My God, if you'd seen him.

I'm glad I didn't, I said.

So am I. You might have done the wrong thing.

How?

You might have tried to help him.

Perhaps I might have, I said, and I felt pleased.

And before you'd helped him fifty yards a policeman would have nabbed him, and maybe you too.

Yes, I said, that's true.

The police would have spoilt a devil of a lot of those New Testament stories, wouldn't they've?

They would. Times have changed.

They have. Police means us, doesn't it? Life now.

Sure, I said.

There's a writer that reckons a drunken sailor's nearer to God than a Presbyterian parson.

That's Chesterton.

Well, he makes out a damn good case for it.

Sure, I said. He does.

And I left a drunken sailor retching his heart out on a rubbish dump. If I'd seen a Presbyterian parson having trouble with his car I'd have offered a hand.

It's the times. They've changed.

People have changed too.

They must have.

That sailor would have hated me if I'd interfered, wouldn't he've? Gosh, say I'd landed him in Court?

You'd certainly have been popular.

It's no good believing in Christianity now, is it?

Not if it doesn't fit in.

Well, it doesn't. I suppose he went back to his ship and skited about the time he'd had.

If he was drunk I suppose he did.

He was drunk. About an hour later I saw him down by the wharf. He was just a bit shaky.

You silly old man, I said. Forget it.

I can't. He might have passed out. I walked up and down and then I walked away.

Times have changed.

Perhaps a few people haven't. Me for instance.

You did the right thing.

I know. By doing the wrong thing.

Forget it, I said.

I can't. My God I wish I could. I just walked up and down and then I walked away. I did the wrong thing and did the right thing. I feel as if I'm going off my block.

Never, I said. We'll have another drink and forget it.

A GOOD BOY

I never wanted to be a good boy. I've got myself into a mess I know, but won't anyone ever understand that? Mother always said, If you take *my* advice you'll always be a good boy. How could I tell her I didn't want to be a good boy?

I was always real sorry for mother and father. They didn't seem to have any pleasure in life. Father never went out after he'd come home from work. He just sat and read the paper. His stomach was bad too, and made noises, and he kept on saying, Pardon. It used to get on my nerves. I used to watch him and mother when I was supposed to be doing my homework. Sometimes the look on mother's face gave me the idea that inside she wasn't properly happy and was wanting pleasure just the same as I was. It used to make me come over all sentimental and I'd have a job to keep myself from crying. She used to say she never had a minute's rest, and she'd keep on darning stockings or something like that right until it was bedtime and she had to go and make father's cocoa. They were good people, both of them. And they expected me to be good too. And how could I tell them that I didn't want to be good?

I couldn't tell them. Instead I pretty often played the wag instead of going to Sunday school and did things like that and they never found out. And when I started going to that billiard saloon I kept that dark too, because father and mother would never have stood for it. It was when I'd left school and could only get odd jobs, and father was

making me swot at book-keeping so I could be an accountant instead of just a dry-cleaner like him.

Gee, but I used to have some fun in that billiard saloon.
Paddy Evans kept it. He'd been a jockey but he'd pulled
a horse and got disqualified. They said it was a crook
business right through like they say all racing is. The trainer
of the horse and the owner and a bookie were all mixed up
in it. You know, crossing and double-crossing each other,
but it was Paddy who got it in the neck. Anyhow Paddy
was a good sort, even though he did have the hardest dial
you ever saw on a man. And so was his wife a good sort
too. Of course they weren't good people like father and
mother, they never went to church or anything like that,
and it's a fact that Paddy ran a book, but they were real
good fun. I'll tell you how fat Mrs. Evans was. She was so
fat she always had to make a split in the top part of her
shoes and sew in a little gusset. She was absolutely full of
fun, made a joke out of everything, and wintertimes when
it was time to close she'd nearly always bring out coffee
and toast.

You know I could never see anything much wrong in
that billiard saloon. Most of the boys never had enough
money to put anything on with Paddy, and billiards is a
good game. It takes a boy's mind off thinking too much
about cuddling girls and other things. And with all those
angles to think about it's as hard as trying to work out one
of those geometry theorems. Me and the boys were all good
cobbers too. They were nearly all boys who worked in
shops and motor places, and they used to ask me things
like what it means when you put & Coy. on a cheque, and
they used to sling off at me when I couldn't tell them.
Well, I don't believe even a bank-manager can say why
you put & Coy. on a cheque. Not properly say. But later
on it was like I've said, I was just one of the boys. They
didn't sling off at me and we were all good cobbers.

Well, of course father found out. I was a bit too big then
for him to give me one of those hidings but gee, the way
he and mother talked at me was like nothing on earth. For

peace and quietness I had to promise I wouldn't go to
Paddy's place any more. Father had his knife into Paddy
properly. He stuck him up in the street and roused him up
hill and down dale, and one day when he happened to see
him riding his bike on the footpath he had him fetched up
in Court. Oh, hang it all, I didn't blame father. He and
mother are both good people, you can't deny it. But it
wouldn't have done any good telling them it's no use trying
to make people good if they don't want to be good.

Another thing, I'd have done anything to please mother
at that time because it was just before my little sister was
born. I'd noticed it was going to happen, and it sort of got
under my skin because there'd been only just the three of
us in our family ever since I could remember. At any rate,
when it did happen it was lucky for me because it gave
father and mother someone else to think about and made
it easier for me to get out at night and see the girl that I've
landed myself in this mess over. She worked in a restaurant
and gee, it was fun to sneak round the back and help her
wash the dishes.

Oh hell, what's the use of going on? I thought while
they're keeping me here in clink I'd write the story of my
life, then perhaps if my little sister reads it when she's
grown up *she* might understand that I never wanted to be
a good boy. But it's all no good. What I've written so far
is all balled up and doesn't explain what I want it to at all.
All I want to explain is that I never wanted to be a good
boy, and how can I explain that?

I killed that girl. Yes. It was because she cracked on that
I was the only fellow she was going with but I found her
out. And what did I do? Did I remember that I never had
been a good boy, and never wanted to be a good boy? Did
I remember how the boys said Paddy Evans' wife used to
go out with a lawyer who bought her a fur coat, and Paddy
just said he wished he'd buy her a muff as well? Did I? No
I didn't. I went all righteous just like father and mother
used to go when they caught me or anyone else playing
them a dirty trick. Gosh, when I killed the girl I felt better

28

and cleaner than I've ever felt in my life. I bet father used to feel just the same as I did then when he used to give me those hidings. I never wanted to be a good boy, but when it came to a sort of test I found I was a good boy after all. I did the right thing. I've told the detectives and the lawyers and the doctors and everybody that over and over again, and they won't believe me. You'd almost believe they think I'm off my block which is just plum ridiculous. I've told them I've never been a good boy, all except that one time when I did the right thing just like father and mother had always tried to teach me. That was the time I killed that girl.

Oh Christ, won't anyone ever understand? I'm all balled up I know, but I'm trying to explain. I never wanted to be a good boy.

I'VE LOST MY PAL

It was early summer, shearing time. Tom and me went into the country and we got a job picking up fleeces in a big shed. After we'd pulled the bellies off the fleeces we had to roll them up and put them in the press. It was a good job. We liked it. We had to work hard and we got covered in sheep grease, but I'll tell you a thing about sheep grease. It comes off best in cold water. And that saves a lot of bother.

I could tell you a lot of things about that shed. You know a lot of lambs are beggars for not sitting still when you're shearing them. There was a shearer who used to go maggoty if a lamb wouldn't sit still. He'd heave it back into the pen. But it's not about the shed I want to tell you. I want to tell you about how I lost my pal Tom.

The shearers used to get tireder than Tom and me did. Evenings they were done in. And most evenings they drank beer and that helped to make them sleepy. All except one. His name was George and he was the one who used to heave the lambs back into the pen. He'd come outside with Tom and me, and we'd sit on the woodpile and smoke cigarettes and tell yarns. Another thing, he'd stand in a tub and wash himself, then he'd dress up. Yes, he'd put on a stiff collar and a go-to-Jesus tie. All to come and sit on the woodpile with Tom and me. We used to think it was funny. He liked himself, we thought. He used to wash himself in the tub in front of everybody, and he was pleased at the things we used to say about the different parts of him. He had a corker body anyhow.

I've Lost my Pal

Well, we used to sit on that woodpile just about every night. I don't know why. It was hot in the kitchen anyhow, and nice and cool out on the woodpile. And of course we were just a couple of kids, and I suppose we felt a bit shy among all those shearers. George used to come and sit there and tell us a lot of yarns. He'd spend a lot of time filing his nails too, and running a comb through his hair. He always wanted to know if he looked nice, and we'd tell him he looked nice as pie. Sometimes he'd go maggoty because one of the dogs would start barking. He said it got on his nerves. He said that was his only trouble in life. His nerves. He said he could stand anything except things that got on his nerves. If anything got on his nerves, well, look out! He said if the dog got on his nerves too much he'd do it in, and he sounded at the time like as if he meant it.

Gosh, I'll never forget those nights on that woodpile. There was a bosker moon too. We were too tired for anything except smoking one cigarette after another, and telling yarns. At least Tom and me were tired. George mightn't have been. I remember he said a bit about how tough he was, and about how no work could ever get him tired. But he said sometimes he sort of got tired inside. It was when he sort of felt everybody he met was too silly to talk to, wouldn't understand him if he did talk. Then, George said, it was the same with him as when anything got on his nerves. So let anybody who made him feel tired like that just look out.

It began this way. George told a yarn about how he'd been stuck up by the police over that old man that was found dead in a swamp. You know, the papers were full of it. There was a bootmark in some mud. George said how the police had looked at his boots but there was nothing doing. He said he had an alibi anyhow. It was the way he told us about it that got Tom narked. Tom reckoned he was making out he did the old man in. Or if he didn't he knew who did. George pretended to get hot under the collar, but you could see he was really pleased the way he'd got Tom thinking things.

Well, the next night George got Tom narked again. Maybe there always was a sort of goody-goody streak in Tom. He told George not to sling off at things so much. It was because George asked him if he wore a white flower on Mother's Day. Tom said he didn't.

Well, I don't either, George said, but if I did I'd have to wear a red one.

And when Tom asked him why, he said it was because he never had a mother. Tom didn't like him saying that. He told him he ought to have more respect for his mother even if she wasn't married. Then George said how he hadn't much time for getting married or regular jobs or anything like that. He said you might as well be dead as work at a regular job and have to keep a nagging wife. He certainly did sling off a lot. Then he wound up by saying he wasn't too shook on women anyhow.

Why not? Tom said. Give me a girl who's on for a cuddle and oh boy!

Right enough, George said, but when I was a kid a joker had me for a pet. See?

Was he a scoutmaster? I asked.

Oh, near enough, George said. He was a Sunday school teacher.

That got Tom narked. He told George he ought to be ashamed of himself for telling things like that.

Righto, kid, George said, forget it. I remember he did a big yawn. It made me think of what he'd said about some people making him feel tired inside. Then he got up off the woodpile and went inside. But first he heaved a few chunks of firewood in the direction of that dog. Off and on it was barking a treat.

Of course I told Tom he was silly to get narked over a thing like that. Just because a fellow told you straight-out about himself there wasn't any need to get hot under the collar. And didn't it take all sorts to make a world, anyhow? I told him he'd get on George's nerves, and hadn't George said look out? And of course Tom argued the point. Mind you, I felt sorry for Tom. He was all the time hoping for a steady job so he could get married. He was a good-looking young chap, Tom was, and mighty fond of loving. Very much so. And naturally he expected everyone to be pretty much like himself. So he didn't like George saying straight-out how he wasn't too shook on women, and how a Sunday school teacher once had him on for a pet. Well, Tom kept on arguing the point, so what with the dog barking fit to get on anyone's nerves I heaved a few more chunks of wood at it and left Tom sitting on the woodpile.

So the next day Tom didn't speak to me much. And this was a day when the lambs that George was shearing were no good at all at sitting still. He kept heaving them back into the pen. One he heaved so far it went whack on the side of the woolshed and fell down whop on the floor. Tom said, For Christ's sake! and George heard him say it. He sort of looked pleased like he had looked that other time when he had Tom thinking things about the old man that was found dead in the swamp. And the next lamb he sheared Tom and I saw him rip the poor little beggar right across the belly. Well, maybe it was an accident, but you sort of felt that George was a bit pleased. Tom went outside and he stayed outside longer than he ought, but I didn't blame him. I didn't blame George either. Well, I did a bit, but you can't expect a shearer to pick up a lamb in his arms and nurse it. Can you now?

As I've said Tom didn't speak to me much that day and I just left him alone. I fancied he didn't want me sitting out on the woodpile with him either, so when one of the shearers asked me to play him whisky poker I said I would. But when I got sick of that I went outside to find Tom. He wasn't on the woodpile, but George was. The dog was barking a treat too, worse than ever before. George was running his comb through his hair and he asked me if he looked nice. I said he did, and he began filing his nails. Then he began crooning a Bing Crosby, but he left off doing that to swear at the dog and heave a few chunks of firewood over that way. I asked him where Tom was and he said he knew but he wasn't splitting.

Well, it looked to me like as if Tom and George had been having another argument. I sat down on the wood-pile and talked to George, and he said how Tom didn't know life, but he believed I did. He told me a lot. Oh, he knew life all right. Maybe he knew too much. At anyrate I could have sat and listened to a chap like that all night if it hadn't been for the way the damned dog was barking. Talk about getting on your nerves! And I thought I ought to be having a look for Tom. I guessed he'd be feeling pretty sore what with me rousing on to him the night before for being silly, and now having another argument with George. So I said I was going to look for him, and George said, O.K. brother. But I hadn't got up off the woodpile before George began walking over to the dog. It barked blue murder the nearer he got to it, and if it didn't do the maddest dance you ever saw on the end of its chain! How George managed to get in on it I don't know, but he did. There was a bosker moon, like I've said, and I just sat on that woodpile and watched George strangle the dog. I couldn't move. I couldn't. You see I knew then what had happened to Tom. For the life of me I couldn't move.

Of course George is going up for it. You'll see about it in the papers. And they're trying to blame him for the old man that was found in the swamp. Maybe he did it but he says he didn't. And he doesn't make any bones about doing Tom in. I don't know. I'm sore at losing Tom. I am that. But I have to admit that he'd sometimes get on your nerves and make you feel tired by arguing silly. Haven't you ever felt like that with anyone? Own up. I bet you have.

THEY GAVE HER A RISE

When the explosion happened I couldn't go and see where it was. I'd been working on the wharves, and a case had dropped on my foot. It put me on crutches for a fortnight.

I was boarding with Mrs Bowman down by the waterfront at the time. She was quite a good sort though a bit keen on the main chance. But I didn't blame her because her husband had cleared out, and to make ends meet she took on cleaning jobs several days a week.

Explosions are like fires, you can't tell how far off they are. But it was some explosion. Mrs Bowman and I were in the kitchen and the crockery rattled, and the dust came down off the light shade. Sally Bowman was working out at the ammunition factory, and Mrs Bowman never said anything but you could see she thought that's where it might have happened. Of course people were talking out in the street and the news came pretty quick.

It was out at the ammunition factory. And they said some of the hands had been blown to smithereens.

Mrs Bowman broke down.

She's dead, she said, I know she's dead.

Well, we couldn't do anything. I went over next door on my crutches and asked the people if they'd find out about Sally and whistle me. Then I'd break the news to Mrs Bowman.

I went back and Mrs Bowman was worse than ever. She'd been getting dinner at the time and she sat there with her head down on the table among the potato peelings. Her hair'd come all unput too, and she looked awful. But she wasn't crying, and you sort of wished she had've been.

She's dead, she said, I know she's dead.

She's not dead, I said.

I know she's dead.

Bull's wool, I said, she's not dead.

Oh God, she said, why did I make her go and work in that factory?

I'll guarantee she's been lucky.

She's all I've got. And now she's dead.

If you don't look out you'll start believing it, I said.

It was no good. She went on a treat. I asked her if she'd like me to get one of the neighbours in but she said no.

I don't want to see nobody no more, she said. Sally's all I was living for, and now she's dead. She was a good girl, she said, she was good to her mother.

Sure, I said. Of course she was good to her mother. So she always will be.

She won't. She's dead.

I couldn't do anything. The worst of it was I had a sort of sick feeling that Sally had been blown up. She was only seventeen and a nice kid too. And Mrs Bowman was as good as a widow. It was tough all right.

Then Mrs Bowman started to pray.

Lord God Jesus, she said, give me back my baby. You know she's all I've got. Do please Jesus Christ Almighty give me back my baby. Please Jesus just this once. Darling Jesus I know I done wrong. I shouldn't ought to have made my Sally go and work in that factory. It was because of the money. I had to make her go, you know I did. But oh sweet Jesus if you'll only give me back my baby just this once I won't never do another wrong thing in my life. Without a word of lie I won't, so help me God.

She went on like that. It sounded pretty awful to me, that sort of praying. Because I'm a Doolan myself, and Mrs Bowman was always down on the churches. You wouldn't have thought she had a spark of religion in her

They Gave her a Rise

at all. Still, it was tough. And I felt like nothing on earth.

The next thing was Sally was brought home in a car, one of those big limousines too. The joker driving had been going home from golf and he'd volunteered. He had to help Sally out of the car and up the steps because she was just a jelly. Her hat was on crooked and she couldn't stop crying. Of course the neighbours all came round but I told them to shove off and come back later on.

Well, Mrs Bowman had kidded herself into believing that Sally had been blown to smithereens. So when Sally walked in she went properly dippy and carried on about her having come back from the dead. So I slung off at her a bit for being dippy and banged about cheerful-like getting them a cup of tea. Sally wasn't hurt at all, but some of the girls had been killed so naturally she was upset. Anyhow I slapped her on the back just to show her mother it wasn't a ghost that had walked in, then Mrs Bowman began crying and you could see she felt better. So both of them sat there and cried until the tea was ready.

I can't believe my eyes, Mrs Bowman said, I thought you was dead.

Well, I'm not dead, Sally said.

I thought you was.

I thought I was too. There's Peg Watson, she's dead.

What a shame, Mrs Bowman said.

And Marge Andrews, she's dead too.

Poor Mrs Andrews.

Mum it was awful. It was just like the noise of something being torn. Something big. A wind sort of tore at you too. And then there was a funny smell.

Anyhow you're not dead. You've been spared.

That wind knocked me over. I thought I was dead then. You've been spared.

Yes I know. But what about Peg Watson and Marge Andrews?

Poor Mrs Andrews, Mrs Bowman said.

Then Mrs Bowman roused on to me for putting too much sugar in her tea.

I thought I'd never taste tea again, Sally said, not when I was knocked over I didn't.

Have another cup? I said.

Mr Doran, Mrs Bowman said, how ever much tea did you put in the teapot?

I made it strong, I said. I thought you'd like it strong.

Anyone would think we was millionaires. Mrs Bowman said.

Sally said she wasn't ever going back to work in the ammunition factory again.

Why not? Mrs Bowman asked. You could see she was feeling a lot better and she spoke quite sharp.

Well I'm not. You never got knocked over by that wind.

I've had things to put up with in my life. Yes I have.

I know you have, mum. But you never got knocked over by a wind like that.

You can't avoid accidents.

I know you can't. But what about Peg and Marge?

Isn't it a shame? Poor Mrs Andrews. Marge was getting more money than you, wasn't she?

Anyhow I'm not going back. So there.

Oh, indeed, young lady, Mrs Bowman said. So that's the way you're going to talk. Not going back! Will you tell me where our money's coming from if you're not? Huh! You'd sooner see your mother scrubbing floors, wouldn't you?

Listen mum, Sally said. Listen. . . .

Well, I left them to it. I went over next door to talk to the people, and you could hear Sally and her mother squabbling from there.

Of course Sally wasn't off for long. And they gave her a rise.

A PAIR OF SOCKS

I wish I'd never gone and bought that pair of socks. That was what started the row between me and Fred.

Fred and me were cobbers right from the time we were kids. We used to go to the same school, and we both used to be little blokes. People used to ask why didn't we grow, and said it must be because we smoked cigarettes. It'd make us lay off smoking cigarettes for a bit. At any rate we always said we'd grow up to be jockeys. And everybody said jockeys had to smoke cigarettes so they'd grow up little blokes. But I suppose it's only a gag like that about Eskimo kids eating candles.

If the teacher would let us we'd always sit together. But it was no good sitting together in one way, because I couldn't do sums no more than Fred could. We'd want to tell each other how to get the sums out right and we couldn't. So we always had to cheat off somebody else or we'd get kept in. But I could do compositions real good and Fred couldn't, so I'd tell him what to put.

You know, its a queer thing that just because a man goes and buys a pair of socks he loses his cobber. But that's what happened to me. I went and bought a pair of socks for Bill Thomas, and Fred turned me down. I'll tell you about it.

Bill was a trainer, and me and Fred used to be his strappers. It was lucky for us we both got jobs with Bill. After we left school we couldn't get jobs nohow. We just used to kick around the town together. Then some days we'd go and hang around the racecourse, and after a bit

Bill wanted a couple of strappers so he took me and Fred on. That was just for a start. He said he'd make good jockeys out of a couple of little blokes like us. Only we'd have to be apprenticed first. Bill used to give us fifteen bob a week and we had most of our tucker out at his place. And after a time we went and lived at his place too, because the racecourse was a good distance out of town, and Bill and his missis rented a house out that way.

Well, if life didn't begin then for me and Fred. Gee, our education began then I can tell you. But maybe I learned a bit faster than Fred did, because Fred always was a shy little beggar. And I wasn't shy a bit. Mrs. Thomas could see Fred was shy too, and she used to tell him he oughtn't to be. She was a real nice woman.

As for Bill, he was the hardest case bloke you ever came across. He was tough. He looked like a racehorse himself. He was all muscle, but not bulgy sort of muscle. And his face was just skin stretched over some bone. He had a gold tooth, too. And the things he used to say. If he saw a lady with a fat stomach he'd say she must have been eating new bread. And if a man had whiskers Bill'd say how he'd swallowed a grey horse and had the tail hanging out of his mouth. He would. Struth, he was a dag.

Bill had some good horses in his stable too. They were bosker horses. Until I went to work for Bill I didn't know how good racehorses are. The way they get fond of a man! They want to lick your hands, and right up your arms too. And bite at you, playful-like. It sort of gets you.

Well, Fred and me had plenty to do. We had to take the horses out exercising, and dress them, and shake their beds up and do things like that. And of course Bill would always come round to give them their feeds, even if some other times he didn't come round much. He was a bit of a one for going on the booze, Bill was. And naturally he had a lot of things to fix up with owners and bookies and other people. But Fred and me always used to get a kick out of him coming round and cracking his jokes. Once we were talking about what it would be like to be dead, and Bill

said, When I go to sleep I want to wake up dead. That's
how I want to die. Struth he was a dag, Bill was.

Of course later on Fred and me used to go round the
meetings with the horses. Those were the times. We'd go
in a G truck with the horses, and most times Bill would
come with us in the truck too. And if he had a win he'd
shout us plenty of beer and cigarettes, though he never
drank anything except gin himself. And didn't Fred and
me get a kick out of taking the horses into the birdcages
and leading them round. I'll say we did. Only Fred
was always a bit shy with so many people looking at
him.

Well, d'you know, now it's all over I can tell you Fred
and me didn't use to appreciate properly those times we
had. Not by a long chalk. It was an education like I've
said. We were so bloody happy all the time. And yet we
didn't know we were happy and that's a fact. And we got
on that well together. Fred was a lot shyer than me. He
was never much of a one to talk and I was. He never even
used to talk to me much. He wasn't so shy if nobody took
any notice of him, but if he saw anyone looking at him too
much, he'd always get in close to me. He sort of depended
on me that way, and I'd always try to take anyone's attention off him that was looking at him too much.

There were times I'd feel like getting off on my own for
a bit but I never used to know how Fred would take it.
You see I used to feel sometimes that I'd like to pick up
with a sheila, so I'd tell Fred I'd be going off on my own,
and he'd say O.K. And I'd ask him, wouldn't he be going
off somewhere on his own too? And he'd say no, he'd be
waiting for me when I came back. And sure enough he
always would be. I'd feel it sort of put me in the wrong,
and I'd feel a bit narked with Fred. But he was such a
decent little beggar you couldn't feel narked with him for
long. Anyhow, when he'd say he'd just wait for me I'd feel
sorry for him, so most times I'd forget about the sheila I
thought I might pick up and tell him to come along too.
Then he'd hop round happy as Larry while he was putting

41

his clothes on, and I'd get a kick out of thinking what a hell of a good joker I was.

You'd hardly credit I could bust up all that life Fred and me used to have just because I went and bought Bill a pair of socks. Would you?

It was one night when Mrs. Thomas and Bill and Fred and me were having a game of poker. Bill kept on cracking his jokes and saying other things, and Mrs. Thomas said how he'd demoralise us. Though I don't know what demoralise means. Bill said, Shut up you old hen. He did. He used to say things like that to her. And she'd just give him a raspberry, or else she'd lean over the table and kiss him fair on the mouth. Anyhow Bill said how we'd have to play good to beat him because the next day was his birthday, so he was sure to be lucky.

Well, I never thought another thing about it, only the next day Bill sent me into town to do a message, and it just came over me like a flash how I ought to give him something for his birthday. So I went into a shop and bought that pair of socks. They only cost me a bob too.

Now you know. It wasn't two weeks after that Bill gave me and Fred the sack. I didn't blame Bill. Fred was awful. He wouldn't do a thing Bill told him to. He'd do things wrong too, and every chance he got he'd pick on me and go off pop. And of course I'd tell him off back. In the end Bill got fed up so he sacked us both.

Of course it's a good while ago since it happened. But I can't get it out of my mind. I never see Fred now. They say he's got a job on a scow. I couldn't get on with any other trainer either. It was because of the slump. I've got a job in a grocer's shop and I'm trotting a sheila. She's a pearl of a sheila too. But when I think of the life Fred and me used to have, gee, if I don't kick myself and wish I'd never gone and bought that damn pair of socks.

42

AN AFFAIR OF THE HEART

At Christmastime our family always went to the beach. In those days there weren't the roads along the Gulf that there are now, so father would get a carrier to take our luggage down to the launch steps. And as my brother and I would always ride on the cart, that was the real beginning of our holidays.

It was a little bay a good distance out of the harbour that we'd go to, and of course the launch trip would be even more exciting than the ride on the carrier's cart. We'd always scare mother beforehand by telling her it was sure to be rough. Each year we rented the same bach and we'd stay right until our school holidays were up. All except father who used to have only a few days' holiday at Christmas. He'd give my brother and me a lecture about behaving ourselves and not giving mother any trouble, then he'd go back home. Of course we'd spend nearly all our time on the beach, and mother'd have no more trouble with us than most mothers are quite used to having.

Well, it's all a long time ago. It's hard now to understand why the things that we occupied our time over should have given us so much happiness. But they did. As I'll tell you, I was back in that bay not long ago, and for all that I'm well on in years I was innocent enough to think that to be there again would be to experience something of that same happiness. Of course I didn't experience anything of the kind. And because I didn't I had some reflections instead that gave me the very reverse of happiness. But this is by the way. I haven't set out to philosophize. I've set out to tell you about a woman who lived in a bach not far beyond that bay of ours, and who, an old woman now, lives there to this day.

As you can understand, we children didn't spend all our time on our own little beach. When the tide was out we'd go for walks round the rocks, and sometimes we'd get mother to go with us. My brother and I would be one on each side of her, holding her hands, dragging her this way and that. We'd show her the wonders we'd found, some place where there were sea-eggs underneath a ledge, or a pool where the sea-anemones grew thick.

It was one of these times when we had mother with us that we walked further round the rocks than we had ever been before. We came to a place where there was a fair-sized beach, and there, down near low-water mark, was the woman I've spoken about. She was digging for pipis, and her children were all round her scratching the sand up too. Every now and then they'd pick up handfuls of pipis and run over near their mother, and drop the pipis into a flax kit.

Well, we went over to look. We liked pipis ourselves, but there weren't many on our own beach. The woman hardly took any notice of us, and we could have laughed at the way she was dressed. She had on a man's old hat and coat, and the children were sketches too. There were four of them, three girls and a boy; and the boy, besides being the smallest and skinniest, looked the worst of all because he was so badly in need of a hair-cut.

The woman asked mother if she'd like some pipis to take home. She said she sold pipis and mussels. They made good soup, she said. Mother didn't buy any but she said she would some other day, so the woman slung the kit on her shoulder, and off she went towards a tumble-down bach that stood a little way back from the beach. The children ran about all round her, and the sight made you think of a hen that was out with her chickens.

Of course going back round the rocks we talked about the woman and her children. I remember we poked a bit of fun at the way they were dressed, and we wondered why the woman wanted to sell us pipis and mussels when we could have easily got some for ourselves.

Perhaps they're poor, mother said.

That made us leave off poking fun. We didn't know what it was to be poor. Father had only his wages, and sometimes when we complained about not getting enough money to spend, he asked what we thought would happen to us if he got the sack. We took it as a joke. But this time there was something in what mother said that made us feel a little frightened.

Well, later on my brother and I made lots of excursions as far as that beach, and gradually we got to know the woman and her children, and saw inside their bach. We'd go home in great excitement to tell mother the things we'd found out. The woman was Mrs Crawley. She lived there all the year round, and the children had miles to walk to school. They didn't have any father, and Mrs Crawley collected pipis and mussels and sold them, and as there were lots of pine trees along the cliffs she gathered pine cones into sugar bags and sold them too. Another way she had of getting money was to pick up the kauri gum that you found among the sea-weed at high-tide mark, and sell that. But it was little enough she got all told. There was a road not very far back from the beach, and about once a week she'd collect there the things she had to sell, and a man who ran a cream lorry would give her a lift into town. And the money she got she'd spend on things like flour and sugar, and clothes that she bought in second-hand shops. Mostly, though, all there was to eat was the soup from the pipis and mussels, and vegetables out of the garden. There was a sandy bit of garden close by the bach. It was ringed round with tea-tree brush to keep out the wind, and Mrs Crawley grew kumaras and tomatoes, drum-head cabbages and runner beans. But most of the runner beans she'd let go to seed, and shell for the winter.

It was all very interesting and romantic to me and my brother. We were always down in the dumps when our

45

holidays were over. We'd have liked to camp at our bach all the year round, so we thought the young Crawleys were luckier than we were. Certainly they were poor, and lived in a tumble-down bach with sacking nailed on to the walls to keep the wind out, and slept on heaps of fern sewn into sacking. But we couldn't see anything wrong with that. We'd have done it ourselves any day. But we could see that mother was upset over the things we used to tell her.

Such things shouldn't be, she'd say. She'd never come to visit the Crawleys, but she was always giving us something or other that we didn't need in our bach to take round to them. But Mrs Crawley never liked taking the things that mother sent. She'd rather be independent, she said. And she told us there were busybodies in the world who'd do people harm if they could.

One thing we noticed right from the start. It was that Mrs Crawley's boy Joe was her favourite. One time mother gave us a big piece of Christmas cake to take round, and the children didn't happen to be about when we got there, so Mrs Crawley put the cake away in a tin. Later on my brother let the cat out of the bag. He asked one of the girls how she liked the cake. Well, she didn't know anything about it, but you could tell by the way Joe looked that he did. Mrs Crawley spoilt him, sure enough. She'd bring him back little things from town when she never brought anything back for the girls. He didn't have to do as much work as any of the girls either, and his mother was always saying, Come here Joe, and let me nurse you. It made us feel a bit uncomfortable. In our family we never showed our feelings much.

Well, year after year we took the launch to our bay, and we always looked forward to seeing the Crawleys. The children shot up the same as we did. The food they had kept them growing at any rate. And when Joe was a lanky boy of fifteen his mother was spoiling him worse than ever. She'd let him off work more and more, even though she never left off working herself for a second. And she was looking old and worn out by that time. Her back was getting bent with so much digging and picking up pine cones, and her face looked old and tired too. Her teeth were gone and her mouth was sucked in. It made her chin stick out until you thought of the toe of a boot. But it was queer the way she never looked old when Joe was there. Her face seemed to go young again, and she never took her eyes off him. He was nothing much to look at we thought, but although my brother and I never spoke about it we both somehow understood how she felt about him. Every day she spent digging in her garden or digging up pipis, pulling up mussels from the reefs or picking up pine cones; and compared to our mother she didn't seem to have much of a life. But it was all for Joe, and so long as she had Joe what did it matter? She never told us that, but we knew all the same. I don't know how much my brother understood about it, because as I've said we never said anything to each other. But I felt a little bit frightened. It was perhaps the first time I understood what deep things there could be in life. It was easy to see how mad over Joe Mrs Crawley was, and evidently when you went mad over a person like that you didn't take much account of their being nothing much to look at. And perhaps I felt frightened because there was a feeling in me that going mad over a person in that way could turn out to be quite a terrible thing.

Anyhow, the next thing was our family left off going to the bay. My brother and I were old enough to go away camping somewhere with our cobbers, and father and mother were sick of the bother of going down to the bay. It certainly made us a bit sorry to think that we wouldn't be seeing the Crawleys that summer, but I don't think we lost much sleep over it. I remember that we talked about sending them a letter. But it never got beyond talk.

What I'm going to tell you about happened last Christmas. It was twenty odd years since I'd been in the bay and I happened to be passing near.

I may as well tell you that I've not been what people

47

call a success in life. Unlike my brother who's a successful business man, with a wife and a car and a few other ties that successful men have, I've never been able to settle down. Perhaps the way I'd seen the Crawleys live had an upsetting influence on me. It's always seemed a bit comic to me to see people stay in one place all their lives and work at one job. I like meeting different people and tackling all sorts of jobs, and if I've saved up a few pounds it's always come natural to me to throw up my job and travel about a bit. It gets you nowhere, as people say, and it's a sore point with my mother and father who've just about ceased to own me. But there are lots of compensations.

Well, last Christmas Day I was heading up North after a job I'd heard was going on a fruit-farm, and as I was short of money at the time I was hoofing it. I got the idea that I'd turn off the road and have a look at the bay. I did, and had a good look. But it was a mistake. As I've said the kick that I got was the opposite to what I was expecting, and I came away in a hurry. It's my belief that only the very toughest sort of people should ever go back to places where they've been happy.

Then I thought of the Crawleys. I couldn't believe it possible they'd be living on their beach still, but I felt like having a look. (You can see why I've never been a success in life. I never learn from my mistakes, even when I've just made them.)

I found that the place on the road where Mrs Crawley used to wait for a lift into town had been made into a bus terminus, and there was a little shelter shed and a store. All the way down to the beach baches had been built, and lots of young people were about in shorts. And I really got the shock of my life when I saw the Crawleys' bach still standing there; but there it was, and except for a fresh coat of Stockholm tar it didn't look any different.

Mrs Crawley was in the garden. I hardly recognised her. She'd shrivelled up to nothing, and she was fixed in such a bend that above the waist she walked parallel to the ground. Her mouth had been sucked right inside her head,

so her chin stuck out like the toe of a boot more than ever.
Naturally she didn't know me, I had to shout to make her
hear, and her eyes were bad too. When I'd told her I was
Freddy Coleman, and she'd remembered who Freddy
Coleman was, she ran her hands over my face as though to
help her know whether or not I was telling the truth.

Fancy you coming, she said, and after I'd admired the
garden and asked her how many times she'd put up a fresh
ring of tea-tree brush, she asked me inside.

The bach was much the same. The sacking was still
nailed up over the places where the wind came in, but only
two of the fern beds were left. One was Mrs Crawley's and
the other was Joe's, and both were made up. The table was
set too, but covered over with tea-towels. I didn't know
what to say. It was all too much for me. Mrs Crawley sat
and watched me, her head stuck forward, and I didn't
know where to look.

It's a good job you came early, she said. If you'd come
late you'd have given me a turn.

Oh, I said.

Yes, she said. He always comes late. Not till the last bus.

Oh, I said, I suppose you mean Joe.

Yes, Joe, she said. He never comes until the last bus.

I asked her what had become of the girls, but she took
no notice. She went on talking about Joe and I couldn't
follow her, so I got up to leave. She offered me a cup of
tea, but I said no thank you. I wanted to get away.

You've got Joe's Christmas dinner ready for him, I said,
and I touched the table.

Yes, she said, I've got him everything that he likes. And
she took away the tea-towels. It was some spread. Ham,
fruit, cake, nuts, everything that you can think of for
Christmas. It was a shock after the old days. Joe was
evidently making good money, and I felt a bit envious of
him.

He'll enjoy that, I said. What line's he in, by the way?

He'll come, she said. I've got him everything that he
likes. He'll come.

It was hopeless, so I went.

Then, walking back to the road I didn't feel quite so bad. It all came back to me about how fond of Joe Mrs Crawley had been. She hadn't lost him at anyrate. I thought of the bach all tidied up, and the Christmas spread, and it put me in quite a glow. I hadn't made a success of my life, and the world was in a mess, but here was something you could admire and feel thankful for. Mrs Crawley still had her Joe. And I couldn't help wondering what sort of a fellow Joe Crawley had turned out.

Well, when I was back on the road again a bus hadn't long come in, and the driver was eating a sandwich. So I went up to him.

Good-day, I said. Can you tell me what sort of a fellow Joe Crawley is?

Joe Crawley, he said, I've never seen him.

Oh, I said. Been driving out here long?

He told me about five years, so I jerked my thumb over towards the beach.

Do you know Mrs Crawley? I asked him.

Do I what! he said. She's sat in that shed waiting for the last bus every night that I can remember.

He told me all he knew. Long ago, people said, Joe would come several times a year, then he'd come just at Christmas. When he did come it would be always on the last bus, and he'd be off again first thing in the morning. But for years now he hadn't come at all. No one knew for sure what he used to do. There were yarns about him being a bookmaker, some said he'd gone to gaol, others that he'd cleared off to America. As for the girls they'd married and got scattered, though one was supposed to write now and then. Anyhow, wet or fine, summer or winter, Mrs Crawley never missed a night sitting in that shelter shed waiting to see if Joe'd turn up on the last bus. She still collected pine cones to sell, and would drag the bags for miles; and several times, pulling up mussels out on the reefs she'd been knocked over by the sea, and nearly drowned. Of course she got the pension, but people said she saved every penny of it and lived on the smell of an oil-rag. And whenever she did buy anything she always explained that she was buying it for Joe.

Well, I heard him out. Then I took to the road. I felt small. All the affairs of the heart that I had had in my life, and all that I had seen in other people, seemed petty and mean compared to this one of Mrs Crawley's. I looked at the smart young people about in their shorts with a sort of contempt. I thought of Mrs Crawley waiting down there in the bach with her wonderful Christmas spread, the bach swept out and tidied, and Joe's bed with clean sheets on all made up ready and waiting. And I thought of her all those years digging in the garden, digging for pipis, pulling up mussels and picking up cones, bending her body until it couldn't be straightened out again, until she looked like a new sort of human being. All for Joe. For Joe who'd never been anything much to look at, and who, if he was alive now, stayed away while his mother sat night after night waiting for him in a bus shelter shed. Though, mind you, I didn't feel like blaming Joe. I knew how he'd been spoilt, and I remembered how as a boy I'd sort of understood the way Mrs Crawley felt towards him might turn out to be quite a terrible thing. And sure enough, it had. But I never understood until last Christmas Day, when I was walking northwards to a job on a fruit-farm, how anything in the world that was such a terrible thing, could at the same time be so beautiful.

COW-PATS

My father was a cow-cocky, but he couldn't make cow-cockying pay. It was because of the mortgages. He had to get the County Council to give him work on the roads, and until my elder brothers got fed up and cleared off to town he'd make them go out and get work too. It meant that mother and we younger children had to do a fair bit of work on the farm, but of course we didn't know any other sort of life. Anyhow we managed to stick on the farm.

We had to get up early to milk, but we didn't think we were hardly done by. As I've said, we didn't know any other sort of life.

But what sticks in my mind are the seasons when our boots wouldn't be any too good. Sometimes they'd leak so much that mother'd tell us we'd be better off if we didn't wear them at all. Of course some mornings there'd be a frost, and our feet would be pretty cold by the time we'd got the cows into the yard. But one of my brothers found out a good way of warming his feet up. He stuck them into a cow-pat that had just been dropped, and he said it made his feet feel bosker and warm. So we all stuck our feet into cow-pats, and after walking over the frost it was bosker and warm sure enough. Mother wasn't too shook on our doing it at first, but afterwards she didn't mind. So on cold mornings we'd watch out, and whenever a cow dropped a nice big pat we'd race for it, and the one who got there first wouldn't let the others put their feet in.

Then there was the season when mother had to have a

spell. She was absolutely done up, and had to go into town for a week's holiday, and as I was the youngest father let me go too. We stayed at the Lion Hotel, which was kept by my Uncle Sam; and Uncle Sam let us stay there for a week for nothing.

Well, it was after we'd come back from town that I turned up my nose at those cow-pats, and wouldn't put my feet in one no matter how cold it was. My brothers reckoned I thought I'd come back from town a bit too flash for a trick like that. That wasn't the reason, though. No, while we were staying at the hotel I'd seen something that I was holding my tongue over.

All during the week at the hotel I'd be up early, as most kids that age usually are, even if they don't have to milk cows. I'd play round the front door while the porter was washing the steps, and I'd ask him what he did this, that and the other thing for. But most of his answers didn't half satisfy me. Then one morning just as the porter was finishing the steps an old man came along the street and asked if he could warm his hands up in the bucket of water. The porter said, Sure, so the old man put his hands in the water and kept them there until they were warm.

Well, that was something I understood without having to ask any questions. Perhaps it's stopped me from asking a good many questions in my life. I believe it's correct to say you get the best answers out of life if you don't ask any questions.

Of course, after so many years I don't look at it in quite the same way. While you're alive you naturally want to keep yourself warm, and it doesn't matter much how you do it. But at that age to see an old man who might be glad of a few cow-pats to warm himself up in was somehow a bit too much for me.

IN THE DEPARTMENT

He didn't have a handle to his name. If you're one of the small fry in a big Government Department you don't have. It's just Beggs get me that file and step on it.

It was like that all day. Beggs got files and stepped on it. He got them from upstairs and down. He arranged them in piles and then he carried them away again.

Files.

Files.

It was a wonderful way the department had of doing things. If you were one of the big fry you never actually did anything yourself. Well, hardly anything. You certainly spent a lot of time writing minutes on files. But the minutes told somebody else to do things. That was why Beggs had so many files to carry around. He had to look and see who the minutes were addressed to. Then he'd carry the files away. And of course the people he carried them to would write more minutes. And that meant more carrying for Beggs to do.

Files.

Beggs didn't know what the files were about. All he knew was that they had to be carried. Beggs saw a file and he had an impulse to carry it. The big fry of the department had files put on their tables by Beggs and they had impulses to write minutes. So it went on. It was work.

Files.

Work.

The girls banging their Burroughs and typewriters.

In the Department

Beggs was kept hard at it all day, but he didn't mind. He'd got used to it. It was just work. You had so many hours of it to do each day. And all afternoon you watched the clock. And it was lucky there were one or two places you could go and loaf in if you got the chance. Because it helped to keep the clock moving.

All day carrying files.

One of the loafing places was the basement. That was where the stationery was kept, and the two old duds were in charge. They were called the two old duds because years ago they'd had every opportunity to learn the knack of writing minutes on files, and they never had. Instead they'd turned out duds. Here they were getting on to be old men, and all they did was look after the stationery. While upstairs quite young men were writing minutes on files, and doing it so well they had chances of a future. In years to come they'd be so high up they'd have to go to the opening of Parliament.

But down in the basement there was no one to see if the two old duds lit up for a smoke, or took their coats off in the hot weather. And they could always look at the newspaper photographs of the opening of Parliament.

Anyhow the two old duds weren't busy all day writing minutes on files, so when Beggs went down there he didn't get his head bitten off. But sitting about, smoking and talking, passing the time of day. It wasn't work. Beggs didn't feel happy about it.

Files.

Carrying files.

The girls banging their Burroughs and typewriters.

The two old duds just wasted time.

And the two old duds had a way of talking. You never heard anyone else talk like it in the whole building. They talked just like your own father and mother might talk at home if they happened to be a bit broad-minded. Only more so. And you could talk the same way back. It gave you a shock. Upstairs nobody talked to you except to tell you to get a file, or to bite your head off if you didn't step on it. But of course there was nothing wrong with that. It was work. It had to be.

Files.

Work.

No time for talking or any silly nonsense.

The basement was a home away from home. The two old duds never talked about stationery and files and writing minutes on files. One of them was Mr Flyger, and the other was Mr Birtleberry. Mr Flyger did most of the talking and he talked like something out of the Bible. Everybody in the building knew the way he talked. He was getting on to be an old man and he sat there licking his thumb as he went through a pile of stationery. Yet everyone knew he'd fallen in love with a young girl. He told everyone about it, and everyone said he had a tile loose.

I've fallen in love with a young girl, Mr Flyger said.

Mr Birtleberry never took any notice. He'd heard it all so often. But Mr Flyger always looked as if he was nearly crying, and Beggs had to look away.

And there was the time this happened.

Whatever shall I do? Mr Flyger said, I've fallen in love with a young girl. I've gone to her people and they say no. My life is dry sand, and my heart has withered up.

You couldn't laugh. Not in front of Mr Flyger anyhow. It affected everyone the same way. Nobody laughed. But behind his back they said he had a tile loose.

Beggs said he wished it was half-past four.

Files.

Upstairs files to be carried.

And the girls banging their typewriters.

Ah ha, Mr Birtleberry said, she waits for you.

Beggs coloured. As a matter of fact she did wait for him, and in the tramcar going home they'd begun holding hands.

My heart has withered up, Mr Flyger said. My soul is in hell.

Well, why didn't a man laugh?

You'd better look out, Mr Birtleberry said, or you'll end up the same way.

And Beggs said, Says you. But he went on colouring.

When I was a lad, Mr Birtleberry said, I learned my lesson. That one and only time gave me hell.

Yes, Mr Flyger said, my soul will abide with the damned for ever.

All my life, Mr Birtleberry said, there's been that one and only time. It got me down that time but it taught me a lesson. Never again, says I to myself, I've had my fill of being miserable.

And Beggs said, Gee, I don't want to be a bachelor all my life.

Well, that made Mr Birtleberry laugh, and Mr Flyger who hadn't been known to laugh since he'd fallen in love with his young girl laughed too.

Boy, Mr Flyger said, I'd have you know our friend here has a missis and a family of five.

Files.

Upstairs files to be carried, and Beggs went upstairs. The files would take your mind off anything you couldn't understand.

Life was dry sand.

Life was files. You didn't know what they were about. You kept on carrying them.

Endless files to carry.

Files.

Files.

THREE MEN

Listen Marge—don't you think a lot of boys are peculiar these days? They treat you just as if you was a lump of dirt, and what I say is if a girl had any common she'd never even speak to the nasty creatures.

There was Hilda and me the day we went to the races—we didn't buy a race card because Hilda said if you didn't have a card you could always ask some boy to let you have a look at his, and if you knew how to do your stuff you never could tell but what it mightn't end up in a date.

Well, Hilda certainly knows her onions because that's just how it turned out. Only there were two boys instead of one which made it a whole lot better, specially as Hilda went nuts on the little fat one that I wouldn't have had on as a gift. But the other one was a proper he-man and a real gentleman too you could see, and it made my heart go pit-a-pat just standing there talking to him, and he could have asked me to leave home just as soon as he liked and he wouldn't have needed to ask me twice.

Anyhow that afternoon went just like magic, you'd never believe it. I could hardly be bothered to look at the races and I don't believe Hilda could be either, and I didn't care if our horses won or not. They didn't win anyhow. The boys had come in a car and between the races they'd take us over to where it was parked and we'd all have a few spots. Though of course I didn't have too many because I'm not a girl like that. But Hilda can never stop herself from having a fling, so one or two times I had to tell her not to forget she was a lady.

Three Men

It was a great afternoon believe me, but when it came to the last race I got a kind of sad feeling inside me because the boys hadn't said anything about making a date. All the same they said they'd take us back to town in the car and so they did. And I got a thrill out of sitting in the back seat with the one who was a proper he-man, and he put his arm along the seat behind me and I'm telling you this without a word of a lie—I could have sat back and he'd as good as had his arm round me. But I'd never do a thing like that without I got the proper encouragement, because a girl like me shouldn't ought to ever forget that she's a lady. Anyhow I didn't sort of feel safe enough to sit back because the way Hilda's boy was driving after having all those spots was giving me the jitters. And seeing the way Hilda was behaving sitting next to him in the front seat I thought I'd better sit up and set an example or anyone that saw us go past might think it was a real rough party.

Well, the car stopped to let us out at the bottom of Queen street, and you know I could have just sat there and died the way that sad feeling had got me. I've never felt the strength go out of me like that before. But Hilda was just carrying on laughing and giggling with her cheeks all red and I never thought she'd say it, but when she slammed the door shut she said, Don't ask me to go out with you tonight boys because I'd have to break a date. And the boys said, Too bad. And I never know how I did it but I said, Yes boys it's her grandfather's funeral she's got to go to and she's taking me along to play gooseberry.

So then the boys said could they ring us up on the phone? And that was O.K. because we've got the phone on at our boardinghouse, so Hilda wrote the number down on the cover of the fat one's cheque book and they said, Be good girls, and we'll ring you about half-past seven—gee Marge, think of him having a cheque book.

Well you know we flew home just like magic and when we got in Mrs Potter was cooking some apple fritters and they tasted real lovely, only Hilda bolted hers too quick and they gave her the stomachache. And we kept on talk-

ing like mad in front of Mrs Potter which we don't generally do because even if she is a bit deaf she hears a lot
more than you'd think. Though neither of us cared because
we knew she wouldn't mind leaving the key out on the
nail, and I told myself to remember and give her a kiss
before I went out and tell Hilda to too, because you can't
help feeling sorry for the poor old thing what with her
being deaf and having that husband who was always going
on the booze until he ran away and left her to shift for
herself. There's not many girls who'd consider other
people's feelings like that, but it's a crying shame because
if we can't be kind to each other what I say is we all ought
to be dead. And even if Mrs Potter is old like that now I
suppose she must have been a young girl once even if it was
a long time ago. And I suppose Hilda and me (and you too
Marge) will be old like that some day ourselves, though I
can hardly believe it myself and anyhow thank God it
won't be for years and years and years.

Anyhow Mrs Potter said she didn't mind leaving the
key out on the nail and Hilda said she was going to have
a bath and I told her she'd better step on it, so we went
upstairs and while Hilda was having a bath I put on my
new organdie cut on the bias. And then just because I had
nothing better to do I read a book that Hilda said was hot,
but every time you came to a hot place you had to read a
row of dots, and anyhow I had to leave off to go and give
Hilda a peppermint for her stomachache.

Well do you know Hilda was drying herself when the
phone rang so I had to go and answer, and Hilda opened
the bathroom door and stood there in the draught without
a stitch on, and my heart was going pit-a-pat so as I could
hardly speak. And I said Hello, nice and ladylike-like.
Hahlu, that's what I said. And for crying out loud if it
wasn't a lady who'd got the wrong number!

Do you know right from that very instant I just had an
idea that something was going to go wrong, but I never
said a word to Hilda and she never said a word to me, so
of course we never said a word to each other. And I just

went on reading that book but there were so many dots I turned over a good few pages each time, and oh, I forgot to tell you I had to read standing up because I didn't want to sit down wearing my new organdie. And Hilda took a good while making herself looking pretty like she always does, and then do you know the most awful thing happened —I broke out all over with sweat. Really I did, though it's perspiration I *should* say. It just dripped off me like water and I was so hot I had to fan myself with a hanky, and Hilda saw me and said I must be getting breezy. And I tried to tell her how I'd got a line on those boys just as if by magic and they were all kidsteaks. I did honest. And the words just stuck in my throat. So I said, What if the boys wanted us to go joy-riding for miles and miles and miles? And Hilda told me not to be a prude or I'd never get anything except a boy like the answer to the Maiden's Prayer. So I never said another word, and I thought, All right, you just wait.

Well do you know Marge, wait was right because we waited until nine o'clock and the phone never rang once. And Hilda looked awful because she had a lie-down on her bed and you'd nearly have thought she had passed out. It fair gave me the jitters because I got sick of standing up and reading all the dots in that book and when I looked at Hilda I couldn't help thinking of her in a coffin and flowers and a hearse and things like that. So I said, How about going down town and having a milkshake? And she said all right we'd go. And when we were outside in the street Hilda said she wouldn't mind betting they were a couple of pansies anyhow. But I said she could speak for the little fat one if she liked, and if she asked me she had just about all her taste in her mouth.

Well Marge, now I've told you—oh and Marge I nearly forgot, I told Hilda to wait because I'd forgot about giving Mrs Potter a kiss, and do you know you mightn't believe it and she tried to make out she wasn't, but when I went in where she was sitting down there doing her knitting she was *crying*!

AN ATTEMPT AT AN EXPLANATION

About the earliest time in my life that I can properly remember was when I was living with my mother in the front room of a shabby old house in the main street of our town. It wasn't a very big room but we had hardly any furniture to speak of. Among other things there were our beds and a table and a gas stove and mother's sewing machine. And hung up on the window was a cardboard notice that faced the street and said, MENS AND BOYS SHIRTS MADE HERE ALSO BOYS PANTS.

Anyhow mother always seemed to get plenty of sewing to do and most times it would keep her busy every minute of the day, though unless we were having just bread and milk she'd leave off towards evening and I'd help her to cook the dinner. And soon after we'd washed up I'd have to say my prayers and go to bed while mother went on with her sewing. And how long she used to keep on I don't know as the noise of the machine never stopped me from going to sleep.

I suppose I was old enough to have started school, but mother said that as I was all she'd got she wouldn't let me go until I was seven, so if it hadn't been for boys who came with their mothers to get fitted for shirts and pants I might have gone short of playmates. But as it was I could nearly always get boys to stop and play. If it happened to be the right time of the year they'd be interested in my silkworms and sometimes mother would let us play in the street outside, though not too often as she said she didn't want me to turn out a little street urchin.

An Attempt at an Explanation

There was only one day in the week when mother didn't do any sewing and that was Sunday. On that day we'd both have our baths in the bath that our landlady let us use, and then mother would put on her best dress and I'd have to wear my best suit and we'd go off to the Methodist church for the morning service. And I didn't mind going as there was always a children's address and I liked to hear the minister read out of the Bible, and if I got tired of listening to the sermon I'd play with the tassels on the end of mother's fur, or she'd let me take her hand and I'd run my finger round the seams of her glove.

Then on Sunday afternoon I'd have to go to Sunday school but I didn't mind that either, and in the evening mother would always read to me out of the big Bible that we used to have, and most of the stories she read me I knew just about off by heart. It was the biggest Bible you ever saw and it had special pages written all over with the names of my great grandfather's children and who they'd married and the dates and the names of their children and so on. And it had pictures of the people in the stories and I remember that pictures of angels would always make me feel envious because of the beautiful way they could tread on the air. And of course I'd ask the usual questions such as whether angels were hes or shes. They looked like shes in the pictures but the stories always said they were hes, yet mother said they weren't either hes or shes and I'd understand about that when I grew up.

Well, taken all round it was quite a good sort of life.

Then there came a day I'll never forget when I told my mother I was hungry and she didn't take any notice of what I said. Other times when I'd told her that she'd always got up from the sewing machine and given me something to eat, but this time she just went on sewing and didn't say a word. I couldn't make it out at all, but for a bit I went on watching a silkworm cast its skin, then I told her again, but instead of giving me something to eat she said that we were going out for a walk.

I couldn't make it out at all, but mother told me not to

ask any questions so I didn't, but it was all I could do not to, especially when I saw mother take our Bible and tie it up into a brown-paper parcel. Anyhow it was all right to have mother go for a walk like that so I told her only once more that I was hungry and after she'd put on her hat and brushed my hair we went along the street and I wanted to help carry the Bible but mother said it was too heavy.

Then we came to a shop that I'd never been inside before, and I can't remember who'd told me but I knew it was a shop where they lent you money. And after mother had waited a bit looking in the window we went inside and when I saw the look on mother's face as she started to talk to the man behind the counter I pretended to look away, but all the time I couldn't help watching out of the corner of my eye. And of course I heard what they said.

Mother started to untie the parcel but the man said it was no good as he didn't lend any money on books and a Bible wouldn't be worth any money anyhow. So mother picked up the parcel again and we came out of the shop, and outside we just stood there watching the people go past, and because of the look on mother's face I felt worse than I'd ever felt in my life up till then. I didn't know what to do or what to say, so I just took hold of mother's hand. And after a bit I asked her couldn't we go for a walk in the park? And mother said yes, so we carried the Bible further along the street and went through the gates into the park.

It was a fine sunny day but there weren't many people in the park, and we walked along the paths and looked at the flowers. And then we sat down on a seat and it was nice and warm sitting there in the sun. There were starlings walking about making pecks at the grass, and blackbirds that hopped along yards at a time and then listened and dug their beaks into the ground and pulled up worms. And I thought it was lovely to sit there and watch the starlings and the blackbirds as I took a great delight in every sort of living creature. At home I had my silkworms and I'd hang over the box for hours at a time watching them eat the mulberry leaves that I gave them, and I knew their life story from beginning to end. And once after I'd been playing at wrestling with another boy I found two little white insects walking across the back of my hand, and before I showed them to mother I watched them for quite a while, and I noticed that you couldn't blow them off with your breath or shake them off just by shaking your hand. They'd just crouch down and hold on tight. But when I showed them to mother she was horrified and said they were lice and they'd live on you, and she told me I was never to play with that boy again. And she gave me a bath straightaway and made me change my clothes. But I thought it was a lot of fuss over nothing. I wouldn't have minded a few lice living on me if I could have found out as much about them as I knew about my silkworms.

At any rate I was having quite a good time sitting there with my mother and I'd forgotten all about being hungry, and that our Bible was lying wrapped up on the seat beside us. Then both of these things suddenly came back into my mind, and it was because our Methodist minister came walking through the park wearing his black hat and his long black coat. Mother and I both watched him coming and he kept on stopping to look at the flowers and touch them with his walking stick, and when he passed our seat and saw who it was he raised his hat to mother and stopped and said what a nice day it was. And then he went on, and right across the park he kept on stopping to look at the flowers and touch them with his walking stick.

Well, I couldn't help it. I started to cry. And of course mother thought I was crying because I was hungry. She said to me, You must stop crying this instant. But I couldn't stop. And I wasn't crying because I was hungry, though at the time I didn't have the reason at all clear in my mind.

I don't know that I can explain it even now, but I know I wasn't crying just because of myself personally. I think it was because for the first time in my life I understood how different sorts of things are all connected up together. I thought of the way my silkworms ate the mulberry leaves that I gave them, and the way the lice had crouched down

65

and held on tight to my hand when I tried to shake them off. And there, right in front of me, the birds were looking for food, and the worms that themselves wanted something to eat were being eaten by the blackbirds. And there came into my heart a pity for all living things that were hungry and needed food.

If I'd been older perhaps I would have made a picture for myself of the earth as just a speck of dirt drifting in space, with human creatures crawling over it and crouching down and holding on tight just as the lice had done on the back of my hand. But I was far too young to make any such picture. All I could do was to see a sort of connection between the lice and the silkworms and the birds and my mother and myself, and then, after you'd taken a sort of jump, our Methodist minister who walked through the park touching the flowers with his walking stick. And as the birds flew away and nobody was there except my mother and myself all my pity was concentrated on my mother. Never in my life did I love her as much as I did at that moment. But it wasn't a personal love. I loved the other things just as much. And I didn't want to take my mother's hand and feel the seams of her glove as I did in church. I didn't want to touch her. And I wished I could have stopped crying as I didn't want her or anyone else to know about the way I was feeling. She didn't know anyhow, because I'm sure she thought I was crying only because I wanted something to eat.

Well, after a while I was able to leave off crying, and it wasn't long before a twelve o'clock whistle blew and people out of shops and offices came into the park to eat their lunches. But my mother and I just went on sitting there being warmed by the sun. And after I'd noticed a few people screw up their lunch papers and put them in the rubbish baskets I went and had a look and found quite a number of crusts and pieces of bread. So I brought them to my mother and she said I wasn't to eat them. But I laughed and said that I was going to. And I did. And soon my mother ate some too, and I noticed that she couldn't

66

help crying a little bit herself. But it only made me laugh all the more, and I went and turned somersaults on the grass and my mother said I was turning out a regular street urchin.

And while my mother was saying that I was turning out a regular street urchin I was laughing to think that we'd had to wrap up our Bible to try to get something to eat, yet our Methodist minister could leave his Bible at home while he went for a walk in the park and touched the flowers with his walking stick.

A GREAT DAY

It was beginning to get light when Ken knocked on the door of Fred's bach.

Are you up? he said.

Fred called out that he was, and in a moment he opened the door.

Just finished my breakfast, he said. We'd better get moving.

It didn't take long. The bach was right on the edge of the beach, and they got the dinghy on to Ken's back and he carried it down the beach, and Fred followed with the gear. Ken was big enough to make light work of the dinghy but it was all Fred could do to manage the gear. There wasn't much of him and he goddamned the gear every few yards he went.

The tide was well over half-way out, and the sea was absolutely flat without even a ripple breaking on the sand. Except for some seagulls that walked on the sand and made broad-arrow marks where they walked there wasn't a single thing moving. It was so still it wasn't natural. Except for the seagulls you'd have thought the world had died in the night.

Ken eased the dinghy off his shoulders and turned it the right way up, and Fred dropped the anchor and the oars on the sand, and heaved the sugar bag of fishing gear into the dinghy.

I wouldn't mind if I was a big hefty bloke like you, he said.

Well, Ken didn't say anything to that. He sat on the

68

stern of the dinghy and rolled himself a cigarette, and Fred
got busy and fixed the oars and rowlocks and tied on the
anchor.

Come on, he said, we'll shove off. And with his trousers
rolled up he went and tugged at the bow, and with Ken
shoving at the stern the dinghy began to float, so Fred
hopped in and took the oars, and then Ken hopped in and
they were off.

It's going to be a great day, Fred said.

It certainly looked like it. The sun was coming up behind
the island they were heading for, and there wasn't a cloud
in the sky.

We'll make for the same place as last time, Fred said.
You tell me if I don't keep straight. And for a time he
rowed hard without sending the dinghy along very fast.
The trouble was his short legs, he couldn't get them properly braced against the stern seat. And Ken, busy rolling
a supply of cigarettes, didn't watch out where he was going,
so when Fred took a look ahead he was heading for the
wrong end of the island.

Hey, he said, you take a turn and I'll tell you where to
head for.

So they changed places and Ken pulled wonderfully
well. For a time it was more a mental shock you got with
each jerk of the dinghy. You realised how strong he was.
He had only a shirt and a pair of shorts on, and his big
body, hard with muscle, must have been over six feet
long.

Gee, I wish I had your body, Fred said. It's no wonder
the girls chase you. But look at the sort of joker I am.

Well, he wasn't much to look at. There was so little of
him. And the old clothes he wore had belonged to someone
considerably bigger than he was. And he had on an old hat
that came down too far, and would have come down further if it hadn't bent his ears over and sat on them as if
they were brackets.

How about a smoke? Fred said.

Sure. Sorry.

And to save him from leaving off rowing Fred reached over and took the tin out of his shirt pocket.

That's the curse of this sustenance, Fred said. A man's liable to be out of smokes before pay-day.

Yes, I suppose he is, Ken said.

It's rotten being out of work, Fred said. Thank the Lord I've got this dinghy. D'you know last year I made over thirty pounds out of fishing?

And how've you done this year?

Not so good. You're the first bloke I've had go out with me this year that hasn't wanted me to go shares. Gee, you're lucky to be able to go fishing for fun.

It's about time I landed a position, Ken said. I've had over a month's holiday.

Yes I know. But you've got money saved up, and it doesn't cost you anything to live when you can live with your auntie. How'd you like to live in that damn bach of mine and pay five bob a week rent? And another thing, you've got education.

It doesn't count for much these days. A man has to take any position he can get.

Yes, but if a man's been to one of those High Schools it makes him different. Not any better, mind you. I'm all for the working class because I'm a worker myself, but an educated bloke has the advantage over a bloke like me. The girls chase him just to mention one thing, specially if he happens to be a big he-man as well.

Ken didn't say anything to that. He just went on pulling, and he got Fred to stick a cigarette in his mouth and light it at the same time as he lit his own. And then Fred lolled back in his seat and watched him, and you could tell that about the only thing they had in common was that they both had cigarettes dangling out of their mouths.

Pull her round a bit with your left, Fred said. And there's no need to bust your boiler.

It's O.K. Ken said.

You've got the strength, Fred said.

I'm certainly no infant.

70

What good's a man's strength anyway? Say he goes and works in an office?

I hadn't thought of that.

Another thing, he gets old. Fancy you getting old and losing your strength. Wouldn't it be a shame?

Sure, Ken said. Why talk about it?

It sort of fascinates me. You'll die someday, and where'll that big frame of yours be then?

That's an easy one. Pushing up the daisies.

It might as well be now as anytime, mightn't it?

Good Lord, I don't see that.

A man'd forget for good. It'd be just the same as it is out here on a day like this. Only better.

Ken stopped rowing to throw away his cigarette.

My God, he said, you're a queer customer. Am I heading right?

Pull with your left, Fred said. But I'll give you a spell.

It's O.K. Ken said.

And he went on rowing and after a bit Fred emptied the lines out of the sugar bag and began cutting up the bait. And after a bit longer when they were about half-way over to the island he said they'd gone far enough, so Ken shipped his oars and threw the anchor overboard, and they got their lines ready and began to fish.

And by that time it was certainly turning out a great day. The sun was getting hot but there still wasn't any wind, and as the tide had just about stopped running out down the Gulf the dinghy hardly knew which way to pull on the anchor rope. They'd pulled out less than two miles from the shore, but with the sea as it was it might have been anything from none at all up to an infinite number. You couldn't hear a sound or see anything moving. It was another world. The houses on the shore didn't belong. Nor the people either.

Wouldn't you like to stay out here for good? Fred said.

Ring off, Ken said. I got a bite.

So did I, but it was only a nibble. Anyhow it's not a good day for fish. It wants to be cloudy.

So I've heard.

I've been thinking, Fred said, it's funny you never learnt to swim.

Oh I don't know. Up to now I've always lived in country towns.

Doesn't it make you feel a bit windy?

On a day like this! Anyhow, you couldn't swim that distance yourself.

Oh couldn't I! You'd be surprised . . . get a bite?

Yes I did.

Same here . . . you'll be settling down here, won't you, Ken?

It depends if I can get a position.

I suppose you'll go on living with your auntie.

That depends too. If I got a good position I might be thinking of getting married.

Gee, that'd be great, wouldn't it?

I got another bite, Ken said.

Same here. I reckon our lines are crossed.

So they pulled in their lines and they were crossed sure enough, but Ken had hooked the smallest snapper you ever saw.

He's no good, Fred said. And he worked the fish off the hook and held it in his hand. They're pretty little chaps, aren't they? he said. Look at his colours.

Let him go, Ken said.

Poor little beggar, Fred said. I bet he wonders what's struck him. He's trying to get his breath. Funny isn't it, when there's plenty of air about? It's like Douglas Credit.

Oh for God's sake, Ken said.

I bet in less than five minutes he forgets about how he was nearly suffocated, Fred said, and he threw the fish back. And it lay bewildered for a second on the surface, then it flipped its tail and was gone. It was comical in its way and they both laughed.

They always do that, Fred said. But don't you wish you could swim like him?

Ken didn't say anything to that and they put fresh bait

on their hooks and tried again, but there were only nibbles. They could bring nothing to the surface.

I'll tell you what, Fred said, those nibbles might be old men snapper only they won't take a decent bite at bait like this.

And he explained that off the end of the island there was a reef where they could get plenty of big mussels. It would be just nice with the tide out as it was. The reef wouldn't be uncovered, it never was, but you could stand on it in water up to your knees and pull up the mussels. And if you cut the inside out of a big mussel you only had to hang it on your hook for an old man snapper to go for it with one big bite.

It's a fair way, Ken said.

It doesn't matter, Fred said. We've got oceans of time. And he climbed past Ken to pull up the anchor, and Ken pulled in the lines, and then Fred insisted on rowing and they started for the end of the island.

And by that time the tide had begun to run in up the Gulf and there was a light wind blowing up against the tide, so that the sea, almost without your noticing it, was showing signs of coming up a bit rough. And the queer thing was that with the movement the effect of another world was destroyed. You seemed a part of the real world of houses and people once more. Yet with the sea beginning to get choppy the land looked a long way off.

Going back, Ken said, we'll be pulling against the wind.

Yes, Fred said, but the tide'll be a help. Anyhow, what's it matter when a man's out with a big hefty bloke like you?

Nor did he seem to be in too much of a hurry to get to his reef. He kept resting on his oars to roll cigarettes, and when Ken said something about it he said they had oceans of time.

You're in no hurry to get back, he said, Mary'll keep.

Well, Ken didn't say anything to that.

Mary's a great kid, Fred said.

Sure, Ken said. Mary's one of the best.

I've known Mary for years, Fred said.

73

Yes, Ken said. So I've gathered.

I suppose you have. Up to a while ago Mary and I used to be great cobbers.

I'll give you a spell, Ken said.

But Fred said it was O.K.

Mary's got a bit of education too, he said. Only when her old man died the family was hard up so she had to go into service. It was lucky she got a good place at your auntie's. Gee, I've been round there and had tea sometimes when your auntie's been out, and oh boy is the tucker any good!

Look here, Ken said, at this rate we'll never get to that reef.

Oh yes we will, Fred said, and he pulled a bit harder. If only a man hadn't lost his job, he said.

I admit it must be tough, Ken said.

And then Fred stood up and took a look back at the shore.

I thought there might be somebody else coming out, he said, but there isn't. So thank God for that. And he said that he couldn't stand anybody hanging around when he was fishing. By the way, he said, I forgot to do this before. And he stuffed pieces of cotton-wool into his ears. If the spray gets in my ears it gives me the earache, he said.

Then he really did settle down to his rowing, and with the sea more or less following them it wasn't long before they were off the end of the island.

Nobody lived on the island. There were a few holiday baches but they were empty now that it was well on into the autumn. Nor from this end could you see any landing places, and with the wind blowing up more and more it wasn't too pleasant to watch the sea running up the rocks. And Fred had to spend a bit of time manoeuvring around before he found his reef.

It was several hundred yards out with deep water all round, and it seemed to be quite flat. If the sea had been calm it might have been covered to a depth of about a foot with the tide as it was. But with the sea chopping across it wasn't exactly an easy matter to stand there. At one moment the water was down past your knees, and the next moment you had to steady yourself while it came up round your thighs. And it was uncanny to stand there, because with the deep water all round you seemed to have discovered a way of standing up out in the sea.

Anyhow, Fred took off his coat and rolled up his sleeves and his trousers as far as they'd go, and then he hopped out and got Ken to do the same and keep hold of the dinghy. Then he steadied himself and began dipping his hands down and pulling up mussels and throwing them back into the dinghy, and he worked at a mad pace as though he hadn't a moment to lose. It seemed only a minute or so before he was quite out of breath.

It's tough work, he said. You can see what a weak joker I am.

I'll give you a spell, Ken said, only keep hold of the boat.

Well, Fred held the dinghy, and by the way he was breathing and the look of his face you'd have thought he was going to die. But Ken had other matters to think about, he was steadying himself and dipping his hands down more than a yard away, and Fred managed to pull himself together and shove off the dinghy and hop in. And if you'd been sitting in the stern as he pulled away you'd have seen that he had his eyes shut. Nor did he open them except when he took a look ahead to see where he was going, and with the cotton-wool in his ears it was difficult for him to hear.

So for a long time he rowed like that against seas that were getting bigger and bigger, but about half-way back to the shore he took a spell. He changed over to the other side of the seat, so he didn't have to sit facing the island, and he just sat there keeping the dinghy straight on. Then when he felt that he had collected all his strength he stood up and capsized the dinghy. It took a bit of doing but he did it.

And after that, taking it easy, he started on his long swim for the shore.

LAST ADVENTURE

The one and only time when I visited a certain seaside place in the far north of New Zealand was when I'd just left school. My mother had had an illness all through the spring, and towards Christmas the doctor ordered her away to the seaside. And as I was finishing with school that summer my father said I might as well have a decent holiday before I started on a job in his office early in the New Year.

In those days it was a quiet place up in the north there, a very old settled place with a row of Norfolk pines planted along the beach, and after living all my life in a country town I thought nothing could have been finer. Although to begin with my mother was rather difficult. She was far from being really well again, and she expected me to stay with her nearly all day while she sat in a deck chair in the shade of the pines. But later on we got to know some of the people in the settlement (they were nearly all retired lawyers and colonels, and people of that type), so most days I could get mother settled in her deck chair among the ladies along at the croquet lawn. They'd promise to keep an eye on her, and then I was free to go off and explore the coast. And it was on one of these occasions that I met the old man my story is about.

You had to walk a fair way along the coast before you came to where he lived. He'd built himself a shack among the sandhills, and he'd mainly used old pieces of corrugated iron. It was a hot sort of place to live in in summer, but then in summer he was hardly ever inside, and wintertime, he said, he could always keep a fire going with the drift-wood that he picked up along the beach.

The first time I came on him he was in having a swim and he seemed to be enjoying himself. He was well sun-burnt, and he had such an extraordinary growth of shaggy hair on his chest that when he stood up chest-high in the water, it floated on the surface like seaweed. He looked very old to me. He had on only a small pair of trunks and he was sunburnt all over, and I thought that at one time he must have been a lot heftier than he was then, as in places his skin hung in folds and reminded me of a rhino-ceros that I'd seen in a zoo. Anyhow we said good-day to each other and he came out of the water and took me up to his shack and gave me a drink of his homebrew. It was the first time in my life I'd tasted any sort of brew, and I must say I found the taste to my liking.

But that first day he didn't open out much, although he told me that his name was Fred Holmes, and he seemed to like having me there to talk to, so it wasn't long before I got into the habit of always heading in his direction when-ever I could leave my mother. He owned an old dinghy and he'd take me out fishing with him, although most of my time I'd have to spend in baling to keep us from sinking. And it was while we were fishing, or while we were lying in the sand after having a swim, that he told me about his life.

He'd been born in a Devonshire market town, and his father had been a solicitor (my own father was a public accountant, I told him), but when he was fifteen he'd cleared out and gone to sea in a windjammer. The trip had been across to New York and he'd got left there. It was over a girl. Her father kept a saloon on the waterfront, and on the night the ship was sailing he thought he'd like to say good-bye to her just once more, even though he'd already said good-bye a good many times over. So he climbed up on some big pipes that were stacked endways underneath her window. But up on top he'd slipped down inside one of the pipes, and that had put the lid on things properly.

The girl's father hadn't taken to him too kindly and he didn't feel like making a row, but there was no way of getting out. So he'd missed his ship, and for a time he'd had a tough spin living from hand to mouth on odd jobs he picked up on the waterfront. But later on he'd got another ship and finished up with her in Fremantle. This time he deserted on purpose. He thought he'd try his luck on the goldfields.

Well, he told me endless tales of his adventures and I suppose they were commonplace enough. I'd read any number of stories of such adventures and had many a wild longing to experience them myself, but they seemed so far removed from the everyday life of a small country town that I supposed I'd never have the courage to make the break. But it was somewhat different hearing them first-hand from Fred Holmes. He had a narrative gift that thrilled me as scarcely any book had ever done, and when I'd go back to the croquet lawn to help mother back to our boarding-house, and be offered a cup of tea when only an hour or so before I'd been drinking the old man's home-brew, I'd feel quite sick at the thought of how tame most people's lives were. Never in my life had I met anyone like Fred Holmes. But I was young, of course, and didn't know much.

The days passed and I could think of nothing but Fred Holmes and his adventures. And each fresh episode that he told me stirred me up more than the one before. His tales were of pearling and wild life in Broome, of life in the mounted police and on the goldfields. Later on he'd come further east and worked on boats running about the islands, for a time he'd run a banana farm in Queensland, and he'd first come to New Zealand in the hope of making a fortune out of picking up ambergris. He hadn't made a fortune, he said, but he'd done fairly well.

I remember particularly one bit he told me about gold prospecting. He told me about the way old-timers would cut a big potato in half and hollow out the centres, then they'd put their mixture of gold and quicksilver in the hollows, bind the pieces together with wire and put the potato in a heap of cinders. The heat would drive off the quicksilver and they'd open the potato and there'd be a lump of gold inside. It was wasteful of course, as you lost the quicksilver, but it was a way. And after a story like that I'd go back to the croquet lawn dreaming of enormous potatoes with enormous lumps of gold inside.

Other times he would tell me grim stories, and I could see that he had a great liking for telling them. There was one about when he was a constable in Boulder City and was sent out with a horse and cart to bring a corpse into town. He picked up the corpse and put it in the back of the cart, and after stopping at every hotel on the way he got back late at night. But when he looked in the cart the corpse wasn't there. So to save himself from getting into trouble he drove back over his route, but without finding the corpse anywhere. Then when he arrived back in the morning the corpse was found in the lock-up. It had fallen out of the cart outside the last hotel he had stopped at. Another constable had found it there, and thinking he was dealing with a drunken man had dragged him along to the lock-up.

But I'm afraid that such stories did not impress me very much. My life up till then hadn't brought me into contact with any corpses, and the sort of adventures that attracted me had no connection with them. And no matter how long I listened to the old man his grim stories would always seem much less real to me than his romantic ones. I much preferred to hear about potatoes with lumps of gold inside.

I had, in fact, almost made up my mind that I'd follow the old man's example and live a life of adventure. He told me that young people hadn't the spirit of adventure in them any longer, and it was a pity that in a new country like New Zealand it had died out so soon. He was quite proud of his life, particularly of the fact that he had been born in a humdrum market town in Devon, and into a very staid and respectable family, yet had struck out for himself and refused to live the tame easy life that he could have lived.

Nevertheless I had my doubts. I asked him whether he didn't wish that now he was old he could live in comfort, and that he'd saved some of his money instead of always spending it on drinking and having a riotous time generally. But he said he had no regrets, and that if you had that attitude to money you'd never get the best out of life. When his time came he would die a free man just the same as he had always lived. Nor had he any intention of ending his days in his shack, he said. He'd been thinking of moving on for some while past, and there'd be lots of exciting times for him yet. It was just that in the meantime he was content to spend his time fishing and swimming and lying in the sun. And on such an occasion he'd always slap himself on the chest and declare that he was still as sound as ever he was. And certainly he seemed to be in the best of health, although there was one time when we were in swimming and after we'd raced over fifty yards or so he stood up rather pale and shaky. I said something about it, but he declared that it was only my imagination. Even so I noticed that he lay down, and was very quiet for a fair while after.

Then it happened that Christmas week began, and a few visitors turned up in the settlement, as well as some of the sons and daughters of mother's croquet-playing friends. So besides croquet there was tennis, and cricket on the beach, and mother insisted that instead of going off so much on my own I should make myself sociable by joining in. And as she was still far from well, and liable to be easily upset I had to fall in with her wishes as much as possible. Several days went by and I didn't get a chance to go along and see old Fred Holmes. But I was thinking of him all the time, and one day when a crowd of us took a launch trip round the Bay I got so sick of listening to back-chat that hardly went beyond tennis and dancing and cricket that I made up my mind. I decided that I would be like the old man and live a life of adventure. I didn't know how or when I

would start on it, but sooner or later, start on it I would.
And perhaps I was helped to make my decision by the
launch's calling in at a place where overseas boats could
come in to load timber. There was a big boat in loading
at the time, and as we went past I watched the men
working aboard. It made my heart beat. Lots of them, I
thought, could tell of adventures as exciting as any of Fred
Holmes's. And some of them looked very little older than
I was. They might be cabin boys or apprentices, I didn't
know what, but if they could get away on such boats so
could I. And I imagined myself persuading Fred to let me
have his dinghy so that some night I could pull out, climb
aboard some such boat, and stow away. Perhaps I could
persuade him to come too and it would be all right, I
thought, to have him with me.

Anyhow, it must have been nearly a week before I got
an opportunity to spend a day with my friend, and it was
early one fine morning when I set out, wearing my bathing
suit, and carrying only a towel and a parcel of lunch. But
just before I was clear of the settlement I had to pass the
little building that was known as the police station, although there was never any constable to be seen, and
whatever duties were necessary were done by the local
storekeeper. Outside was the storekeeper's old Ford truck,
and as I passed the man himself came out of the building
and asked me if I'd lend him a hand. I went inside and
there was a coffin wrapped round with mourning crepe,
and you could see it was just a long box made out of rough
boards. Well, the storekeeper got me to help him to carry
out the coffin and put it on the truck, and I felt rather
uncomfortable having to do such a thing dressed only in
my bathing suit.

The old bloke's not so heavy as I thought he'd be, the
storekeeper said, and as he lit his pipe before driving off I
said I supposed it was somebody local.

Yes, he said, the old bloke who was living just up the
coast. Fred Holmes.

I was too upset to say anything. I just stood there and

watched the storekeeper crank up and drive away, and there were so many ruts in the road I wouldn't have been surprised to see the coffin bounce off the back of the truck.

And thinking the matter over all these years, I've never yet been able to decide why that sight of a coffin bouncing about on the back of an old Ford truck should have had such a profound effect on me. After all, an expensive funeral wouldn't have made things any better. I suppose it was just the shock of waking up to the fact that no matter what sort of life you have, there's always the catch at the end of it.

MISS BRIGGS

There's a woman who lives in my street. Her name is Miss Briggs.

There must be thousands of such women. Such streets too. If you take the whole world, hundreds of thousands.

Miss Briggs rents a room from an old woman who rents an old house from an old man. The old man doesn't rent anything from anybody. Unless you can call taking a taxi renting anything. Or buying a grandstand ticket to see the Springboks.

The house is a very old house. Once it was a grocer's shop with rooms to live in upstairs. But the grocer went bankrupt and the old man couldn't get another shop-keeper to take it. So he had the verandah roof pulled down, and the front altered a bit, and a few rooms added on the back. Then he got the old woman as a tenant, and she got a signwriter to paint up the words, GUEST HOUSE.

But the old woman won't take you as a boarder. You have to rent a room. Though she'll always sell you a pig's trotter. I don't know how big a trade she does in pigs' trotters, but she's always got a window full of them, marked 2d each.

Whether or not Miss Briggs eats pigs' trotters I can't say. I shouldn't think so.

I've never spoken to Miss Briggs, although I see her nearly every day. Except on Sundays she's always carrying two suitcases. They're heavy by the way they drag down her shoulders. She's a mere sprig of a woman.

The queer thing is I don't know what Miss Briggs sells. She's never tried to sell me anything. I wonder why. Perhaps she deals in ladies' requisites.

If it's anything masculine why has she never called at my place? Pooh, she needn't think I'm all that hard-up. If I wasn't frightened of frightening her I'd stop her in the street and ask her what she means by it.

Now, would anyone whose line was ladies' requisites be likely to eat pigs' trotters?

Miss Briggs is a goer anyhow. You want to see her on a wet day.

The ladies along at the croquet green have to brave out the wet days too. They have to talk and eat all day without taking any time off to play croquet.

I think I'll write to Mr Ezra Pound about the ladies along at the croquet green. He might like to put them in his next Canto.

On a wet day Miss Briggs gets wet. Well, when you've got rent to pay what can you expect? Even the doctors can't put off their calls just because it's raining.

You know those patent windscreen wipers that doctors have on their cars. Miss Briggs would get on much better if she had the same sort of patent for her glasses.

Miss Briggs never smiles. I've never seen her talking to anyone, and who her customers are I don't know. You'd think she'd go to church but she doesn't go, although one night she went past my place singing Abide With Me.

Love?

Who can say? Could a person go through life without loving somebody?

Sometimes I think Miss Briggs is something I'm always dreaming. But if that is so why don't I dream her coming out of the Guest House eating a pig's trotter?

Miss Briggs?

My goodness yes, Miss Briggs.

TOOTHACHE

He stared hard at the dark but he couldn't see anything. And there wasn't a sound. Yet he knew he
was awake by the feel of the bed and his toothache.
Granma, he said, granma.

There wasn't a sound and he could see only the dark.

Granma, he called out, granma.

And he began crying.

Then he knew his granma was coming, but he didn't
leave off crying. And then he shut his eyes because his
granma was standing there with a candle, and he told her
he had the toothache.

So his granma picked him up and carried him and put
him in her bed. And he stopped crying and watched her
get out a tin full of powder and put it on the chair beside
the bed. She was an old woman with only a few bits of hair
hanging down, and she was big and fat in her white
nightgown.

Then he felt the toothache again and cried, but his
granma blew out the candle and the bed went up and
down as she got in. And a moment later her finger slid into
his mouth and rubbed some of the powder into his hollow
tooth. First it gave him a taste in his mouth and then he
didn't feel the toothache.

His granma was big and fat and warm. She held him in
her arms and he pushed his face into her fat. She had a
certain smell but he liked it, and it couldn't have been
longer than a minute or two before he'd gone to sleep.

D   85

But his granma didn't go to sleep. She was just a fat old woman with a few bits of hair hanging down, and she lay there, quite still, holding the boy in her arms.

And all night she was staring hard at the dark.

TOD

The little boy and his sister, somewhat younger, stood by the fence and sang out, Tod! You sing out, he said. And she sang out, Tod! Then he sang out, Tod!

The kitten came treading over the grass towards them, but when the little boy made a grab it bounded off sideways, its tail in the air, its back arched in a hoop. It stopped to cuff at a dandelion—once, twice, three times, then it ran up a post of the fence and clung there.

The little boy and his sister squealed with delight. They forgot to sing out, Tod!

Kitty, the little boy said, and he made another grab.

This time he caught the kitten. He held it by the loose skin on its back, the kitten struggling, and his sister trying to snatch it from him. The kitten got away and then the little boy hit his sister in the face with both hands. She sat down with a bump and yelled.

Her brother went and stood by the fence. Tod! he sang out. And he kept on singing out, Tod!

The little girl stopped crying and her brother went over and got down beside her. He put his arms round her and tried to give her a kiss, but she turned her face away. So he went and picked the dandelion that the kitten had cuffed.

Here you are dear, he said.

He put the dandelion in her hand, and she let him give her a kiss.

Over by the fence again the little boy sang out, Tod!

87

come on over. Go on, he said, you sing out. And she sang out too. And then they both sang out together.

They went on singing out until the little girl began to hiccup.

Stop doing that, her brother said.

His sister hiccupped and he thumped her on the back.

Leave me alone, she said, and she hiccupped.

He thumped her, and then he swung his arm right back and thumped her as hard as he could.

She yelled again. I'm going to tell on you, she said, and crying for all she was worth she trotted off into the house.

But her brother stayed by the fence, singing out, Tod! Everything would be just all right if only Tod would come on over. And he was far too young to know that he hadn't got the name exactly right.

BOY

For my twelfth birthday my father promised me a box of paints.

If he behaves himself, my mother said.

I didn't say anything. Instead I did one of my famous big sniff-in sniffs. It was a case of urgent necessity.

Wipe your nose, my mother said.

I began counting the days to my birthday, and at the rate they went I didn't see how I'd reach my birthday this side of being an old man.

With a week to go I reckoned it was time to remind my father about the paints just in case he'd forgotten. But it turned out I didn't remind him because that afternoon after school I broke the window of the shed in our backyard. It wasn't the first time either, though always an accident of course.

But the last time was almost too long ago to remember. That's how it seemed to me anyhow, though I did sort of somehow remember clearly enough that I'd been promised a thrashing the next time it happened. So I got quite a surprise when all my father did was to promise me a thrashing if it happened again.

It had me properly worried. Things being what they were I didn't feel like reminding my father about the box of paints, but I thought if he could forget one promise he could just as easily forget another.

Anyhow years and years went by and one morning I woke up and found I was twelve years old. It was all too marvellous for words. At breakfast mother gave me six new handkerchiefs and said that no decent twelve year old boy ever went anywhere without a clean handkerchief in his pocket. And father told me that he'd bring the box of paints when he came home from work that evening.

Well, that afternoon after school I was out in the backyard with my shanghai, and when I took a shot at a thrush that came and sat on our gooseberry bush you can guess what happened. My hand slipped of course.

Mother heard the noise and came to the kitchen door.

You know what your father said, she said, and went inside again.

When my father came home I was in my room lying on my bed. I heard him put his bike away in the shed and then I could hear him and mother talking in the kitchen. And then mother called out for me to come to my dinner.

I went, and my father was sitting in his place taking a look at the paper before he carved the meat. I sat down and we had dinner and I never said a word and father and mother never talked much either. And I could see the box of paints wrapped in brown paper lying on the top of the sewing machine.

When he'd finished his dinner my father took out his pipe and pointed.

Your paints are over there, he said.

First you can help me with the dishes, my mother said.

But I dropped the tea-towel when I saw my father light a candle and go out to put another piece of glass in the window.

I'll hold the candle father, I said. And here's the putty-knife father, I said.

I helped him a lot I can tell you. I helped him until he growled at me for helping him and told me to go and help my mother instead.

Later on that evening I painted a thrush in mid-air with a most painful look on its face and half its feathers flying. I told my father and mother it was because I'd landed it with my shanghai.

Neither of them seemed to think much of my painting.

It's half an hour past your bedtime, my mother said.

I felt like telling her it was only twenty-five minutes, but I somehow thought with my father there I'd better not.

But it was only the next day that my father heard me answering my mother back, and oh gee if he didn't lay it on.

A HEN AND SOME EGGS

I think that one time when my mother set a hen on some eggs was about the most anxious time I've ever experienced in my life.

The hen was a big black Orpington, and mother set her inside a coop in the warmest corner of our yard. My brother and I went out one night and held a candle, and mother put the hen in the coop and gave her thirteen eggs to hatch out. And the next morning we ran out and looked inside the coop, and it was wonderful to see the hen looking bigger than ever as she sat on the thirteen eggs.

But besides being wonderful to see the hen sitting on the eggs, it was a worry to see that she had one egg showing. And it was the same way each time we looked. It wouldn't have been so bad if we could have been sure that it was the same egg each time, because mother had put the thirteenth egg in just to see if thirteen was an unlucky number, and if it hadn't hatched out it wouldn't have mattered much. But we couldn't be sure, and we'd go to school thinking that if our hen was silly enough to let each one of the thirteen eggs get cold in turn, then we wouldn't have any of the eggs hatch out at all.

Then an even worse worry was trying to get the hen to eat. We'd put her food just by the hole in the coop but she'd take no notice. And after we'd got tired of waiting to see her come out and eat and had gone away and left her, sometimes the food would disappear, but as often as not it wouldn't. And when it did disappear we could never be sure that it wasn't the sparrows that had taken it. So each time we looked inside the coop we thought our hen was getting thinner and thinner, and if there happened to be two eggs showing instead of one we were sure that it was so, and we said that after all our trouble there probably wouldn't be one egg that'd hatch out after all. And we thought that our hen might be even silly enough to let herself starve to death.

Then one Saturday morning when it was nearly time for the eggs to hatch out, something terrible happened. My brother and I were chopping kindling wood in the yard and suddenly my brother said, Look! And there was the hen walking up and down inside the wire-netting part of the coop, something which we had never seen her doing before.

We thought she must be hungry, so as fast as we could we took her some wheat. But the hen didn't seem to be hungry, and instead of eating the wheat she started cackling, and if we stayed near her she'd run up and down inside the wire-netting instead of just walking. Well, we went and told mother, and mother told us to leave the hen alone and she'd go back to the eggs. So we stood in the yard and watched, and the hen went on walking up and down, so we went and told mother again. And mother looked at the clock and said, Give her five minutes from now and see what happens.

Well, the hen went on walking up and down, and we could hardly bear it. It was awful to think of the thirteen eggs getting colder and colder. Anyhow mother made us wait another five minutes, then she came out and we tried to shoo the hen back into the coop. But it was no good, the hen went on like a mad thing, and mother said we'd just have to leave her alone and trust to luck. We all went inside to look at the clock and we reckoned that the hen must have been off the nest for at least twenty minutes, and we said that the eggs couldn't help being stone cold by that time.

Then when we came outside again we saw the most astonishing thing happen. The hen suddenly left off cackling and walking up and down. She stood there without moving just as if she was trying to remember something, then she ran for the hole in the coop and disappeared inside.

Well, it was ourselves who went on like mad things then. But after a few minutes we started talking in whispers, and we chopped our kindling wood round the front of the house so as not to disturb the hen, and we'd keep coming back into the yard to creep towards the coop and look in from a distance, and it was more wonderful than ever to see the hen sitting there, even though she had the one egg showing as usual.

And a few days later twelve of the eggs hatched out, but the thirteenth egg was no good. To this day I've wondered whether it was the same one that was always showing, and whether that was the one that was no good. My brother said that the hen knew it was no good and didn't bother to keep it warm. He may have been right. Children are rather like hens. They know things that men and women don't know, but when they grow up they forget them.

SALE DAY

Victor poked his head in the kitchen door.

Anybody home? he said.

Elsie told him there wasn't. She was putting some chops on to fry, but the fire wasn't going any too good.

Victor pulled his shirt off, and went to have a wash in the scullery sink. There'd been a fire through the fern that he'd been cutting and he was pretty black.

It was sale day, and except for Victor the family had gone into town in the car. Before he'd gone the old man had sent Victor away up to the back of the farm to cut fern. He'd had to take his lunch which meant that Elsie had been left on her own all day. Usually there'd have been the cat for a bit of company. But it happened to be spring. And the cat was a tom.

Out in the scullery Victor made a lot of noise puffing and blowing and slopping water about, then he came back wet and soapy, and groped for his towel. He went over to the stove to dry himself, and Elsie got out of his way. She didn't look at Victor. She finished setting the table.

After a bit Victor flung the towel at a peg and it stuck on. Good shot, he said. He stood there slapping himself on the chest. He was a rather fine-looking young chap and he had plenty of muscle. Elsie turned round and looked at him.

You'll get your death of cold, she said.

Victor didn't say anything.

You ought to put your shirt on, Elsie said.

I will in a mo.

95

Your mother wouldn't have you standing about like that.

Mother doesn't appreciate a man's figure.

Elsie looked at him.

I like myself, I do, she said.

The chops began to sizzle a bit so Elsie went over to look at them and Victor moved aside. Then the cat walked in. It looked pretty thin on it. It stood just inside the door and made a meow at Victor, but you couldn't hear anything.

Hello cat, Victor said.

Silly, Elsie said, call him by his proper name.

Victor stamped his foot at the cat and it crouched but it didn't run.

He stinks, he said. He's randy.

Puss, Puss, Elsie said.

The stinking brute. Don't encourage him.

Pussy cat, Elsie said.

I don't like randy tom cats.

Come on pussy cat, Elsie persisted, where've you been all day?

You'd hate him if he was a she.

Go on, Elsie said, I'm fond of animals.

Elsie turned over the chops with a fork. They weren't sizzling any too good, so she put the pan over the open fire.

I don't particularly like myself, Victor said. Any more than I like that cat.

I'll believe you if you put your shirt on.

I thought you were fond of animals.

Well, I am.

Only randy tom cats.

Elsie didn't say anything.

The cat was pruning its whiskers against the leg of the table. Its tail stuck up straight. Elsie went on talking to it and the cat said meow, but you couldn't hear anything. It was so thin it looked silly.

I hate the sight of it, Victor said. It's randy.

If I hadn't had jobs in hotels I wouldn't know what randy is.

Sale Day

It's just a word, Victor said. A bloody good one.

He left off slapping himself and stroked his muscles instead. The chops were sizzling properly now, and Elsie gave them another turn over.

D'you know, Elsie, Victor said, I nearly came home for lunch.

Elsie didn't say anything.

Yes, I did, Victor went on.

Elsie looked at the clock.

It's time they were home, she said.

High time, Victor said.

The cat came and rubbed itself against Elsie's legs, and she bent over to stroke it.

Don't touch him, Victor said. The randy brute stinks.

It's only nature, Elsie said.

You're nature too, Elsie. So am I.

Well, what about it?

That's what I say. What about it?

Pussy cat, Elsie said.

Nature's bloody awful, Victor went on.

Oh, go on. Put your shirt on.

In a mo. I've got a sensitive nature, Elsie.

Didn't I say you liked yourself?

You're wrong Elsie. And I don't like you kidding to randy tom cats.

Elsie looked at him.

I believe you're cracked, she said, and she picked the cat up and nursed it.

Living all your life on a farm you see too damn much of nature, Victor said. It's no good if you've got a sensitive nature yourself.

You want to take life as it comes.

I bet that's what you did. You're engaged, aren't you Elsie? Give us a proper look at the ring.

No I won't. You can see it good enough.

Well, tell us about the lucky bloke.

That's my business.

O.K. Have it your own way.

97

They stood there, and Victor went on stroking his muscles. Elsie stroked the cat and it started to purr.

I jolly near did come home for lunch, Victor said.

I wouldn't have cared, Elsie said.

That's what you say.

Well, you heard me.

Say I had come home for lunch, Victor went on. The cat wasn't home then.

Elsie poked at the chops with her fork. They were doing now a bit too fast.

I'll hold the cat, Victor said, and he took it. He held it up by the legs with both hands and the cat hung down in a curve, but it didn't leave off purring.

Filthy brute, Victor said.

They're done, Elsie said, poking at the chops. I wish they were home.

She lifted the pan a bit and you could see that the fire was hot underneath.

You want to lift the pan right up, Victor said. They're burning.

Well, Elsie lifted the pan and Victor dumped the cat in the fire. Elsie just stood there, and Victor grabbed the pan and jammed it down on top of the cat.

Then, not far away, you could hear the car, and Victor went over to put his shirt on.

Look here, Elsie, he said, it's a fortnight to next sale day. If I was in your shoes I'd look round for another job.

THE MAKING OF A NEW ZEALANDER

When I called at that farm they promised me a job for two months so I took it on, but it turned out to be tough going. The boss was all right, I didn't mind him at all, and most days he'd just settle down by the fire and get busy with his crochet. It was real nice to see him looking happy and contented as he sat there with his ball of wool.

But this story is not about a cocky who used to sit in front of the fire and do crochet. I'm not saying I haven't got a story about him, but I'll have to be getting round to it another time.

Yes, the boss was all right, it was his missis that was the trouble. Some people say, never work for a woman, women'll never listen to reason. But that's not my experience. Use your block and in no time you'll be unlucky if you don't have them eating out of your hand.

But this time I was unlucky. This Mrs Crump was a real tough one. She and the boss ran a market garden besides the cows. She'd tie a flour-bag over her head, get into gumboots, and not counting the time she put in in the house, she'd do about twelve hours a day, and she had me doing the same. Not that I minded all that much. The best of working on the land is that you're not always wishing it was time to knock off. Nor thinking of pay-day, either, particularly if there isn't a pub handy. I'm not going to explain. If you don't believe me, try it yourself and see.

But twelve hours a day, every day. I'll admit I used to

99

get tired. Mrs Crump would see I was done in and tell me to stop working, and that was just what I was waiting for her to do. But there'd be a look in her eye. She'd say that I wasn't built for hard work, but she wasn't surprised because she'd never met a man she couldn't work to a standstill. Well, after she'd said that I'd just go on working, and if I was feeling cheeky I'd tell her I didn't mind giving her a run for her money. And before those two months were up I was feeling cheeky pretty often. Once she got going about my wages and everything else she had to pay out. She couldn't keep the wolf from the door, she said. Well then, I said, if you can't you'll just have to keep the door shut.

Now I'm running on ahead so I'd better break off again, because this isn't just a no-account story about how I began to get cheeky and put wisecracks across Mrs Crump. It's not about Mrs Crump, she only comes into it. I'm not saying I haven't got a story about her too, but it's another one I'll be getting round to another time.

What I want to tell is about how I sat on a hillside one evening and talked with a man. That's all, just a summer evening and a talk with a man on a hillside. Maybe there's nothing in it and maybe there is.

The man was one of two young Dallies who ran an orchard up at the back of Mrs Crump's place. These two had come out from Dalmatia and put some money down on the land, not much, just enough to give them the chance to start working the land. They were still paying off and would be for a good many years. There was a shed where they could live, and to begin with they took it in turns to go out and work for the money they needed to live and buy trees.

All that was some years before I turned up. The Dallies had worked hard, but it wasn't all plain sailing. They had about twenty-five acres, but it sloped away from the sun. They'd planted pines for shelter, but your shelter has to make a lot of growth before it's any use on land with a good slope to the south. And it was poor land, just an inch or two of dark soil on top of clay. You could tell it was poor from the tea-tree, which made no growth after it was a few feet high. Apples do best on land like that, so it was apple-trees the Dallies had mainly gone in for.

Of course Mrs Crump gossiped to me about all this. When I was there the Dallies weren't keeping a cow, so she was letting them have milk at half the town price. She didn't mind doing that much for them, she said, they worked so hard. And my last job each day was to take a billy up to the back fence. I'd collect an empty billy that'd be hanging on a hook, and I'd always consider going on and having a yarn with the Dallies. It wasn't far across to their shed but it would be getting dark, I'd be feeling like my tea so I'd tell myself I'd go over another time.

Then one evening the billy wasn't on the hook and I went on over, but the door was shut and there was no one about. The dog went for me but he never had a show. He'd had distemper, he couldn't move his hind legs and just had to pull himself along. I had a look round but there wasn't much to see, just two flannels and a towel hanging on the line, and a few empty barrels splashed with bluestone. Close to the shed there were grape vines growing on wires, then the trees began. They were carrying a lot of fruit and looked fine and healthy, but just a bit too healthy I thought. You could tell from the growth that the Dallies had put on a lot of fertilizer. For a while I waited about, kidding to the dog until he wagged his tail, then I went back.

The next day one of the Dallies brought the billy over but I didn't see him. When we were milking Mrs Crump told me. He was the one called Nick, and the evening before he'd had to take his mate into hospital. He'd had a spill off his bike and broken some ribs and his collar-bone. Mrs Crump thought perhaps there'd been some drinking, she said they made wine. Anyhow Nick was upset. If his mate died, he said, he would die too. He'd have nothing left, nothing. And how could he work and live there by himself when his mate was lying all broken up in the hospital? Every afternoon he would leave off working and ride into town to see his mate.

There's a pal for you, Mrs Crump said.

Well, up at the fence the billy would always be on the hook, but if Nick was in town seeing his cobber I'd think it would be no use going over. Then one evening he was just coming across with the billy so I went over to meet him. We greeted each other, and I think we both felt a bit shy. He was small and dark, almost black, and his flannel and denims were pretty far gone the same as mine were. I gave him my tin and told him to roll a cigarette, and when he lit up he went cross-eyed. I noticed that, and I saw too that there was a sort of sadness on his face.

I asked him how his cobber was, and he said he was good.

In two days he will be here, he said. You could see he was excited about it and his face didn't look so sad. In two weeks, he said, it will be just as if it never happened.

That's great, I said, and we sat down and smoked.

How's the dog? I said.

He is getting better too, Nick said.

He whistled, and the dog pulled himself over to us by his front paws and put his chin on Nick's leg, and somehow with the dog there it was easier to talk.

I asked Nick about his trees and he said they were all right, but there were too many diseases.

Too much quick manure, I said.

He said yes, but what could they do? It would take a long time to make the soil deep and sweet like it was in the part of Dalmatia he came from. Out here everybody wanted money quick, so they put on the manure. It was money, money, all the time. But he and his mate never had any. Everything they got they had to pay out, and if the black-spot got among the apples they had to pay out more than they got. Then one of them had to go out and try for a job.

It's the manure that gives you the black-spot, I said.

Sometimes I think it is God, Nick said.

Well, maybe you're right, I said, but what about the grapes?

Oh, Nick said, they grow, yes. But they are not sweet. To make wine we must put in sugar. In Dalmatia it is not done. Never.

Yes, I said, but you don't go back to Dalmatia.

Oh no, he said, now I am a New Zealander.

No, I said, but your children will be.

I have no children and I will never marry, Nick said.

No? I said, then your cobber will.

He will never marry either, Nick said.

Why? I said, there are plenty of Dalmatian girls out here. I bet you could get New Zealand girls too.

But Nick only said no no no no no.

If you were in Dalmatia I bet you'd be married, I said.

But I am not in Dalmatia, Nick said, now I am a New Zealander. In New Zealand everybody says they cannot afford to get married.

Yes, I said, that's what they say. But it's all wrong.

Yes, Nick said, it is all wrong. Because it is all wrong I am a Communist.

Good, I said. Well, I thought, spoil a good peasant and you might as well go the whole hog.

I bet you don't tell Mrs Crump you're a Communist, I said.

Oh no, Nick said, she would never be a Communist.

No fear, I said.

I will tell you about Mrs Crump, Nick said. She should go to Dalmatia. In Dalmatia our women wear bags on their heads just like her, and she would be happy there.

Yes, I said, I believe you're right. But Nick, I said, I thought you'd be a Catholic.

No, Nick said. It is all lies. In Dalmatia they say that Christ was born when there was snow on the ground in Palestine. But now I have read in a book there is no snow in Palestine. So now I know that they tell lies.

So you're a Communist instead, I said.

Yes, I am a Communist, Nick said. But what is the good of that? I am born too soon, eh? What do you think?

Maybe, I said.

You too, Nick said. You think that you and me are born too soon? What do you think?

He said it over and over, and I couldn't look him in the face. It had too much of that sadness. . . . I mightn't have put it the way Nick had, I mightn't have said I was born too soon, but Nick knew what he was talking about. Nick and I were sitting on the hillside and Nick was saying he was a New Zealander, but he knew he wasn't a New Zealander. And he knew he wasn't a Dalmatian any more.

He knew he wasn't anything any more.

Listen, Nick said, do you drink wine?

Yes, I said.

Then to-morrow night you come up here and we will drink wine, Nick said.

Yes, I said, that's O.K. with me.

There is only to-morrow night, Nick said, then my mate will be here. We will drink a lot of wine, I have plenty and we will get very, very drunk. Oh, heaps drunk.

Yes, I said. Sure thing.

To-morrow night, he said.

He got up and I got up, he just waved his hand at me and walked off. He picked the dog up under his arm and walked off, and I just stood there and watched him go.

But it turned out I never went up to Nick's place. When I was having my tea that evening Mrs Crump told me about how a woman she knew had worked too hard and dropped dead with heart failure. But there's nothing wrong with my heart, she said.

No, I said, except that maybe it's not in the right place.

Of course it must have sounded like one of my wise-cracks, but I was thinking of Dalmatia.

Anyhow Mrs Crump said she'd stood enough from me, so when I'd finished my tea I could go.

I wasn't sorry. I stood on the road and wondered if I'd

go up to Nick's place, but instead I walked into town, and for a good few days I never left off drinking.

I wanted to get Nick out of my mind. He knew what he was talking about, but maybe it's best for a man to hang on.

AN ENGLISHWOMAN ABROAD

That little piazza in Genoa was a popular place in the evenings, quite a lot of people would be strolling there. There were several cafes, and one side was a terrace where you could lean over the parapet and see the people in the streets lower down, and the harbour in the distance. Of an evening I often went there to stroll and lean over the parapet, to sit at a table and smoke and drink coffee. Sometimes an enormously fat man who carried a straw hat in his hand would go among the tables outside the cafes and sing *La donna e mobile*. That wasn't so good. But if you gave him a few *lire* he'd soon move on, though nobody took much notice of him, and the less money he got the more renderings he'd give.

It was outside a cafe one evening that I met the two girls, Mathilde and Madeleine. They were young, quite nice looking in their own way, done up to the nines—nails lacquered and plenty of make-up. They came and sat at my table and asked me to buy them wine and cigarettes. They were quite cool about it, no beg your pardons. But they were quite good company. We sat in a row with our backs against the cafe, the girls one on each side of me, and they passed remarks about everybody that went by. They weren't Italian, they came from Marseilles. They said they didn't like Italy, or Italians. They'd turn round and make faces at the Duce's picture stencilled on the cafe wall. Discreetly though, so as not to attract attention. Mathilde said her father was a socialist, and Madeleine said hers was too.

So he called you by a saint's name, I said.

It's a good name, she said. It suits me.

She looked straight at me, and I didn't feel like contradicting her.

After the first evening they'd come along fairly often, but not every evening. I used to look forward to their coming even though it cost me more than I could afford in wine and cigarettes.

But before I met Mathilde and Madeleine I had made another acquaintance in the piazza. She was much older than the two girls and quite plain, with her hair done into a bun at the back; and compared to the girls you might have said that she was prudishly dressed. She wore always the same plain white dress that reached from her neck to her ankles and had sleeves that were tight round her wrists. She looked quite odd, and I think I would have been interested in her anyhow, but it happened that she was English. The first evening I noticed her she came and leaned over the parapet beside me. She smiled, yet not confidently—she seemed to be very shy. I offered her a cigarette, but she said she didn't smoke.

You are English, she said, I can tell, I am English too.

I asked her to have something to drink, and she said she'd have only coffee as she never touched anything stronger. We went and sat outside the cafe and she didn't give me much opportunity to talk, she talked herself. She told me her name was Rose, though now she called herself Rosa. She asked me if I was born in the country, and said she was. She was born in Devon, her father had been a farmer, and she spoke of the cows and the fields and the flowers in the hedges. Tears came into her eyes and I felt most uncomfortable. When the fat singer came along she told me it made her think of the time when she had sung in the choir of the chapel she had gone to many years ago. Her eyes filled again and I managed to change the conversation. Presently she said she must go, but perhaps she would see me another evening.

So it happened that sometimes I would see Mathilde and

Madeleine, and sometimes Rosa, but for quite a number of evenings the three of them were never in the piazza at the same time. And the difference between them was astonishing—it was like being in two separate worlds. Mathilde and Madeleine would walk into the piazza as though they owned the place. Taking no notice of anybody, they'd make straight for my table and call the waiter and order what they wanted almost before they had greeted me. Then they'd sit back and begin their comments. Italian women were so stupid, they had no idea how to dress. And Italian men were pigs, they were mean with their money, and they ate sausages that made them smell. They were no better than beasts. They were even worse than that, they were *bourgeois* beasts, which besides being something unmentionably low, was the reason for their all having turned into fascists.

But it was all quite pleasant to listen to. It would be a change from the tears that had been in Rosa's eyes an evening or so before.

I don't think I could have stood Rosa for long if it hadn't been that she was English. I was curious. No matter how much she told me about herself it was always of her life long ago. I had no idea how she came to be living in Italy, and she brought Genoa into the conversation only to remark that the Italians spelt it Genova. I could only guess what her life was like at the moment. She never came into the piazza in the confident way that Mathilde and Madeleine did. I would see her in the distance, walking slowly, looking at everyone that passed, perhaps stopping to speak to some man who might be leaning over the parapet. But I never saw her make a hit. The man would move away and she'd turn and look across to see if I was in my usual place, then she'd slowly work her way round to me. And if she talked of the people in the piazza while she sat at my table her attitude would always be sympathetic. Didn't I think that young woman who went by had such a sweet face? And that old man at the table over there, what nice eyes, but so sad and tired—what a lot of sadness there was in the world, yet one met people who were kind, too. Oh yes, she had had her ups and downs, and such a lot of people had been kind to her. I'd avoid looking at her for fear of seeing the tears. Conversation was difficult. She embarrassed me as much by her sympathy for other people as for herself.

Then the crucial evening arrived when Mathilde and Madeleine and I were sitting in a row and I saw Rosa enter the piazza. As usual she moved slowly, and over by the parapet she looked across our way. She looked for some time, apparently not seeing me, but made her way round until she was quite close. Then I heard the girls exclaim.

Look! Mathilde said.

It is that *bourgeoise*, Madeleine said.

She is disgusting, Mathilde said.

For some moments Rosa didn't come any closer. She stood there smiling at me, looking helpless and forlorn. I tapped the table in front of me, inviting her to come and sit down. She came closer, but the girls protested.

Go! Mathilde said.

Quick! Madeleine said. Or we will call the police.

Rosa walked away slowly, looking back, and Mathilde and Madeleine made faces at her.

What manners! Mathilde said.

To address you in front of us, Madeleine said. It is truly disgusting.

I didn't comment. Mathilde and Madeleine ordered more wine, and Rosa went on round the piazza. It was some time before she was near again, and this time she hurried towards us. The girls became quite excited, but Rosa sat down and leaned across the table towards me..

I must tell you something about these two poor girls, she said.

Won't you have some coffee? I said.

Please no, she said. You see, you are so kind and good, and so innocent.

Thank you, I said.

The girls were shouting at her, and people were looking

at us, and I was wondering what sort of a situation was going to develop, but just then there passed in front of us a hotel porter, with the name of his hotel written across his cap. He was carrying two portmanteaux, and followed by a woman who was begging him to give the portmanteaux back to her. She was frightfully distracted, almost in tears, and you could tell from her voice that she was American. A little girl clung to her skirt, and Junior, who was somewhat older, followed behind with a pair of binoculars slung over his shoulder. He was the only one of the group who didn't appear at all upset. Quite close to us the porter stopped to argue with the woman, shouting that it was a good hotel of the second class he was taking her to, but she only begged for her portmanteaux.

Mathilde and Madeleine were amused, but Rosa's sympathies were aroused.

Oh, the poor soul, she said.

She left us and went over to the group, and when she spoke English the anxiety of the American woman was very much relieved. Rosa began to argue with the porter and wasn't long in getting rid of him, and while she talked to the American woman Junior inspected us all through each end of the binoculars in turn. Then Rosa came over to wish me goodbye.

The poor soul, she said. She's a Mrs Wentwater, and she's so frightened. I'm going to take care of her.

That's kind of you, I said.

She's such a nice lady, Rosa said. Her hubby's waiting to meet her in Geneva, but when the boat got to Marseilles, what do you think she did? She went and took the train to Genoa by mistake.

Too bad, I said.

Yes, Rosa said, Mr Wentwater's a minister in the Baptist Church, and he's been sent to a big meeting at Geneva.

You must tell her how you used to sing in that choir, I said.

Yes, Rosa said, won't it be nice? She's going to stay with

me, because I have a big room, and the children can sleep on the floor.

You're a real friend in need, I said.

Yes, she said. Aren't I?

She went back to her friend and they took a portmanteau each and walked along. Rosa put her spare arm round Mrs Wentwater's waist, and Junior, several paces behind, turned round for a last look through the binoculars.

It was not until some weeks later that I left Genoa, but I never saw Rosa again. One evening in the piazza I enquired from Mathilde and Madeleine, but they had not seen her either.

Without doubt she is in gaol, Mathilde said, because certainly she would rob the American woman.

And Madeleine was of the same opinion.

But I thought perhaps Mrs Wentwater had engaged her as a companion. Who could say? Perhaps she was on her way to America, where she would sing in Mr Wentwater's choir.

A MAN AND HIS WIFE

It was during the slump, when times were bad. Bad times are different from good times, people's habits aren't quite the same. When the slump was on you didn't have to worry about certain things. The way you were dressed, for instance. Along the street you'd meet too many who were as hard put to it as you were yourself. That's one thing the slump did, it put a certain sort of comradeship into life that you don't find now.

During the slump people had to live where they could, and a lot of them lived in sheds and wash-houses in other people's backyards. I lived in an old shed that had once been a stable, and it was all right except for the rats. It was out towards the edge of the town, and there were two of us living there, and my cobber was on relief work like myself. There'd been some trouble between him and his wife, so when he had to get out he came and lived with me. It cut the rent in half, and there was room enough. And Ted was quite a good hand at rigging up a table and suchlike out of any odds and ends he could pick up. He got quite a lot of pickings from a rubbish tip that was handy, and with me giving him a hand we made a fireplace and got the place pretty snug, which it needed to be for the winter. It wasn't a bad sort of life. We never went short of tucker, though a few times we had to raid a Chinaman's garden after we'd spent all our money in the pubs. As a single man, I'd only get about a day and a half's relief work a week, and drew fourteen shillings. Ted got more but of course there was his wife, and he had to part up.

A Man and his Wife

I knew Ted only casually until I struck him on relief. He hadn't long been in the town. He'd had a good job in a pub, but he went on the booze once too often. To start with he wasn't so hot with a shovel, and the gang used to pull his leg, but he was a good-tempered bloke, and as I say there grew up that comradeship when the slump was on. It was pretty hard for him when his wife got her separation, because it was all in the paper, and everybody started making jokes. When she got in Court his wife certainly got going about the sort of husband he was. Besides always getting drunk, she said, he kept a dog, and he'd talk to the dog when he'd never talk to her. He was always taking the dog for walks too, and once when she tried to go along as well he locked her in the wash-house and never let her out until he came home. Well, our gang certainly thought up plenty of jokes about that dog.

When he came to my place, Ted brought the dog. It was nothing special, just a dog, but Ted was certainly fond of it. He had it sleeping at the foot of his bed, and I only put up with it because it was good for the rats. But later on it got under a bus along the road and that was the finish. Ted took it pretty hard, but he wasn't the sort that ever says much. He never told me anything about the trouble he'd had with his wife. There are men who'll talk to you about such things, but it's more often you find women that way. And Ted's wife was the sort. She'd call sometimes to collect her money, though if Ted saw her coming up the road he'd hook off if he could before she got near. And if he couldn't I'd hook off while they had their barney. But usually Ted would have a fair idea when she was coming and wouldn't be around, and then Mrs Watts would talk to me. She was quite all right, quite a nice woman, though always a bit on edge so to speak. She'd say quite a lot. Ted spent too much money on drink, she said, but it was the dog that was the trouble. A man ought to put his wife first, she said. She wouldn't have minded so much if it had been another woman. She couldn't understand it, she said. Well, maybe I couldn't either, so I felt sorry for Mrs

Watts. But I felt sorry for Ted too, so I never told her when the dog was done in. I thought maybe things would come right if they were just left alone.

It didn't work out though, because one day Ted came home with a canary, and he certainly began to think the world of that canary. It just about made me think that he might be a bit unnatural, though I didn't think he was, because one night when some of the gang were round and we were all a bit stonkered, Ted told about how his missis once ran a fish shop and had a girl serving behind the counter for a pound a week. And it was only a shame she was worth the money, Ted said. His wife used to complain that the pound made too big a hole in the profits, but as for him he reckoned the girl was well worth the money. But of course we all chipped in to say he was a dirty old man, and it was no wonder his missis had kicked him out.

But about the canary. Ted loved that bird. He worshipped it. And anyway, it certainly could sing. Ted'd make himself late for work in the morning talking to it and seeing it was all O.K., and he paid a neighbour's little girl sixpence a week to always run over and put the cage inside the window if it came on to rain. And when we got home it was no good expecting him to lend a hand because he'd just want to sit down and kid to the bird. I'd tell him he was a goat, but it did no good. Even when the dinner was cooked it was no good telling him to come and eat, he'd sooner just sit there and kid to the bird.

There was another thing too. Ted'd get all hot and bothered if anybody began to take too much of an interest in his bird. He didn't mind me so much, though I sort of felt I had to keep off the grass. It was when there was a crowd round that he'd get properly hot and bothered. We'd have some rare old times some evenings when there was a crowd round, usually some of the boys in the gang. We'd fill up the baby. We had a big demijohn that we used to call the baby, and we'd all put in and then toss to see who'd go and get her filled up. And an old suitcase that

A Man and his Wife

Ted'd got from the rubbish tip came in handy for the purpose. Well, evenings when we'd had the baby filled would get Ted all hot and bothered. Because once they were a bit stonkered the boys would want to have a bo-peep at the bird while he was asleep. If you were careful you could look under the cloth Ted put over the cage at night and see him standing on one leg with his head tucked in, and his feathers all fluffed up. And it was certainly great to see him sleeping there, specially considering the noise and the smoke. He'd always be a bit unsteady on his one leg and the boys'd argue about that, some saying it was because of his heart beating, and others that he was only balancing. But of course Ted'd be all on edge trying to keep everybody away, and he'd go crook if somebody moved the cloth too much and woke the poor little blighter up, which was usually what happened.

Well, for months on end Ted just about lived for that canary. Then later on he decided it didn't get enough exercise inside the cage, so he tried a stunt. We'd shut the door and the window and Ted'd let the bird out of the cage, and it certainly seemed to enjoy the outing. And Ted thought he was a clever bloke when he'd taught it to sit on his shoulder, though when he put seed in his hair to get it to go up on top it wasn't a success, because the bird got its feet tangled, and I had to cut off some hair to get it away, which reminded me how once on a sheep farm I found a little skeleton tangled in the wool on a sheep's back. In the end though, Ted did a stupid thing, he left the window open while the bird was having its outing. I said wasn't he taking a risk, but he said no, the bird loved him too much ever to fly away. And certainly for a time it just did its usual stuff, sitting on Ted's shoulder and hopping about on the table. Though when it decided to go it didn't waste any time. It up and nipped out that window just as fast as if it was a sparrow that had blown in by mistake. For a time it hung about in a tree while Ted walked round and round underneath with the cage in his hand. And watching the pair of them I thought the bird was rubbing it in, because

115

up in the tree it sounded to me as if it was singing better than ever it did before.

The next morning Ted was gone before I was awake. The cage was gone too, and Ted never turned up at work and lost a day's pay. It was no good though, he never found the bird. Later on we talked it over and I said he'd better try another dog, but he said no. I've still got the wife, he said. Yes, I said. The wife never let me down, he said. No, I said. It was all I could think of to say. He put his things together and went right away, and it wasn't long before I was going round regularly twice a week for a game of cards with the pair of them. But right until the finish of the slump I was living on my own, and occasionally I'd sort of wish that Ted hadn't been so careless with his canary.

OLD MAN'S STORY

He was sitting there on the waterfront, and off and on I watched him while he read the newspaper. He looked a frail old man, I don't mean feeble, just frail. Delicate. You see such old men about and you wonder how it is they've lived so long, how it is that some sickness hasn't carried them off long ago. You think perhaps life has always been easy for them, you look at their hands and feel sure about it. Though hands will sometimes deceive you just as much as faces.

It was good to be sitting there on the waterfront. Besides the old man there were ships alongside the wharves to look at, and the sea, and seagulls. The seagulls were making their horrid squabbling noises. It was because of a slice of buttered bread lying close to our seat, the butter gone soft and yellow in the sun. The seagulls wanted it, but didn't dare to come so close to us, and I watched them, wanting to see if they'd have the courage. Then the old man frightened the birds away by saying the word, Terrible! I looked at him and his cheeks had turned red, and I understood it was because of something he'd read in the newspaper.

Have you seen this? he said, and I leaned over to see the column he was pointing to.

Yes, I said. It was about a man, an adult man and a young girl. A Court case.

Terrible! the old man said.

Yes? I said. Maybe you're right. Anyhow, I said, five years in gaol is terrible.

Yes, the old man said, five years in gaol. Terrible!

Oh, I said, I get you. I don't go much on putting people away, I said.

No, the old man said, it's terrible.

But people say, I said, what can you do?

I don't know, the old man said. But I knew of a case once. It didn't get into the newspapers.

Well, the old man told me, and it was quite a story. It had all happened when he was a boy, fourteen years old perhaps, or thereabouts. He'd just finished school and for a time he went and worked on his uncle's farm. It was a nice place, he said, an old place in a part of the country that had been settled very early. The farms round about were all old places, most of them were run by the families that had been the first to settle there. There were old orchards everywhere, and plenty of trees, English trees that had been planted right at the beginning. Some people went in for crops and some ran cows, but besides they'd have poultry and bees, and everybody had an orchard. Life was pretty quiet there, the old man said, there wasn't any hurry and bustle, it was just real old-fashioned country life. Now and then there'd be a picnic in the school grounds, where the trees were very thick and shady, or perhaps they'd hold a dance in the school itself, but that was about all. You couldn't have found a nicer place, the old man said. His uncle's house was an old place just about buried in a tangle of honeysuckle and rambler roses, not the sort of farmhouse it's so easy to find nowadays. The railway ran alongside but it was a branch line, there weren't many trains and they'd run at any old times. Why, the old man said, he could remember one time when the driver stopped the train to get off and buy a watermelon from his uncle. But nobody worried, because people took life differently in those days.

As a boy the old man used to spend his school holidays there, and he'd enjoy himself no end, so when he finished school his people sent him to help his uncle. They thought perhaps he might turn out a farmer. Anyhow it suited him

fine. There were just his uncle and his aunt (they'd never
had any children), both easy-going, good-natured sorts,
and a man they'd had working on the place for years. This
man was a little wiry fellow with a mop of curly hair that
he never brushed, and a wrinkled face that was always
grinning at you. It was a wicked grin, the old man said,
one eye'd close up a lot more than the other. Anyhow he
was quite a character. He'd turned up one day with a swag
on his back, been given a job, and never moved on for
years. He was no chicken, in his fifties perhaps; and they
used to call him Bandy; though one leg was a lot bandier
than the other. He'd had that one broken more times than
he could remember was the yarn he told. When he was a
boy he'd gone to sea, he said, and several times he'd fallen
from aloft. But he told so many yarns about his life in
different parts of the world it was hard to say whether they
were all true. He was Irish, the old man said, and had the
real Irishman's way of telling you far-fetched yarns. Anyhow he milked the cows and was generally useful about
the place. He taught the boy to milk and the two of them
were in each other's company the most part of each day.
Once you got to know him, the old man said, he was a
regular hard case to talk to, his aunt would have had a
blue-fit if she'd found out. But of course it was only natural
for a boy that age to listen to Bandy and never let on. He
was curious about life, he had to find things out sooner or
later, and thinking it over later on he reckoned he'd
learned more from Bandy than he ever had out of his
Sunday school books. It was pretty strong stuff, granted,
it had a real tang to it, but it was honest stuff all the same.
Nor did it ever get him excited so far as he could remember,
not in a physical way anyhow. When Bandy'd tell him he'd
been with white black brown and yellow and was still
clean, he never had any other feeling except a sort of hero-
worship for him. It was the same as if Bandy had said he'd
had fights with all colours and had always knocked the
other fellow out without ever getting a scratch himself.
People forget when they grow up, the old man said. Maybe

they've learned to play safe by shying away from the strong stuff, but they forget it would never have appealed to them as children in anything like the same way. Children live in a different world, the old man said.

Anyhow, that was the position when the old man was a boy of about fourteen working on his uncle's farm. He was enjoying the life in that old-fashioned neighbourhood, and he was great cobbers with this Bandy, this hard old case; and besides teaching him to milk cows Bandy was every day telling him what was what. Neither his uncle nor his aunt had any idea, he said, they never seemed to worry about his always being with Bandy, and he never told them a thing.

But it turned out things didn't stay like that for very long. One day the boy's aunt went up to town for a holiday, and when she came back she brought home a girl with her. She was quite a young thing, thirteen or fourteen years old perhaps, and small for her age. It seemed she was an orphan and someone had persuaded the old man's aunt to be a good soul and give her a home, to try her out anyhow. Well, her name was Myrtle and she was nothing much to look at. She wore glasses and had curls that hung over her forehead. They made her look a bit silly, the old man said, you felt you'd like to get the scissors and clip them off. She'd annoy you too by always asking, Why? She didn't seem to know much about anything, and you could hardly do a thing without her asking, Why? Still, she seemed to be quite harmless, she helped with the housework and did everything she was told without making any fuss about it. Nobody took much notice of her but she didn't seem to mind.

Later on, though, the boy noticed that a change had come over Bandy. To begin with he'd been like every one else and hardly taken any notice of Myrtle. Then the boy noticed he'd become interested. Up in the cowshed he'd ask, How's Myrtle this morning? Or picking fruit in the orchard he'd say, We'll keep that one for Myrtle. And the curious thing was, the old man said, Myrtle showed signs

of being interested the same way. If Bandy was working in
the garden anywhere near the house Myrtle would be sure
to start banging about on the verandah with a broom.
Bandy'd grin at her (that wicked grin, the old man said),
and they wouldn't say much, but you could tell there was
a sort of situation between them. One day when Myrtle
was out on the verandah Bandy suddenly left off digging
and picked a bunch of roses (which he wasn't supposed to
do) and gave them to the girl. And instead of saying anything she just dropped the broom and ran inside, and
Bandy was sort of overcome as well and went away down
the garden leaving the boy to dig on his own. It was the
kind of thing a boy notices, the old man said, even though
he mightn't be able to make head nor tail of it. Another
thing was that Bandy wasn't the company he'd been before. He'd be a bit short with the boy for no reason at all,
nor would he talk in the old way. If the boy tried to get
him to talk on the old subject he wouldn't bite, or else he'd
tell him he'd better behave himself or he'd grow up with
a dirty mind. He couldn't make it out, the old man said.
The idea he'd got of Bandy right from the beginning made
it just impossible for him to make it out. And you only had
to look at him and look at Myrtle. So far as they were
concerned, one and one didn't make two at all.

Then it happened his uncle began to get an idea of the
way the wind was blowing. Perhaps he'd been told about
the bunch of roses, the boy didn't know. Bandy began to
spend his spare time making a garden seat (one of those
rustic contraptions, the old man said). It was on the edge
of the orchard, but right up against a hedge where you
couldn't see it from the house. And one day when it was
about finished the boy tried it out by taking a seat. Well,
Bandy told him off properly. He hadn't made it for him to
sit on, he said. No, he'd made it for Myrtle. But the boy's
uncle just happened to be coming up on the other side of
the hedge at the time, and he came round and Bandy got
told off properly. The boy only heard half of it because his
uncle sent him away, but after that nobody could help

seeing the difference in Bandy. He went about looking
black, the old man said, he'd be always muttering to himself and he'd make a mess of his work, spilling buckets of
milk, putting the cows in the wrong paddock and that sort
of thing. And by the way Myrtle looked she must have got
a talking to as well. She looked scared, the old man said,
and often enough she'd look as if she'd been crying. Nor
were the pair of them the only ones you could see the
difference in. Everybody in the house was affected. The
boy couldn't sleep at night for thinking it all over, and
he'd hear his uncle and aunt talking in bed in the next
room. And he was pretty certain he knew what they were
talking about. Why Myrtle wasn't packed off back where
she'd come from he couldn't make out, but that didn't
happen and for some weeks things just drifted along as
they were. He felt very unhappy, the old man said, he was
all the time thinking of writing his people to say he was
sick of farming and wanted to come back home.

All the same things couldn't last as they were. Myrtle
wouldn't eat her meals and Bandy did his work worse and
worse. You felt something was going to happen, the old
man said, things were absolutely ripe so to speak.

Then one evening the boy saw something. It was one
evening when he'd been across to a neighbouring farm for
a game of draughts. His aunt didn't like him being out at
night on his own, but he'd begged to go, he wanted to get
away from what was going on in the house. He couldn't
stand it, the old man said. Every night Myrtle'd be sent off
to bed immediately she'd done the dishes, and you'd hear
Bandy muttering to himself in his room which was a lean-to
up against the kitchen wall. Anyhow, coming home this
night the boy took a short cut through the orchard, and
looking along a row of trees he saw that somebody was
sitting on the seat Bandy had made. There was a bit of a
moon and he could see something white. He thought of
Bandy and Myrtle, of course, and for a time he waited, not
knowing whether it would be safe to go closer or not. He
thought his heart was beating loud enough to give the show

away on its own, and in the dark he felt his cheeks begin
to burn. He was thinking of what he might see. But he
couldn't help himself, the old man said, he had to go
closer. And Bandy and Myrtle were sitting on the seat.
Bandy was in his working clothes but Myrtle seemed to be
in her nightgown, at anyrate the boy could tell she had
bare feet. And they were sitting there without saying a
word, the old man said, sitting a little apart but holding
each other's hands. Every now and then the girl would
turn her face to Bandy and he'd lean over to kiss her; or
Bandy would turn his face and she'd lean over to kiss him.
That was all there was to see, the old man said. Nothing
more than that. It amounted to this, that bad old Bandy
had got the girl, this young Myrtle, with her silly curls, out
on the seat with him, and there was nothing doing except
those kisses. And the whole time the boy stood there
watching he never heard them say a thing.

It was a tremendous experience for a boy, the old man
said, too big for him to be at all clear about until later on
in life. All he understood at the time was that he had
somehow managed to get life all wrong. Like all boys he
thought he'd got to know what was what, but as he stood
there in the dark and watched Bandy and Myrtle he understood that he had a lot to learn. He'd been taken in, he
thought. It wasn't a pleasant thought, the old man said.

Well, the old man told me the story sitting there on the
waterfront. It had all happened a long time ago, and he
didn't tell it exactly as I've written it down, but I felt
there was something in the story that he wanted to make
me see. And I felt it was mainly connected with the part
about Bandy and Myrtle sitting on the garden seat, because
when he'd told me that part the old man seemed to
think his story was finished. He stopped talking and
began to fold up his newspaper. But I couldn't leave it at
that.

What happened? I said.

Oh, the old man said, my uncle caught the pair of them

in Bandy's room one night, and the girl got packed off back where she'd come from.

I see, I said, and the old man got up to go.

And what about Bandy? I said, and I got up to kick the piece of buttered bread over to the seagulls.

Oh, the old man said, one morning when he was supposed to be milking the cows Bandy hanged himself in the cowshed.

BIG BEN

He was a tremendous big man, the name all us relief
workers used to call him by suited him fine. He had
good features too. But his wife, besides being just a
little thing, was about as plain-looking as a woman can be
without being actually disfigured in some way.

I never knew exactly when they arrived out here, but it
must have been a good few years before the slump. They
had three children, all boys, and I remember Ben said his
kids were all Pig Islanders. When I first got to know them
the oldest boy was about ten, so it must have been early in
the 'twenties. One time on the way home from work he
came into my bach to crack a bottle of homebrew, and
after that I began going along to his place sometimes of an
evening.

They'd managed to buy their own house but it wasn't
anything to write home about, just a big wooden box with
trimmings, and badly in need of a coat of paint. Though
maybe it was better than what they'd been used to back in
the Old Country. It was right at the end of the street,
where the street took a quick slope down to a creek that
ran into the sea. The sea came up the creek at high tide
and then you didn't see the mud, though even at high tide
the water didn't cover all the tins and rubbish that everybody seemed to come along the street to dump there.

On the slope alongside the house there was room enough
for a fair-sized garden, and that's where Ben put in a lot
of his time. He didn't know a thing about growing vegetables, you could tell that at a glance. But he was keen so

I showed him a thing or two, though in a hundred years he'd never have got the knack of getting things to grow. But as I say he was keen, and there were times when the pair of us would put in whole days in his garden, yarning about this and that while we worked, and leaving off occasionally for a bite and a cup of tea. It was easy to talk to Ben, not that he talked much, but I did, and he was good at listening, and his missis would be at the kitchen door nursing the youngest kid while she listened as well.

But if Ben was a quiet sort of joker I don't know what you'd call his wife. She never said a thing, and if she did she had such a Cockney way of talking you had to think twice before you knew what she meant. I can't stand people who don't talk, so I'd never have been able to get on with her on her own, but with Ben there it was all right. Sometimes I'd strike her down the street going shopping and we'd walk along together, but with her having nothing to say I'd feel awkward, though usually she'd be pushing a go-cart with the youngest on board, who'd be someone to talk to. I mean someone that you didn't expect to talk back anyhow. All the same she wasn't dumb, you could tell that. It was just that you felt she couldn't make head or tail out of colonial ways or people. She was a fish out of water, so to speak. She usually wore a kid's cotton hat which somehow didn't seem to improve matters either. And sometimes I'd think she must be about as lonely as it's possible for anyone to be without actually being on a desert island or something equally drastic.

If it comes to that, Ben was lonely too, though you couldn't get the hang of his feelings as easily as you could of his wife's. One trouble was they were living in the fag end part of a posh suburb, there weren't so many people more or less of their own sort living around, and they somehow didn't seem to cotton on to the few that were. At times it would make me feel real blue thinking about it all, though that was usually when I'd be recovering from a bout of homebrew.

But if it wasn't so good for Ben and his missis it was O.K.

for the kids. The eldest one, young Ben, was quite a bright lad, a regular New Zealand kid with just a touch of Cockney talk that he'd picked up from his mother. He and his next brother fitted in all right with other kids, and they'd be off down to the beach every opportunity they got, and I think they had quite a good time even if the tucker would be sometimes a bit too short to fill their bellies to the limit.

Well, it must have been about the middle of the slump when I got to know Ben, but he didn't seem to be worrying particularly about the slump. He was a fitter by trade, and having a trade he thought he'd get a job all right when things began to improve. Though it turned out they were a long time improving, and I gathered he was slipping back more and more with his payments on the house, which must have worried him quite a lot, particularly when it was a question of deciding on mutton flap for dinner, or a few pence saved to keep the roof over your head.

But often of an evening we'd forget all about that. I'd take along some of my homebrew, and with a few in even Ben's wife would have something to say. And if it hadn't been for the homebrew I don't think I'd ever have discovered much about what their lives had been like in the Old Country. Ben'd sit there smoking his pipe and talking mainly about Douglas Credit, and it was his missis who'd tell me such things as how he'd been an Old Contemptible in the last war. One night she brought out his medals to show me. Once Ben got talking about the old days though, he'd open out. He hadn't liked the war, he said, but he'd had four years of it. Afterwards he'd travelled about a bit and found jobs in his line weren't so easy to get. And he'd a notion that the way things were going there'd be trouble in Europe again before long. He was married then, and he thought if he had any kids he didn't want them to go through all he'd been through, and that was the main reason why he'd decided to try his luck in New Zealand. And his luck had been pretty good until like so many others he'd got hit slap-bang by the slump.

I'm not altogether sure what it was that happened eventually (perhaps their house was going to be taken off them,
I don't know), but as things began to improve a bit Ben
didn't seem to be happy at all. Not even when he got a
job. And even that turned out bad, because he'd hardly
got into his stride when the boss went broke, and Ben never
got some of his wages. But maybe it was something deeper
than that. Maybe Ben began to feel that living in New
Zealand he'd always be sort of living on a desert island.
Perhaps even his experience of gardening had told him
he'd never really get the hang of colonial life. It was O.K.
for the kids, he certainly knew that, but what about his
wife? He certainly must have had a pretty good idea what
it was like for her. After all, he could go out working
alongside his mates but his wife hadn't a friend. She hardly
ever spoke to anyone outside the house except when she
was buying the mutton flap and suchlike. You'd hardly
believe it, but it just happened to be that way. Somehow
her looks, the way she talked, everything, was against her.
And I'd noticed right from the start that Ben thought the
world of his missis. You sort of felt like telling yourself it
was against all reason yet it was pretty plain for anyone to
see.

Anyhow, I certainly got a shock when I went along one
evening and found them packing up. There were candles
stuck on the lids of tins all over the house, and even young
Ben and his brother were being kept busy. Ben himself was
hammering away making boxes, and he wasn't short of
material because years ago he'd made a lot of their furniture out of packing cases. All he said was he'd decided to
try his luck over in Australia, and he asked me to come
round the next morning and help to get the boxes on the
carrier's lorry.

And next morning I knew, because there were Orient
Line labels on the boxes. But Ben never said anything more
about where they were going, and I knew he couldn't
stomach telling me he was going back to the Old Country.
It would have been too much like telling a man you'd been

licked in a fight. And where he got the money from I don't know, but it must have been sent out by his people, because I'll swear he never had any nest-egg of his own.

It wasn't so good later on saying goodbye along where they got on the bus. It just happened to be a great day, and you could hear the sea breaking on the shore. And young Ben began to cry at the thought of what he was leaving, though we cheered him up by telling him the fun he'd have going over the sea in a big boat.

For months and months I didn't hear, then Ben wrote a letter that I've always meant to answer but never have yet. They were back in London, living off the Mile End Road where he and his missis had lived when they were first married. He'd got a job during the first week, he said, and things were booming properly. The missis was well, and happy to be back among her own people. Young Ben wasn't taking to the place too kindly, though he'd soon get used to it. The other kids were doing fine, and there was another on the way. About the only thing that can worry me now is another war, he wound up.

September 1940

PARK SEAT

I didn't go much on the look of the old man making my way, he was the sort that makes you think poor old devil. But then you think my God say I get to be just like that, and then you don't mind so much if he is making your way.

It's fine weather, he said, good for old bones.

Too right, I said.

The sea looks nice from here, he said. Reminds me of when I was a sailing man, he said. One time we were sailing up the St Lawrence, do you know that river?

Canada, I said.

That's right, he said. It was freezing cold and we reckoned we weren't getting enough tucker. One night a couple of us went and broke in where the stores were kept, but we'd hardly got away with the stuff before it was found out. So what did we do, we heaved the stuff overboard—

and coming down the river again not long after the ship went right past a piece of ice with the things they'd heaved overboard lying there, and everybody tried to pretend they didn't notice any difference between that piece of ice and all the rest, and there was the Boxing Day picnic dinner spread out underneath the pear tree in the garden not forgetting the bucket of whipped cream, and I was being given a piggy back round the croquet lawn by the sunburnt young man who'd been to sea and was going again although everybody said wasn't it a pity he was so wild he ought to settle down now, gee up I was saying

—Could you spare me the lend of a bob? the old man said.

TWO WORLDS

My granpa Munro was a Belfast man. He was also a Loyal Orangeman, and I think I first became aware of these facts when I asked why granpa was dressed in a fancy apron in a photograph that hung on the wall. Granma explained to me, but I was too young to have much idea what it all meant.

Then one time during school holidays, when my brother and I were staying with granma and granpa Munro, we found a string of beads in the street. I say we, but my brother said he saw it first. I said I did.

Neither of us had ever before seen such a string of beads. Instead of their being all of an even size, or else threaded so that they began small and grew large and then got small again, this string was made of a number of small beads that were interrupted at regular intervals by a big one. We counted the number of big beads and the number of small ones in between, and the number altogether, and this kept us busy for quite a time. Then we squabbled over who was to be the owner, but my brother was the older, he had the advantage of me, and the findings disappeared into his pocket.

I got my own back by saying they weren't worth anything anyhow. And as soon as we were home I said that we'd found something, and told my brother to show granma. He gave me a look that told me plainly what he thought of me but he brought the beads out, and granma hardly had them in her hand when she gave a sort of groan and dropped them on the table. She spread out her arms to keep us from going near, and granpa got up from his chair and looked at the beads over the top of his glasses. Granma said we were not to touch and she took the tongs and would have put the beads in the fire if granpa hadn't stopped her.

Well, granma went on getting the tea, we asked her what the beads were and she said they were a Catholic thing. I don't think that meant a great deal to us. We knew what Catholic churches looked like from the outside and that was about all, though at school we'd learned to say a rhyme:

> *Catholic dogs don't like frogs,*
> *And won't eat meat on Friday.*

Meantime granpa was walking up and down, stopping now and then to look at the beads. I suppose there must have been quite a tug of war going on between the man who was a loyal Orangeman, and the man who didn't want to do anything dishonest. Finally he pushed the beads on to a piece of paper with one finger, and put them on the mantelpiece.

I don't think we thought about the beads for very long that evening. My main feeling about them was quite a satisfactory one. My brother had prevented me from being able to say they were mine, now he couldn't say they were his either. I felt that we were quits.

When we came home from going to the butcher's for granma the next morning we found that granpa had the horse harnessed in the buggy, and was waiting to take us for a drive. We ran and put our boots and stockings on, which was the rule whenever we went out driving, then we climbed up and sat beside granpa. He touched Beauty with the whip, and driving out the gate we waved to granma who was standing at the door to watch us go.

Granpa turned in the direction of the main street, and at the corner a man was lighting his pipe in the middle of the road.

By your leave! granpa shouted out, and he made the
man jump. But my brother and I turned round and saw
him laughing, and we knew it was mainly because of the
straw hat, with holes for his ears to stick through, that
Beauty wore. On hot days granpa always put it on, and it
was supposed to keep him from getting sunstroke.

All the way along the main street granpa shouted out,
By your leave! to people that were crossing the street, even
though it didn't look as if any of them were going to be run
over. And my brother and I saw so many people laughing
that we felt a little shy and uncomfortable until we were
through to the other end of the town.

It was a part of the town we didn't know very well, the
houses were smaller and closer together than in the part we
knew, though granpa pulled up outside a big house with
a lawn and trees in front. He gave us the paper that he had
wrapped the beads in, and told us we were to go and knock
at the front door and ask for Mr Doyle. When Mr Doyle
came to the door we were to say we'd found some beads,
give him the parcel, and come straight back again.

We went up a path that wound through the trees and
took us out of sight of the street, and when we knocked at
the door it was opened by a fat lady with a red face.

Please is Mister Doyle in? my brother said.

Mister Doyle? the fat lady said, and we were frightened
by the way she looked down at us.

Do you mean the Very Reverend Dean Doyle? she said,
and what she said made us more frightened. I looked at my
brother, my brother looked at me. Neither of us had a
voice any more.

Then a voice from behind the fat lady said, Well boys?

The fat lady stepped back and in her place was a white-
haired old man wearing a parson's collar.

My brother held out the parcel, and I was quite surprised to hear myself speak.

We found them, I said.

Did you now? the old man said, and he looked at me as
he unwrapped the paper.

I found them, my brother said, and the old man looked at him.

We both found them, I said.

Well indeed now, did you both find them? the old man said, and he laughed as he put the beads in his pocket.

Would you boys like some lemonade? he said, and he told the fat lady to bring some, and then he leaned against the doorpost and asked us what our names were. He certainly had a way with him and he soon had us talking.

My brother said he might be getting a bicycle for his birthday, and I said he'd promised to let me ride it. This wasn't quite true, but I was hoping it might have some effect on my brother.

Then the fat lady brought the lemonade, with a straw in each glass, and when I'd finished I asked if I could keep the straw. My brother, who'd given his glass back, said I wasn't to, but the old man gave him his straw. Then he said, Goodbye boys, and remembering granpa we both began to run down the path.

But round the first bend we came to a standstill. Granpa was coming up the path. There was a look on his face we'd never seen before, and he had the buggy whip in his hand.

A MAN OF GOOD WILL

When I was a boy at school our family lived some way along the road from a tomato-grower who was supposed to be eccentric. Among other things it was said that he didn't eat meat, neither had he ever been known to smoke or drink. Neither, as I found out for myself later on, did he use certain words or tell the usual sort of stories. But a lack of the more obvious vices will make people talk just as readily as the reverse, so I suppose it was only natural for some such word as eccentric to be passed round the neighbourhood.

He was a single man, this David Williams, and well on in years. He was so dark in colouring that people said he had a touch of the tar-brush, but if his name was anything to go by he probably got his dark skin from Welsh blood. He was a sketch of a man to look at, he walked pigeon-toed, and he was so thin his clothes seemed to hang on a framework of sticks. When you talked to him he laughed a lot, pushing his face in yours, and catching hold of your arm. Over one of his eyes he had a drooping eyelid, and it didn't fit in too well with the rest of him because it rather suggested wickedness. He had his sister living with him, attending to the house and helping with the outside work, and to look at she was very much the same kind as her brother. Though if anything, there was even less of her.

On their place there was a tremendous lot to do. They had a big glass-house for winter growing, and as soon as the warmer weather came there'd be the outdoor work as well. One winter I earned a few shillings by helping a milkman during my school holidays, and driving along the road in the small hours of a frosty morning we would see a light moving inside the glass-house. Some mornings there would be two lights, and that meant Miss Williams was working with her brother. But no matter how early they started you'd see them working until well on into the evening, when they must have been too tired to do another stroke.

The Williams were grafters, everybody agreed about that. They never seemed to have any time for recreation, unless that was the name you could give to the time they put in on their flower beds and keeping the place tidy. They never went to socials or dances, they never even went to church, so nobody got to know them at all well. But they had people's respect for being such hard workers. Occasionally it would be said they were a pair of money-grubbers, living only to rake in the cash, but I think that would usually be said by somebody who wouldn't have minded being able to do the same thing. That is, if they were doing it. Nobody knew for certain.

Then after they had been on the place for a number of years Miss Williams became ill. She was taken to hospital and died after a few days. The funeral was a private one and her brother had her cremated, and a story got about that he afterwards took the ashes and threw them into the air to be scattered by the wind. I heard people talking about this and some said it was a horrible thing to do. They said it didn't show much respect for the dead. I remember my mother said that the thought of it was enough to give her the creeps.

Miss Williams's illness had happened round about Christmastime, when the outdoor tomatoes would soon be coming into bearing. Her brother was away for about a week after the funeral, the house was locked up and everything was neglected. Then it was noticed he was back again and he seemed to be just the same as ever, but he had about double the work to do. It was too much for him and one evening he came along the road to see my father. He

A Man of Good Will

wanted to know if I would like a job, and I think my father was a bit doubtful. He wasn't the sort of man to approve of queer fish, but I'd just left school and hadn't found anything to do, so finally it was all fixed up. I went over the next morning and began by following my boss about, watching until I got the hang of things, and after a week or so I began to develop into quite a capable lad. I couldn't keep up with the speed my boss worked at, but we got on all right together, and besides teaching me the work he told me all his theories. He was against the use of quick manures, he said, it meant that tomatoes grown that way didn't feed you properly, though what was a commercial grower to do? If he didn't do as the next man did he'd go broke. And he was against all the expensive and complicated business of spraying. He said it wouldn't be necessary if you had healthy plants that weren't forced. He didn't even approve of the poisonous spray for caterpillars, and as we worked along the rows he taught me to watch out for the moths' eggs, which you found underneath the leaves and on the flowers. It was quite a good method perhaps, but it took up a lot of time.

To begin with I'd go along the road home to my lunch at midday. But later on I'd stay and eat with my boss, he seemed to like my company and he got a butcher to call sometimes and leave a piece of sausage, though he never ate any himself. And it was mainly during our times of eating together that he began to tell me about how he had come to be a tomato-grower. Probably he said much that I was too young to understand, but it was all so different from what I was used to hearing in my own home, that I could always listen without feeling impatient. Also it fascinated me to watch him. He'd walk pigeon-toed across the kitchen to fill the tea-pot, or he'd bend his head back to look out at me from under his drooping eyelid.

He'd begun life in a draper's shop, he said, and for a number of years he'd liked the work quite well. He had the knack of arranging things so he was put on to dressing the window, and he did so well it wasn't long before he was

137

able to get a job in a big store. He stayed there for years, finding the work quite to his liking, and getting more and more money, but at the same time he wasn't happy and he wasn't satisfied. Deep down he wasn't, he said. He'd begun to feel it was wrong of people to shut themselves away from the sun and fresh air by working in such places, except that you went home at night it was just as though you'd been put in gaol. As for people who worked inside cages behind the counters of banks, or sat all day going up and down in lifts—well, you might just as well live in a cage out at the zoo. And such ideas had kept coming into his head, until he decided he'd cut out all his pleasures and save hard so that he could set himself up in a new way of living. Why, he said, it had even meant he'd had to change his mind about getting married. Then later on when he'd got started he found out the life meant much harder work than he'd ever imagined. Yet he'd liked it all right, he said. He'd feel prouder over the sight of a good bunch of tomatoes, with the top ones just beginning to colour, than he'd ever felt over any window he'd dressed. And another thing, it was an education, because it had taught him things he never knew before.

If you grew something for sale, he found out, particularly if it was something that wouldn't keep, you mainly had to take just what people would pay for it, even though you might get a lot less than would pay for the work and expense it had cost you. And that was a different thing from what happened in the big store he had worked in, where you usually managed to buy at one price and sell at another that would always keep you on the right side. You didn't wait until you were offered a price, no, you mainly got the price you asked for. Well, the world was a funny place, he said, you'd strike people who'd grumble over the price of tomatoes when it hardly paid you for the work of picking them, yet if you'd asked these people to work for such little return they'd have properly hit the roof. And most of them you couldn't blame, because they could never have afforded to buy at a fair price. Well, well, he said, the world was all wrong, men couldn't be brothers to each other when they spent so much time worrying over the prices they were going to pay or get. It made you feel unhappy, but when you'd puzzled your brains you asked yourself what could you do? You could count yourself one of the lucky ones if you got plenty to eat and a good share of sunshine and fresh air, and didn't have to dress up to go to work. The only thing that worried him, he said, was that he hardly ever had enough spare time to read a book. And the joke of it was he'd thought when he started out he was going to have plenty.

All this and a lot more I mainly listened to during the half hours when we knocked off for lunch. A few things would sink in, and from time to time I'd be liable to fetch them up at home. Mr Williams says, I would begin, and sometimes I'd annoy my father by contradicting him with something my boss had said. I'm afraid my father was the sort of man who gets upset if people say things that aren't like what the newspapers say. One evening I heard him talking to my mother, telling her that I was under a bad influence, and that I'd better look round for another job. That was all I heard, but I knew my mother would be on my side. She was easy-going, and I knew she liked me to come home and tell her what I'd had for lunch, and what the inside of Mr Williams's house was like. It made her feel important to be able to tell people about how he did all his own cooking, washed and mended his clothes, and managed to keep everything tidy even to polishing the floors. What an eccentric man! Though I remember she hadn't got the word quite right and said *es*centric.

So in the meantime my father didn't interfere with my job, and it was lucky for my boss because the season was turning out a good one. Every day was a real scorcher. I lived with the strong tomato-smell always in my nose, and the hot smell of the earth that we were forever sprinkling with manure and drenching with water until it was soaked right through. I'd start early, stay late, and get paid extra, but we never seemed to be able to catch up with what had to be done. On top of the other work was the marketing, and tomatoes that were still warm from the sun hours after they'd been picked, seemed always to be layers deep on the floor of the packing shed. Like all good seasons it had benefited everybody's crops alike. It was one right out of the box, and my boss told me he'd never known so many tomatoes about at so cheap a price. Sauce factories that had contracted for whole crops had landed themselves in the cart, he said, deliveries were more than they knew what to do with, and they were buying dearer than they could have bought on the market. So the growers who had contracts were all right, but as for the rest of them, well, my boss reckoned a bad season of blight couldn't have been a worse blow than such plenty was.

Then one morning I turned up to work and got a surprise to find my boss hadn't even finished his breakfast. And instead of telling me what to get busy on he asked me inside. Have you had a good tuck-in? he said, and I said I'd had plenty. Go on, he said, I know what boys' appetites are like, and he made me sit down to a poached egg on toast. He sat there with his arms folded, and I'd never seen him taking it so easy. It's a silly game, this working so hard, he said, look what it did to my poor sister. With my mouth full I mumbled something, and he began to tell me about a growers' meeting that had been held the night before. He'd been along, he said, and they had a scheme for each man to dig a pit and throw away half his crop. But I'll guarantee they won't be able to trust each other enough to make that idea work. Besides, it would be a wicked shame. I got up to speak, he said, and the words wouldn't come. I just stood there like a fool with my mouth open, and the chairman told me to sit down. He told me this several times over, and he laughed as though it were a great joke.

When I'd finished eating he still didn't seem to be in any hurry. Instead of leaving the dishes until lunchtime he started on them right away, throwing me a tea-towel. Or don't you like women's work, my boy? he said, and laughed. Then he got me to wait while he swept the floor, and when we were finally out in the garden he just walked about saying that no man could help being happy in a garden on a day of such weather. A man in the garden, a woman in the house, and a child in the cradle, he said, that's what God put us on the earth to make come true. And then, just as if he hadn't said anything at all out of the ordinary, he told me what he wanted me to do. But don't work too hard, he said, and laughed. And if it had been anyone else but him I'd have thought he was slinging off.

He left me to go ahead and never came near me all morning, and I had no idea what he was doing. He should have been nailing up cases in the packing shed but I didn't hear him, though when he called me to lunch I noticed as I went past that the tomatoes we'd picked the afternoon before had all disappeared. He was drying his hands out on the verandah, and straightoff he said, Come and tell me if I've made a good job. So we went down the length of the glass-house to the front of the section, and there, just inside the gate, he'd put all the tomatoes in a heap. Not just an ordinary heap though, he'd built them up into a sort of pyramid, the way you see them in the shop windows, only this one was a monster. He asked me if they looked nice, and I thought they certainly did. And it wasn't just because they made a pretty picture, each one a perfect specimen that showed a wonderful red polish in the sun. It was something more than that. I'd helped him do the work, and just to stand and look at the result gave me a wonderful feeling of being satisfied. Perhaps I'd never before understood what deep feelings you could have over things you'd made happen under your own hands. Perhaps I understood even more than that. I may have understood that the feeling had nothing to do with the money you could sell such things for. I'm not quite sure, but I know I had the feeling, and I knew my boss had it too, and that it was tremendously deep in him. And I think he knew about me as well, because instead of saying anything much he put his arm round my shoulders, and I wasn't at all keen about him doing this but I let him leave it there.

Once we were back up at the house he talked and acted just the same as usual, yet it turned out that day was the first of some very queer days for me. My boss would leave me to work on my own, while he spent most of his time sitting down at the gate in an old easy chair he took off the verandah. And besides leaving the heap of tomatoes there, he was all the time making it bigger with every fresh lot that we picked. One morning I turned up to work and struck him having an argument with our carrier. It was our main market day, and the carrier had made his call to pick up the cases we'd normally have been sending into town. My boss was saying he wasn't sending anything in, and the carrier was pointing to the heap and asking what the big idea was. I stood listening, and my boss just laughed and said, No, my friend, until the carrier got annoyed, and drove off after shaking my boss's hand from his arm, and telling him he was clean off his rocker.

Then stories about what was happening began to get around. Probably the carrier talked, but it wouldn't have made any difference if he hadn't, because anybody could look over the gate and see the heap, and my boss sitting in the old chair. More and more people began to stop and stare, and later on there'd sometimes be quite a crowd. I noticed people began to look at me in the street, and although I hadn't said a word at home, my father wanted to know what Mr Williams thought he was up to. I didn't know what to say so I didn't say anything, but I must have gone red because my mother suddenly changed the subject. Though when she got me on my own she asked me what Mr Williams was doing with that heap of tomatoes. I said I didn't know, and it wasn't exactly the truth, but I could never have explained, even if I'd wanted to try.

Then for a couple of days everybody had something else to talk about. The weather broke. All of a sudden there came a terrific gale that blew one way one day and the other the next, and in between there was a downpour that measured several inches in just a few hours. The wind lifted the roof off a house in our road, so it was no wonder my boss's tomatoes were all flattened out. The tea-tree sticks were dry and brittle from so much sun and the wobbling weight of the great top bunches was too much for them, they snapped off and the flax ties that held only meant a worse tangle. If it hadn't been for the rain the damage wouldn't have been so serious, but the sun came out hot again, and that sea of green tangle, lying thick on the wet ground, meant we had to go for our lives if we wanted to stop the blight from setting in. My boss never had time to sit in his chair for days. We'd both of us begin at daylight and work ourselves to a standstill, and after about a week it was certainly wonderful the way we managed to get things pretty straight again. Though of course a lot of damage had been done. All over the country it was the same and I read about it in the newspaper. Tomatoes were specially mentioned, and it was said that prices would go up.

Yet once things had been got straight my boss left me to work on my own again, while he went back to his chair, taking time off only to put more and more on the heap. Though by this time it had gone properly rotten inside, and was getting smaller if anything. Also it was smelling bad and bringing the flies around, and the sanitary inspector came and said it would have to be shifted into a hole and buried. And he didn't like it when my boss laughed and said it was a good smell, it meant that the earth was getting her own back again.

Nor was he our only visitor. They started driving up in their cars every day, looking as smart as if they'd just stepped out of bandboxes, and my boss would look a cut talking to them in his denims and sandshoes, and his shirt full of holes that he'd left off mending. There was a man from my boss's bank came, and a man from the markets, and a policeman along with one of our local doctors. But I never heard what they talked about, and I never said a thing to anybody, not even the Sunday morning when my mother came in from next door, and said they were taking Mr Williams to the hospital in an ambulance. They'd found him lying just inside the gate, she said, and he'd had a stroke.

I ran along the road and I was just in time to see my boss lying all tucked up on the stretcher. He couldn't move and he couldn't speak, and he didn't seem to be able to hear. The drooping lid was right down over that eye, but the other one was wide open. I got right in front of it, but he didn't seem as if he could see me.

THAT SUMMER

It was a good farm job I had that winter, but I've always
suffered from itchy feet so I never thought I'd stick it for
long. All the same I stayed until the shearing, and I quit
after we'd carted the wool out to the station, just a few
bales at a time. It was just beginning December and I had
a good lot of chips saved up, so I thought I'd have a spell in
town which I hadn't had for a good long time, and maybe
I'd strike a town job before my chips ran out.

The old bloke I was working for tried hard to get me to
stay but there was nothing doing. I liked him all right and
the tucker was good, but him and his missis were always
rowing, and there was just the three of us stuck away there
with hardly any company to speak of. I had to sleep on an
old sofa in the kitchen because it was only a slab whare
they lived in with two rooms, and I got a bit sick of hearing
them fighting every night when they'd gone to bed. The
old bloke told me he'd had money enough to build a
decent house long ago, but his missis said if he did she'd be
there for keeps. So she wouldn't let him, but they'd gone on
living there just the same.

I had to get up early to walk the six miles to catch the
train, and I never saw the old bloke but his missis came out
just when I was going. She had a little bag of sovereigns
that I'd never seen before and she made me take one, only
she said it was to keep and not to spend so as I'd always
remember her. And when I got down the road she came
running along and grabbed hold of me for a kiss, and then
she stood in the road and waved. She looked a bit of a

sketch I can tell you, with her hair hanging down and her old man's coat on over her nightgown. I felt a bit sorry and wished in a way I wasn't going, because the farm away back there in the valley looked sort of nice and peaceful with the sun just getting up on such a fine morning, and only a sheep calling out now and then, and the dogs barking because I hadn't let them off the chain when I started down the road. And I looked at the hills and thought what a hell of a good worker I was to have cut all the fern and scrub I had in the winter. But I thought no, I've got to be on the move. Many a time I've wished I didn't have my itchy feet, but it's never much good wishing for things to be any different.

So I caught the train all right, but I had a few minutes to spare and I talked to the porter. He'd been to a dance the night before, he was yawning his head off and looked as if he needed a wash.

The old bloke giving you a spell? he said.

No, I said, I'm going out for good.

What, he said, turning it in. You'll never get another job.

I'll be O.K. I said.

So he told me about how he'd got a letter from his sister, and her husband was out of a job and things couldn't be worse in town. But he hadn't finished telling me when the train came in. So I got on board, but it was a slow train that stopped to shunt all the way along the line, and I was pretty fed-up by the time I got into town early that afternoon.

I left my bag at the station and after I'd had a feed I just walked about the streets looking at the shops and the people. I thought to myself, now I'll have a good time. I thought maybe I'd pick up with a girl, and with the chips in my pocket I knew I could kick around for a good many weeks before I'd need to think about getting a job. I thought I'd go to the flicks, but it seemed better just to be in the streets. I'd have plenty of time to do all the things I wanted to do, so there wasn't any need to go rushing things. Because things never turn out as good as you think they will, so it's always just as well to get all the fun you can out of thinking what they're going to be like beforehand. I went and sat in the park, and whenever there was a girl came past that I thought might have me on I'd watch out to see if she'd look me over. But there was nothing doing. And I said to myself well, a knock-back from one of yous isn't going to make me lose any sleep. But I hoped it wouldn't be long before I had a bit of luck all the same.

After I'd had another feed I thought I'd better look for a place to sleep, so I went and got my bag from the station, and then I found a joint that was kept by a Mrs Clegg and I thought it would be O.K. It was a two-storeyed place standing in between a butcher's shop and a brick warehouse. You paid for your bed and had to get your meals out, but there was a gas ring at the top of the stairs, and Mrs Clegg said I could borrow a spare teapot and make myself a cup of tea if I wanted to. So I thought that would suit me fine, because I could buy myself a couple of buns and have a lie-in some mornings just for a change after the farm.

Mrs Clegg was quite a decent sort, but she had a glass eye that was cracked right down the middle, and it was funny the way she sort of looked out at you through the crack. Her old man was out of a job and that was why she was running the joint, though seeing she only had three rooms to let she said she wasn't making a fortune.

When she'd fixed my bed up she took me down to the kitchen to give me the teapot, and her old man was reading the paper, and their little girl was saying pretty boy to a budgie that was answering her back. Though sometimes it would ring a little bell instead. Mr Clegg told me he'd been a cook on a boat but now he couldn't get a keel. It was hard, he said, because he liked being at sea, though I thought by the look of him it must have been only a coastal or even a scow he'd worked on. He was pretty red too, though he said he hadn't been until he'd had experience of being on relief.

Of course it was the sort of talk I'd heard a good many

147

times knocking around, so I didn't take much notice. Mrs Clegg kept on chipping in and they'd squabble a bit though not as bad as the old couple on the farm, and the little girl left off talking to the budgie and started asking her mother if she could have some money to spend. She asked about fifty times before her mother said no, and asked her if she thought money grew on trees. So then she began to ask if money did grow on trees, and when she'd got to about the fiftieth time I chipped in myself and said I'd have to go.

But it was only to go down the street and buy what I wanted so I could lie-in if I felt like it, and then I turned in, because walking about the town in my good shoes had made me feel tireder than if I'd done a day's work on the farm. And I thought I wouldn't need any rocking to get to sleep, but my room was right over the kitchen and I could hear the pair of them going it hammer and tongs, and then the youngster got spanked and the way she yelled gave me the dingbats. It was too much like what I'd been used to, and for the first time that day I didn't feel so good about throwing up my job and coming to town. Because I thought there wasn't any sense in having itchy feet if they only got you out of a steady job and into a place like Mrs Clegg's. And there wasn't any sense in having them anyhow, because they never gave you any peace. Yet all the time I was thinking like that I was asking myself whether I'd get up and clear out right away, or whether I'd wait until daylight, and I knew that wherever I went I wouldn't go back to the farm. But while I was trying to decide I must have gone to sleep because I don't remember anything more.

But it turned out I never shifted from Mrs Clegg's, not for a long time as I'll tell you.

The first morning I stayed in bed, and I thought nobody could be any better off than I was. It was a good bed to lie on after the sofa on the farm, I had my chips, and there wasn't a job I wouldn't take on if I got the chance. But for a while I was going to have a good time just kicking

around. I laughed when I heard Mrs Clegg chase her old
man out of the house, and I tried to get an earful when I
heard somebody out on the landing place. There were only
two other rooms upstairs but Mrs Clegg hadn't said if they
were let. I didn't see anyone that first morning anyhow,
because every time I told myself I'd better get up I thought
no, it's too good where I am. Though once I sat up to look
out the window, and the weather was good, but there was
nothing much to see except the butcher's backyard on one
side and the wall of the warehouse on the other, and Mrs
Clegg's washing hung out in between.

It wasn't until late that I'd had my tea and was all
flossied up, and by that time there was no one about the
house except the little girl, and she was hanging the budgie's cage on a nail on the front of the house. She was the
thinnest kid you ever saw, with legs like sticks, and a real
old woman's face. She said her name was Fanny and asked
me what mine was. So I told her to call me Bill, and she
said, Does money grow on trees Bill?

It might do, I said, I couldn't say for certain.

We've got a tree, she said, so you can mind the house
while I go and look.

No, I said, but hang on until tomorrow and we'll both
have a look. See you mind the house, I said, because I
don't want anyone to break into my room.

Then just along the street I passed Mr Clegg. He had a
waistcoat on over his flannel, and he was leaning up
against the wall of a pub talking to the taxi-drivers. I
bought a newspaper and one of the taxi-drivers asked me if
I wanted to take a double, so I took a half dollar one even
though all the good ones were filled up. Because taxi-
drivers are good blokes to keep in with, they usually know
of a house to take you to if you don't happen to know of
one yourself. And I thought I ought to stand Mr Clegg a
drink, but what with the taxi-drivers there were too many
around, so I put it off until another time. You could tell by
the look of him he got a good few anyhow.

There wasn't much I could do before it was time to eat,

F

so I went into the park to read the paper, but instead I watched an old man who was having a wash in the fountain. After he'd finished washing he looked in the water and spent a lot of time combing his hair, then he came past my seat and asked me if I'd done with the paper, so I said I had and gave it to him. But a young joker got up from the next seat and said he wished I hadn't done that, because he was going to ask me for the paper himself.

Stiff luck, I said.

He said he'd had a date with a sheila the Sunday before but she hadn't turned up. It was right there where he'd been sitting, and he'd been waiting at the same time every day ever since. She might have put an ad in the paper, he said. I felt like telling him to forget it but he was taking it pretty bad, so instead I asked him if he'd come and eat, because by the look of his clothes I'd have said he was up against it.

I shouted him a bob dinner and I could tell by the way he ate he was in need of a binder, but he never said whether he was out of a job or not. He just wanted to tell me what a great sheila she was that had let him down, so to shut him up I said we'd go to the flicks. But it was a mistake, because after the lights went out a girl came and sat in the seat next to me, and when I put my leg over her way she was willing. I pushed and she pushed back, and it wasn't long before I had hold of her hand, and what with holding her hand and wondering how I'd get rid of this fellow Sam if she looked any good when the lights went up I never had much idea what the first part of the programme was about.

Well, the lights went up and she certainly looked good. She gave me the onceover and maybe she thought I didn't look so bad either, but she could tell I was with Sam and Sam didn't look so good. I said if he liked he could take my tin and go out and roll himself one, but he said no, he could wait till after. He just wanted to talk about his sheila, she was a bit like the girl in the big picture he said. It made me properly narked but I hadn't got the heart to tell him

off. Me and the girl got to work again while the big picture
was on and this Sam was that thick in the head I bet he
never guessed a thing, but soon as the lights went up she
went for her life while Sam was saying he'd have a fag if it
was O.K. with me. So I gave him my tin, and I thought
that's that, but I could have crowned him all the same. He
wanted to get going about his sheila again but I said, To
hell with all that, let's go and have a drink.

So we got in a pub and we both had a good few in by
closing time, and then they said we could carry on upstairs
if we liked, so it wasn't long before we were properly
canned. Sam talked about his sheila and once I'd got
canned I didn't mind. I didn't mind doing all the paying
either, though I spent a lot more money than I intended,
and when it was about ten o'clock we took a taxi and went
to a dance that Sam knew about. It was a pretty flash
turnout with a lot of streamers and balloons, but what with
Sam looking like a proper bum and the both of us being
canned they wouldn't let us in. So we went to another
place that was a lot tougher, and nobody said anything,
not even when we started butting in on other blokes'
sheilas. We got a couple of them to come outside for a spot,
but they went crook when we spilt beer over their skirts,
and in the end there was nothing doing. And so far as I was
concerned it didn't matter because I was that canned I
wouldn't have had a hope of doing anything. And I don't
remember getting home to Mrs Clegg's but I was there the
next morning when I woke up.

It was Sunday and the church bells were ringing, but
after the night before I didn't feel so hot until I had a drink
out of a bottle I found in my pants' pocket. Then I felt
better, and I looked out the window and the weather was
still good, and Mrs Clegg's washing was still hanging on
the line. I thought I might go and lie on the beach in the
sun, but Fanny came and asked if I'd go and look at the
tree to see if there was any money.

There was nobody about upstairs but Mrs Clegg was in

the kitchen, and her old man had put his chair on the
bricks outside and was reading the paper. Fanny and I
went down to the fence where there was a pretty good
smell, because a heap of sawdust out of the butcher's shop
was over the other side. We couldn't see any money hanging on the tree and Fanny was disappointed, but I said
maybe it was the wrong time of the year. Fanny said
perhaps it had fallen in the grass, it would if it was ripe, she
said. So we looked and I had my fingers on a sixpence in
my pocket, and then I thought no, I'll give the kid a real
thrill, I'll make it a bob. So I dropped the bob and so help
me if it wasn't the sovereign the old lady had given me on
the farm. I put my foot out but Fanny was too quick. She
didn't know what to make of it but she wouldn't let me
have a look, and before I could stop her she'd run up the
bricks singing out that it was a money-tree. Her old man
looked over the top of his paper and held out his hand, but
Mrs Clegg suddenly showed up and got in first. And then
there was a proper hullabaloo, the two of them going it
hammer and tongs, and Fanny howling and jumping up
and down on the bricks.

Come on Fanny, I said, those legs of yours will snap off
at the knees if you're not careful.

I got her to come back and we had another look, and I
took jolly good care it was only a sixpence this time. Her
old man wanted to take it off her but Mrs Clegg wouldn't
let him, so there was another hullabaloo. And Fanny
wanted to keep on looking but Mr Clegg said if he caught
her near the tree again he'd tan her hide.

Well, I felt a bit sore over the sovereign, but I thought if
Mrs Clegg put it towards buying a new glass eye I wouldn't
mind so much. Fanny had just about decided I was her
property and wanted me to play penny catches, but her
mother came out and started to weed round a row of
tomatoes she had growing up against the fence, and I said
if she'd tell me where the spade was I'd make a proper job
for her. Fanny went to get the spade but Mr Clegg came
out and said he was going to do a bit of digging himself.

That Summer

You're going to do a bit of digging, Mrs Clegg said, but he didn't say anything.

It was under the tree that he went to dig and off and on he'd be down there for a good few weeks after.

I wished I'd gone to the beach because the sun was real hot and there wasn't a cloud. It had been a dry spring and everybody said it was going to be a hot summer. There was the yarn they always say about how the Maoris had said so. Though it was getting a bit late in the day to go off to the beach so I played penny catches with Fanny, but the ball kept on banging into the washing and in the end Mrs Clegg went crook, though she needn't have done because her clothes weren't as clean as all that. So then I told Fanny I hadn't any more time to go on playing, but it was really because I'd seen a smart-looking piece of goods dry-ing her face and having a bo-peep out the bathroom win-dow, which was upstairs next to mine. I went up the stairs about six at a time and she was crossing the landing place with only a sort of kimono-thing on. Hello, I said, but she only said, How do you do, and went inside and slammed the door of her room. She didn't look nearly so good as she'd looked through the window anyhow, she was a little piece that somehow made you think of a kid's doll and not my type at all. So of course I told myself I couldn't be worried.

I began to feel empty so I went down town and had some dinner in a place that was run by a Dalmatian. Being Sunday there wasn't much doing, so he brought out his two little boys to show me, though one was so shy he got behind his father's legs and only put his head out now and then. And when his missis brought the tucker he said how she wouldn't learn to speak English. You could only grin at her, though I talked to the kids and they were great kids, the sort of little blokes I wouldn't mind if I had myself.

My wife thinks always of our country, the Dally said. She says that if she learns to talk here I will not take her back to our country.

And will you? I said.

Yes I will, he said. But first I must have a lot of money. My wife she wants us to go now but I say no. It is lonely for her when she will not talk but she has her little boys and soon they will take her shopping which she will not go now, because she does not talk.

Anyhow *he* talked, and I liked listening to him, and I'd grin at the wife now and then just to sort of include her in the conversation, and the kid that wasn't shy sat on a chair with his legs stuck out and took it all in. I thought they were a real nice family, I promised I'd go there again, and when I came out I was wishing in a way I was settled down myself, because here I was in town all on my own, and that afternoon I felt at a bit of a loose end. Sunday afternoons on the farm when there was nothing else doing I'd go and shoot pigeons away up in the bush, and I wouldn't feel as much on my own as I did now in a town full of houses and people. But it's no good letting those things get you down, so I went back to Mrs Clegg's to lie on my bed and read a True Story. I read them sometimes though the yarns are all a lot of baloney, nothing like real life at all. But I'd hardly got started when Fanny came in and I didn't shoo her out because I wanted to do a bit of fishing.

Fanny, I said, who lives here besides me?

Terry, she said.

Terry? I said. Isn't there a lady?

That's Mrs Popeye, she said.

That's a funny name, I said.

Mr Popeye doesn't live here, she said, because he's a sailorman. But he comes sometimes.

I see, I said. And I got the idea all right but I didn't have a chance to ask her any more because Mr Clegg came up and asked if I felt like having a drink. He'd had a shave and put on a collar, though without any tie.

Yes, I said. But can you get one?

Come on, he said. And you clear away out of here, he said to Fanny. Look at her legs, he said.

I've got nice legs, Fanny said, and she pulled her dress up to her waist to show me.

154

Of course you have, I said. Only you want to be careful they don't snap off.

Her old man told her off for pulling her dress up, and we left her talking to the budgie which was kidding to itself in a piece of looking-glass. But all the way along to the pub Mr Clegg kept on about her legs.

You look at them, he said, it just shows you the way a working man gets it put across him every time.

Too right, I said, but I wasn't anxious to start talking politics.

We went along to the pub where I'd seen Mr Clegg the day before and the pub-stiff that was on the door told us to go upstairs where there was quite a few, including all sorts, men and women. And we hadn't been there long when the barman got the tip and we were all shoved up a little stairway on to the next floor. But that was the only scare, nobody was caught, and by the time it was dark the pair of us had a good few in, and each time I paid because there never was a time when Mr Clegg even looked like paying. And things being what they were I was beginning to feel like calling it a day, only just then a bloke came in that was a cobber of Mr Clegg's.

He was a cook off a boat too, a tremendous big man, but dressed more like a stoker in dungarees that would hardly button across his chest. He didn't have any singlet on underneath and his chest was all hair, and when he'd had a few drinks he started to sweat, and you could see it oozing out and running down under the hair until it soaked into his trousers. I shouted him and Mr Clegg and he shouted back, and then I got talking to the barman and dropped out while the cook went on shouting Mr Clegg. The both of them talked politics and the cook sounded a good deal more bolshy than Mr Clegg was. And then a tall bloke joined in. He'd been sitting there on his own listening, and he started off by saying he didn't see anything wrong with capitalism. Well, that got the cook going good and proper, he paid for whiskies for the three of them and they went on and had one after another, the cook always paying and calling the big nobs that run the world for all the names he could think of. Me and the barman just listened, and after the cook had spent about a quid him and Mr Clegg went off together, and then the tall bloke came over and asked the barman what the cook's name was. But the barman said he didn't know.

Come on, he said, you know.

I don't know, the barman said.

You heard what he was talking about?

Sure, the barman said.

He's a bolshy.

Maybe, the barman said.

What do you reckon's wrong with capitalism? the tall bloke said, but the barman wouldn't answer. What's the name of his cobber? he said.

I don't know, the barman said.

Well, instead of saying anything more he went downstairs and the barman winked at me and said he was a demon, and I wasn't surprised because I'd picked there was something wrong with him right from the start. But it wasn't long before he came back with the boss.

Terry, the boss said, you know the name of that big fellow.

I don't know, the barman said.

You better tell.

No I don't know, the barman said, and considering the way they were picking on him I felt like having a go at cleaning up the pair of them.

Anyhow the boss saw it was no good so they went out and I asked the barman to have a drink. You could see it had shaken him up and we both had double gins. And seeing there was nobody else there just then he said we'd have another two on the house. It would be good for his cough, he said. He had an awful cough. And once having got started we kept on for quite a while. He was a lot older than me, with one of those hard faces all covered with wrinkles like Aussies have, but I sort of had the feeling he was a decent bloke.

156

You've got a hard dial, I said, but I bet you've got a kind heart.

I'll say, he said.

I bet you have, I said. But of course I was stunned. Anyhow, I said, isn't your name Mr O'Connor?

Sure, he said.

Well, I wanted to tell him I'd been sort of trying to place his face right from the jump, and now I'd suddenly remembered. One time when I was working on a farm he brought out a racehorse to graze. It was a good while ago but I knew he was the same bloke, though I didn't get the chance to make certain because a crowd came in and he had to get busy. He pushed me over one more double gin which he only pretended to ring up on the peter, but there wasn't a chance to talk. So I thought I'd better shove off or I'd be ending up tight as I was the night before. I said so long to the barman and that I'd be seeing him, and it was only when I was trying to walk straight along the street, just to see how tight I was, that I remembered the boss had called him Terry. Which made me pull up while I tried to figure out whether he might be the same bloke as Fanny's Terry. I thought maybe I'd go back and find out, but instead I kept on along the street to find out how tight I was. I could walk straight all right but it didn't mean anything, because sometimes you get head-drunk, and sometimes you get leg-drunk, and there's a lot of difference between the two.

I thought I'd better cry off the booze for a bit, so all next week I went to the beach. It was too good to miss, specially as it was so baking hot round the streets. The asphalt went soft and there were marks of motor tyres all over the road, and away in front of you the heat made it look as if water was lying on the road, so you'd naturally think of the beach. And it was certainly great to be out there. I'd go on a tram as far as it went, and then I'd walk on to a quiet bit of beach that I knew about.

Most days nobody'd come around, but I had company,

because the first morning on the tram I met a bloke named Ted who was doing the same as myself. I'd meet him every day, and I'd always bring a couple of riggers and he'd buy some buns, and it was certainly nice to have his company. He never had much to say so I couldn't make out hardly anything about him, though I thought he looked a bit of a hard-shot. He wasn't a rangy specimen like me, no, he was nuggety, with one of those faces that is flat on the front of your head. And being dark he didn't get sunburnt nearly so bad as I did. To kick off with we'd fool about in the water, and if there was nobody around we wouldn't worry about any togs. Then we'd fool about on the beach and lie in the sand, and when it was time for the buns and the beer they'd go down well, and in the afternoon we'd just about go to sleep. It was a great life I can tell you, though coming home in the tram we'd be properly tired out, which is what lying in the sun always does to you. Ted'd say, So long, see you again tomorrow, and I'd be too tired for anything except a feed and a talkie, and if the talkie wasn't any good I'd just about go to sleep. And one night the joker sitting next to me had to poke me in the ribs because I was snoring.

Well, it was like that for a whole week, and some nights my sunburn was that bad I could hardly sleep. By Sunday I thought I'd better give it a rest, but the weather was still holding out so I thought no, the going's good, I'll give it one more pop.

And that day Ted was there as usual but he had his girl with him. I didn't feel like butting in but he called me over and gave me a knock-down, and she was certainly the goods, a good-looker and a great figure, sort of streamlined all over, though you could tell she had a temper. She wasn't like Ted, she was a mag, and all the way along until we got to our beach she talked about how nice the water looked, and she'd make us stop to pick up shells and look in the pools to see things. But it wasn't long before we were undressed and in the water, and nearly all morning we had a great time just fooling about. Mavis was the girl's name

158

and she'd brought a thermos and plenty of sandwiches, and she made me have some. I'd brought my riggers as usual but Mavis wouldn't have any, because she said drink only brought sorrow into people's lives. Ted said he was willing to take the risk so we drank the beer between us, and then Ted lay on his back with his togs rolled down and said this sort of life would do him for keeps. Mavis kept on looking his way and you could tell she was nuts on him, but I knew there was something wrong because she couldn't help picking on him every chance she got.

Yes, she said, you can be a sand-boy every day while I go and work in that damn shop.

Forget it kid, Ted said.

Listen to him Bill, she said. The first time we made a date he turned up tight in a taxi. He was broke too, and I had to pay five shillings for the fare.

And instead of saying anything to that Ted just rolled over and curled himself round Mavis.

Don't make out you're a smoodger, she said, because you're not.

If anyone knows anything better than this sun lead me to it, Ted said.

He's a baby over the cold Bill, Mavis said. Last winter I knitted him a woolly and he used it to go to bed in, with his underpants on too. And what's the good of a man when he goes to bed like that?

Ted rolled away from her then, he lay on his side with his back to the pair of us.

Look at that sea, he said.

But Mavis couldn't stop herself from trying to put nasty ones across him, though I bet she knew she was making him feel sore.

Yes, she said, it's all right for you, but what's a hot day in that damn shop. It only means us girls have to let our stockings down to try and keep cool. If they didn't let you go home at night you might just as well be in gaol.

You'll get over it kid, Ted said.

Listen to him Bill, Mavis said. He works about three

months a year, so where would he be if he hadn't got me?

You get your money's worth sweetie, Ted said.

Listen to him Bill, Mavis said. That's what he says. When I knitted him a woolly and he used it to go to bed in.

Well, Ted got up and went away and tried to see how far he could throw stones up the cliff. And Mavis kept on talking, but I pretended to go to sleep and when I gave a few snores she didn't say anything more. But I looked and she was crying, though when I looked again she was reading a True Romance, but it wasn't long before she gave that up and just stretched herself out in the sun. Ted came back and stretched himself out too, with his arm round Mavis, and we must have all gone to sleep because for a long time nobody moved or said anything.

But when we were sitting up and talking again Mavis must have temporarily got all the dirt out of her system, because instead of picking on Ted she made us laugh with yarns about people she served in the shop, and the way they talked and carried on, and what she'd do with the money if she ever won an Art Union. And afterwards we all went in for another swim, and Ted said he'd bet me I wasn't game to swim round a buoy that was anchored a good way out from the shore. So I took him on, but when I was out there hanging on to the buoy for a rest I got a bit of a surprise, because they'd both gone out of the water and were just about dressed. I swam back fast, but by the time I touched bottom they'd climbed nearly to the top of the cliff, and I could hear Ted swearing at Mavis and telling her to come on. And when I sang out for them to wait Ted sang out that they'd wait at the tram.

Well, I didn't hurry myself. If they waited at the tram that would be all right, but if they didn't that would be all right too. Because I thought it wouldn't be long before Mavis was picking on Ted again, and I wasn't anxious to be there when she started. And it was only when I'd finished dressing that I found out my money was gone.

Of course it was a knock and I certainly felt bad. I

thought well, I hope poor old Mavis gets her whack, but Ted being the sort of joker I'd gathered he was I didn't suppose she would. She probably wasn't in the joke. What's money anyhow, I thought. I'd been in town just over a week and had a good time, even if I hadn't had any luck so far as a girl was concerned. To hell with Ted and Mavis, I thought.

But it was hard all the same. I thought I could go into every shop in town until I found out where Mavis worked. But I knew I wouldn't do that. Ted might be no good but I could tell she was nuts on him, and it'd be rocking it into her properly to put the police on to him. I'd never be able to prove anything anyhow, and my idea of the johns is that a man wants to keep well away from them no matter what goes wrong.

My sugar's gone, I thought, that's all there is to it. Now I've got to look for a job.

Well, it wasn't the first time I'd been broke, and I knew I'd feel better if I went home and slept on it. The main thing was to stop myself from doing any more thinking. I didn't have the price of a tram fare because Ted had left me a skinner, so I started to walk into town. But I didn't hurry myself, and I kept stopping to look at everything I saw going on in the streets just to keep my mind occupied.

And as it turned out it wasn't long before I got a notion. I went past a house that was hidden behind some trees and just over the fence there was a garden. So I walked up and down and when there was nobody in sight I hopped over the fence and pulled up a plant that looked as if it might be growing into a little tree. I wrapped it in a sheet of newspaper I was keeping because of the acceptances, and I'd only gone a few more streets when I met a lady that looked as if she might do a bit of business.

Excuse me lady, I said, but maybe you're interested in gardening.

Yes, she said, I am.

Well, I said, I'm off a boat and I got this in Jamaica.

Why, she said, it looks like a something or other.

I don't know what you call them, I said, but I've never seen them out here and you never saw such a pretty flower.

So she asked me if it had got long red petals.

No, I said, the flower's blue-coloured and as big as my head. You don't see many of them even in Jamaica, I said, so I reckon it ought to be worth a good five bob out here.

So then she said she hoped I wasn't telling her a story.

Oh no lady, I said, I wouldn't do that.

We had a bit more barney and finally she took it for three and six, and soon as I'd got the sugar in my pocket I didn't lose any time in shifting along. But I didn't take a tram, no, I kept on walking and slowed down again after a while, and got into town pretty late, so although I was feeling a bit empty I went straight home to bed and was lucky enough to get to sleep before I had a chance to start doing any more thinking.

And next morning I woke up early and the weather still looked good, though of course I didn't think it looked quite so good as it had other mornings. I hadn't anything to eat but I made a cup of tea, then I thought I'd better get down town to see about a job. I looked at the paper in the Library but there was nothing doing, and I spent the morning going round the registry offices but there was nothing doing in any of those places either. And in the afternoon it was just the same. I tried all the registry offices again, and when it was time for the afternoon paper to come out I waited outside where they always stick up the front page to let people see the ads. But I could hardly get near for the crowd, and when I did get a bo-peep there weren't any jobs that I thought I'd have a chance of getting. So I went inside to look at the file, because I'd missed seeing the results of the double I had on with the taxi-driver, and what with going to the beach all the week before, and having plenty of chips in my pocket, I hadn't worried. Well, I'd picked a first and a second, and the second had only got beat by a head. It was the first time I'd ever got so close and I got a bit excited, because I thought if I could get that close I could pick two winners, so I decided I'd see the taxi-driver and take another instead of breaking into my three and six, which I hadn't done even though I was feeling pretty empty inside.

But first I hung round the streets a bit longer, standing on the corners to roll cigarettes and watch the crowd, though seeing I have my itchy feet I never can stand still for very long, particularly when everyone else is on the move. Then I went up to see the taxi-driver but he wasn't on the stand. His cobbers said he'd be back soon so I waited but he didn't turn up, and I had to go into the pub because I wanted to pick up a bit of counter-lunch. I saw Mr Clegg there with a half-handle in front of him and he looked as if he was making it last a good long while, but I dodged about in the crowd to keep him from seeing me and asked for a half-handle myself. The eats were late coming out and I had to make my drink last a lot longer than I thought I would, but when the trays did come I was one of the first to be in, and I finished up by putting away quite a good feed. The barman took my half-handle to fill it again but I said, Wait a minute, where can I see Terry?

Terry? he said, Terry's left here.

All right, I said, fill her up. Where's he working now? I said.

The barman didn't know, so I had my drink and came out. The taxi-driver was there and I took the double, and he said I was lucky because it was a new chart he'd just got out. There were hardly any taken certainly, so I picked a good one, but at the last moment I decided I wouldn't cough up the sugar just then. The taxi-driver didn't look any too pleased but he said O.K. boy, I'm a sport.

Then I didn't know what to do. I didn't know whether to blow in a bob on a talkie or not, so to put off trying to decide I thought I'd go and have a lie-down on my bed. But Fanny was just taking the budgie inside, and she showed me the way it could swing a ping-pong ball that was tied to the top of its cage. She'd bought it with the money from the money-tree, she said.

The old man isn't home yet Bill, she said, so we can go and look.

No, I said, not just now.

But she pulled me by the hand, so I gave in and we had to walk on the ground that Mr Clegg had dug to get under the tree, but it was only a tray bit that I dropped. Fanny danced up and down and went to show her mother and I went upstairs, and when the old man came home I heard them having a row. And later on I looked out the window and he was down there digging.

But being all on my pat up there that evening somehow gave me the dingbats properly. I couldn't decide what to do to fill in the time, and I couldn't keep my mind off thinking about a job. I tried reading my True Story but it was no good. I'd just lie on my bed but that was no good either, and I'd have to keep getting up to walk up and down. I'd stop in the middle of the floor to roll a cigarette and listen to them downstairs. I'd think, my God I've got to have someone to talk to, but even after I'd turned out the light and had my hand on the doorknob I'd go back and just flop on the bed. But the last time I flopped I must have dozed off, because I woke up lying in my clothes, and I wondered where the hell I was. I'd been dreaming, and I still seemed to be in the dream, because there wasn't one sound I could hear no matter how hard I listened. Then somebody started coughing and I knew where I was, but next minute I was back in the dream again, and I kept on dreaming and waking up right until it began to get light, though the last time I dropped off I slept a long time and never dreamt a thing.

It doesn't matter what sort of a night you have, things are always different in the morning. I didn't waste any time hopping out of bed because I didn't want to give myself a chance to start doing any more thinking. And I didn't have much of a chance anyhow, because while I was mucking about getting my bed made, I heard Mrs Clegg come upstairs and start giving somebody a tongue-banging.

It developed into a real ding-dong row, and so help me if the other voice didn't sound like Terry O'Connor's, and so far as I could tell he was giving just about as good as he got.

Shut the door, was the last thing he sang out. And Mrs Clegg sang out, Shut it yourself.

So I went out to get an eyeful and there was Terry sitting up in bed reading the paper.

Gee, I said, so this is where you hang out.

Hello boy, he said, and I went and sat on his bed and said I'd heard he'd left the pub.

That's right, he said.

You know Terry, I said, I remember you. You remember Mr Fletcher's farm?

Sure, he said.

Well, I said, I remember when you brought out a horse.

That's right, he said. Well, he said, it looks like another scorcher, and he threw the paper away and did a big stretch and we yarned for a bit and I asked him who the dame was that lived next door.

That's our Maggie, he said.

She's not my type, I said.

No, Terry said, nor mine either, and he said he wouldn't have her on if she was hung with diamonds. Well, he said, I suppose a man's got to rise and shine.

I've got to go and look for a job, I said. And Terry said he was looking for a job too, and while he was getting dressed I looked in the paper but there didn't seem to be any jobs going. We went down town together anyhow, and I thought it was certainly great to have a bit of company. We passed a coffee and sandwich place and Terry asked if I felt like a bite.

Not specially, I said, but I'll have one.

So we had coffee and sandwiches, and I paid because the girl was waiting and Terry just went on eating. And when we came out we ran right into the taxi-driver that had the double chart.

Hello Terry, he said, how's things?

A box of birds, Terry said, and the taxi-driver brought out his chart. But Terry said he was stiff because the one he would have picked had been taken. Too bad, the taxi-driver said, and I told Terry the double I'd picked, and he said I'd beaten him to it and I'd be in the money there was nothing surer.

So that was all right, Terry made me think my luck was going to be in, and we went round all the registry offices together but there was nothing doing. So I asked Terry if he couldn't go to his Union, but he said it wouldn't be any good.

I had something to say about the Union boss last meeting, he said, and that's why I'm on the street. That and not letting that bloody dee bulldoze me.

Gee, I said, that's hard.

But Terry said it was best to forget it, and I asked him to come to the Dalmatian's for a feed. So we went along and the place was pretty full, but the Dally was working the peter and he remembered me.

You are back again, he said. That is good for me.

Good for me too, I said, because I want to eat.

Good, he said, good. It is good to eat.

Too right, I said.

Well, we had three courses and it certainly felt good afterwards, and after we'd rolled cigarettes I told Terry to wait because I wanted to speak to the Dally. Terry said O.K. and I barged into the kitchen and the Dally didn't look any too pleased.

What do you want? he said.

Well, I said, sort of embarrassed a bit.

Be quick, he said.

Well, I said, I suppose you couldn't give me a job.

No, he said, I cannot give you a job. Already I have too many to pay. They are not too many for the work, but they are too many to pay.

Yes, I said, but I thought if anybody turned it in.

You think somebody will walk out, he said. But nobody will walk out. It is always easy to walk out but today it is hard to walk in, so today nobody will walk out even if it is easy.

Then his missis put her head in the door and he told me to wait a minute. And soon as he'd gone the cook, who was a fat little joker and walked like a proper queen, came over and asked if it was a job I was after.

You come back tomorrow, he said. And when I asked him why tomorrow he said the bloke they had washing dishes out in the pantry would have to go to the quack.

What's he got? I said.

You know, the cook said. He showed me this morning and he's got it pretty bad.

Good, I said, and thanks for the tip.

And then the boss came back. You are still here, he said, but I cannot give you any work.

Never mind, I said.

You can pay now, he said. One dinner one shilling, and he held out his hand.

No, I said, two dinners two shillings, and I'll pay you tomorrow.

And he certainly didn't look any too pleased over that, but I walked out the door and picked up Terry, and the Dally came after us right on to the street but he never said anything. Then just to get out of the streets for a bit the pair of us went down on the wharves, and half-way along one wharf we watched while a lot of wharfies worked on a boat that was unloading guano.

There's your chance, Terry said. You get extra pay for working that stuff.

What about you? I said.

No, he said, the dust's no good to me.

I asked a man and he told me to go on board and ask, and I went on board but I couldn't find the man I had to ask for. I looked down the hold and the wharfies were shovelling the stuff into bags, but you could hardly see them for dust. They looked as if they hadn't got a stitch on and they were sweating properly and the dust was sticking to the sweat, and it was certainly a sight because all you could see was a tangle of bodies nearly the same colour as the guano, except that the colour was darker where the sweat was collecting and running down. The stuff smelt like the bird-dung it was too, it got up my nose and all over me just looking down, so I went back to Terry.

I can't find the man, I said, but the job don't look any catch.

I bet it don't, Terry said, and we walked on to the end of the wharf and sat on the edge with our legs hanging down. And it was great to be sitting there too. For the first time for days a wind had got up and you could sit in the sun without feeling too hot. There were big woolly clouds in the sky, and blowing up against the tide the wind was making the sea choppy, and I thought no man whose belly was full could have said it wasn't good to be alive. I wondered if Terry was thinking the same way, but a man never does ask those sort of questions, so instead I asked him if he'd have a smoke, and he made one but it made him cough. He threw it away and I asked him hadn't he got rid of his cold.

It's not a proper cold, he said.

No? I said.

It was the war, he said.

I didn't say anything but I thought it was rotten. Terry looked hard and tough, but his face was sunk in, and maybe the wrinkles didn't improve it either, and there was only enough of him to cover his bones and nothing over. But when things are rotten like that what can a man say? But it sort of made it not so good to be just sitting there on the end of the wharf, and so help me if I didn't begin to start thinking about how I was broke, which I didn't want to do.

Come on, I said. And I wanted to do the registry offices again but Terry said once a day was enough and we had an argument, and in the end I said I was going to do them anyhow, so Terry came along and waited outside. And so help me if there wasn't a job going at the second one I tried. It was a farm job a good way out of town and you had to pay your own fare, but I knew if I took it on I'd get there all right. But I somehow just couldn't say I'd take it on, and it was mainly because I couldn't help thinking of Terry waiting for me in the street outside. So I got the woman to promise she'd keep it open for me if I came back inside a couple of hours. And I never said a word to Terry but when he stopped outside the next registry place I said no, because I'd got to go back to the last place later on. So to pass the time we went and had a lie-down in the park and Terry put his hat over his face and went to sleep.

But I didn't feel like sleeping. I kept looking at Terry and I kept wondering what the hell would become of him, and I couldn't make out why he wasn't racing horses any more. He looked sick anyhow, and I was practically certain he was a skinner. Of course it was none of my business, but I thought he was a decent bloke and it was certainly nice to have his company. I thought damn it all, it's none of my business, but I couldn't make my mind up all the same. Then while I was wondering what the hell was wrong with me there was a joker came and sat on the grass right alongside.

I say mate, he said, could you give me the lend of a bob.

No, I said, and you needn't wake my cobber up.

Sorry mate, he said, and he went and sat down further off.

Well, I thought that showed a sort of nice feeling so I went over.

I'm on the beach myself, I said, but I can make it a deener.

Never mind mate, he said.

No, I said, you take the dough.

God bless you mate, he said.

That's all right, I said.

Then he got talking and he said he felt like calling me Bill, because I reminded him of a mate of that name. It was quite a yarn he got telling me. This Bill was a pretty good mate, he said, and when they were up against it he didn't mind going shares with any money he got. Though later on it was different, it was the joker telling me the yarn that usually did the shelling out. He didn't mind, he said, though he reckoned he shelled out a lot more than Bill ever did. And Bill would admit that. Bill'd say never mind, because he'd make it up when his ship came home. Well, it finally turned out that once when he was away in the country looking for a job he read in the paper how Bill had won a prize in an Art Union. And it made him think. He'd been thinking he'd like to make the break with Bill if he could without letting him down, so now was a good opportunity. He was up against it at the time and Bill had promised to make it O.K. with him when his ship came home, but he had the feeling that a man can say those things, but it's different when you actually have the dough. So he thought of a stunt, he thought he'd do Bill one last good turn. He sent him a letter and said he'd heard of a job away down south, so he'd decided to go and so long and good luck, and he never mentioned a thing about the Art Union. But he'd hardly posted the letter when he got one from Bill saying so long and good luck because he was getting out of the country and sailing that night. And Bill never mentioned a thing about the Art Union either.

It just shows you, he said.

Yes, I said.

A man wants a mate that won't let him down, he said.

Yes, I said. But I wasn't paying much attention because Terry had woke up.

I've got to go, I said.

Wait a minute mate, he said.

No, I said, I've got to go.

Listen mate, he said.

No sorry, I said, and I went back to Terry, and we went down town again and Terry waited while I went in and told the woman I wasn't taking the job. When I came out I told Terry there was nothing doing and he said I was stiff.

It's O.K. I said, and when I turned into the first pub we came to Terry said he knew of a better one, and it was certainly a good one for a feed. The counter-lunch had just come out, and for the price of our half-handles we put away just about as much as we could hold. Then we had another two half-handles which meant I hadn't a razoo left. Terry said let's go, and to finish up the day there was nothing to do except kick around the streets. We'd stand in shop doorways and Terry'd pipe off everyone that went past, and outside the picture theatres he'd make me wait to watch people getting out of their cars.

See that old duchess, he'd say, she wants you to look at her now she's got her feathers pruned, but when she wakes up in the morning she won't look so hot, she won't want anybody looking at her then.

I bet she won't, I'd say, and I'd forget about being broke thinking what a funny joker Terry was. He didn't seem to be worrying about anything, and we carried on joking all the way up to Mrs Clegg's.

But when we got to the top of the stairs it was different, because all Terry's gear was in a heap outside his door and the door was locked. And Terry got excited and said he'd bust in the door. But I said he'd better not, he could doss in with me, I said, and have it out with Mrs Clegg in the morning. So while I made us a cup of tea he put his things in my room, and then we managed to get pretty comfortable in the bed even though it was a pretty tight fit.

Terry didn't waste any time going right off to sleep either, but I couldn't get to sleep. After all, considering the two of us were broke, and what with turning down a job, a man would have been lucky to get to sleep without doing any thinking. It was one of those hot nights too, and I started to roll round and woke Terry up. So I tried to lie still but when I got the cramp I thought no, this is no good. I waited until Terry was snoring again and then I managed to get out without disturbing him. I went and leaned out the window and I could see Fanny's money tree in the moonlight, and maybe that's what gave me the notion how to pick up a little money before morning. I got into my clothes and borrowed a pair of sandshoes that were among Terry's gear, and out in the street it was nice and quiet and a lot cooler. And a clock said it was going on for one o'clock.

I did a long trek out to one of the suburbs and then I didn't waste any time getting round the back of the houses to clean up any money that had been left out for the milkman. Some places I couldn't find any billy, or a dog would bark and put the wind up me properly, but I kept on until I got nearly ten bob all told. Then it wasn't so good doing the long trek back again, and I couldn't stop myself from worrying a bit over pinching money. But I thought when a man's in a jam he oughtn't to let himself be worried, and besides, there were the two of us to consider. Then when I got back to Mrs Clegg's I knew as soon as I was inside the room that Terry was awake. So when I got back into bed I said I'd had to do a job for myself, and when I was nearly asleep Terry said that sort of job didn't usually take several hours to do.

Oh I don't know, I said, they say a dog will travel five miles.

No, Terry said, more than that.

Well, you mightn't believe it, but I woke up early feeling just like a box of birds. And it was certainly great to have somebody to talk to, though Terry didn't look any too good so I told him to stay in bed, and while the kettle was boiling I went out to buy him a newspaper, and we looked at the jobs but there didn't seem to be any going. So Terry sat up and read the news out while we had our tea. Then I told him I'd be back in a minute, and I went downstairs and barged right into the kitchen where Mrs Clegg was getting the breakfast.

Mrs Clegg, I said, Terry's shifted his gear into my room.

Then he can shift it out again, she said.

No, it's stopping there, I said, and I suppose you don't happen to have another bed.

Who's paying the rent? she said, and I said I was.

All right mister, Mrs Clegg said, only it'll be extra for the room.

Good, I said, but what about the bed?

Well, we fixed it up. Mrs Clegg said we could have
Fanny's bed and Fanny could sleep on the floor. And
seeing it was just a stretcher we could fold it up for more
room during the day if we liked. I said wasn't it a bit tough
on Fanny, but Fanny jumped about and said she *wanted* to
sleep on the floor.

So that was all right, and when I went back to Terry
there was Mrs Popeye sitting on the bed in her kimono-
thing.

Our Maggie's come to see us, Terry said.

Good, I said. How are you Maggie?

I'm feeling fit, she said, and the way she sort of slowly
blinked her eyes made me think of a kid's doll.

We know what you're fit for, Terry said.

That's right, Maggie said, and she asked how was her
back hair.

Bitch, Terry said, and he went on reading the paper.

That's no way to talk to a lady, Maggie said. Me being a
married lady too.

Well, Terry said something pretty rude to her then but
she didn't seem to mind. What with her fringe she certainly
looked like a sort of cheap doll, though she showed real
rabbit's teeth when she giggled.

Fancy you two boys sleeping here together, she said.

That's all right Maggie, I said.

Yes, she said, two's always better than one if you don't
like a crowd.

I don't get you Maggie, I said, but just then Terry hit
her whack over the head with the paper.

Get out, he said.

But Maggie didn't seem to mind. She said she'd be
seeing us again and cleared off to her room, and I told
Terry I wouldn't mind trying her out even though she
wasn't my type, though her being married made a bit of
difference. And Terry said she was no more married than
he was, and anyhow he wouldn't have her on if she was
hung with diamonds.

I thought it was about time I was getting along to the Dally's, so I told Terry I wanted to get down town but he needn't worry about getting up until he was ready, and I told him about what I'd fixed with Mrs Clegg.

I'll meet you at the Dally's at twelve o'clock for dinner, I said, and I gave him half a dollar. And I went off whistling and feeling life was good when a man had a cobber like Terry to kick around with, and maybe I was feeling good because I was thinking what a hell of a good joker I was. Though if I was I was kidding myself, because when all said and done I was only doing what I was to please myself, though it might have been a roundabout way of doing it.

I went along to the Dally's anyhow, and besides everything else the weather was still staying good, so I didn't leave off whistling, and the Dally was standing in front of the peter with his hands in his pockets. And he looked a bit worried.

Hello, I said, here I am and I'm after a job.

He looked a bit more cheerful when he saw me but he looked suspicious.

How did you know? he said.

Know what? I said, sort of innocent.

Never mind, he said, but what do you know? Have you ever done the work? he said.

Sure, I said, I've helped the cook in camps out in the bush.

It's not the same, he said, but he told me to come with him and he took me out the back and told me to get busy on a bag of potatoes.

Wait a minute, I said, what are the wages and how long do I work?

He didn't look too pleased over that, and instead of telling me he said it was no good me starting if I hadn't got an apron. But just then the cook came out of the kitchen and said he'd lend me an apron, so the Dally said what the hours and wages were, and then I got the apron from the cook and got busy on the spuds. And by the time I'd done

174

a few benzine tins full time was getting on, and I had to get the sink all clear to be ready for the twelve o'clock rush. And when the whistles blew I went outside and Terry was waiting, so I gave him the works and told him to meet me when I knocked off. Then I had to get inside again and get busy, and what with being new to the work, and except for time off to get outside the two meals that were thrown in with the pay, I was kept busy without hardly a minute to spare right until the time I knocked off.

It was good having the job though. I came out feeling everything was O.K. and I met Terry and after we'd splashed on a talkie we went home and the two beds were all set, and Terry had cleaned up the room and made everything real tidy. There was hardly any room to move about certainly, but we didn't let that worry us, no, we made us cups of tea before we went to bed and I said it'd be beer once I got my pay. And I wasn't long going to sleep, though I remember Terry woke me up several times with his coughing, and each time I could see the red dot of a cigarette in the dark, and I supposed he felt the need of it but it only made him cough all the worse.

Then each morning it was the same. I'd wake up feeling good and I'd put the kettle on and go and buy Terry a paper, and maybe Maggie would come hanging around cadging cigarettes, and sitting on the beds while she talked. And I wouldn't have minded taking it easy but I'd have to get off to the Dally's, and the morning I went after I'd given Terry my last half dollar I was a bit worried because it was still a good few days to payday, and Terry hadn't managed to pick up any sort of job. He just kicked about the town all day and came into the Dally's for his meals, and I didn't blame him if he wasn't trying much for a job because every day he looked more sick, and at night the way he coughed was something awful. I thought if I could get Maggie on her own I might ask her for the lend of a few bob, but I changed my mind because I thought of another stunt.

I got up before it was light and Terry never woke up, and this time I picked on a different locality. It was just getting daylight when I got there, and I picked on a street that ran off the main road from near a bus-stop, and sure enough the papers had been delivered. So I collected the lot and parked them in a heap in a shop doorway, then when the buses began to run I stood at the bus-stop with the papers under my arm, and it wasn't long before I'd nearly sold out. Of course I thought the stunt was a good deal more risky than the last one, specially as a good few jokers came out of the street I'd been down, and went very crook about their papers not being delivered. So between buses I put what was left back in the shop doorway, all except one which I kept for Terry, and then I had to do the long trek back because I didn't like the idea of being seen on a bus. And it took longer to do because I kept off the main road as much as I could. So it was late when I got back to Mrs Clegg's, and I only had time to look in and give Terry the paper and half a dollar and then get along to the Dally's. And I felt a bit windy all the rest of the day, and off and on for a few days after. But nothing happened, so I was lucky, and what with a half-dollar I borrowed from Maggie Terry didn't go short of any meals before payday.

But by the time my second payday came round I was well sick of working for the Dally. He was certainly tough to work for. He was tight with the hot water, and it was hard to make a job of the dishes when there was grease floating thick on the top of a sink full of dirty water. And there were things I saw that put me right off the tucker. If the pumpkin wouldn't cook the cook'd put it out on a big dish and work it through his fingers until he'd squeezed all the lumps out. And a man hardly had time to wipe off his own sweat, let alone roll a cigarette, so for a spell I used to go out the back and pretend to do a job for myself. But I couldn't do that too often, because if there wasn't any cleaning up to do there was always the spuds to keep ahead with. You had to put them in a machine and turn the handle to knock the worst of the skin off, and with the weather like it was it certainly made a man sweat doing the turning.

I never got much chance to talk to any of the girls either, and it was a disappointment because there were several good-lookers among them, and I wouldn't have minded trying to fix a date. But with all of us going for the lick of our lives there'd only be time for a wisecrack now and then, though one of them began pinching me on the backside every chance she got. I didn't mind, though I'd rather have done the pinching myself, but the cook got my goat when he started trying to do the same thing. He was a tonk all right, just a real old auntie, and I'd met the sort a few times before. Right from the jump he'd come hanging round me if the boss wasn't about. He'd want me to let him do things for me, so just to keep him quiet I brought along a big bundle of washing which included Terry's as well, and so help me if instead of turning it down he didn't do the best job I've ever seen done. And it was then he started doing the pinching, which made it mighty awkward for me seeing I'd let him do the washing. And what with working alongside him every day he had me a bit worried, and what with the tough work I knew my feet would get itchy and I wouldn't be able to stick it out at the Dally's for long.

And I haven't mentioned it before but it was coming on to Christmas, and it worked out that payday came just the day before. So after I'd knocked off me and Terry had a spree up in our room. We got Maggie to come and be in as well, and so help me if she didn't know how to drink beer. And when the party was going properly we got Mr Clegg to come and be in too, and even his missis came and had a few. So that night we were all happy.

Then when I knocked off Boxing Day Terry was waiting to tell me I'd landed the double I had on with the taxi-driver. So that was a bit of real All Right. We decided to have another spree, which we did with the same crowd, and we were all happy a second time. Then the next morning I decided to turn in the job at the Dally's. What with my wages and winning the double, I had a fair bit of sugar in my pocket even though the two sprees had knocked me back considerably. And Terry said why not try my luck at the Races. Well, the weather was still staying good as gold, and I thought it would be great to have a day out at the Races with Terry. So I told the Dally a yarn about how I had to go and see my mother because she was sick, and he let me finish up that evening. And when the cook found out I could hardly stop him from sort of getting all over me, and you can believe it or not but he went out and bought me a bunch of flowers. I thought he must have heard the yarn about my mother, but when I said something so help me if he didn't begin to cry. He hadn't bought the flowers for anyone except me, he said.

It turned out a bosker day the day I went out to the Races with Terry. Though it hadn't rained for so long each day was just about as good as the one before if you didn't mind the heat. I paid Mrs Clegg some rent in advance just in case, then we went out in the tram and there was a tremendous crowd going, all flossied up for a day out and looking a lot different from what they looked like coming home. Though of course I wasn't thinking of that at the time. No, like everybody else Terry and me were out for the day, and you know the feeling. Terry looked good and didn't cough much, he was funny the way he piped off people he saw in the crowd, and I could have grabbed him round the waist and chucked him up in the air, I was that full of beans I was sort of feeling that way.

But once we were on the Course, which had all the grass burnt off by the sun and looked hard-going for the horses, it was easy to see that going to the Races wasn't exactly a holiday for Terry. He took it all very serious. And if I said anything when he was standing in front of the Tote trying to figure out what he'd back he'd go crook and tell me not to be a nark.

Well, I said, put on ten bob and we'll go down and see them at the barrier.

No, he said, you go.

No, I said, you come too.

No, he said.

So I said O.K. and gave him a couple of smackers. And after he'd been up to a window we went and got a good possie, and it wasn't long before the balloon came down and then they were off. And it was certainly great to watch, you could see the colours on the jockeys coming round the rail smooth as if they were birds flying, and I wished Terry had said what we were on, but I felt that way I didn't care. It was only ten bob anyhow, and I got all worked up just out of the fun of the thing, though Terry didn't look any different, not even when they were coming down the straight. Of course I thought he'd say if we were in the money once they'd passed the post, but he never said anything so I thought we must be stiff. He just waited until the judge's placings went up, then we went down to the birdcage to watch the horses coming in for the next race, and I forgot all about being stiff because I was thinking what real good horses they looked. There were a couple I thought I wouldn't have minded backing if I'd been there on my own, but I thought no, Terry knows his stuff so I'll just leave it to him. But when the prelims were over and we were going back to the Tote, Christ, if Terry didn't pull out four tickets that were duds.

Gee four, I said. But I knew I'd torn it soon as I spoke, because Terry pretended he was too busy with his card to take any notice. So I just said too bad, and I gave him a couple more smackers.

And so help me if this time it didn't turn out that Terry was on a good thing. But gee, I felt sore I'd opened my trap, because it turned out he'd gone easy with only ten bob and it was a pretty good divvy. All the same we went and had a few beers on the strength of it, and I was feeling that sore I had to make Terry let me shout. Then next race he went in solid but he had no luck, and after that it didn't matter what he did, he couldn't do anything right. And I was trying all the time to laugh it off, but there were times when I'd be feeling bad at the sight of people coming away from the pay-out windows. Because they'd be sticking money in their pockets and looking that pleased with themselves. I knew I'd have looked the same way myself, but I couldn't help thinking it just showed what money does to you.

Then it came on to the last race and Terry hadn't had any luck so I told him to take my last quid, though I didn't tell him it was the last. He didn't want to take it but I had to make him, because I was still feeling sore over not keeping my mouth shut.

We better quit, he said.

No, I said, give it one last pop.

No, Terry said, better not.

Go on, I said, you take the sugar.

Well, Terry put the quid on but we didn't go down to our usual possie. Terry said he was getting done-in, and you could go round the side of the Tote where the pay-out windows were, and see the finish of the race pretty good from there. So we stood on a seat under the trees and joked about how we'd be first to the pay-out windows anyhow.

But I never took much interest in the race because I was busy getting an eyeful of a joker that was already waiting over by the pay-out windows. He looked a weak sort of joker, just a little runt, though all turned out in his Sunday best. And to begin with I thought he was canned, because fast as he was eating a sandwich it came out his mouth again. I told Terry to look but just then they were coming down the straight, then when I turned round again the joker was coming over our way.

What won? he said, and he stood there with lumps of chewed bread coming out of his mouth.

Teatime won, Terry said, and I believe the joker would have fallen down if he hadn't grabbed us round the legs. So we got off the seat and sat him down, and for a while he looked real sick.

I knew he'd be tough, he said. I saw the way he lifted his

feet up in the prelim, he said, and he had me and Terry staring at a handful of tickets.

I put a tenner on, he said, and he'll pay that.

Maybe, Terry said, and then the figures went up and Teatime had paid a tenner sure enough.

Twenty tickets, the joker said, it was all the money I had. I lost my job, he said, and I've got my mother to keep, but I did like the way he lifted his feet up.

Well, we got introduced all round and the joker said his name was Reg, and Terry began to get sort of friendly with him, and maybe I began to get an uneasy sort of feeling. But I'd had enough experience of opening my mouth for one day so I didn't say anything.

Terry said we'd take Reg over to collect his dough, so we went over and got first at a window, and we all stood in the queue, this Reg in between the pair of us, and Terry talking nineteen to the dozen about racehorses. I'd never heard him say so much before, though I noticed he never said a word about how Reg was going to collect a hundred quid.

Then after a bit the windows went up and Reg got his money and Terry took us out a gate where he said we'd get a taxi, and sure enough we were lucky enough to get one. And the first pub we came to Reg wanted to stop for a drink, but Terry said leave things to him, and we finally pulled up at the biggest pub in town. Reg paid for the taxi and inside there was a crowd, but Terry pushed up to the counter and Reg stood us drinks just as fast as we could get the barman to serve us, and although it wasn't far off closing time we all had a good few in by then.

But right until we were turned out I hadn't sparked up much. Because Terry was still doing all the talking, and he was getting that friendly with this Reg. He certainly had me thinking things, though I admit I couldn't properly get a line on what it was all about. But I didn't want to interfere, so when we were all standing outside in the street I said I was going home.

No, Terry said, you come and eat.

No, I said, I want to have a lie-down.

What you want is a bellyful of tucker, Terry said.

No, I said, and I said so long and shoved off, and I thought Terry would go crook but he just let me go.

I wasn't happy about shoving off, but I was in one of those moods you get in sometimes. Before I turned the corner I took a look round and Terry and Reg were still standing outside the pub, and it looked as if Terry was still doing all the talking. It made me feel sore, though I couldn't get things at all straight in my mind. Terry's after that boy's dough, I told myself, but I didn't believe it all the same. No, I thought, Terry's a decent bloke and I don't reckon he'd do a thing like that. On the other hand what did I know about Terry? He wasn't the sort that ever lets you know much about himself, though you could tell he always had a lot going on in his mind, even if you had to guess what it was about. Terry wouldn't do a thing like that, I kept telling myself, but I sort of felt it was no good telling yourself that about anybody. Anybody is liable to do anything, I told myself, particularly where there's money concerned. And I remembered how out at the Races I'd been thinking what money does to you.

But what was I worrying about anyhow? Because Terry could do what he liked so far as I was concerned. He was up against it the same as I was, and when things are tough a man can't be worried. That's what I'd thought when I pinched the money out of the milk billies, so where was the difference? And then I thought maybe I was only feeling sore because I was jealous of this Reg. Because I'd thought Terry was the sort of joker who'd go solid with a cobber, and quite apart from the money business I didn't like the way he cottoned on to Reg.

But it was no good letting myself be worried, and I wasn't doing myself a bit of good standing there watching the pair of them. So I turned the corner thinking I'd go to the flicks, but then I remembered I only had a few odd bits of chicken feed left in my pocket, and that made me start thinking all over again. Oh hell, I said to myself, I'll go and have a feed.

So up towards Mrs Clegg's place I turned into a quick-lunch eating joint, and so help me if I didn't run into Maggie.

Hello Maggie, I said. All on your pat, I said, and seeing she was eating a pie I asked for one myself.

Fancy meeting you without your boy-friend, Maggie said.

That's all right Maggie, I said. And who's my boy-friend anyhow?

As if you don't know, she said, and she started doing the blinking doll stunt.

No Maggie, I said, I don't know.

Go on, she said.

So I told her not to talk like a blinking idiot and that sort of shut her up, though it was a blinking doll I should have said. And I started to kid to her a bit and you could see she was in the mood for a bit of kidding to. I put my hand on her leg underneath the table, and instead of carrying on and acting silly she just let it stay there, so when we'd finished eating I asked her what she was doing to put in the evening.

I got nothing on, she said.

Then let's go somewhere, I said.

No, she said, I better not. My husband's ship comes home any day now, so I better be a good girl.

Sort of save up, I said.

That's right, she said. Matelots have got to save up so I ought to too.

Do they save up? I said.

Well, she said, you're asking me.

And what about you? I said.

Well, she said, sometimes. It all depends. Anyhow, she said, what about yourself?

You can save up too damn long Maggie, I said.

I know, she said. My God, she said.

Come on Maggie, I said.

So I paid for the pair of us which left me practically a

skinner, but what with the way things were I was too far
gone to care about almost anything, except maybe whether
I could do a line with Maggie.

Do you want to go to the pictures? she said.

No, I said, let's walk, and we just walked and Maggie
was sort of serious, I'd never struck her in the same mood
before. She didn't seem to be taking notice of anything I
said, and we just kept on walking and turning corners. But
she was the one who sort of decided which corners to turn,
and seeing I hadn't taken much notice where we were
going I got a surprise when I discovered we'd parked
nearly outside Mrs Clegg's. But I hadn't time to say anything before Maggie said no, let's keep on walking. So we
kept walking, but now I was a wake-up to what was in
Maggie's mind. I was sitting up and taking notice so to
speak while we went on turning the corners, and I wasn't
surprised when we pulled up outside Mrs Clegg's a second
time.

And this time Maggie said come on up, and she went up
the stairs pretty fast with me following. And upstairs I
followed her straight into her room and she shut the door.
Then when I looked at her and saw the way she was
breathing I knew she wouldn't be able to stop herself, so I
naturally felt my heart begin to beat a bit.

Take it easy Maggie, I said, and we sat on the edge of the
bed and she was shivering, but I told her to take it easy,
and I put my arm round her and she cuddled up until I got
my hand on her bubs. But so help me if she wasn't that
flat-chested I couldn't even feel anything. And seeing I
didn't know what to say I said something about that. But it
made her go crook as anything.

You needn't be personal, she said, and she jumped up
and stood there looking at me, and she looked properly hot
and bothered.

Don't be silly Maggie, I said. Come over here, I said.

But she went on standing there and I was wondering
what I did next, though as it turned out she didn't waste
much time deciding things for me.

That Summer

Take it easy Maggie, I said. Struth, I said, but she was too keen. So I just lay back, I thought I'd let her work off steam a bit. And it was just as well I did back-pedal, because the pair of us were wake-ups when we heard somebody coming up the stairs, and when the door opened we were just sitting on the edge of the bed, though I suppose a man has to admit we must have both looked considerably hot and bothered.

Anyhow it was Maggie's bloke Bert. And he was a big matelot, though not a Pom, it was easy to tell he was a Pig Islander.

Hello, he said, but he didn't look at all pleased to see me there, though of course Maggie jumped up and began to make a fuss of him.

You're looking good Bert, she said, and Bert said he was a box of birds, and until Maggie chipped in he began telling her how his ship had got in late that afternoon and he'd got leave.

Bert, Maggie said, this is Bill.

How are you Bill, he said, and I got up off the bed but he didn't shake hands or anything, he just went on talking to Maggie, and I could tell she was worried over the way he was taking it.

Things didn't look any too good to me so I thought I'd best clear out. I said I was going and Maggie said hooray Bill, and I went over to my room. And there wasn't any sign of Terry so I sat down for a bit. I felt I needed to pull myself together, because what with running into Reg at the Races, and now this Maggie business coming afterwards, everything seemed to have gone wrong. And the last few weeks things had been that good.

It wasn't a bit of good just sitting there though, I knew I'd have to get out in the streets. But I'd hardly made up my mind to go when I heard an argument start over in Maggie's room, and I opened the door a bit so I could listen. And to begin with I couldn't hear much, and later on when they'd got to arguing loud enough for me to hear I didn't want to hear. In a way I didn't anyhow, because my name was being brought in, and the way things were developing it sounded as though there was going to be a serious row. Things didn't ease off any either, they got a lot worse. It was you did and I didn't more and more and louder and louder, and when it developed into let me go and you're hurting me I knew things were getting serious. He's going to beat her up, I thought, and I thought it was about time I got off down the street. Because what could I do? Terry'd always reckoned Maggie wasn't married but who could say? No, I told myself, I'm not going in there. I felt sorry for Maggie naturally, but I thought it was no good trying to do anything if I was the cause of the trouble. So I went out, and in the street you could still hear the pair of them tearing into each other, and it only took a minute or two before Maggie began to yell. Christ, I thought. But I knew it was best to keep out of it, and I began walking the streets just the same as I'd done with Maggie.

And I didn't go home for a long time that night. I thought I'd wait until Terry was sure to be home, so I kicked around the streets until it was well after midnight, and it did me good because there's always plenty to see going on round the streets, and it takes your mind off things when they go wrong. There's lots of other people in the world you tell yourself, and you start wondering what they're like. And maybe you decide everybody must be pretty much the same in most ways if you could only find out. That's my idea anyhow, though I admit I may be wrong.

I walked about for quite a while, then I decided I'd go and sit on a seat on the waterfront. And down there I watched some white patches that you could just see rocking on the water, and I decided they must be seagulls. I wondered why you never see them sitting on wires like you do other birds, and I decided it must be because of their feet. And thinking of birds made me remember about the pigeons I used to shoot in the bush, and next minute I'd started calling myself a fool for wanting to come into town. Town's no good, I told myself, a man doesn't have any

say, he just gets pushed about. And when I started to go
the length of the main street just once more, I was thinking
I'd go and try for a farm job first thing next morning. But
next minute I was remembering how I'd nearly come a
thud over Maggie, and then I forgot everything else because I was thinking about Terry again.

But I got a knock, because up at Mrs Clegg's there still
wasn't any sign of Terry, and all the stuffing sort of went
out of me so to speak. I certainly felt blue. But I thought
chin up, a man can't be worried. I listened but there
wasn't any sound from Maggie's room and it sort of
cheered me up. I bet it all ended up in a good old kafuffle,
I thought. Good luck to them anyhow, I thought. Then I
turned in and I never thought I would, but I went right
off to sleep without doing any more thinking.

But when I woke up late next morning Terry still wasn't
there. It made me feel bad, but I thought never mind,
he'll turn up. Yet I felt sort of jumpy. All sorts of things
that might have happened kept coming into my head, and
just because there wasn't any sign of life from Maggie's
room I worried over that as well. Though I told myself I
needn't, because they'd naturally be sleeping in, that was,
if Bert hadn't had to go back to his ship.

Then when I'd had a cup of tea I didn't know what to
do. I didn't want to go out and miss Terry, yet I knew it
would give me the dingbats if I just stayed on there waiting. So I decided I'd leave a note and then go out. Which
is what I did, and along the street I caught up to Mrs Clegg
who'd gone out ahead of me and was pushing an old pram.
And walking along I looked in the pram and it was filled
with things out of the kitchen, including a good few tools
that must have belonged to her old man.

Gee, I said, selling up the home.

Not yet, she said. It's this weather, she said, it makes
that man think he can take things easy.

It makes me lazy, I said. I wouldn't mind if it rained.

You know, she said, he never done that to her before.

Mr Popeye? I said.

If it wasn't for the money I'd turn her out, she said.

Yes? I said.

Then next minute she pulled up outside a pawnshop I'd noticed there before.

I go in here, she said, and she wheeled the pram inside. Things must be tough, I thought. And then I turned the corner and ran right into Terry.

Hello boy, he said, and I couldn't help it, I had to tell him I was that pleased to see him.

How are you feeling? I said.

Good, he said, but I thought he looked pretty crook on it.

Have you had your breakfast? I asked him.

No, he said, I haven't had anything.

Come on, I said, and when we passed the pawnshop I could see Mrs Clegg was still inside. Let's step on it, I said, and soon as we got in I let Terry go upstairs while I went into the kitchen. I couldn't find anything to eat though, there was nothing that would have fed even the budgie. But Terry said never mind, he couldn't eat anything anyhow. So I made him a cup of tea and he drank that, then he took off his coat for a lie-down, and I was all the time wanting to ask him if he had any money but I didn't like to.

It was good having him back though, but while I was wondering whether I couldn't think up another of my stunts for picking up a little ready cash he went off to sleep. So I thought I'd walk about in the streets for a bit and maybe I'd get an idea. But when I got downstairs there were two jokers knocking at the door. I picked them for what they were right away, and so help me if it wasn't me they were looking for, and when they said they wanted to ask me a few questions I told them to go ahead, but I admit I had the wind up considerably.

You'd better come along to the police station, they said.

All right, I said, but what's it all about? And they said I'd soon find out about that.

O.K. I said, but first I want to speak to my cobber
upstairs.

Then I thought no, why worry Terry when he needed to
get some sleep. And I wouldn't be away long, I thought.
So I told them it didn't matter about my cobber.

Well, they walked one on each side of me, and I tried to
talk to them now and then but they took no notice. Though
sometimes they'd have some joke on of their own, they'd
talk across me just as if I wasn't there, and it made me feel
as if I was some sort of wild animal they were taking
through the streets. And occasionally I'd see people we
passed who'd pick them for dees, and I knew they'd be
turning round for an eyeful. So all things considered I
wasn't feeling so good by the time we got to the police
station.

I didn't feel any better there either, because it was a big
place, not at all the sort of place you feel you can make
yourself at home in. We went up a lot of stairs and finally
they took me in a room and we all sat down round a table.

You've been interfering with a woman, one of them said.

Go on, I said. Have I?

But you'd never have guessed the way I was feeling from
what I said.

It won't do you any good telling lies, the same one said,
and he looked at some papers and said it was a serious
something or other. Anyhow, he said, all we want you to
do is answer a few questions.

All right, I said, first you give me the works, then I'll
tell you my story.

And it was Maggie who'd been putting it across me,
which is what I'd guessed, though how it had all come
about I didn't know. You'd have thought they'd have told
me that, but they never did. Instead they just sort of threw
out hints, and the way they made out they knew everything that had happened just about had me thinking they
must have had somebody there watching.

There's no question about what happened, one of them
kept on saying, and they kept on at me until I said, All

right, I'll tell you my story. Which is what I did, though I didn't say anything about Bert beating her up afterwards.

So then they sort of went over it all again.

You admit you put your hand on her, the one who did nearly all the talking said.

Yes, I said, but she didn't object.

She objected all right, he said.

Well, I said, maybe she did, but afterwards she didn't.

No? he said. Then why did her husband come in and find her fighting to save herself? And that was a new one on me because they certainly hadn't told me that part of Maggie's story.

That's just baloney, I said.

Well, he said, she can show the bruises.

So then I said how Bert had beaten her up. But they said I'd only just made that up, if I hadn't why hadn't I told them before? And they said it would make things a lot worse for me if I told lies.

Well, I tried to explain but it did no good, they just went on saying I'd admitted I put my hand on her and she'd objected. And I got that fed up of arguing I felt that way I didn't care much if they believed me or not, though I sort of woke up when they said they were sorry but they'd have to bring a case against me.

And it was certainly a knock because up till then I'd never realized I was properly in the cart, I certainly had no idea it was going to end up in a Court case. And it naturally made me begin to worry about Terry. I didn't know what to say, and they said I was lucky it wasn't a more serious charge, and seeing I'd admitted what I'd done and hadn't told any serious lies I'd probably get probation.

I still sort of had too much stuffing knocked out of me to say anything, but probation didn't sound so bad, and maybe I wouldn't have minded so much if I hadn't been thinking of Terry. All the same I didn't see how they could prove anything against me, but when I told them they said there wasn't any question about it because of what I'd admitted. And finally they said it would be best for me if they put it all in writing. And after we'd argued a bit more I got that fed up I thought writing it down wouldn't make any difference, so I went over it all again while one of them did the writing. And I admitted I put my hand on her, and I admitted she objected, and I admitted I let her go when I heard Bert coming, but I never admitted anything more, and besides other things I wanted them to put in about Bert beating her up, but they said it had nothing to do with it, and I couldn't say I'd actually seen him do it anyhow. Then when it was all finished they got me to sign, and I could sort of tell they were thinking they'd done quite a good stroke of work. But I was so fed up I was past caring about anything much.

They wouldn't let me go away then, no, they said they'd try to have the case brought up in the Police Court that afternoon, but it mightn't be until the next morning. So I asked them if I could send a message to my cobber, I wanted him to come and see me I said, and they said that would be O.K. they'd see Terry got the message. Then I asked them what the time was, and I'd no idea it had all taken hours and hours. The twelve o'clock whistles must have blown and I'd never even heard them.

I'll admit another thing, I said, I'm feeling empty.

We'll soon fix you up, one of them said, and they took me downstairs and turned me over to a john who wrote my name down in a book and told me to hand in all my money, but there was nothing doing because I didn't have any. Then when he'd taken my belt off me (it was so as I couldn't hang myself I suppose), he took me along a passage and locked me up. I sat down to save myself from holding my pants up, and I was sitting there thinking how it was the first time I'd ever been in one of those places, when the john came back with a tray that was loaded up with a big dinner. It was a real good dinner too, two courses and plenty to eat, and I could have eaten the lot and more, but I thought gee, so far as tucker goes I'm better off than poor old Terry is. I might be anyhow, I thought, because I remembered I didn't know whether he'd got any money out of Reg. All the same I didn't like to think of Terry going hungry, so I tore some pages out of a Western that was in the cell, and wrapped up half of both courses and put the parcel in my pocket. All in together it certainly looked an awful mess, but I thought Terry wouldn't mind if he was feeling empty.

Then when I'd got outside the tucker I felt a lot better. I stretched myself out on a sort of long seat that was the only bit of furniture in the cell, and I thought if only a man never had any cobbers or anything, getting picked up by the police would take away some of your worries anyhow.

I must have gone to sleep because it seemed no time before the john was unlocking the door and telling me to come along. And along at the end of the passage Terry was waiting for me. And if I wasn't pleased to see his wrinkled old Aussie's face! I certainly was. He grinned back at me too, and the john let us sit together on a seat there and I asked him how he was feeling now. And he said he was feeling good.

You don't look any too good, I said, but he said not to worry about him.

I'm in a jam, I said, and I gave him the works, and Christ if he didn't begin to laugh when I told him how I'd nearly had Maggie on.

How far did you get? he asked me.

This far, I said, and I showed him. But I never even felt anything, I said.

I bet you didn't, he said. But go ahead, he said, and I told him the rest and when I'd finished he said some pretty rude things about Maggie.

But don't you worry, he said, because there won't be any case.

They're going to bring one, I said.

Don't you worry, he said.

I'll need to get a lawyer, I said.

You won't need any lawyer, he said. Listen boy, he said, you don't need to worry, because I'm promising you there won't be any case.

All right Terry, I said, but are you sure?

Shake, he said.

All right, I said. And I certainly felt bucked, though I had no idea what he was going to do, yet I felt dead sure I could depend on him all the same, which was a peculiar feeling to have after the way I'd been feeling only the day before.

When does the case come on? Terry asked me. And he said there was just one thing. I've got to get hold of Maggie, he said, and he told me if he couldn't get hold of her by next morning the case might go as far as the Supreme Court, which meant they'd keep me in clink until the sittings came on unless somebody would go bail.

Do you know anyone? I said, and he said yes, maybe he might be able to fix things.

All right, I said, I'm leaving it to you. But Terry, I said, how are you off for sugar?

I'll be O.K. he said.

Have you got any? I said.

I've got a few bob, he said.

What about Reg? I said, and I couldn't help asking him but I bet I went red in the face.

I won't be seeing Reg, he said. He sounded a bit annoyed, and I didn't know whether I felt glad or sorry, because Reg might have been good for a loan.

I'll be worried about you Terry, I said.

You got no need to worry, he said, and I knew I'd better lay off, because I was getting him narked.

So I said O.K. and I told him not to move, and it was easy to put the parcel in his pocket without the john seeing. Then I couldn't think of anything more to say, so we just sat there, and I wouldn't have minded if it had lasted like that for hours. But the john said if we'd finished talking I'd better come along, so we shook again and Terry said he'd tell Mrs Clegg some yarn if she asked. Then we said cheers and I went along and was locked up thinking everything was going to be O.K.

Nothing happened that afternoon. I had a lie-down on the seat again and I must have gone to sleep, because I don't remember anything until the john brought me another feed. And it was just as good as the one before, and I thought it was no wonder there were such a lot of cases when they stood you good tucker inside.

Then when the john came for the tray he brought me the blankets to sleep in, so after I'd had a read of the Western I decided to turn in, and I'd have had quite a good night if I hadn't been waked up by somebody who started kicking up a row somewhere along the passage. And by the sound of the voice I thought it must be some old girl who'd been picked up for being tight. It kept me awake for hours anyhow, but when I woke up at daylight everything was quiet.

And I woke up still feeling that everything was going to be O.K. so I was sort of impatient for them to take me into Court and get it over. I had bacon and eggs for breakfast, then the doors all along the passage were unlocked and we all came out and they collected us along at the end where Terry and me had done our talking. There was a fair collection too, I'd had no idea, though only one woman, and if she was the one who'd kicked up the row you could hardly believe it, because she looked quite all right. I thought she might have been any man's own mother, but of course it's a fact that nobody's the same person once they've sobered up.

We all had to stand there with a crowd of jacks in plain clothes standing round, and one in uniform called out our names and said what we'd been picked up for. And I didn't know what it was all about, but I suppose it was so as they could get us taped and pick out anybody they had anything else on. It made me go red though when I heard what it was I was charged with. It didn't sound too nice I can tell you, and I thought damn it all, why give it that

194

sort of name? Anyhow, I thought, I bet all those jacks have done plenty they wouldn't like anybody to know about, particularly when you can give it such a rotten name.

Still, there was nothing I could do about it, I just stood there with the rest, and when it was all over they put us back in our cells again. Then when I was beginning to get the dingbats through being there so long on my own I was taken out by the two demons who'd picked me up. It was time to go over to the Court they said, and they asked me if I'd got a lawyer.

No, I said, I don't want any lawyer.

All right, one of them said, but don't say we didn't ask you.

Then they told me to come along, and it wasn't far to the Police Court but I wished it could have been further. Because it was a fine summer's day (though no different to what it had been for weeks), and we cut across an open place where there were flowers and trees. The grass was all dried up by the sun yet it looked nice and cool there, just seeing a hose going made you feel cool. And it was nice to see some kids that were cutting across on their way to school, but I thought if a pair of dees hadn't been taking me to Court I might never have noticed these things.

But as I say the walk was over too soon, and when we got inside the Court we had to wait quite a time before my case came on. First there were traffic cases, then after a few drunks had been hauled up an old man that nobody could have much liked the look of was told off by his Nibs for trying to do himself in. The bandage round his neck didn't improve his looks either, he looked sick I can tell you, and you'd have thought no man would have treated him as rough as the Magistrate did. But I bet he thought he was treating him good by letting him off.

Then after the old man it was my turn, and I'd been sitting down with one of the dees while I kept my eyes open for Terry. And there wasn't much of a crowd that'd come to watch, so it was easy to tell he hadn't turned up. I had to stand there while they told the magistrate the case and then Maggie was brought in to say her piece. And she only took one look at me and never looked my way again. And you'd hardly believe anyone could tell a story that was all baloney as well as she did, and it certainly knocked me plenty. She was all flossied up and to begin with you sort of felt she was enjoying herself properly. But when she'd got nearly to the end something went wrong, because instead of answering a question she suddenly went white and hung on to the rail in front of her. And his Nibs said to let her take her time, and he looked at me as if he thought I needed to be watched or I'd be trying to swing another one across her. But it never worried me much because it was just then I spotted Terry. He was standing in front of the crowd with a grin a mile wide, and when he saw me looking at him he winked and jerked his head over towards Maggie. And it certainly gave me a nice feeling to know he was there, but things were sort of going round in my head so much I couldn't even wink back.

Maggie got going again and I fixed my attention on her, and when she'd finished one of the dees went into the box and read out what they'd written down. Then there was some talk about Bert, his ship was away, they said, but the magistrate said it didn't matter about Bert because of what I'd admitted in my statement. And then he went on and said a whole rigmarole about what he was going to do, and what would happen if I said I was guilty or not guilty. But I never had much idea of what he was saying because I was suddenly a wake-up to what I'd let myself in for when I signed that statement. I understood things then I can tell you, and it made me feel hopping mad. Instead of listening to his Nibs I just couldn't take my eyes off the two demons. And Christ, I thought. And I couldn't think of anything except, Christ!

But I knew it was no good letting my feelings get the better of me. So I told myself to hang on. I said not guilty all right, and when he asked me something about bail I said I didn't want any bail, because I'd looked at Terry and he'd shaken his head. I remembered how he'd said the

case might go as far as the Supreme Court anyhow, and
way at the back of my mind I was still feeling dead sure of
Terry even if things had got in a worse tangle than I'd
expected.

All the same it was a hard job trying to stop my feelings
from getting the better of me when I was walking back to
the police station with the two dees. Because I thought
they'd played me a rotten trick. But I didn't say anything
except ask them what happened next.

You wait, one of them said, we'll look after you.

Yes, I said, I'm reckoning on that.

But I needn't have tried to be sarcastic, because a man
needs a lot sharper tongue than I've got to get under any
dee's skin.

It was all right being back though, because of the tucker.
I asked the john who fetched the tray what happened next,
and being quite a decent bloke as I'd thought he was right
from the beginning, he stayed and talked and told me a
lot.

They'll take you out there, he said, and he said it might
be in a taxi or it might be in the Black Maria. And when I
asked him what it was like out there he said he didn't know
much about it, but he reckoned they'd treat me all right
until I got convicted.

I'm not getting convicted, I said, but he only said, Good
luck boy, and shook hands.

Well, it wasn't until late in the afternoon that the Black
Maria came for me. It had blokes on it dressed more like
soldiers than cops, and another joker was taken out and
put inside as well as me, and there wasn't much room
inside because it was chock full of stuff they were taking
out to the gaol, and I had to sit right up behind the driver's
seat where I could look out a little window and see what
streets we were going through. And instead of going
straight out to the gaol we went down the main street and
pulled up outside a butcher's shop while they put some
boxes of meat on board, and it looked more like dogs' meat

to me. But while we were waiting I looked out the window, and so help me if Maggie didn't go past. She stopped to cross the road too, and watching out for the traffic it seemed as if she looked right at the window. I don't suppose she did really, and it was only for a second, but it made me feel very funny inside.

There were no more stops though, after that we kept right on to the gaol which was a long way out of town, and soon as we were out there we had to help unload the stuff. Then they took us inside and put our names down, and after they'd put black stuff on our fingers and got our fingerprints, they took us into a big sort of hall with iron doors along both sides, and locked the pair of us up on our own.

So there I was. And I'd only had time to look out through the bars and see there was nothing to see except a concrete wall and some sky above, when they brought me a hunk of bread and a pannikin of tea, which was certainly not so good after what I'd been getting. Then after a bit the light went on, and to stop myself from doing any thinking I had a read of a detective mag that was lying there. But the yarns were all about crooks and I reckoned they were a lot of baloney, nothing like the real thing at all. So I chucked the mag away and walked round a bit, and I may as well tell you that when you're in clink there's always a spyhole in your door. You can't see out, but if you keep your eyes skinned you can always tell when anybody has come along for an eyeful. And that first night I just happened to be watching when somebody came along and moved the slide, so I asked could I have a dab of vaseline to put on my piles. And mister peeping Tom said he'd have to see about that.

Of course it was mainly a gag just to have somebody to speak to, though as a matter of fact my piles were hurting pretty bad. And while I was waiting I thought I'd have a read of what was left of a Bible, and I'm blowed if I didn't strike the yarn about Joseph and his coat of all colours. It was a real good yarn too, I liked reading it a hell of a lot, but before I'd got through the light went out, and there I was in the dark and it didn't look as if the vaseline was going to turn up. So I thought I'd better turn in, and it sounded as if the jokers locked up alongside were doing the same thing because I could hear their beds creaking.

And maybe it was because of the way those beds creaked that I couldn't get to sleep. They didn't stop creaking, and I thought maybe they were jokers like me who'd been locked up for the first time. It made me start thinking about what makes a man get tough and land himself in clink. Because all those jokers must have been the same as I was once too, just kids. And I started to remember about when I was a kid. I remembered the times when I'd get a kick on the behind for pinching out of the bin where they threw the rotten fruit along at the auction mart in the town where I lived. And the times when the old man would come home tight, and us kids'd go out in the morning and find him lying in the onion bed without hardly a stitch on. And I remembered other times too, and I never thought about Terry or Maggie much. I just couldn't take my mind off the jokers that were locked up alongside me, because their beds never left off creaking all night.

I was glad when it was morning, because as I say it doesn't matter what sort of a night you have, things are always different in the morning. When I heard a noise of doors being unlocked I got up and put my pants on, and when the doors were all unlocked you had to stand outside while a sort of procession came round. First you had to empty your jerry into a can, then you got your tins of porridge and stew off a tray, and last you got your pannikin full of tea out of another can. Then you had to be locked in again while you ate your breakfast. But that first morning I couldn't eat much of it, because they might have called it porridge, but you couldn't tell by the taste. You could hardly tell the tea by the taste either, but I'm not going to tell all about what it's like in clink. Most things you soon get used to, if you don't eat you feel empty, so it's best to eat and after a while you never leave any. And maybe the main reason why I couldn't eat my breakfast the first morning was because I was wondering whether they'd leave me locked up on my pat all day. Also I was beginning to worry about Terry again. I wondered how the hell he'd get on for chips, and I was hoping to God they'd give me his letter if he wrote one, though it turned out I needn't have worried about that.

It wasn't long before the doors were unlocked again and they took us out in a yard with concrete walls all round, and I thought it was all right because of the company, though a screw shouted out we were not to tell each other about our cases. Everybody had plenty to talk about without talking about their cases anyhow, and when it got too hot in the sun we all went under a little roofed-in part, and with everybody squatting down and taking it easy while they talked the usual sort of talk, it might have been any crowd of jokers that were cutting scrub or working on the roads on relief. Because they all had ordinary clothes on, and up till then I hadn't found out they were all jokers that were waiting to come up in court, though a few were dinkum lags who were all togged up to go into town in the van because they needed to go into hospital.

But as I say I'm not going to tell all about what it's like inside just because I was in for a few weeks. There'd be too much to tell anyhow.

I never got any letter from Terry the first day or the day after, and I felt if one didn't come soon I'd have the dingbats worse than I'd ever had them before. What with hardly getting any sleep and listening to the beds creaking all night I thought I'd go silly, and then maybe they'd have to take me away to the rat house. But a letter came all right. And was it a relief! Terry said chin up and cheers and I needn't worry because he'd fixed things, though he couldn't get anybody to go bail, he said, but he was still trying and maybe he'd have some luck. And he wound up that I was not to worry if he didn't write again because things were fixed for sure, (with a line under the word sure), and I needn't be worrying about him either because he'd be O.K.

So while I was feeling the relief I wrote back saying what a great cobber he was, and how he certainly had my thanks. And I put a letter inside for Fanny. I told her I'd gone away for a few weeks so I was leaving her to look after Terry. Get your mother to give him something to eat sometimes Fanny, I said. And I put in a bit about the money tree, and how I knew for certain it liked little girls that were kind to people. I didn't think it would do much good but maybe it was worth trying. And I asked her in a P.S. if she'd taught the budgie to do any new tricks.

And it wasn't until several days after I'd written the letters that I began to get the jitters again. Because Terry didn't write any more, and even though he'd told me he mightn't I couldn't make it out. And lying in bed at night when I couldn't sleep I'd start thinking he might only have pretended to help me, while all the time he hadn't done anything at all. I hadn't said anything about my case to anybody inside but quite a number had told me about theirs, and they all said you were a goner once you'd signed a statement admitting anything you'd done. There was no way of getting out of it then, they said, and they'd be that certain they knew the whole works I'd get the wind up considerably. So lying awake at night I'd start thinking rotten things about Terry. He wants me put away, I'd tell myself. Yes, I'd think, that's what he wants, because I'm the only bloke that knows he was with Reg after he collected the hundred quid. And once I'd got as far as thinking that way I'd sort of let myself go, and work out all the different ways he might have used to get the money out of Reg. And I'd tell myself I could bet he'd left Mrs Clegg's and I'd never see him again. Because say they put me away for five years? I'd think. And I couldn't help it, I'd break out in a sweat.

But of course it was mainly during the night time that I'd be thinking these things. When it was daylight I'd sort of feel maybe I'd gone off to sleep without knowing, and only dreamed all I'd been thinking. I'd go out into the yard thinking everything was going to be O.K. and I'd be all right unless any joker said something that was liable to start me worrying again. Some days they'd talk about their lawyers, and they'd all reckon they'd got good ones. If they didn't get off, they reckoned, they'd get only a light stretch. And I hadn't got a lawyer. I had the law dead against me, and instead of trying to do anything about it I was just relying on Terry. And I'd ask myself what could Terry do against the law all on his own any more than I could? But then I'd think if I tried to do anything I might only spoil what it was that Terry had said he'd fixed. So there I was, sort of feeling I was liable to be caught which ever way I went, and some days I'd feel if things didn't stop going round in my head I'd end up in the rat house for sure.

I've never known time drag like it did during those weeks. Some days were that long I thought they'd never finish, and the nights were worse. Yet it seemed no time when they started taking away a few jokers each morning to have their cases tried. And when I sort of woke up I found I'd got easy about things. I felt I didn't care what happened. When they asked me didn't I want a lawyer to defend me, because the country would pay if I couldn't, I still said I didn't want any lawyer. Because I'd worked myself into a state. Things couldn't be any worse than they were, I thought, and if Terry was going to let me down it was just too bad. Yet even though I'd got to the stage of thinking I didn't care what happened to me, I'd be liable to break out in a sweat at the thought of what might be happening to Terry. He might be no good, I thought, but he was sick anyhow, I'd liked having him for a cobber and we'd had some good times together. And the thought of him having nothing to eat was the one thing I could never make myself feel easy about.

You could feel the difference in the place once the van started going in each day with a few jokers to be tried. All the rest were wondering which day it was going to be their turn, and that's the sort of thing that would give any man the jitters. We'd always be keen to find out how things had gone yet we never got much chance. Because several got off and never came back, and those who'd got convicted would be wondering how long a stretch they'd get, and that's the sort of time when you don't feel like asking a man too many questions. Or if their cases hadn't finished they'd be in just as rotten a state, so it wasn't easy to find out anything much.

Then the morning came when it was my turn, and I was told to get myself shaved and make myself look respectable. And I was just a bundle of nerves waiting to be taken out of the yard, but once we were in the bus, three of us, each with our pannikin and a hunk of bread to eat at midday, I didn't feel so bad. I was lucky enough to be sitting up by the window again and it was good to look out and see the places we went past.

We didn't see much of the outside world though, because the bus backed right in at a door, and we were taken out and locked in a cell right away, all of us in together. And it was easy to tell the courtroom was somewhere upstairs because of the sound of feet moving. My two mates were going up for sentence and it wasn't long before they were taken out. I was left there on my pat so just to calm myself down I walked about the cell, and it was a terribly dirty place, nothing like what I'd been used to. All over the walls there were drawings that must have been done by jokers who'd had to wait there, and they were nearly all drawings of jokers being hanged or lying on their backs with knives stuck through them. And underneath it would say, NEVER MAKE A STATEMENT TO A DEE. Or, THIS IS A BLOODY DEE AND THIS IS WHAT HE'S GOING TO GET. And calling the dees for all the names you can think of.

But it wasn't long before one of my mates was put back in again, and I didn't know what he'd got but he took it pretty hard. He just sat there with his head in his hands and didn't say anything, and I would have liked him to talk because it was hard to bear the sight of him sitting there. I'd been told he had a missis and several kids too. But I didn't have to put up with it for long, because my other mate came back and then it was my turn. I said O.K. but before I got out the door the first joker jumped up and gave me his fist to shake. Good luck boy, he said, and I thought it mighty nice of him. It made me feel as if I was nearly going to cry.

Well, the screw took me along a passage to the bottom of a little stairway and I had to sit there and wait, and another joker was waiting there as well, and when he looked at me so help me if it wasn't Ted, the bloke who'd pinched my money that day on the beach.

Well I'm blowed, I said, and just for a second I thought he was going to pretend he didn't know me.

No talking about your cases, the screw said.

O.K. brother, I said, and I asked Ted how things were, though it was a stupid question to ask.

Not so good, he said.

I'm telling you in your own interests, the screw said.

That's O.K. brother, I said, and I told Ted I was pleased to see him anyhow. Though that was a stupid thing to say too, because before I could say any more another screw came down the stairway to fetch Ted, and I thought he might be going up thinking I was trying to rub it in over pinching my money. Which I hadn't intended to do at all, no, it was just that seeing somebody I knew I was only trying to be friendly.

And waiting there on my own I began wondering what had happened to his girl Mavis, but it seemed hardly more than just a few minutes before he came down again, and this time I didn't say anything because he looked well shaken up. He certainly looked white. The screw took him straight off down the passage and he said something as he passed me, but he seemed to be only talking to himself. And I was wondering why I'd never struck him out there, he'd been out on bail I supposed, when it was my turn to go up the stairway.

And it was a surprise to find I'd come out right inside the
dock where I had to stand while my case was on. It wasn't
so good standing up there with the court full of people that
had come to watch, all sorts, besides men for the jury and
all the officials and lawyers. But after a time I had a look
round to see if Terry was there, though I soon turned
round again, because there were too many that were looking me straight in the face and taking me in as if they'd
never seen anyone like me before.

There was nobody on the jury I could have said I'd ever
seen before and I had to wait a fair time while it was being
called. I thought things would never get started, but they
did at last when the charge was read out and I was asked if
I pleaded guilty or not guilty. Then a lawyer got up and
said what my case was about, and after the judge had said
something, sort of saying it so nobody could get the guts of
it at all, Maggie's name was called out and she came in
looking all flossied up. She had to swear on the Bible and
the lawyer asked her her name and other things about how
we'd been living at Mrs Clegg's. Then he asked her to tell
about the night of such and such a day, and he gave the
date, and how anybody had remembered I don't know,
because I hadn't. And Maggie said how I'd come into the
quick lunch place and started talking to her, and afterwards we'd gone up to her room.

Did you invite him to go with you to your room? the
lawyer said, and Maggie said she didn't remember.

I didn't mind him coming, she said, and the lawyer said
oh. Then he blew his nose and looked at his papers before
he said anything more.

Well, he said, what happened?

There wasn't anything happened, Maggie said.

You must tell the court what he did to you, he said.

He never did anything, Maggie said, and the lawyer
said oh again.

Come along now, he said, we can all understand your
feelings, and he sort of looked round at everybody. But you
must tell the court, he said.

And Maggie began to go red but she still said I never did anything. And you could tell it was a surprise to everybody. They stayed that quiet listening you couldn't hear any sound except the sound of breathing, and when the lawyer blew his nose it sounded that loud everybody jumped, and after that it wasn't quiet any more. You could hear people talking and they had to be told to pipe down.

Maggie didn't go any redder than the lawyer did anyhow, he started to get in a temper I can tell you, but the judge chipped in and started to talk to Maggie, but she went on saying no and no. Then the judge said something to the lawyer and he went on asking Maggie questions. Hadn't I done this to her? he said, and hadn't I done that? And Maggie got a bit rattled but she still went on saying no.

So in the end the judge chipped in again, and I couldn't hear all he was saying, nobody could, but he said something about wasting time, and when the lawyer said something about what I'd admitted in my statement he said he wasn't going to let the case go to the jury just on that. And he went on and said a lot more that I couldn't get the guts of at all, but in the end he did say I'd have to be discharged.

And he'd hardly got finished before the screw that had been sitting on the stairs, where he was just out of sight of everybody, told me to come down, and while I was going down he grabbed me by the hand and said I was the luckiest bloke he'd ever known in his experience.

You mind your step in future boy, he said, and going along the passage I was in a sort of daze. All the screws came round to shake me by the hand and I had to sit down because my legs felt as if they wouldn't hold me up.

When I was outside I was still shaking, but I felt a lot better after I'd taken a few big lungfuls of air. And I reckon that's what anybody would feel the need of if they'd just walked out of court without getting a stretch.

But of course I was thinking of Terry, so I didn't waste any time getting round to the front of the court. There were people standing about talking and a few recognised me, and I noticed that now I wasn't standing in the dock they looked at me in quite a different way, but I couldn't be bothered because I had Terry on my mind. I looked inside but there was no sign of him, the place was empty, so just as fast as I could travel I made tracks for Mrs Clegg's place.

The budgie was out on the front of the house, but inside it was all quiet down below. I went up the stairs a good many at a time and Terry's and my room was empty, the bed was made up but the stretcher was gone and there was no sign of anybody's things, and I couldn't help noticing a smell of disinfectant. So without hardly knowing what I was doing I went over and opened Maggie's door, and there was an old man lying on the bed with only his shirt on.

Sorry, I said, and I said, Where's Terry? But instead of saying anything he just heaved a half-eaten apple at me. So I slammed the door and called out sorry again, then when I looked out the window of the other room I saw Mrs Clegg along at the end of the clothes line, and I didn't waste any time in getting down to her.

Hello, I said, and straight off I said, Where's Terry?

But she bent down and put a clothes peg in her mouth, and I had to wait until she'd pegged it on the line before she answered.

He's in the hospital, she said.

Where've you been? she said, and I looked her straight in the eye even if I did pick on the glass one.

I've just been away, I said.

Look at that, she said, that's where he coughed up his blood, and she pointed to a sheet on the line.

How long ago? I said, and she said two days, and I turned round to go without saying anything more. But Mrs Clegg called out.

There's rent owing mister, she said.

O.K. I said, I'll come back.

And making fresh tracks for the hospital I felt in as bad a daze as I'd felt in only a short time before.

Up at the hospital they wanted to make a fuss about me seeing Terry.

Are you a relative? they said.

No, I said, just a cobber.

And the bloke on the other side of the counter looked at me as if he was down on anybody that was just a cobber.

Well, he said, don't you come here again out of visiting hours. And he told me the number of the ward and said to ask for the sister.

The sister wasn't a bad sort, she gave me a smile and took me out on the verandah, and there was old Aussie face sitting up and leaning on a heap of pillows. He grinned when he saw me too, but Christ, if he didn't look crook.

Hello Terry, I said, and he said Hello boy, and for a while we didn't seem to have anything else to say. I just sat there holding on to his hand, and after giving us a few looks the jokers in the other beds looked away, and I thought it was mighty nice of them.

You're not feeling too good, I said, but just as usual Terry said there was nothing wrong with him.

I want to get out of here, he said.

You better stay if you're crook, I said.

I'm not crook, he said. Listen boy, he said, tomorrow they're going to put me down in a shelter, and he sat up further to look over the verandah rail, and I could see the little shanties he was talking about. It'll be easy to walk out from there, he said.

But can you walk Terry? I said.

I can walk, he said. You come up tomorrow afternoon. They can't keep me, he said.

All right Terry, I said, but I knew I'd have to think it over.

You fix things, he said.

I'll have a try, I said, but have you got any chips?

No, he said.

Never mind, I said, I'll fix things.

So you got off all right, he said.

How did you work it Terry? I said.

I worked it, he said, and he wouldn't say anything more. Forget it, he said.

Then the sister came back and said my time was up. So I said so long to Terry, and caught up to the sister and asked her a few questions. Terry was pretty bad, she said.

How bad? I said, but she said I'd better ask the doctor if I could find him.

And my luck was in, because going down the stairs I stopped a young joker in a white coat, and he just happened to be Terry's doctor.

That man's in a bad way, he said.

That's no good, I said, but will he get better?

No hope, he said.

Well, I said, how long will he last?

Too hard to say, he said. It's just like that, he said, and he ran on up the stairs.

And it's too hard to say just how I was feeling when I came out of the hospital. I got the feeling again that my legs wouldn't hold me up, so I went and sat on a seat in a bus-stop shelter shed, and I remember I was in such a daze I didn't seem to be thinking of anything at all, not even Terry. Nor noticing anything either. Because people would go past, or they'd come in and sit on the seat and talk, but I never moved or took the slightest bit of notice.

I sort of began to take notice when a dog came up and started sniffing me. Hello dog, I said, and he stood there in front of me with his tail going. And after a bit his mouth started dribbling. You're thinking of tucker are you? I said, and I remembered the piece of bread I had in my pocket, and when I took it out the dog's tail wagged faster. I didn't know the time, it must have been well on in the afternoon, but I hadn't felt hungry. The bread tasted good though, and I broke off small pieces and gave them to the dog, and when I had no more to give him he went down on his belly with his paws stretched out in front, and his tail swept a clean place on the floor of the shed.

But when I'd eaten I decided I'd have to do something,

so after I'd kidded to the dog a bit I went down town and waited until I got the chance to use the phone in a pub. Then I looked in the book and rang up a parson that came visiting once while I was out there. I got him all right and he said he remembered me, and after he'd talked a lot of palaver I said I'd got no money and was in need of a job.

Well, he said, I know a gentleman who helps young fellows in your position. He's a very fine gentleman indeed, he said, and he told me the name and I waited while he looked up the phone number.

You ring that number, he said. And remember, he said, any one of us may stumble if we depend on our own strength alone.

That's right, I said.

Goodbye, he said. May you receive grace and strength, he said.

Yes goodoh, I said, and thanks very much.

Then I rang the other number but a girl said the joker wasn't there. She told me to ring his house number which I did, and got on to his missis. And she said he wasn't home but he would be in the evening, and instead of ringing again I'd better call and see him.

So I promised I would, and then I went into the bar but the counter-lunch hadn't come out. I went outside and waited and then I went back and picked on a pretty classy joker that was there on his own. I just went straight up to him and asked him if he'd stand me a half-handle.

Sure, he said. Have a large one, he said, and he called the barman and got the drink.

Things a bit tough? he said.

I'll say, I said, and he talked about the depression and I made the drink last until the tucker arrived. Then we both went over and I put away quite a lot in quite a short time, and when the joker saw the way I was eating he sort of turned the plates round so as the biggest pieces were next to me.

Eat up, he said.

But next minute some of his cobbers came in. They were

all classy jokers too, and the first one didn't take much
notice of me because he was too busy talking. I stood there
finishing the drink, and so help me if I didn't hear them
start talking about the Court cases. And by the way they
talked I thought they must be lawyers. It made me feel a
bit nervous because I thought they might say something
about my case, so when they had more drinks all round,
and my joker turned and asked if I'd have another, I said
no thanks and shoved off.

I thought I'd need somewhere to sleep that night, though
I wouldn't have minded flopping in the park with the
weather so good, but of course there was Terry to consider,
so I thought it wouldn't do any good to put off trying to
fix things with Mrs Clegg.

But soon as I got up there I ran right into Fanny, and
it was a hard job getting her to put off paying a visit to the
money-tree.

You promised Bill, she said.

Yes I know, I said, but did you look after Terry?

Yes, she said, because he was sick.

You're a good girl Fanny, I said. And seeing I was
feeling glad that Terry had been looked after I said that
later on I might buy her another budgie, though I told
myself I oughtn't to be making any rash promises.

Then I went in and Mrs Clegg and her old man had
finished dinner and were having a cup of tea. So I sat down
and had a cup and we had quite a long talk, though Mr
Clegg was all the time going on about politics and rocking
it into the government. Off and on he was reading the
paper too, and I had the jitters wondering if he might come
across my name.

If things don't improve there's going to be hell to pay,
he said.

You may be right, I said.

Yes, he said, when the winter comes there'll be trouble.
And it was a fair dinkum prophecy, though I had no idea
at the time.

But later on when he went off down the street I had Mrs

Clegg on her own, and it was a hard job putting it up to her.

I have to think of the money, she said.

I know, I said. But listen, I said, you've got two rooms empty now, because when people can live in wash houses and sheds for a few bob they won't rent rooms. So why not take Terry and me?

You mightn't pay, she said.

I'll pay, I said. Look, I said, I've got hands, I can work. If I don't pay today I'll pay tomorrow.

And in the end I got her to say yes when I promised I'd let her have ten bob just to show her first thing in the morning.

Well, that was something off my mind, and when I looked at the clock I thought it was about time to go and see the joker the parson had put me on to.

I had to walk a long way to get there, and it was a posh house, one standing in a big garden. But I thought well, he can't eat me, and I rang the front doorbell. It was his missis that opened the door though, and she took me inside into a big room that was fitted up like a sort of gymnasium. Over in a corner there were parallel bars and all that sort of gear, and a heap of things like soccer balls crash helmets and golf-sticks. And all round the walls were pictures out of the Bible with texts underneath.

She made me sit down and then she said she was sorry but her husband had gone out.

He's so busy, she said, and she asked me if I'd ever been there before.

No, I said.

Well, she said, my husband is such a busy man. I'm sure you wouldn't want to come and take up any more of his time, she said.

So I asked her how did she mean.

My husband is so good to all his boys, she said, but if he doesn't give it all up I think he'll have a breakdown. I do really, she said.

I said I was sorry to hear that, but I was only being

polite because it was her I felt a bit sorry for. She looked pretty sick on it. I've never seen anyone look as black round the eyes, and besides everything else she looked a bit batty because her hair was all over the place.

I only wanted to know if he could get me a job, I said, and I told her how the parson had put me on to him.

Yes I know, she said, he sends so many, but she smiled and said of course it wasn't my fault.

Couldn't you go away and do farm work? she said.

Yes, I said, I'd like to, but just now I haven't got a penny to my name.

Then if I give you a pound, she said, will you promise you won't waste it or spend it on drink?

Yes, I said, I'll promise that.

And you'll try very hard to find a place on a farm? she said.

Yes, I said, I'll do that.

Very well, she said, here's more than a pound, and she got up and took thirty bob off the mantelpiece. Though she held on to it until we were out on the verandah, and before she handed it over she said there was just one more thing.

I want you to promise you won't ring my husband up any more, she said.

All right, I said, I'll promise that.

The poor man, she said, he's just wearing himself out.

You want to get him to take a holiday, I said.

She said it was nice of me to say that, and I went down the path thinking she must be a bit crazy. But I had the thirty bob in my hand.

Well, it was late by the time I got to bed, and when I woke up in the morning I felt done. Another day, I thought, and I sort of didn't want to face it, so I kept my eyes shut and turned over and tried to go off to sleep again. It wasn't any good though, I was only kidding myself and I knew I'd better get moving. I hopped out of bed, and while I was stretching I looked out the window at Mrs

H   213

Clegg's washing which was hanging on the line just like it was on the first morning I stayed there. The weather didn't look any different either, it was just as hot, and I wasn't sure but I thought I could get the whiff from the heap of sawdust in the butcher's backyard. And just for a second it all gave me a sort of peculiar feeling. Because it seemed to be that first morning all over again, and as though I'd gone back and started again, and nothing had happened in between.

If only it hadn't all happened, I thought, but then I thought if one thing doesn't happen another one does, so what's the difference? But I couldn't help feeling there's always a difference all the same.

I went downstairs and collected my things and Terry's from Mrs Clegg and borrowed the teapot again, and she lent me a few teaspoonfuls of tea. And she looked bucked when I gave her half a quid. I fixed up with her about the stretcher and told her I'd be bringing my mate home later on. Though I didn't say anything about how I was going to manage about his tucker if he had to stay in bed. I thought it best to leave that over in the meantime.

Then when I'd had my tea and was out in the streets I felt life wasn't so bad, though I had a longing to go up and see Terry right away. But I'd looked in the phone book and found out the visiting hours, so I was putting it off until the afternoon.

I went and looked at the paper in the library but there didn't seem to be anything doing, so instead of trying the registry offices I decided I'd go and have a shot at getting on relief. And after a long wait in a queue down at the place I got to a window, and the joker there said right away that as a single man they wouldn't consider me unless I'd go to a camp in the country.

Yes, I said, but I've got a sick cobber.

That's nothing to do with us, he said.

No, I said, but I've been sick myself.

What's wrong with you? he said. And I didn't know what to say so I said I'd strained my heart.

Who's your doctor? he said.

Well, I said, I haven't been to one here, and I told him I'd had a job in the country which I'd had to give up because of my heart.

All right, he said, we'll see if you're fit. And after he'd written on a form he gave me a slip of paper and told me where to go.

If you go now, he said, he might put you through this morning.

So what was I to do? I'd told the yarn about my heart but I didn't think there was anything wrong with me. Yet I thought I might as well go and give it a pop, so I went round to the place, and it was a broken-down building in a back street, and when I looked inside there was a big dark room with rows of jokers sitting on wooden seats. They didn't look any too cheerful either, no, most of them were old jokers, and they all looked as if they were properly up against it.

And while I was standing there a door opened up the far end, and an old joker came out buttoning up his strides. Then a young fellow came out and called a number, and another one of the crowd got up and went in, after which he called me up and changed my slip for a piece of cardboard with my number.

Sit down and wait your turn, he said.

So I went back and sat with the last row of jokers, and the one next me started talking.

Wait your turn's right, he said. That's what I've been doing all my life.

It's no good, I said.

Yes wait, he said. You can wait here or you can go home and wait, it don't make no difference. It might as well be your funeral you're waiting for, he said.

It's certainly no good, I said.

Wait, he said, yes, wait till the guns go off. You wait boy, he said, you'll find out you were born just at the right time.

But knocking around I'd heard all that sort of talk, so I asked him how long you had to wait.

It depends, he said, you can never tell. We might have to come back tomorrow if the quack's not through by the time he feels like having a bite. I bet he has a good bite too, he said.

I bet he does, I said. Anyhow, I said, I'm going out for a breath of air, and he said I'd better be careful if I didn't want to miss. You can't ever tell, he said.

I went outside anyhow, and just across the road there was a parking place for cars, and up against the wall of a building I noticed a lot of bikes were parked. And so help me if I didn't get one of my notions.

I picked one of the bikes and rode off, and not far along there was a street that cut right up through the park. And I pedalled up that hill just as fast as I could make the bike go. When I got to the top I was done, and I turned round and let her run down again. I parked the bike outside the place and looked inside, but there was still nearly the same number of jokers, not counting a few more that had turned up. So I came out and repeated what I'd done, and kept on several times over. Then I reckoned I'd have time for just one more, and when I got back I was that done I could hardly stagger over and put the bike back where I'd got it from.

Well, I timed it pretty nicely. I just had time to cool off and get my breath under control when it was my turn, and once inside the room the quack asked me straight off what my trouble was.

I've got a bad heart, I said. And without saying anything he put the things in his ears and had a listen. He listened for quite a time too, then he stood back and looked at me.

Who's your family doctor? he said.

You are, I said.

You look all right, he said.

I don't feel too good, I said.

So then he had another listen.

Breathe naturally, he said.

I'm trying to, I said.

And after a bit he sat down and wrote, and before he'd finished writing he told me to go back to the office next morning.

Next, he said, and the young fellow shoved me out, and I came away without having any idea how things had gone.

It was over anyway, and next minute the whistles blew and I decided I'd go a bob dinner. It seemed a mean thing to do, considering the hole Terry and me might be going to be in, but I thought it might be as well if I kept my strength up. I risked going to the Dally's, and as usual at that time he was standing behind the peter, and he seemed as if he was quite pleased to see me.

Is your mother better? he said.

And I had to think because I'd forgotten that yarn.

She's fine, I said.

Good, he said. That is good for you. And it is good for me now you are back to eat here.

Yes, I said. And I sort of realized for the first time he must talk about it being good for somebody to just about all his customers. And I thought that seeing he hadn't said anything, it was no good asking him about a job just then.

After I'd eaten I just slowly worked my way over to the hospital. Visiting time hadn't started when I got there but I risked going round the building, and I found Terry all right after I'd looked in a good few shelters. He had one all to himself, though there was another bed and he said he'd have a mate by tomorrow. But he started on right away about how he wasn't going to be there tomorrow.

There's nothing wrong with me, he said.

Did you walk down here? I said.

I can walk, he said.

Have you tried? I said.

Listen boy, he said, there's nothing wrong with me except I feel a bit done-in.

O.K. I said, because it wouldn't have done any good telling him he looked awful, and I knew if I kept on I'd only get him narked.

I never could stand being kept in at school when I was a kid, he said.

No, I said, no more could I.

How did Mrs Clegg take it? he said.

She took it good, I said. She's a real nice woman, I said.

She's all right, Terry said.

Listen, I said, I've got enough chips for a taxi, so why not come now?

No, he said, because I don't want any fuss. And you hang on to your chips, he said.

So I said O.K. again and he started talking horses, and all the time I was hearing about which ones would win the autumn meetings I was wishing he'd give me the works about Maggie instead, because I still couldn't get that business out of my mind. But Terry was still talking about the horses when a bell rang and a nurse came past and said visiting time was over. And Terry told me to come up again after nine o'clock when lights were out.

Nobody will see you if you come up from the bottom of the hill, he said.

And I thought that was a good idea, so I said so long and went straight over the grass and down the hill from where I was, just so as I'd have an idea of the way in the dark. And I knew it would be easy, because I could turn round and wave to Terry almost until I was down on the road.

It was lucky I went that way too, because some relief jokers that were working on the road had just finished up for the day. They were locking their shovels in a box and putting their barrows all together, and as I went past I couldn't help thinking that one of those barrows might come in handy.

Well, I kicked about the streets until it was time to pick up the usual bit of counter-lunch, then I went up to Mrs Clegg's and got her to lend me a piece of dripping, which I thought I might need just in case the barrow wheel started squeaking. And I took the blanket off my stretcher and carried it folded up over my arm, though I thought Terry wouldn't need it on such a warm night.

Then time began to drag pretty badly while I was waiting to bring off the stunt, but I went and had a cup of coffee in a coffee and sandwich place, and a hard-case old sheila in sandshoes came and sat next to me. She was the sort you see going into pubs carrying shopping bags with good wide mouths. She kept putting her hand on my arm so I bought her a cup of coffee, and she said wouldn't it be nice to go for a run in a taxi.

Sorry, I said, nothing doing. But with things as they were, I thought maybe I wouldn't have minded if I could have got her to pay *me*.

By nine o'clock though, I was up on the road below the hospital, where it was pretty quiet at that time of night. I tried the barrows until I got the one that ran easiest, and after I'd greased her up and left her by the fence, I climbed over, and Terry saw me coming up the hill and struck a match so as I wouldn't mistake his shelter.

And everything went O.K. though all the time we were a bit windy in case some joker in one of the other shelters might ring his bell and give the show away. Terry had managed to hang on to his clothes and they were folded in his locker. He could hardly stand but I got him dressed, and before we shoved off he left a note he had written all ready. Then I got him on my back, and it was easy taking him down hill because he didn't seem to be any weight at all.

We've got our taxi waiting, I said, and he said oh yeah, but he thought it was a great stunt when he saw the barrow.

He didn't need the blanket but he sat on it folded up, and to begin with it was easy because it was still downhill. But then there was a long hill to go up and I had to keep stopping for rests, and Terry joked about how I needed more benzine, and said horsey keep your tail up. And a few people passed us, though no cops, and if we saw them coming I'd have a rest, and Terry'd get out and sit on the edge of the barrow just so as not to attract too much attention.

We had to get across the main street though, and that was worrying me considerably. But we took the barrow down pretty close and parked it on the edge of the footpath, then Terry got out, and with me hanging on to him he could walk, though only slowly, but I got him across, and propped him up against a railing where he could sort of half sit down while I went back for the barrow. And wheeling the empty barrow across didn't attract much attention, and we were lucky, because there weren't any cops.

And we got up to Mrs Clegg's all right, and I got Terry on my back again and carried him up the stairs, though when I'd put him on his bed I just had to flop myself, because I was nearly busted.

Maybe it was the joke of my weak heart that helped me to get my strength back, and I certainly needed it because Terry was lying there helpless just like I'd dumped him. And I thought I could bet he looked a long sight worse than I did, even though I'd been doing all the work. So I doubled his pillow up and used my own as well, then I got him undressed, and I'd never noticed it before but there was a string round his neck with a medal-thing at the end of the loop. I had a look and it said, I AM A CATHOLIC IN CASE OF ACCIDENT SEND FOR A PRIEST.

It was a new one on me, but I asked him if he wanted me to.

If you like, he said, and he closed his eyes again and I had to pull him about until I finished off trying to get him comfy.

Are you all right? I said.

I'm O.K. boy, he said, and I turned off the light and left him, because I knew I'd better go and put the barrow back, even though I was feeling more like leaving it until the morning.

Gee but I was tired the next morning. My head felt as if it was stuck to the bed, and my eyes felt as if they'd had some glue used on them as well. But there was Terry with his wide open, and that was always one thing about him, no matter how crook he was, his eyes always looked bright and lively as a bird's.

I just lay there trying to get over the tired feeling, and after a bit I started joking with Terry about how we only needed to ring a bell and we'd get our breakfast brought in, and in the end I hopped up feeling quite lively.

You won't be getting up today, I said.

Not today, tomorrow, he said.

So I mucked about and got two cups of tea, and then Terry said how about the paper? I went out and got him one, and bought a loaf of bread and a quarter of a pound of butter as well, and he said he didn't want any breakfast but he ate some. And while he was eating I got him to look at the jobs, but he said there didn't seem to be any going.

Then when I'd got myself looking tidy I told him I was going out but I'd be back to see him at midday, and I gave him the tobacco I had left, and he was sitting up reading the paper and looking as if he never had a worry in the world when I went out. Except that he looked so crook.

I went straight down to the unemployment office and waited in the queue, and when I got to the window the joker looked up my papers, and then I had to go round to a counter and wait to see another joker. And he said they wouldn't send me to camp, instead they'd give me about a day and a half's relief work a week, and I'd draw fourteen shillings. I thought that would be all right because it would pay the rent with quite a few bob over, but when I'd filled in the papers he said I'd have to wait a fortnight before I began. And I tried to argue it out with him but it did no good, he said I could take it or leave it. So there wasn't anything I could do, but I came away feeling sore over having to wait a fortnight.

Except for a ten bob note and some chicken feed I had hardly anything left in my pocket, so I went down on the waterfront for a sit-down while I tried to decide what I'd do next. Though what with the ships and the wharves there was so much going on down there, my mind would sort of shy away from trying to decide anything for me.

And I was just beginning to think I'd better get off up the street again when a young joker came and sat next to me. We got talking and he said he was out of a job but he'd soon be going back on a farm again. He'd been working there before, he said, and the farmer bloke had sent him a letter to say he could come back if he liked to break in twenty five acres of rough land, and take it over on easy payments. He told me all about it, and if there wasn't any catch it sounded as if there might be something in it. So I told him the jobs I'd had on farms.

Well, he said, how about being mates and going together?

And I liked the look of him so I said O.K. right off, and the thought of being back working on the land again made me feel suddenly all worked up. But next minute I remembered, so I said wait on a bit, because I'd need longer time to decide.

Where can I see you tonight? I said.

Well, he said, it will have to be early, and he said how he was sleeping in a railway carriage, but you needed to be early if you wanted to get a decent possie. So we fixed a date for the afternoon.

Where do you eat? I said, and he said he went on the ships, there were some of them that stood you quite a good feed, he said.

I'm going on now, he said, so you come along.

Sure, I said, and we'd got a fair way along the wharf before I remembered again. I stopped and said I'd changed my mind, and I suppose he thought I was batty, because he went on without stopping. And I suppose he knew I'd never turn up at the place where we'd fixed the date.

But I put it all out of my mind and went up the street and spent my chicken feed on a couple of pies, and got the girl to put on tomato sauce just to give them a taste. Then coming out I ran right into Maggie, and she went red but she stopped and said she'd been wanting to see me.

How are you anyway? I said.

I'm feeling good, she said.

You didn't look as if you were feeling any too good in that witness box, I said.

And she looked away and said wasn't it a pity, and she'd been wanting to apologise.

He beat me up that bad, she said.

He certainly did, I said.

He was a brute, she said. I ran away right into a cop, and he stopped me and I said a man had tried to put one across me.

Too bad, I said.

I didn't know what I was saying Bill, she said. He wouldn't let me go, he made me go to the police station so he could give me to those awful men.

The two demons, I said.

Yes, she said, they kept on that long I had to say it was you.

You didn't have to Maggie, I said.

Yes I did, she said, and she went red again. I didn't want to get Bert into trouble. Bert's all right, she said, I like Bert, he's been good to me.

So I said I supposed that was why he beat her up.

I can't help liking him Bill, she said.

All right Maggie, I said, let's forget it. You put things right again anyhow.

But I had to, she said. Terry said he'd put me away if I didn't. I'd forgot about Terry, she said.

I don't get you Maggie, I said.

Yes you do, she said. You can't tell me you don't know.

Skip it Maggie, I said.

Of course you know, she said.

Cut it out Maggie, I said, and I was feeling pretty annoyed.

All right, she said, but you can't kid me.

Well, I didn't know what she was driving at, and I thought the pies would be getting cold. I said I'd have to go, and Maggie asked me how Terry was keeping and I told her the way things were.

Poor old Terry, she said, I might come up and see him

sometime. I might bring Bert and some beer, she said.

Beer mightn't be good for him Maggie, I said.

Aw heck Bill, she said, beer's always good for everybody.

All right Maggie, I said, I might be seeing you.

I said so long and I hurried up to Mrs Clegg's and found Terry half asleep, though he was lying on the top of the bed. It was too hot under the blanket, he said. He certainly looked hot and I was worried, because I didn't think eating a pie would do him any good. But he didn't complain and he ate bread and butter as well, and drank two cups of tea afterwards.

I was worried about leaving him again and he didn't want me to go either. He got me to get a pack of cards out of his suit-case and I played him whisky poker for matches. But after a few games he said he felt like having another sleep, so he settled down and I got him to let me put his overcoat on top of him just in case he caught cold.

I didn't stay long down town anyhow, because kicking round the streets I couldn't think of a single thing to do. And in the end I began to feel reckless and decided to blow in nearly the whole of my last ten bob. I went to cheap places in back streets and bought mutton flap, and things from the grocer's, besides a few nice things for Terry. And when I got up to Mrs Clegg's with an armful she hummed and hahed, but I said everything was for her as well as Terry and me, and in the end she said she didn't mind putting on a bit extra, though she said she hoped Terry wasn't going to be in bed for long.

I thought I'd done a great stroke, I did the vegetables, then I went upstairs to lie on my stretcher and yarn to Terry. And while we were waiting for Mrs Clegg to call out we joked about how it was just as good as staying in a flash hotel.

But later on we'd hardly finished eating when there was a noise on the stairs, and a second later it sounded as if somebody had fallen down. I went out and it was Bert and Maggie, and Bert had slipped on the stairs and was trying to get up, while at the same time he was hanging on to an armful of riggers. I went down and took the beer off him and with Maggie shoving behind we got him to the top. Then he was O.K. he had a good few in certainly, and so had Maggie, but they weren't all that tight. They'd brought a lot of riggers and I was worried, because I thought beer wouldn't do Terry any good, but I couldn't do anything, because he looked that bucked when he saw the pair of them. And he said straight off he was feeling dry.

It gave me a rotten feeling watching Terry put away the first few drinks, but once I had a few in myself I felt different. Way at the back of my mind I was remembering what the young hospital quack had said. And I asked myself who was I to be interfering with anyone's pleasure in a world like this? Though it wasn't too nice remembering what the quack had said, and I told myself the sooner I got lit up the better for my own peace of mind. And it wasn't long before I was telling myself it was nice to see a bit of colour in Terry's cheeks anyhow.

It turned out quite an evening, though the pair of them stayed on far too long for my liking. Among four of us the beer didn't last any too long, and when there wasn't any more Bert turned sort of sour, and the way he started picking on Maggie reminded me of Ted and Mavis, though with them it had been the other way about. Maggie was silly the way she took it too, she tried to throw everything back and that only made Bert worse.

I'll make a proper job of you if I start this time, he said.

You better not start, Maggie said, and Bert said wouldn't he start?

You do, Maggie said, I'll put you away.

And maybe Bert would have started on her right then if Terry hadn't managed to grab hold of his two arms.

No rough house, he said.

No, I said, because we don't want any more cot cases.

But Maggie was too far gone to hold her tongue.

Anyhow, she said, I'm sick of wearing these glad rags round my legs.

You shut up Maggie, Terry said, and he spoke mighty sharp.

I won't shut up, she said. What do I care? she said, I'll put the both of us away.

And Bert tried to go for her then, but with Terry and me holding on Maggie got quite a good start down the stairs before he could tear himself away.

Terry and me just lay back on our beds, and it was mighty nice to lie there listening to the quiet after all the row. And I didn't feel like saying anything, because all of a sudden I was a wake-up so far as Maggie was concerned. I lay there thinking back and trying to put two and two together. And I dozed off to sleep thinking unless you do it on paper, it's not always so easy to make two and two add up right.

I could go on and tell a lot more but I don't see the use. Terry never picked up after the night of the party, no, he just sort of went steadily downhill. And there was hardly a thing I could say or do, though he never went short of tucker if he felt like eating.

I'd look at him lying there.

Terry, I'd say.

What is it boy? he'd say.

Nothing, I'd say.

And then I'd say, Terry.

And instead of answering he'd just have a sort of faint grin on his face.

Terry, I'd say.

But I never could get any further than just saying Terry.

I wanted to say something but I didn't know what it was, and I couldn't say it.

Terry, I'd say.

And he'd sort of grin. And sometimes I'd take his hand and hold it tight, and he'd let it stay in my hand, and there'd be the faint grin on his face.

Terry, I'd say.

I'm all right boy, he'd say.

And sometimes I couldn't stand it, I'd have to just rush off and leave him there.

And one night when I came back again I looked at him and knew it was the finish.

Terry, I said, and he didn't answer.

Terry, I said, and I said I was going to get the priest.

Cheers boy, is what I think he said, and I rushed off without even saying goodbye.

I found the place and the priest said he'd come. So I waited and took him along and showed him Mrs Clegg's, and told him where to find the room upstairs. Then I went along the street and the taxi-driver I'd won the double with was on the stand.

Do you want to take one? he said.

No, I said, and I'd only got a few bob, but I asked him if he knew of any decent sheilas.

He grinned and put away the paper he was reading and told me to hop in.

You surprise me, he said.

And it was a fine warm night for a drive. Maybe if only it had rained, I remember I thought.

1938–1941

'GODS LIVE IN WOODS'

After they'd finished a late breakfast Henry put some more fire on and filled up the kettle. Then he brought out a big thermos and began to cut slices of bread. Roy still had plenty to say, but Henry interrupted him.

I'm going to bring some sheep down from the back, he said.

Good, Roy said, and he went on talking.

Roy was one of Henry's nephews and it was donkey's years since he'd been down to the farm, not since he'd been a lad. The previous evening he'd driven down for the Easter weekend. He'd arrived late, but full of talk, and they hadn't gone to bed until long after midnight. Anyhow it made a change for his uncle Henry, he was a bachelor, and except when he had somebody there helping him on the farm he lived on his own. It was years since he'd finished breaking in his farm from heavy bush country.

Come on, Henry said, or it'll be lunchtime before we start.

He put what they were taking to eat in a *pikau*, and they went outside. There had been rain in the night but now it was a fine hot day, one right out of the box. As much of the sky as you could see between the sides of the valley was a wonderful blue. Henry let the dogs off the chain, and they bounded about until they were sure where the boss was going, then they went on ahead along the road that led up the pumice floor of the valley that was Henry's farm. And it was only a few minutes up the road to the woolshed, its pens overshadowed by huge willows. Roy remembered the woolshed from the time he had been there as a lad, but the willows had only just been planted then.

By Jove uncle Henry, he said, they make a man realize he's a lot older than he feels.

Not far beyond the woolshed the road ended. Here the valley began to close in and there were no more pumice flats, the spurs being thicker and coming down right to the creek. And above the creek the track that began where the road left off was cut into the spurs. It was really what was left of a tramline that had been used for bringing out logs. Nor was the country so good up here, it was even steeper, and on the shady faces the fern had properly got away. And places where the grass still held were scarred by slips that showed up the clay and papa. One of these had come down from above the track, and piled up on it before going on down into the creek. A chain or so of fence had been in its way and it had gone too. You could see some posts and wire sticking out of the clay.

That one came down in the flood last winter, Henry said. A man is lucky to have any farm left. But what was it you were saying? he said.

And Roy went on to say what nonsense it was for Easter to come at the wrong time of the year. It's to do with re-birth, he said. Springtime. It's a pagan ceremony really.

Yes? Henry said.

And Roy said he didn't go to church any more, he'd joined the Rationalists instead.

His uncle listened while he went on to explain himself, and by that time the valley had begun to widen out again. All the same it was the end of it, the side ridges joined up in a tremendous circle, and the basin that they made was broken up by spurs coming down off the skyline. And filling a long wide gully between two of the spurs was the only piece of bush that was left on the farm. Everywhere else you saw only the grass, sheep and cattle dotted about, fern and manuka getting away, the fire-blackened skeletons of trees still standing, and the great bare faces with the clay and papa showing. It was as though everything there was to see was there to be seen. But looking up towards the bush wasn't at all the same, you couldn't help but feel that it was quite different.

It's an easier climb up this way, Henry said.

He turned off towards the bush, and they crossed over the creek just above where another one came down from the bush and joined in. And you couldn't help noticing that the water was cloudy in one and clear in the other. At that moment Roy was saying that religion didn't have any meaning any more, but his uncle interrupted him. He was standing on top of the bank where he could watch the two streams mix.

A man can stand here and watch his farm going down to the sea, he said. But carry on with what you were saying, he said. And going up to the bush Roy went on to say how science had got the wood on religion properly. Yet believe it or not, uncle Henry, I know a crazy sort of guy who reckons things'll crash, and then there'll be a return to the old pagan religions. But can you see people going back to believing in gods and dragons? Well, I'm blowed if I can.

But for some time the dogs had been out of sight somewhere ahead, all of a sudden some sheep moved, and by the time Henry had got the dogs to come behind they were on the edge of the bush. And for a while inside the going was tough. There was the sloping ground for one thing, but it was mainly because, years before, the biggest trees had been taken out. The stumps still had rows of spikes across them, where the sloven had broken away, though they were covered over with moss now. And there was the litter of the tops, and the logs that hadn't been worth while, all overgrown now, rotting, and hung with moss.

Roy didn't talk any more. He followed along behind his uncle and the dogs came after, panting, flattening themselves on their bellies to squeeze under the biggest logs, jumping on to the smaller and then down. Henry knew his way though, the tough part didn't last long and then it was a fairly easy grade up what seemed to be the back of a side spur. It was more open bush too, nothing had been taken out, and every here and there they'd come on great barrels that were springing up, up, until they passed out of sight above the lighter stuff. Henry said that climbing the hills made him feel a lot older than looking at the willows did, and he'd keep on stopping for a breather, and they'd stand there without even Roy talking. After the sun it was all very cool and dim, with the smell of damp and rot, and still, except for the birds, and the sound of the creek somewhere down below. The dogs stopped too, and panted with their tongues hanging out. Nor did they wander, they were content to follow along close behind, as if they too had the feeling that this wasn't at all like being in the open country.

Then Henry said, Do you remember the time you thought you were lost?

I had the wind up that time, Roy said. But dash it all uncle Henry, remember I was only a kid then.

And it started him off talking again. He said he'd often thought about how frightened he'd been that time, when really there'd been nothing to be frightened of.

Well, Henry said, it isn't too nice getting caught in the bush overnight.

Still, Roy said, you know there's nothing that can hurt you. I wouldn't mind spending a night in the bush. Not now, he said.

No? Henry said. But the wetas come out at night. And he laughed. The Maoris call them taipos.

And Roy said that was just a piece of superstition, and he was going to explain about that when his uncle said, Listen!

Quite close to them something was moving, then there was the stillness again. The dogs peered. They pricked their ears, left off panting to sniff, and you could see the hair bristling on their backs. Then Henry took Roy's arm and pointed. See, he said. For a moment Roy couldn't see, then he did.

Good God! he said.

From only a few yards away the face of a bullock with big curving horns was staring at them. And from what you could see of the rest of it, it was a wonderful great dark-red beast.

I need a fence down below, Henry said. The sheep don't come up through here but the cattle do. And I've got to have the cattle to help me keep the fern down.

He stooped to pick up something to throw but the beast suddenly turned round. There was a crash, a sway of small stuff, and it was gone.

Roy wanted to know, didn't he feel like cutting the bush out?

No, Henry said, I've done enough of that.

Why? Roy said. Wouldn't it pay?

Oh yes, Henry said, there'd be money in it all right.

And they started climbing again and it wasn't long before they came out of the bush without having gone through very much of it. They'd come out high up on one side, and stopping for another breather before going out of the shade Henry took a couple of apples out of his *pikau*. And while they ate them he explained to Roy that this strip of country running round the back of the bush was the hardest place on the farm to muster. If the sheep ran down into the gully, where the creek started on its run through the bush, it was almost impossible to get them out.

But I'll show you, he said.

It was rough country, and they were quite a time working their way round behind the bush, until they came to the edge of the gully Henry had told about. He stopped then and said they were lucky. There were no sheep down below, they were all feeding higher up, and it looked as if they'd probably run the right way.

But if you don't mind, he said, you go down to the bottom and try to stop anything that comes.

He waited until Roy had got to the right place, then he sent one of the dogs out. It had a long way to go and the sheep never saw it coming, and it didn't bark until just at the right moment. The sheep began to move, and a string of them crossed over the top of the gully just as Henry wanted them to. But the dog went back out of sight, you could hear it barking, then three more sheep showed up in a great hurry, and Henry quickly called the dog off. The sheep started to run across but halfway over they stopped. Henry began calling out, *Ho, ho, ho,* but the sheep didn't move, and the dog was too sudden when he told him to fetch them on. In its fright the last sheep turned down towards Roy, and although he did his best it was no good, the sheep beat him. It was a big wether too, and it never stopped until it finished up right down in the hollow by the creek where it went into the bush. And down there it became even more upset at finding itself without any of its cobbers.

Never mind, Henry said.

But Roy was excited too. He ran down after the wether and was lucky enough to grab hold of it first go. He sat over it, holding on tight, and as he tried to get the beast to move uphill his face looking up at his uncle showed how proud and excited he was feeling.

It's no good, Henry said, let him go.

Roy said, say he took it down through the bush? It ought to be easy along the creek, he said.

And Henry laughed.

There's bluffs forty feet high, he said.

Well look here uncle Henry, Roy said, d'you mind if I have a go?

No, Henry said, it would be a proper mug's game.

But instead of saying anything to that Roy worked the sheep round until it was facing downhill. All of a sudden it tried to make a break but he held on, riding it, then they were hidden by the first trees. The next moment Henry could hear them splashing in the creek.

That evening Henry had his dinner and cleared away afterwards before he showed any signs of doing something. And by that time it had been dark for several hours. First he took Roy's dinner off the rack and put it in the oven, then he made some fresh tea and filled the thermos. And after he'd found a torch that would work he went out and let the dogs off the chain. It turned out that he needn't have bothered though, because he hadn't got as far as the woolshed when the dogs barked. He coo-eed, and Roy answered, and coming round a bend in the road Henry caught him in the light of the torch. He didn't keep it on him though, he quickly turned it away.

Are you all right? he said.

Right as rain, Roy said.

But Henry had seen the wreck that he was, his face bleeding, and his clothes filthy and torn.

He didn't say anything, and going down the road Roy said only one thing, You know uncle Henry, I'd certainly get rid of that bloody bit of bush if I were you.

LETTER TO A FRIEND

. . . You ask me whether I found any material for writing while I was down in that seaside place, so perhaps I'd better tell you about how I met a boy named Paul. Then I can leave you to judge for yourself.

I found Paul at my table one evening when I went in to dinner. He looked quite a nice sort of lad, thoughtful, rather shy, and quite good-looking with dark curly hair and a clear skin. I thought he couldn't be more than seventeen, though he looked older in his double-breasted suit. When our soup came he crossed himself before he began to eat, and while we were eating we told each other our Christian names, and he told me what school he went to. But apart from this our appetites seemed to be too healthy to leave us much time to talk. After the meal I went out on the verandah with my pipe and he came with me. Somebody had left a copy of Poe's *Tales* on a chair, and he wanted to know if I'd read them. I told him yes, and he said he had too, and his next question was a surprise. He wanted to know, did I agree that it was because the author was so very much interested in the problem of evil that he wrote horror stories?

I said yes, I thought so. But I asked him whether he'd thought that out for himself.

Well, to be honest, he said, and he coloured rather, I read it in a book.

So I tried to put things right by saying that was O.K., years ago I'd probably done the same myself. Then he went on to say the problem interested him very much because he wanted to be a priest, but his father had decided to take him into his business. It was on the tip of my tongue to remark that in that case he might have some splendid opportunities to study the problem firsthand. But I didn't. He was too nice a lad.

Anyhow, his next remark was another surprise. Yes, he said, when you think of the war you can't blame Edgar Allan Poe for writing those stories.

I agreed, but this type of New Zealand schoolboy was rather a new one on me, and I found myself too busy with my thoughts to pay much attention while he told me his father would be down the following evening, and was hoping to hire a launch so they could do some deep-sea fishing. . . .

Next morning he was down to breakfast before me, and just crossing himself before he began his porridge. He had on a silk shirt and white trousers that went well with his dark hair. This, I notice, is the second time I've mentioned his clothes, and I suppose it's because he was such a contrast to myself. I was making the most of my holiday, so I was going bare-footed in knockabout trousers and an old shirt, and I used to get stared at in the dining-room. Everybody else would be all togged up, particularly for dinner in the evening. But unlike everybody else Paul seemed to take no notice at all of what I was wearing, and didn't make me feel the slightest bit self-conscious.

Anyhow, it was a wonderful morning, not a cloud to be seen, and a cool breeze just barely lifting the curtains. From where we sat we could look out and see the planes slowly rising and sinking above the trees that hid the aerodrome further down the coast. But none of them had so far come over our way, so the buzz was like something happening 'off'—something important no doubt, but not yet claiming any serious attention.

It was certainly a day, and I told Paul that as it was my last I was going for a last walk away along the ocean beach. He said he'd like to come too, so after breakfast I went out and bought some onions and a loaf of bread at the store. I put them in my rucksack, then we went down on the beach and found quite a crowd collected there already. Near where we jumped down off the breakwater there were a pair of Yanks and a girl. She had on a two-piece sun-suit, a big hat, big round black sun-glasses and tons of make-up. She was sitting absolutely still, holding on to the shaft of a beach parasol, and the Yanks were one on each side of her, one with his arm around her and the other with his hand on her leg. But sitting there so still and silent she didn't seem alive. I thought she could easily have been a dummy figure in a set-up staged for the benefit of newspaper readers interested in the decay of morals.

I said to Paul, I believe that's the way they do up a corpse for an American funeral. But, nice lad that he was, he said, I beg your pardon. He didn't know what I was talking about, and it seemed to me that even if he'd noticed the tableau he hadn't attached any point to it—which somehow seemed to me faintly surprising in view of what he'd said about the problem of evil. (Or is it, maybe, that my notions about the problem of evil are far too much tainted by my puritan upbringing? I leave this question for you to decide.)

However, we were soon round the point and away from the crowd, and there ahead of us was the long empty beach with the sea on one side and the sandhills on the other. The tide was going out, and black-backed gulls were walking on the wet sand, some of them taking off now and then to carry up pipis to drop and follow down to the sand again. The glitter on the sea was dazzling, and high up above the gannets were flying in great curves, sinking and rising, catching the sun in a flash of white, hovering with beating wings before they dive-bombed that glittering surface. I thought of Blake's lines, '. . . the starry floor, the watery shore, is given thee till break of day. . . .' But away over at the back of the sandhills, above the trees, you could still see the planes. . . .

Well, as far as we could see into the distance there was

237

nothing ahead of us but that empty beach. Yet we took all day over it and it wasn't half long enough. Paul soon lost his shyness and was quite keen to tell me his ideas about this and that. Then when we got hungry we lit a fire, grilled pipis on hot stones until they opened, and ate them with the bread and onions. Paul said he had no idea that such a meal could taste so good. He ate heartily, but not, I thought, so heartily as I did—as you know my insatiable interest in concrete things has always included things you can eat. But Paul at the age of seventeen has developed a remarkable talent for the abstract. For instance, while we were lying stretched out after the meal, a cicada flew on to my arm and sat there, stridulating and clicking its wings with tremendous gusto. I caught it and got Paul to look at the three extraordinary rubies they have in their heads, and he was interested but not so very interested. He was much more interested in what he'd been telling me about the difficulties you get into if you separate philosophy from religion—God is liable to become an absolute, he said, quite remote from a world in which everything that we experience is relative.

Yes, I said, as I let the cicada go, I see what you mean. As relative beings everything depends on our viewpoint. But an absolute being would have no viewpoint at all.

He seemed pleased that I was capable of showing some intelligence in the matter, and he went on, quite eagerly, to tell me some more. And I listened until a plane came over very suddenly, flying low over the sandhills, and passing right over us before it went out to sea. As always I was fascinated by the thing, and only became conscious that Paul had gone on talking when the noise had died away enough for me to hear his voice again. But somehow the plane had killed my interest in his theorising. It was brutal of me no doubt, but I said that immediate things had always interested me most. And I quoted Blake, 'Turn away no more; why wilt thou turn away? the starry floor. . . .' But, I went on to say, that up in the sky was the sort of immediate thing you were faced with these days, and you just *couldn't* turn away.

So he thought this over for a moment or two, then he said nearly all the boys at school wanted to be airmen, but he didn't. He said that if he had to go to the war he'd try to get into the ambulance. As he'd done the previous evening he coloured a little as he said this, and I thought perhaps it was something he'd never said to anyone before. It affected me anyhow, but I could only bring myself to say I thought it a good idea. . . .

It was close on dinnertime when we got back, and Paul's father had arrived and was sitting on the verandah. Paul introduced us (he had to ask me for my name, and up till then I hadn't known his), then he was told he'd better go and tidy himself up for dinner. I sat down for a rest, and his father talked to me. I don't intend to tell you his conversation though, you know the sort of thing off by heart. There was nothing at all special about him. He sprang the usual awkward question on me—what line was I in? And he said that after the war property down in those parts should be valuable. He thought the place was wasted as it was, but perhaps the Yanks might help us to make it more attractive—he could see no reason why it shouldn't become one of the most popular playgrounds of the Pacific. . . .

Listening to him I'd now and then catch myself out feeling sorry for him. Or Paul would flash across my mind and I'd feel even sorrier for *him*. And maybe all the time it was myself I was feeling sorriest for. There's just one last point though. There was salad for dinner, and round the edge of the dish were chunks of raw carrot. Paul's father used his knife and fork to eat these with. I was quite cheered up when I noticed Paul follow my example and use his fingers. . . .

SHOWERS

This big fellow got the name of Showers, because he would never answer anything else whenever he was asked what the weather was going to be. Also he worked for the town board, and in the dry weather he'd have to drive about the streets on the water-cart, and that sort of fitted in with his nickname as well.

Anyhow, Showers was a man who was said to weigh just on twenty stone, and as he wasn't specially tall you can imagine what he looked like. He was a good sort though, everybody liked him with his big red face that was always breaking into a grin, and he never seemed to mind when you pulled his leg by asking him what the weather was going to be.

Showers lived with his mother, just the two of them living in a small house, and there were all sorts of yarns about the size of his appetite, and the quantity of meat his mother was always buying. The butcher, having his drinks along at the pub, would say how it was nothing unusual for Showers' mother to buy half a fair-sized sheep on Saturday, and then be back again on Monday morning wanting another half. But everybody always said the butcher was exaggerating, because it might take a lot to feed Showers, but not as much as all that. The butcher would say no, it was the fair dinkum truth, and he'd get annoyed when he couldn't get anyone to believe him. And then one day he told an even better one. He said that one Friday late shopping night Showers' mother had bought a whole calf and had it delivered early Saturday morning, and on Sunday morning early she was round at the butcher's house asking him please would he get something for her out of the shop, because she was right out of meat.

But there was nobody along at the pub at the time who would swallow that one, and the butcher got very annoyed, and it led to a lot of argument. A cow-cocky who was reckoned to be pretty well in said he'd killed and eaten a lot of meat in his time, and he knew for a fact that no man, not even with the help of his old mother, could eat a whole calf in practically one day. So the butcher said all right, was he prepared to bet on it? And after a lot of talk it was all fixed up. The bet was to be a tenner, and Showers was to eat a whole calf, bones not included of course, between sunrise and sunset on anniversary day. The way they fixed it was like this: the day before the holiday the butcher was to deliver the calf to the pub-keeper, and he was to get the cook to make the meat into patties, and all the holiday a plateful of them was to be kept on the bar counter, and nobody was to take anything from that plate except Showers; though it was decided Showers wasn't to be in the know, and nobody was to let on to him, but there'd be no trouble because he was fond of his beer, and if he was stood enough drinks it was reckoned he'd stay in the pub long enough to give the calf a fair go.

So everything was fixed up, and on anniversary day, sure enough, Showers came along to the pub soon after it opened up in the morning. Of course the news about the bet had got around, and there were quite a few side-bets on the go as well, so quite a crowd was there to see if Showers would fall down on the job. But he didn't show any signs of it all through the morning, though just before midday the cow-cocky took the butcher by the sleeve and led him round into the kitchen, and people said the butcher came back pulling a long face. And others went to look and came back winking at their cobbers, and said he'd never do it, because he hadn't finished off nearly half a great big trayful so far, and there was another big one still to go.

Though it wasn't long before things began to look up for

the butcher, because Showers let himself be persuaded that, seeing it was a holiday, he might as well make a day of it and cut out going home for his dinner. And once having made the decision he whacked into the patties a good deal faster, though his backers weren't any too pleased when, instead of sticking to the patties, he'd once or twice reach out for a piece of bread and cheese off one of the other plates.

Then he slackened off again, which after all was hardly anything more than was natural, but his backers got windy when he said maybe he'd better be going home for a snooze now, because later on he wanted to do a bit of work in the garden. But he couldn't resist having another few drinks first, and he'd eat a patty now and then, though sometimes he'd nearly break a number of hearts by taking one up while he talked—but only to put it back on the plate again. Later on though he began to get hungry again, and when it was getting on towards evening and the pub-keeper said free drinks all round, and let everybody eat up too—well, Showers just went right ahead. And packed to the doors though the bar was, you could have heard a pin drop when he took the last patty on the plate, and everybody knew there wasn't a single one more to come.

Of course the next moment there would have been wild cheers and a great hullabaloo, but some wag picked up a plate with one last piece of bread and cheese and held it out to Showers. And he didn't speak very clearly (after all, besides the patties, he'd put away quite as much beer as was good for him), but he was understood to say no thanks, he didn't think he ought to, because he'd heard a yarn about somebody having a bet on to get him to eat a whole calf before sundown.

THE HOLE THAT JACK DUG

Jack had got a pretty considerable hole dug in the back-yard before I knew anything about it. I went round one scorching hot Saturday afternoon, and Jack was in the hole with nothing on except his boots and his little tight pair of shorts. Jack is a big specimen of a bloke, he's very powerfully developed, and seeing he's worked in the quarry for years in just that rigout, he's browned a darker colour than you'd ever believe possible on a white man. And that afternoon he was sweating so much he had a shine on as well.

Hello Jack, I said, doing a spot of work?

And Jack leaned on his shovel and grinned up at me. The trouble with Jack's grin is that it shows too many teeth. It's easy to pick they're not the real thing, and I've always thought they somehow don't fit in with the rest of him. Also his eyes are sky-blue, and it almost scares you to see them staring out of all that sunburn. I don't say *they* don't fit in though. They always have a bit of a crazy look about them, and even though Jack is my closest cobber I will say that he'll do some crazy things.

Yes Tom, he said, I'm doing a job.

But it's hot work, I said.

I've said it was scorching hot and it was. We'd been having a good summer, the first one after the war broke out. You'd hear folks say what lovely days we were having, and you'd be somehow always telling yourself you just couldn't believe there was any war on, when everything round about you looked so fine and dandy. But anyhow, I was just going to ask Jack if he wanted a hand, when his missis opened the back door and asked if I'd go in and have a cup of tea.

No thanks, Mrs Parker, I said, I've only just had one.

She didn't ask Jack, but he said he could do with one, so we both went inside and his missis had several of her friends there. She always has stacks of friends, and most times you'll find them around. But I'm Jack's friend, about the only one he has that goes to the house. I first ran across Jack in camp during the last war, though I only got to be cobbers with him a fair while after, when we lived at the same boardinghouse and worked at the same job, shovelling cement. In those days he hadn't started to trot the sheila he eventually married, though later on when he did I heard all about it. It knocked Jack over properly. He was always telling me about how she was far too good for him, a girl with her brains and refinement. Before she came out from England she'd been a governess, and I remember how Jack said she'd read more than ten books by an author called Hugh Walpole. Anyhow Jack was knocked over properly, and I reckon she must have been too. Or why did she marry him? As for me, I reckon it was because she did have the brains to tell a real man when she saw one, and hook on to him when she got the chance. But all that must be well over twenty years ago now, and it's always a wonder to me the way Jack still thinks his missis is the greatest kid that ever was, even though she couldn't make it plainer than she does, without a word said, that she's changed her mind about him. Not that you can altogether blame her of course. Just about any man, I should say, would find it awfully trying to be a woman married to Jack. But for a cobber you couldn't pick on a finer bloke.

One thing Mrs Parker's always had against Jack is that he's stayed working in the quarry year after year, instead of trying to get himself a better job. Meaning by a better job one that brings in more pay, without it mattering if it's only senseless and stupid sort of work you have to do. Of course, Jack knows that to run the house, with the snooks growing up fast, his missis could have always done with considerably more money than he's able to let her have. He lets her have the lot any way, he never would smoke or drink or put money on a horse. But he isn't the sort that's got much show of ever being in the big money, and any case it would need to be pretty big, because his missis is always coming to light with some big ideas. Not to mention a car, one thing she's always on about is a refrigerator. It would save money in the long run is what she reckons, and maybe she's right, but it's always seemed too much of a hurdle to Jack.

Do you know dear, I heard him say once, when I was a little boy, and my mother opened the safe, and there was a blowfly buzzing about, it sometimes wouldn't even bother to fly inside.

And Mrs Parker said, What's a blowfly (or your mother for that matter) got to do with us having a refrigerator? And Jack went on grinning until she got cross and said, Well, why *wouldn't* it fly inside?

Because dear, Jack said, it knew it was no good flying inside.

And you could tell it annoyed his missis because she still couldn't work it out, but she wasn't going to let on by asking Jack to explain.

But I was telling about that Saturday afternoon when we went inside, and Jack had his cup of tea and I wouldn't have one.

Well, do sit down, Mrs Parker said to me, but I stayed standing. It sounds dirty I know, but I'd had years of experience behind me. I've only got a sort of polite interest in Jack's missis and those friends of hers. They're always talking about books and writers, but never any I know anything about. Henry Lawson now, that would be different. Though I've always remembered that name Hugh Walpole, and once I started one of his, I forget the name, but I never got past the first chapter. I only go there because I'm Jack's cobber, but Mrs Parker is a mighty good-looking woman, so I suppose she's always naturally expected everybody of the male sex to be more interested in her than in her old man. Everybody is anyhow, except me. But still she's never seemed satisfied. And with things that way I've usually always picked on fine weekends to go round and see Jack, because then the pair of us can work in the garden, and I don't have to listen to his missis all the time nipping at him. And times when it comes on wet I've usually shoved off, though sometimes we've gone and sat yarning on the camp stretcher in the little room off the back verandah where Jack sleeps. Jack mightn't have the brains that his missis has but he isn't dumb, and I've always liked to hear him talk. He's such a good-natured cuss, always wanting everything in the garden to be lovely for everybody that walks the earth, and he'll spout little pieces of poetry to show what he means. Years before the war broke out I was listening to him talking about the way things were going with the world, and saying what he thought was going to happen. After all, the pair of us had been in the last war, and I agreed when Jack said he could see it all coming again. And he had more to worry about than I had, because his eldest one was a colt. (I say was, because later on it was rotten to get the news from Italy about him.)

Anyhow, one reason I stayed standing when Mrs Parker asked me to sit down, was because I thought I'd get Jack back into the garden sooner if I didn't sit down. And although he grinned round at the company, looking aw-fully hairy and sweaty though not too naked on account of his dark colour, and even spouted one of his pieces of poetry (which his missis several times tried to interrupt), he was all the time gulping several cups of tea down hot, and I reckoned he had that hole he was digging on his mind, which as it turned out he had.

That hole!

It was right up against the wash-house wall, and we went out and looked at it, and Jack said it would take a lot of work but never mind. He said he hadn't thought about me giving him a hand, but never mind that either. We could widen it another four feet so the pair of us could work there together. And he went and got the spade, and I began by taking the turf off the extra four feet, while Jack got down below again with the shovel.

Now I've known Jack a longer time than his missis has, so maybe that's the reason why I know it's never any good pestering him with straightout questions, because if you do you only get an answer back like the one I'd heard his missis get over the refrigerator. Only seeing Jack knows me pretty thoroughly, he'll probably make it a lot more difficult to work out than that one was. So if he wanted to dig a hole that was all right with me, and I thought if I just kept my mouth shut I'd find out in plenty of good time what he was digging it *for*. To begin with though, I don't know that I thought about it much at all. It was Jack's concern, and he didn't have to tell me.

But I admit it wasn't long before I began wondering. You see, when we finished up that Saturday afternoon Jack said we'd done a good job of work, but how about if I came round and we carried on one night during the week? And that was all right, I said for one night I could cut out taking a few bob off the lads that were learning to play billiards along at the room, and I'd make it Wednesday. And Wednesday after work I had my wash but didn't change out of my working clothes, and after dinner I got on my bike and went round to Jack's place and found him hard at it. Also it was easy to tell this wasn't the only night he'd been working because already by now it was a whopping great hole he was working in. Anyhow we had our usual yarn, then the pair of us got to work and kept on until it was too dark to see any more. And just about then Jack's missis came round the corner of the wash-house.

Whatever are you two boys doing? she wanted to know.

We've been working Mrs Parker, I said.

Yes, she said, but what are you digging that hole for?

You see dear, Jack said, some people say they don't like work, but what would we ever have if we didn't work? And now the war's on we've all got to do our share. Think of the

soldier-boys. Fighting's hard work, and Tom and me want
to do our bit as well.

But before he'd finished Mrs Parker had gone inside
again. I was putting my bicycle clips on my trousers, but
Jack was still down the hole, and he asked if I'd mind
handing him down a box with a candle and matches that
I'd see in the wash-house. I watched while he lit up and
fixed the box so the light shone where he wanted to work.
And for a few minutes I stayed watching, the shovel going
in deep each time under his weight, the candle-light showing up the hollows and curves made by his big muscles,
and the sweat making him look as if he was all covered
with oil. I left him to it, but said I'd be round again
Saturday afternoon, and going home I thought perhaps it
was a septic tank he was putting in. Or was it an asparagus
bed? Or was he going to set a grape vine. It was evidently
going to be a proper job any way, whatever it was.

Well. The job went on for weeks. As far as I could make
out Jack must have come home and worked at it every
night until late. He didn't like taking time off to shift away
the spoil from the edge, so that was the job I took on, and I
must have shifted tons of the stuff down to the bottom of
the garden in the wheelbarrow. Nor would Jack let me go
down the hole any more, he said it was too dangerous, and
it certainly looked like it. Because once he'd got down deep
he started to under-cut in all directions, particularly on the
wash-house side, which seemed pretty crazy to me. Once
he struck rock, so brought some gelly home from the quarry
and plugged a bit in and set it off, and it brought a lot of
earth down on the wash-house side. Then he had to get to
work and spend a lot of time rigging up props in case the
blocks that were holding the wash-house up came through.
I was hanged if I could get a line on what it was all about,
and it was beginning to get me worried. His missis didn't
ask any more questions, not while I was there anyhow, but
I noticed she was getting round with a worried look, and
I'd never felt that way before but I did feel a bit sorry for
her then. About the only ones that got a kick out of the

business were Jack's youngest snooks. The gelly he set off had been a real bit of fun for them, and they and their cobbers were always hanging around in the hope of another explosion. One that would finish off the wash-house, no doubt. Another thing was that for several weeks Jack hadn't done a tap of work in the garden, and one afternoon when Mrs Parker came out with cups of tea for us, she said he must be losing his eyesight if he couldn't see there was plenty just crying out to be done.

Yes dear, Jack said, in that good-natured sort of loving tone he always uses to her. Things being what they are between them, I can understand how it must make her want to knock him over the head. Yes dear, he said, but just now there are other things for Tom and me to do.

He was sitting on the edge of the hole, and after the strain of a long bout of shovelling his chest was going like a big pair of bellows worked by machinery. The day was another scorcher but blowy as well, and the dust had stuck to him, and run and caked, and stuck again, until about all you could see that was actually him was those eyes of his. And the bloodshot white and pure blue staring out of all that was something you almost couldn't bear to look at.

Yes dear, he repeated, we have other things to do.

And it was just then that half a dozen planes flying down quite low happened to suddenly come over. And of course we all of us stared up at them.

You see dear, Jack went on saying, though you could hardly hear him for the noise of the planes. You see dear, he said, we have more important things to do than those boys flying up there. Or at any rate, he went on, just as important.

But since we were watching the planes we didn't pay much attention to him. And it wasn't until they were nearly out of sight that I realized he'd disappeared down the hole again. You could tell he was there all right. The shovelfuls of spoil were coming flying up over the edge at a tremendous rate. And it was only afterwards, thinking it over, that I remembered what he'd been saying.

Well. This is the end of my yarn about Jack and the hole he dug. Next time I went round he was filling it in again, and he'd already got a fair bit done. All he said was that if he didn't go ahead and get his winter garden in he'd be having the family short of vegetables. And his missis had told him he'd got to do something about the hole because it was dangerous when there were kids about. So I took over wheeling the stuff up from the bottom of the garden, and Jack rammed it back in so tight that by the time he was up to ground level again there was practically nothing left over.

I must end up with a joke though. It was only a few summers later we had the Jap scare, and Jack earned a considerable amount of money digging shelters for people who were wanting them put in in a hurry, and weren't so particular how much they paid to get the work done. His missis appreciated the extra money, but she was always on to him to dig one for the family. All her friends agreed it was scandalous, the callous way he didn't seem to care if his own wife and children were all blown to bits!

As for me, I'm ready to stick up for Jack any time. Though I don't say his missis is making a mistake when she says that some day he'll end up in the lunatic asylum.

THE UNDERTAKER'S STORY

A stocky powerful man somewhat gone to seed, he was thrown out of a seaside pub one fine Saturday afternoon when I was sitting on the verandah.

The bar had been too crowded and noisy, too intolerably hot and sticky, and I had taken my beer outside, where the sun would be some time yet before it hit the bench against the front wall. A breeze off the harbour kept the high tide slapping at the sand, which sloped up until it met the concrete verandah flooring, but the glare and glitter was too trying on my eyes and I turned sideways on. The noise from within was a babble and roar, but the moment my ears began to pick out the sounds of a quarrel, it was strange to see how the backs that curved from the wide-open windows began to straighten. As the moment of climax approached they all disappeared.

Spluttering and blowing, his face red unshaved and swollen, he braked with his feet and grabbed at the jamb of the doorway, but so many were pulling and shoving he hadn't a chance. He went limp as they heaved him down the slope, and he lay like something washed up by the tide. It was as though he knew himself to have been defeated beyond all question.

They all turned and went inside again, dusting and straightening their clothes. There was no fuss, no sign of either malice or sympathy. A quarrelsome drunk had been dealt with. The faces at the windows looked the other way, and the backs curved out again.

There were two of us outside now, and while I was

trying to work out the problem the incident had presented me with, there appeared in the doorway an elderly under-sized man, very tidy in a panama hat a maroon blazer and flat rubber-soled shoes. With his white tooth-brush mous-tache as well, he looked as though he had by some mistake dropped in instead of going to bowls. He had with him an old felt hat, which he dusted with his handkerchief as he went down the beach, and for quite some time he kept turning it in his hands as he sat beside the heap of discarded humanity. When he began to speak I could not hear what he said, but the heap immediately came to life. The hat was accepted, and soon they were sitting side by side with their backs to the pub as they talked. Or rather, while the older man went on talking.

I was moved, but perhaps my strongest feeling was one of gratitude that my problem hadn't had to be solved.

When they at last stood up and parted, it seemed that the drunk was perhaps not so drunk. Quite steady on his feet, he returned from along the beach for the ceremony of trust and friendship. Hands were gripped and held, placed on shoulders and left there. It was a sort of tableau, or they might have been figures on a frieze. Beyond them the sea's dark blue suggested melancholy, and the unceasing move-ment seemed not to hold out any promise of permanency for their bond, but at least they stood on sand that was solid and clean after the high tide, and there was the sunlight for an impartial golden blessing.

The elderly man gave me a nod when he re-entered the pub, and I was not surprised when he brought out his own beer.

Ay, he said, quite without any preliminaries as he sat down alongside, ay. It is a sad thing when a man cannot forgive himself for his own failure.

This was direct and intelligent, somewhat unusual. Also, he spoke with a slight Scottish burr, which is often sup-posed to go with reticence.

I said I thought I understood.

Duncan, he said. I knew him when he was a Highland

lad, a sturdy young bull of a lad that lived his days on the hills with the sheep. I remember well I saw few lads of his like when I went on my rounds to those Highland places.

Ay, he said—and it seemed not unlikely that the hills he looked at across the harbour, were re-shaping themselves into something rather different.

You're not a Highland man yourself? I asked.

No. I was a Paisley boy. My people settled from Lancashire, Manchester. I grew up a Lowland Scot, but except for a manner of speaking there's not all that difference. The Lowland Scot is Anglo-Saxon as you may remember from your schoolbooks, and much the same by nature according to the way I figure it out. But there is much to separate him from the Highlander.

You visited the Highlands? I prompted him.

I was a young man travelling with a line of knick-knacks. For the most part it was jewellery, cheapjack stuff. There was money to be had by my boss in Glasgow, but nothing much for a young fellow working on commission. The Highlanders were hard folk to persuade, and if it had not been for the lassies, with their liking to deck themselves out with a bit of finery—well, the order sheets I sent back to my boss would never have added up to much of a turnover.

But this Duncan? I prompted again.

Duncan, he said. I remember well I said to his mother, a Mrs McGowan—I said the land's poor and the season is bad, and I don't forget there is always the landlord, but remember Mrs McGowan I said, it's the townsman in the big city that's first to go without his supper when times are bad. I said it was goodbye to Scotland, for I was off to New Zealand, where by God's help and good luck I would make my fortune.

It must have been a long time ago, I said. How is it you remember so exactly?

Duncan, he said. It was Duncan. The boy was there in the yard, feeding a handful of grain to his mother's hens while I talked at the doorstep. He heard me say the name of this country.

How could I know, he continued, how could I know that name would never shift from the boy's memory?

So he followed you out here? I questioned, thinking I might cut down some of the story's trimmings.

It would be wrong to say that. He never remembered my face, and I did not recognise him until I heard his name called out and took stock of him. You see, I had not made my fortune after near on twenty years, and I had trouble enough to put thoughts of Scotland far from my mind. It was bad luck I took up with my old line of commercial travelling, although it did not look like bad luck at the time. I was employed by a grocery warehouse, and glad of my opportunity to see the country, but there is temptation for a young man when it is rare for him to sleep in any bed except what he can get at the country pubs. I don't mean to say I went to the bad with the drink, because your Scot is canny as a rule, and he has a great respect for book-learning. Many a night when there was drinking it would be no attraction for me, because I was lying on my bed with a book, and to this day I am a great reader of good books. But there is the temptation of women, and that our Maker has decreed for the population of the world. No man may refrain, as you a young man will understand. But no great amount of looseness was ever in my nature, and I took my wife from a pub where I was in the habit of staying, a grand girl with a good hand for cooking, and a full bosom where any man might wish to pillow his head for his contentment.

Yes yes, I said, but what about Duncan?

Duncan, he said. If you are not in a hurry there is time to tell you about Duncan—and he was silent a moment while he appeared to gather up his threads.

My wife left me, and she took away the wee boy. I had never settled in this country, do you see?—even though it was ten or twelve years since I landed. I was still on the road, and it was no life for my wife. A woman should not be exposed to temptation when she has a husband to tend her. I tried, but I could not mend my situation, so I swore by God's help I would mend my ways in case I had another opportunity for settling. I thought hard and deep, and I decided to give up the road. I sat and looked at my soft hands, and I remembered about my grandfather. He was a master spinner, and he settled in the North because he hoped to better himself at the fine Paisley work. There was none of that sort of thing in New Zealand, but I remembered my bachelor uncle gave me a cardboard box of carpenter's tools for my birthday when I was ten. It was because I had said I was going to be a carpenter. The tools were toys, which I was proud to bring out to show the visitors, but although there was a book of directions, and my uncle brought me pieces of wood, I was never known to try to use those tools. It all came back to me in my distress, and I decided (when I was near to turning forty, mind you), I decided I would make myself into the carpenter I said I was going to be.

And? I had to prompt.

Did you not see the big sign as you came through the town?

I thought a moment, and replied that apart from the hoardings, the only sign I could remember was the undertaker's.

That's it, he said. Robert Wilson is my name.

But, I was about to say, when he continued.

You see, I was a very determined man and I had made my decision. I learned the carpentry, and I did more by learning the joinery and cabinet-making. I discovered I had nimble hands when a delicate job was called for. I came over to the coast here, and I set myself up in the furniture line of business, but it would be untruthful to say I prospered. I made none of your cheapjack stuff, which the public preferred because of my prices. I remember well a customer said when I showed him a kitchen cupboard—he said I had put in enough work to make it watertight. He said I should have been a boatbuilder. Ah, but it was about that same time my opportunity came to me. There was just one other furniture-maker in the township as it was then, and he was the undertaker. He died, he was undertaken himself as you might say, and I made my arrangements to take over his business. Now wasn't that a strange thing?—it was honest work for living folk I had done, but the public wouldn't have it on account of the prices. I did not prosper until I worked for the dead man that could have no argument about the price, and no say about what I provided.

He paused, but he held up his hand when I opened my mouth to speak.

Duncan, he said. It was about that same time when I began the undertaking. It was unbeknown to me that Duncan was living behind the hills you see eastwards yonder as you come up the coast. He had taken up a bit of land in a ballot. It was O.R.P. if you understand, occupation with right of purchase, what is reckoned third class land. But alongside of him being hampered for lack of ready money, the floods washed out his fences, and the wind blew a gale that carried away his cowshed, and the lean-to where he lived until he could prosper. I learned the story of his misfortunes one day when I had business at the Court-house, and heard his name called out before the Justices for sheep-stealing. Duncan, I said, when they allowed me to talk with him, before he was taken away to be tried at the Supreme Court—Duncan, I said, do your time as you must if the judgment of the law goes against you, but don't lose heart man. Stand up on your two feet and look folks in the face, for it is in the nature of man to fall according to the law of God. But all may hope to raise themselves by the help of God and man, and if the Almighty does his share so will I too.

You see, I am none of your strict Calvinists in my belief, he broke off to say.

I told Duncan I had not made my fortune, but I stood in a fair way to prosper, and if he would return to the district I would do everything on his behalf that lay in my ability.

And he did return, I said.

Yes. But not before I had lost sight of him for close on ten years. He was not much changed in his appearance, but I never knew a man so reluctant to speak. He scarce spoke a word to me as a boy, and I forced the answers from him that sad day he was brought to the Court, but now he spoke up only one answer when ten might be required. And not to hear his wife answer at all was very aggravating.

You see, he said after a pause, he had taken a wife, and the pair were like foreign immigrants to America that have not learned to speak the English language. But what was the more strange, it was rare you heard them say a word to each other—no, not even upon an occasion of importance as you will hear.

Now do you see? he went on, I had my doubts about them being married. They were matched like to like if you understand, and in the marriage state it is best for the dark to be set against the fair, and the light and merry against what is more sober. But I did an injustice. Duncan had his bit of money saved up, and wished me to help him on to the land according to the word I had promised. I had prospered and I was willing to honour my bond, and indeed it suited me well, because I had bought up sixteen acres of good dairy country going cheap beyond the town boundary. If Duncan would settle, he and his wife could milk for the town supply, and by delivering to the householder as well the profit would be increased. So we made an arrangement, but first I told Duncan there was just one matter. He was a man with a conviction, but that would never be held against him with me supporting him—and I explained how I now had the honour of sitting as a J.P. But there must be nothing irregular in addition that might cause people to talk, and if he would pardon me for mentioning it I would be favoured if he would show his marriage certificate.

Good Lord! I couldn't help exclaiming. And did he crack you?

I was aware of the risk, he went on. But do you see?—I knew if the marriage lines were shown swiftly, I could fairly reckon it was because they were in the possession of

Mrs McGowan, and instead of free choice, I could infer the probability of what the young people nowadays speak of as a shotgun marriage. And in the event, it turned out that Duncan's wife visited me immediately with the document I wished to see.

But there was no child, I said.

Ah, I'm coming to that. I supposed the child had miscarried, and there I had the explanation of two people, man and woman, bound up together as man and wife for no reason but the child. There was no child, but they were still bound. Duncan, a fine strong handsome man, was bound to a poor creature that carried scarce a hint of feminine flesh anywhere on her bones.

His pause was so long I had to say, And?

And I was deceived. They settled nicely, putting heart and soul and all the strength of their two bodies into the work on the land. But I confess I was very surprised to hear there was to be seen a wee boy running about the place, and sometimes riding on the float when Duncan came to town for the early delivery. I inquired, and I found he had been left with his grandmother, Duncan's mother-in-law, until they were settled. Not that I counted the circumstance against them, but it irked me to be deceived when I was right in my reckoning. And I still could not understand why they did not speak to each other, whatever the wrong that had been done, when they had the boy to compensate them for being bound. He was a merry lad, too young for his schooling, but fine strong and healthy. And he was equally fond of Duncan and his mother. He would run from one to the other, and although his frolics never persuaded either to speak except perhaps a syllable, I marked it one day when Duncan placed his hand on the child's head—because Duncan smiled, and that was a thing I had never known him to do.

Ah, but then it all happened, and it was sudden like the plagues visited on the Egyptians by the God of Israel. I have no evidence that Duncan was in the habit of taking liquor privately, but occasionally of an afternoon, perhaps

one day a fortnight, he would ride into town and drink
until closing time. It was never reported to me he drank to
excess, and indeed it was complained by the barmen that
he was the slowest drinker on record. But it did not matter
how much he drank, he would never seek company in the
bar. For my own satisfaction I ascertained that his wife did
not sit wringing her hands waiting on his return, on the
contrary she would have the milking done and everything
washed up ready for the morning, so I did not consider I
had any grounds for complaint. But so far as I can piece
together the happenings, one late winter evening Duncan
rode home and heard the cows bellowing on account of not
being milked. His wife's excuse was Jock, the laddie—he
had been taken ill with a bad stomach pain in the afternoon. He was tossing and delirious with fever, and the wife
dared not leave him to walk some considerable distance
where she could ring up the doctor. She asked Duncan to
go and ring, but he was obstinate and said the boy would
be well by the morning. He went to milk the cows, first
forbidding his wife to leave the house, and swearing he
would have no doctor calling, with authority to poison the
boy with his medicines. The poor creature was distracted,
but she obeyed her husband, and Duncan delayed returning to the house until the evening was well spent. She
thought from the delay he had been for the doctor after all,
but it was not so, and immediately he returned she risked
disobedience, because although the boy had turned quiet
he lay cold in a sweat—and when the doctor came at last,
husband and wife were sitting each side of the bed, not
speaking, but each clasping upon the boy's hands. And the
boy was dead.

He was silent a moment, and the noise from inside the
bar seemed suddenly very loud. I did not know what to
say and said, I see.

But, he went on, there was more happened that winter
night. The doctor got me out of bed to notify me on the
phone. I could not sleep after such news, accustomed
though I was to notifications of the kind, so I dressed

myself and drove out to the farm. I shut off the engine to
coast down the hill to the gate, and I considered returning
to town, because there was no glimmer of light to indicate
they were not in their bed. But a light commenced to shine
beneath the macrocarpas that separated the garden from
the paddocks, so I walked up the track and rounded the
house but I went no further. There was toi-toi I could
stand behind, and I could see well that Duncan's wife was
holding a storm lantern while Duncan dug and chopped at
the roots of the biggest tree. I heard him grunt at his work
but he never spoke, and he worked hard and fast until
there was a big hole tucked well in under the tree. Then I
had to hold in my breath as they passed near returning
into the house, but immediately they came again, Mrs
McGowan still carrying the lantern but Duncan bearing a
rough timber box. He placed it well in the hole, and when
he had finished throwing back the earth and was stamping
it with his feet, then his wife placed the lantern on the
ground and returned into the house. Neither had spoke a
word, but as for Duncan, when he had finished stamping
he picked up the lantern and stood before he returned into
the house. And I heard him say, Jock! my Jock.

For quite some time we were both silent, but the spell
was broken when he had to respond to greetings from a
group which came round the side of the pub to enter by the
front door. It was in any case high time for me to be out on
the road, to wait for the bus that would take me further up
the coast.

I shouldered my rucksack.

Are they still living together? I asked.

Never. She left him after the inquiry.

And is Duncan still on the farm?

Never, never. He earns his bit of money here and there.
He is tipped for marking the scores in the billiard saloon.

Tell me, I said, did you ever marry again?

Ay, he replied. I married my housekeeper. It was in
keeping with my position when I was appointed a Justice
of the Peace. My wife is a fine figure of a woman.

There was an indefinable something about his eyes—what is called a twinkle, I suppose.

And she has an excellent hand for cooking.

Yes, I said as I raised my hand for a goodbye. I'd expect that.

THE COLONEL'S DAUGHTER

When I went in to dinner, the manager of the little tourist hotel left the table where he sat with his family, to come over and introduce me to the old lady whose table I was to share. Miss Smith. A moment later she surprised me by saying that she remembered me perfectly.

You were a Waikato boy, she said, and then she named the town.

Yes, I said, but I don't remember you. I'm sorry.

But surely, she said, surely you remember my orchard!

I exclaimed. It must have been forty years ago that I had helped Miss Kate Smith to beat out a fire in her orchard, one scorching hot summer's day. She had been burning a heap of prunings in droughty weather, and the fire had spread. There was fortunately no wind, and very little dry grass underneath the trees to burn; but upon my looking through the bars of the gate as I passed, I had been called in to help. When we had poured a bucket of water on the last smouldering patch, Miss Smith remarked the fire was a very good servant, but a very poor master. She also asked me my name, and left off calling me Boy; and after a few days I received through the post a bright silk handkerchief, wrapped round with a card which thanked me for my kind help.

I was staring, trying to reconcile a stiff-backed, white-haired, rather prim-looking old lady, with the woman who might have been any age at all to a child of ten, who had worn gardening gloves, and a wide-and-stiff-brimmed straw hat tied on with a veil, and who had vigorously whirled an empty sugar-bag to whack at the flames.

Of course you remember, she said.

Yes, I replied, but I can't remember I ever saw you again from that day to this.

Ah ha, she said, nobody saw me very much. Not in that town. No, she went on, I don't live there now, I got sick of it at last. I live in a flat in the city, but I come here regularly for six weeks in the off-season. I like it quiet.

Wasn't it quiet in the old town? I questioned.

It was and it wasn't. Tell me, she said after a pause, did your mother object to the handkerchief I sent you?

Not that I can remember, I said. Though I seem to remember she wasn't exactly pleased.

I'm sure she wasn't pleased.

We were interrupted while we decided about our soup and what was to follow, and then she asked:

Did your mother ever tell you anything about me?

Nothing that I can remember.

What else did you hear about me?

I thought for a moment, and said I could remember nothing except what everybody seemed to take for granted.

You mean, she said, that I was an aging spinster with plenty of money, an eccentric woman who lived alone in a large house and never went out.

Well, I said, perhaps. Something like that if you must put it that way.

She seemed a little disappointed, and I added:

You see, I got out of the town before I reached my twenties, and I never went back.

I don't blame you, she said. It was a very proper little town. No place for anybody with spirit. Still, she went on, *I* had spirit when I was a girl—at least I thought I had. I do think I might have been talked about, she said in tones that suggested complaint. Tell me, did you never hear any scandal about me at all? Really and truly?

I shook my head. I was beginning to feel a little uncomfortable.

Of course, she went on, your family was as proper as any, but I have always understood that scandal is the main topic of conversation among people of that kind. Or should I say gossip?

I decided to take it good-humouredly.

Perhaps, I said. Probably. But of course not in front of the children.

Your mother's sister now, a Miss Bertha Topp, a maiden lady—as the dubious saying is. She reclaimed a friend of mine, a Daisy Willoughby, she turned Daisy's feet away from the primrose path.

My aunt Bertha, I said, lived with my aunt Daisy, yes, but I think we children all understood that aunt Daisy was not our real aunt. She was a Mrs Clouty, and we played with her dark-eyed little girl, although she was some years older than I was.

Exactly, she said. But how did Daisy Willoughby come to be Daisy Clouty?—tell me that.

Well, I began, and then I said, No, it's too obvious.

Marriage. Of course. You never knew Clem Clouty?

I tried to remember. Certainly I had never *known* him, and yet there was a thread of memory, his voice on the phone perhaps, and a message I was to remember to give. I could connect him with whispers and winks and disapproving looks and—that was it, he drank! But I said:

Didn't he play the piano?

Anybody can play the piano, she said severely. I mean anybody could in those days. I played myself. Probably you did too. Do you know, she said with immense conviction and seriousness, apart from Pachmann, I never heard anyone play with a finer feeling for the instrument than Clem Clouty?

I felt myself impelled to demonstrate that I was knowledgeable in these matters, and said:

You mean he played Chopin?

Ah, she said, and her eyes opened wider, you know!

I once heard Pachmann, I said. In London. Where did you hear him?

264

The Colonel's Daughter

In Germany. It must be going on for half a century ago. It was before my father died—I expect it would be when you were a very small boy. My father was a gentleman, he was Colonel Smith, retired from the Imperial Army. Our name is really hyphenated, my father was Porterhouse-Smith. He took me on a tour, to mend my morals if you please.

Dear oh dear! I pretended to be a little shocked. Were they as bad as all that?

I was carrying on with Clem Clouty.

I see, I said. I expect you mean after he was married to my aunt Daisy.

Ah, but how did he come to marry her? I'll tell you, it was those proper people.

She paused, and I said, Yes, do tell me. After all, we were about to enter upon the cabinet pudding stage, and my slight feeling of irritation had mellowed with the food, and the not unworthy bottle of dry wine Miss Smith had insisted on my sharing.

Daisy Willoughby and I were inseparable, she said. Of course, she really belonged among the proper people, and I didn't. My father was never in trade or anything of that kind, he had money and property, and he drank his bottle a day—and I don't mean cheap brandy. He went to Church only once a year, at Easter, and to the Church of England of course. But I admired Daisy for her spirit. It was more difficult for her, after all as my father's only daughter, indeed his only child, he rather expected me to be high-spirited. He himself had had the spirit to charge the enemy—but I always forget whether it was the Crimea or China. I think it was those Taipings. But you know in a town like that a girl with high spirits could come a cropper —and Daisy did. You see, except for the dances there wasn't a great deal to be high-spirited about. Daisy wasn't supposed to go, but she defied her parents or else she deceived them—I'm not sure now exactly which. Clem Clouty worked in some mercantile establishment, I forget what it was, but he played the piano for our dances, and a

265

few violins and some woodwinds and brass were raked up as well when we held our big balls. Clem used to come to the house to practise on our grand piano, and when my father's rheumatics didn't make him too irritable we used to have some really lovely parties. I mean for a town like that in those days.

I envy you, I interrupted. I can remember only the Bible class socials. Once we were allowed a moonlight picnic on the river, but the paddle-steamer nearly capsized when it broke down and ran on a sandbank. All our bottles of soft drink were broken.

The dear old days! she exclaimed. It is wicked to deceive ourselves about them. And others too. But don't imagine I am deceiving you about Daisy—and myself. This is quite an occasion, and I am deceiving nobody.

Shall we take our coffee on the verandah? she interrupted herself to say, and she looked at her watch. The moon will be up quite soon and I like to see it—but from behind glass at this time of the year. Perhaps if it was a new moon I should feel a little superstitious, but of course it is not.

There was nobody on the verandah, so we turned off the lights to wait for the moon, and while we sat and smoked in easy chairs, her voice in the dark sounded astonishingly fluent. What she had to say seemed quite released from all considerations of reserve or constraint.

Yes, she said, Daisy Willoughby—have you seen her lately by the way?

I said I hadn't seen my aunt Daisy for thirty years.

Well, she said, she's quite gone to pieces now—she's nothing but an old bag, though I expect I sound horribly vulgar. Perhaps it was a mistake to turn the lights off, but leave them as they are. And I must sound as though I am ending my story when I am only in the middle. You see, Daisy was as keen about Clem Clouty as I was, at least I am sure she would have claimed to be if we had ever discussed the matter, which we never did. Probably she would have attempted to depreciate my own feelings by claiming to be even keener. I must admit that it was a shock to me when she owned up to being in a certain condition—as the curious saying is. The fact was not shocking in itself, not to an Army gentleman's daughter, but I could not refrain from calling her a little devil for my own personal reasons. However, I laughed it off. I proposed a trip to Sydney for both of us until it was all over, and I even undertook to pay every expense from money which I hoped to get from my father. I was even prepared to persuade him, if he should be reluctant, by declaring myself to be the guilty one. But all my plans on Daisy's behalf came to nothing. The poor girl's mind turned constantly on the dreadful fact that she was a fallen woman, and she could not forgive herself for straying from her proper environment among the proper people. I didn't mind so much her throwing me over, but I thought her reasons for doing so were most uncomplimentary. Her dearest friend in those circles was Bertha Topp, your proper aunt in two senses of the word. Miss Topp was a girl a good ten years older than Daisy, and on account of her displeasing appearance (I do hope you won't mind my speaking frankly) —but on account of that she had never, I am sure, had to take any serious steps in defence of her personal virtue. But she was perfectly prepared to go into action on behalf of Daisy when she heard her confession. She planned and led a campaign against Clem Clouty whom I have never to this day forgiven for capitulating. The poor boy was persuaded and bullied by Miss Topp until he agreed to go to the altar, or whatever it is they have in those Nonconformist places—I believe it sometimes resembles a card table. But no doubt any piece of furniture will serve as a site, once a human sacrifice has been agreed upon. I remember I had my twentieth birthday on the day of the wedding, and it was deplorable weakness on my part, which I still don't forgive myself, to spend the whole of it face down on my bed while I drenched the pillow with my tears.

She appeared to meditate for a moment or two, and I did not interrupt her.

It is curious, she said, but I don't remember that I ever saw the wedding photographs. I expect there was a careful arrangement of Daisy's bouquet—I believe photographers who do that sort of work are always tactful and understanding.

I remember, she went on, that for quite two years afterwards, I was, at least once a week, galled to hear some fresh piece of news about the happy married life of Clem and Daisy Clouty. I knew it couldn't last, but that didn't help me. Daisy's father and mother had bought the couple a house, right next door to their own. It was so that Clem might be constantly protected against backsliding. But they refused to buy him a decent piano, because that instrument was associated with his life of wickedness, from which Daisy had providentially rescued him. Yes, it is curious the way the minds of some people work. Daisy had been transformed by her marriage into an angel of providence. Can you believe it?—she was said to have risked soiling herself with pitch, in order to fetch up Clem from the depths of the pit. I of course was the woman who had done the most to drag him down there, and Daisy avoided me when we met in the street. It was expecting much too much to expect her to rescue *me*.

Again she was silent for a moment while she finished her coffee, and then she remarked that the moon seemed not to be on time.

But never mind, she said, when it's the moon one can be sure it won't miss an appointment, even though it may turn up late.

But where was I? she went on. Oh yes, about the piano. Well, in all the town I was the only person, the *only person* mind you, who was fully alive to Clem's talent for playing. Also, my father's grand (it had been my mother's poor dear, before she was thrown from our four-wheeler when the horses bolted—but that was when I was a baby, and fortunately I wasn't in the carriage)—my father's grand was the only instrument of its kind in the town, and I should think almost the only one in the Waikato. It broke my heart to be cut in the street by Clem as well as Daisy, but there *was* a difference. I knew it, and I knew that he knew it too. The poor dear boy, so handsome and unusual with his long dark hair and his really beautiful whiskers, I think the style was known as the King Edward—the poor boy did not cut me because he believed me to be a brand that was unreclaimed, and still burning. Indeed no. He was purely and simply ashamed of himself for neglecting his great talent. And how right he was! I was never much of a church-goer myself, but I was by no means unfamiliar with Scripture, and I did know about the awful punishment that was visited on the man who wasted his talents. I would lie awake at nights thinking what I could do to save poor Clem, who was not even permitted to tinkle away at the piano for our dances, and at last I hit upon a plan. It cost my father a lot of money, but it worked brilliantly. A Continental pianist (if I told you his name you wouldn't believe me)—this famous man was visiting the country on a concert tour. He wasn't booked to play in the town, but he had to pass through on his way, and he consented to play privately on my father's grand, naturally for a very substantial fee. Of course I included Clem among the very few people I invited, *and* I didn't invite Daisy. I don't forget the agonies I suffered, wondering whether he would turn up—and yet I knew he would, and he did. Alas, my poor father, he never knew I paid that famous man a fee nearly double the amount he had agreed to fork out. I had to sell half my mother's jewellery to get the money. I was sure that such a fabulous payment would induce the man to listen to Clem for five minutes after the guests had gone —I was even sure that he would feel obliged to say a few kind words. I was not mistaken, and dear Clem was transported into the seventh heaven. Even my conscience was perfectly at ease, because I was convinced that besides being kind, the words were absolutely true.

Her silence was prolonged, and I seemed to startle her with my, Well?

Well, that is the end of my story. Or very nearly. You

might almost say that Clem abandoned his marriage with Daisy, to engage in a liaison with our piano. He was never out of the house, and indeed it was impossible for him to be when he was never off the piano stool. As for the rest, it is just sordidness. Miss Topp violated the sanctity of our home by forcing her way in on behalf of Daisy. And there was such a rumpus, my father, who never really noticed anything, except perhaps when his rheumatics weren't troubling him too badly, which was very seldom—my father, I say, could scarcely continue to be unaware that Clem was actually living in the house. We had a frightful row and I was threatened with the European tour, but in the meantime I managed to put it off. Clem, even though he had given up work, had to appear in the streets some-times, and he was persistently waylaid and molested by Daisy and Miss Topp, not to mention the in-laws. They even attempted to thrust his daughter into his arms in public. And when he eventually gave in and returned to Daisy, he revenged himself by taking to drink. So far as I know, he told nobody about his plans when he decided to leave Daisy, and leave the town. He just disappeared. And after six months, when nothing had been heard of him, I agreed with my father about our European tour. It turned out to be quite wonderful. If I had never gone, I should never have heard Pachmann.

But, she said after a moment, I am getting quite worried about the moon.

And aunt Daisy's husband? I asked. Was he never heard of again?

Clem? Oh dear no, not at all—though it wasn't for many years, indeed it was only quite recently.

Whatever do you mean? I asked.

He is a man in a very big way. He imports crockery, or perhaps it is hardware—I fancy it is something to do with cooking. I have a friend in the city who knows the family. There are two girls, and they both married very well. Professional men, I fancy. Their father sent them to the very best of schools, but do you know?—I was told he put his foot down, and absolutely forbade them to learn the piano. He would never allow any sort of musical instrument in the house. It *is* rather strange, isn't it?—I believe Daisy's parents lost all their money, bad investments or something of that kind. I have been told that your aunt Bertha left a will in her favour, but it was very little, and with the cost of living what it is, poor Daisy half-starves on the pension. They say that her daughter treats her abominably.

Oh, but do look! she exclaimed. The moon at last. How very, very, beautiful. You must be silent, and I will promise to be. We must forget all about this sordidness—I can't think what could have come over me.

Do you know? she said in a whisper—I can't explain why, but it always gives me the curious fancy that I am listening to Chopin.

JUST TRESPASSING, THANKS

Very early one fine summer morning Edward Corrie, a suburban recluse with the tall and distinguished appearance of a retired statesman, discovered from the doorway of his ancient two-roomed cottage, that the stretcher bed on his verandah was occupied. But it was difficult to decide much about the three people who were asleep on their backs in a row, since besides being covered to the chin by the bed-rug they were all wearing dark glasses. It was nonetheless Edward's belief· they were unknown to him: it also somewhat troubled him that they had very little room. Most uncomfortable, very hot and sticky at this time of the year. But the thought was distasteful, and he passed on out of doors in his soft slippers. Nothing was clear to him except that his visitors were young, although he could be tolerably certain the one in-between was a young woman.

The large area enclosed by an untidy hedge was known to the inhabitants of the suburb as Corrie's corner; but to Edward it was all that remained of his grandfather's farm, the scene of summertime explorations during school holidays sixty years ago and more. He remembered paddocks with creeks and creekbanks; trees, some of them native; scrub on the hillsides; besides his grandfather's cows there had been an orchard, and one season a crop of wheat. Many abstract forces had been at work since those days, and bulldozers and builders had done all the rest: in every direction variety had been replaced by rolling hillsides covered with tiled roofs. It was not a view for

which Edward had any affection and he preferred as a
rule to remain indoors, apart from an early half hour
beneath his pine trees before the whosh of an occasional car
along the motorway had multiplied into the commuting
roar. If the wind was in the wrong direction there would be
a smell of fumes. Eye ear and nose offended—what was the
world coming to! It had been his habit to walk late at
night, stirring with his feet the smell of pine needles in the
damp air; but along with the motorway had come strings
of powerful lights—to remind him that to hang up lamps
had been in his day a signal for the freedom of gaiety and
laughter. Except for the flying cars the motorway was
empty: it was seldom that anyone strolled on the concrete
of the adjacent streets: the lights promised joy only to reveal
there was nothing human there.

When he returned to the cottage it pleased him to
discover that his visitors had departed. The rug required
straightening, and he looked briefly for signs that his spare
bed had been used for purposes additional to repose. It was
satisfactory not to discover any. But on the table indoors he
immediately noticed a pair of dark glasses alongside his
loaf of bread—which had diminished by several slices; and
after crossing to his bedroom doorway he remained
transfixed, with his eyes upon the bedside table from which
some odd pieces of change had disappeared—until he began
to tremble as he became abruptly aware that a figure com-
pletely enveloped by the bedclothes was occupying his bed.
To step across and reach an unsteady hand to investigate
was to reveal a young man with freckles and a head of
ruddy-gold hair, who appeared promptly to wake and
answer his stare with the friendliest of smiles from a pair of
blue eyes and a row of unblemished teeth. But without a
word spoken his young visitor again enveloped himself in
the bedclothes and rolled over to resume his sleep.

All that day Edward was about his usual occupations.
Attending to his needs he tidied himself and his living
room, and he sparingly ate. Much of the time his long
frame, a structure which appeared to be composed

exclusively of skin and bone, was accommodated by his easy chair while he engaged his attention upon a book of Latin grammar. He had lately occupied himself with problems of syntax; and once again the thought passed in his head that all boiled down to a question of the best means of communication. In the heat of the afternoon, when his attention flagged and wandered to the curtain hung across his bedroom doorway, it occurred to him that all day he had not heard one sound from his sleeping visitor. Before he abandoned the book he idly turned over the pages from syntax to prosody. Ruricolae, sylvarum numina, Fauni / et Satyri fratres. . . . While he was putting his feet up he glanced out the window, where countryside had been replaced by cement and tarmac: wilderness was perhaps the appropriate name for what had once been woodland—and hardly the right kind of breeding-ground for a race of deities. It occurred to him that he could make use of the dark glasses, and he adjusted them across his eyes against the light. As he settled to sleep the defensive asceticism of his superior features was slowly dissolved: it perhaps disconcerted a little that he was revealed as vulnerable.

There was nothing furtive about the movements of the young man who emerged from behind the curtain despite the silence of his bare feet; nothing about his glance at Edward to suggest that he was in any way glad to have discovered him at a disadvantage. The emphasis of his glance about his surroundings suggested that he would be held by the titles on the bookshelves, but he settled instead for a showy soft cover which he drew from his hip pocket. The protective gloss had failed to preserve the inside pages from being reduced to disgraceful rags, and it was not until he had fingered among them that he could focus his attention. While he sat facing Edward with his legs extended from the edge of a stiff-backed chair, his lips began a rapid motion as he mouthed the words he read; nor did he desist when it became apparent that Edward was awake (the lines of his face betrayed him as his defences were reconstituted, a knowledge which was perhaps too difficult for him to come by).

From behind the dark glasses Edward was busy with the preparation of a judgment. Cheek, cool cheek—and yet there was something remarkably open. In presenting himself before his judge the young man had had the wisdom to bring only his naked humanity except for a rag of shirt—and a pair of trousers so remarkable that they almost destroyed Edward's serious thoughts about the judgment he would presently deliver. Fancy material stove-pipe cut and front pockets, the fashionable kind of thing he had been accustomed to among the young rips of his own day. But a well set-up young man—measured out on a small scale perhaps, but neatly put together. It was unfortunate that his vivid colouring of hair and countenance was destroyed by the dark glasses; but Edward removed them not to restore to his visitor his colour, rather it piqued his curiosity not to be able to decipher the title of the dreadful book. A Deadwood Dick no doubt, an illiterate young man despite the qualities which recommended him.

But the book's title and the young man's reaction to his coming alive were a double astonishment.

Listen to this, Mr Corrie, he began. And after a gesture which sought to impose silence with ·authority he read from Matthew Arnold; concluding the passage with, He too upon the wintry clime / Had fallen—on this iron time / Of doubts, disputes, distractions, fears.

Now sir, he went on, don't you reckon? . . .

While he referred the poet's words to time past and time present, Edward's attention was for the most part taken by recollections of gown and mortar-board worn by the women, and one man—who had also dared sometimes to seat himself with his book on the college steps, an exhibit for passers-by: he too had read poetry aloud and argued about it afterwards. But the mockery had been severe, and it had been a relief in the end to retreat into disputes about

275

free trade and protection. Yet away in some remote corner of himself he could still blush. Perhaps in those days and circumstances cap and gown had been an extravagant badge to wear, but poetry had moved him and his retreat had been cowardly, a shameful denial which had persisted until the dogged recovery of these latter days: the dead stick had flowered.

It struck him as a very curious experience to listen as his own voice said, Matthew Arnold wrote a number of very fine things.

He had intended to enumerate, but the young man again employed his gesture and read from *Switzerland*, from *Empedocles*. . . . And again Edward failed to halt his wandering attention. If he was put to it he too could quote from Arnold, and from memory . . . though long wanderings intervene / They recognise a former scene. . . . His personal history was repeating itself, he had acquired the ability to observe himself as a young man. It did not greatly matter that the locale was not the same, that the badge had been replaced by stove-pipe trousers—the potent essence remained: poetry. But if he was obliged to name the force that had proved itself even more powerful he would say, Social Resistance! And that, he told himself with a dismaying sense of transposition, was now located in himself. Despite his late flowering he remained more or less identical with the environment which had first defeated and then digested him: from this young man's point of view he would be, without any doubt at all, an environmental fact.

It was with a flooding sense of anguish that he reacted from these thoughts to discover himself again in his character as judge. Poetry was all very well, but intruders in the beds of other people must be resisted: the young man together with his vanished companions (and unless the world had returned overnight to its condition of pristine innocence one of the three was the doxy of the other two), must be called smartly to account.

Do you expect me? he began—and he was aware of his

barbarism: he was interrupting verses which compellingly rendered the frustration which the poet had experienced as a monstrous agony. And yet he continued, Am I expected to accept you without question as a lodger in my bed and a boarder at my table?

I was born in there, Mr Corrie, the young man replied. And while he employed his smile he pointed in the direction of the bedroom. Then he obliged Edward by supplying some elucidation of words which might have been either profound mad or just plain silly. That's what my grandmother told me, sir. She used to keep house for your grandfather, Mr Corrie.

And having put to Edward's thoughts the match which exploded them in all directions, he returned his attention to Matthew Arnold. His gesture remained poised, as though held in reserve until he alighted upon the passage which would again demand to be read aloud.

From appearances it might have been supposed that Edward, with his eyes closed and his long fingers crossed against his hollowed chest, was depicting a man relaxed as he recovered after sustaining an injury. But in fact it had not been wholly disagreeable to be reminded of the young man's grandmother, who without much doubt would be identical with the young woman he had familiarly known as Fanny. Also, it satisfied the mature moralist in him to recollect that he had not impaired the young person's virtue—although there had indeed been an occasion when, underneath a row of pine trees long since cut from beyond the motorway, he had pressed matters strongly enough to induce what he had at the time been misled into believing was 'a fainting fit'. By his ignorance or by his timidity, perhaps even by Fanny herself (though from later experience he judged that to be unlikely), he had been denied Fanny. And although he had no regrets he nursed a resentment, for it was on account of Fanny that he had afterwards come to expect all such kindred occasions to be accompanied by the redolence of pine needles. They never had been, and he had arrived at the climax of his disappointment in his marriage. In all his years of bedroom relations he had never been rid of a sense of suffocation until (his son established overseas as a botanist, and his sons-in-law having assumed responsibility for his daughters), he had welcomed the day when his wife intimated that she had never been rid of a sense of having made a mistake in preferring him to the man she had not married. It had been remarkably easy to say to her with an easy conscience, My dear, I have no such reciprocal confession to make, but I do have a sense of regret over devoting many good years of my life to managing the local affairs of an oil company. I would like in my last years to revive interests not much connected with the marketing of petroleum derivatives, and I would prefer in this matter not to be hampered by any further experience of matrimony. In short. . . .

And with a surprising absence of fuss it had all been arranged. He had been glad to provide generously for his wife so long as he might retire undisturbed to the cottage which had remained intact from the days when it had housed his grandfather's share-milker. It had been his folly not to reckon upon the growth of the suburb and the coming of the motorway, but his complaints were trifling apart from his regret that he had never encountered anyone who might have seriously shared his interests; and indeed, unless he was mistaken, there was nobody of his acquaintance who even respected them. In any case, regrets were not for people of his age: his contemporaries who were not already dead must certainly be preparing to be—that was to say, he would permit himself the hope that a sense of preparation was active, although it was no proper concern of his by what way other people made their approach to final dissolution: it might be drink, or debauchery, or prayer, or whatsoever; no doubt all had their uses, and perhaps also their wisdom. . . . By some unusual good chance even this strange young man appeared to have discovered his own wisdom.

While his eyes remained closed he said, I congratulate

you upon your appreciation of poetry.

Just a kind of second nature wouldn't you reckon, Mr Corrie? You mightn't remember but I used to deliver the newspaper right to your door if the weather was wet. I used to step inside and borrow a book if there was nobody about—thinking you wouldn't mind, Mr Corrie.

Edward opened his eyes to stare, and he smiled.

It was you helped to start me off, Mr Corrie. Then I went to the university but I didn't stay. Everybody went for the ticket. It only takes a few years and you see them everywhere. They sit in buses and talk to you out of the newspaper. The forty hour week and all that crap, I didn't want to have it on.

It was with a strong sense of having aimed at saying something quite different that Edward said, What were you doing in my bed?

We're hot, Mr Corrie.

In his slovenly speech he had said something which sounded like an abbreviated, We were hot; but Edward couldn't be sure. He shifted his glance to the window, wondering whether any such young man would be spawned under a tiled roof. Or was the story alleged by his grandmother to be believed?

I daresay, he said.

But it was time now for the young man to stand up and return *All the Poems of Matthew Arnold* to his back pocket; and then, without any sign of self-consciousness or uncertainty to go to the cupboard for the loaf and butter the slices he cut.

I presume you have an occupation of some kind, Edward said; and he declined the slice of bread that was offered him.

The young man was cramming his mouth so he vigorously shook his head—for the first time it was even evident that he was displeased.

No, Mr Corrie, I told you. I'm not going to have it on. I never used to deliver the bread when I had to write my poetry. People complained. There might be a password in any bit of poetry, Mr Corrie. It'll send you. Nobody wants to stay always what they are. All right, okay, call it crap, call it what you like. So what?

As he finished the bread and butter he said, By God, I'm *never* going to have it on!

And Edward was deprived of the exegesis which all this difficult language appeared to demand by the arrival of the young man's ex-bedmates. Or so he might presume them to be—not to mention concede them to be a handsome couple if allowance were made for the show of eccentricity from which all surprise had been emptied by the events of the day. The young woman in her crash helmet, and wearing over tight trousers a kind of leather armour (though evidently not, he told himself, for defence of her chastity), might have arrived from that region which was increasingly mentioned in the newspapers as Space, and which would always demand from Edward such a mental exercise: it was by no means easy at his time of life to replace a nebulous kind of Nowhere with a positive and even precise Somewhere. But he could without difficulty recognize the Space creature's companion as belonging to Earth. Of a height which exceeded his own, and of probably Polynesian extraction if one judged from hair authentic tint of skin and carving of feature, he wore what had always been known in bygone years as dungarees. He was burdened by a large carton which shortly turned out to contain a great quantity of food in tins, and he appeared to be possessed of a grinning good nature which radiated a comprehensive warmth. Edward was involuntarily moved by his own inclusion, and astonished that within himself an area might have been pin-pointed which glowed in return: but all this was not to say that any of them paid him more than passing attention, and indeed, after his tin-opener had been located, they were much too busy consuming vast amounts of mixed food at a speed which Edward judged to be ruinous to the human digestion. He was not however excluded from the banquet, for in quick succession he was offered baked beans, apricots in syrup, Japanese caviare, sausages in spaghetti, processed cream, asparagus tips, fruit salad, Californian tuna; on each occasion from an opened tin with a spoon standing upright as though urgently at attention to serve the cause of human nourishment.

Such unceremonious untidy eating might well have tried Edward's patience if it had gone unaccompanied by the interest of their conversation. (Although the Space woman had nothing to say: she ate certainly, and voraciously, but her only additional function was to select and hand up tins from the carton as she sat on the floor.) Edward was reminded of distant parts of the earth's surface he had visited on oil company business: his ears were constantly registering sounds from which he might reasonably infer that he was listening to a language composed of English words; but at that point all clear understanding of the matter ended, for many words were apparently unrelated to meanings which it had long been his habit to take for granted; and he was sharp enough to be aware that questions far beyond restricted matters of etymology were implied. It was a case in point that, despite the present satisfaction of appetite, his young visitors were much preoccupied with talk of food; and although he could be certain that animal and vegetable matter suitable for the sustenance of human life was signified, it was also strongly implied that this matter was primarily to be thought of as deriving from tins: he was in addition greatly puzzled to gather that nobody with any brains would ever make the mistake of reckoning these tins to be items of commerce. Prominent among other words which appeared to have been subjected to related mutations of meaning were car gas tyre and girl. And yet it astonished Edward's puzzled wits that the most prominent of all words was poetry. It was even a transcendent marvel that the word's meaning had not greatly altered, and might be investigated in language well within his range of habit and understanding. Each time the two young men swapped their quotations he was conscious that he possessed a sense of hearing which had been unaccountably sharpened. It was as though he was determined to miss nothing. And yet he was prompted not to believe his ears when he at last gathered that the quotations read from scraps of lavatory paper discovered in the depths of their pockets were in fact verses of their own composition. Of softest substance, cassia and rain / Thy body is composed, my love: the dark-skinned young man pronounced the lines to be acceptable, although a Parnassian flavour was to be regretted: but presently a contribution of his own (Shatter the ice-casked heart / Send me the avalanching thunder), was held to be of some merit if it was possible to overlook its corny rhetoric.

It was now that Edward felt himself powerfully impelled to intervene. The young people were licking their fingers as they put empty tins together in a convenient heap. Poetry was dropped from their conversation in favour of remarks about getting cracking taking off and shooting through. Several times it was insisted, All right, remember we're hot. There were calculations to do with time speed and distance. But Edward, although he continued to register the words, was much too preoccupied to persist in his attempts at penetrating their meaning. The glowing area within himself which might previously have been pin-pointed had expanded, seeming now to lodge in his throat and prompt him to speech. He felt strongly that if he spoke he would speak with the tongue of an angel, and that what he spoke would be poetry: dredged up from among his memories and held suspended now in his mind were some verses of his own, things not nearly so good and beautiful as these young people were apparently capable of, but which might perhaps contribute worthily to the events of a strange day. All these events appeared now to have united to create a country of the imagination, a transfigured region illuminated by shafts of light which had their origin in poetry: it was a region that was permanent although entirely without substance, and inviolate even though readily accessible. Had not the young man spoken of a password? . . .

Just Trespassing, Thanks

The young people were waving him goodbye as they crowded at the doorway. They were leaving him what remained of the tinned food, they said. Edward felt in his pocket and they declared, No, no, Mr Corrie, you have them. They were gone, and he recollected that unless he was greatly mistaken they already had his loose change. He discovered himself to be exhausted and profoundly satisfied, a satisfaction which he had previously experienced only after carnal union on very rare occasions. To look out the window and discover the tiled roofs were still there was a surprise. Sylvarum numina. Perhaps the day had arrived for Ovid to be rewritten. It was not difficult to understand that deities would expect to be paid token money: but they on their part could hardly be expected to pay their regards to worldly morality.

CITY AND SUBURBAN

To me, it more or less fixes the time I belong to if I say there was always a war in progress when I was a schoolboy. To be more exact, though—the Armageddon I refer to was the second one this century. I remember particularly a teacher who plugged a line about my lucky generation. Last time there had been some mistake about the war to end war. But now, let there be no mistake about it! There was a good time coming for all young people—golden opportunities, glittering prizes later on; more to the point, generous bursaries for all students with ambition. But in those days my ambition was an opportunity denied me by the school leaving age. My elder brother, a little too young for any of the services, was establishing himself in a milkround which could have been profitably extended if I had joined in as a junior partner. I was told that in the meantime I must remain a schoolboy. It was suggested that for compensation I might usefully dig for victory in the vegetable garden.

Whenever there is any kind of petty crisis in my life that milkround will return into my mind as something I regret having missed out on. Let's face it, I'm average. I have my university qualifications, I am by profession an accountant, that's to say a partner in a public accountancy business. I am the end product of what may happen if you raise the school leaving age. Instead of neglecting the opportunities provided (drawing my bursary for beer money), I worked hard and I still do. I'm a married man with two youngsters a home of my own and of course the car. Nothing alters the fact that you have only to strip away the higher education to find me average. If you like, the *new* average—the latter-day common man, the runner among the ruck in the urban rat race. In secret I yearn for something less complicated, let's say a milkround and an unworried living in a small country town. For committing myself to paper I have the good excuse that I am at present enduring another of my crises.

But first I must say that it was only gradually during my years of exposure to the higher education that I discovered its two-sided character. It takes you on a stroll through civilization's flower garden (and I'm not being ironical—I am ready at any time to applaud the man who decides there's nothing in life to compare with reading, say, history); and on the other hand it leads you to believe you are being singled out, made to feel important, assisted to get on and make a career—earn good money. So the question eventually comes up whether you can have it both ways; whether, having been shown around the garden you don't visit there any more, or whether (I am aware that I am changing the metaphor), you endeavour to arrange an uneasy marriage between what is of perennial appeal, and what has its day to day uses in keeping the wolf a long way from the door—in my own personal case one party to the marriage a business career, and the other, well, history. (That study does in fact happen to be my special cup of tea; but with my enthusiasm only moderately abated I could mention others, and will even go so far as to specify theology. Granted free choice of a career I might well have preferred to all others that of a learned clergyman—and the advantage of an efficient curate to attend to parish duties would have clinched the matter beyond all question.)

Now I have aimed at establishing myself as a man who can appreciate that some very attractive flowers grow on what used to be a kind of dung heap, sometimes called by fanciful names (such as Leviathan); but which is nowadays more aptly described as a combined junk and gadget heap, praised-and-damned as the welfare state—or sometimes just praised as the affluent society. What are the advantages I derive from that appreciation? Has the higher education sold me an outsize pup or not? Answers to these questions wouldn't be just for me—as an accountant I would say that to reckon accurately the number involved could be a pretty sizable job of computing, one requiring to be served by the latest model electronic machine if the population explosion and all such kindred phenomena are to be taken into account.

I expect my use of the marriage metaphor is significant. After all, everything we endure in this world is rooted in the married state—I mean it's the reason we are here unless we happen to be literal bastards. And I will say at once that I have no petty complaints about my wife. Since I began with women I have never been able to do without having one around. Pam is nicely put together, and I am confident about wearing qualities which should ensure that she remains for many years easy on the eyes. Also, being one hundred per cent woman, I can never see her landed in my own sort of jam—I mean to say I sometimes foresee the day when my life will be largely composed of an attempt to deal with long hours of boredom occupying the empty space between the morning and afternoon newspapers. That sort of horror will never be Pam's cup of tea, and even if it was she would never recognize it as such. There's a phrase (if I remember it was plugged by Spinoza), sub specie aeternitatis. To my certain knowledge Pam will never be plagued by the itch to relate her experience to any principle—I mean anything that might tend to upset her certainty about what is important in life and what isn't.

But it's time I came to the point—after all, I have mentioned a crisis.

It *would* be on a day like this (by far the best of our summer holiday), that our youngsters should come up the beach at low tide, and bring with them the finger they had found in one of their favourite rock pools.

Mummy, look! That was our boy, Happy. The pair of

them had been disagreeing over who was to carry their
find, which was cupped by Glad in her two hands. To me,
it was as though I had never seen a finger so astonishingly
large despite the wrinkles. The nail was intact and all had
been washed white and clean. As an object composed of
alabaster or translucent wax it could have been attractive
—but there was no mistaking what it was.

As usual Pam was quicker than I was, and her technique
within its own limitations couldn't be faulted. While she
whipped out a handkerchief she agreed with the young
'uns that they had found something very precious (Why!
of all things! a new kind of shell—a *finger*-shell! Well!),
and at the same time quite desperately fragile. Mummy
would keep it for them. And now please would they go
and find Mummy another of those pretty red and green
stones—but wait a minute. . . . And as the handkerchief-
draped horror went into the picnic bag, out came the
transparent packet of chocolate biscuits.

In the meantime I had been trying very hard to rid
myself of the impression that what our children had found
was somebody's severed phallus; and I recovered my
speech only to say a thing which to Pam would be irritating
and silly, and which in the circumstances she was quite
right to ignore.

For God's sake, Pam, I said, why ever in the name of
heaven and earth did you insist they be called Happy and
Glad?

The children had obligingly trotted off as suggested,
and now Pam remarked that we must stroll casually
about the rock pool area, just to be satisfied about any
more human remains. And after that I must take the car
to the nearest phone box and ring the police. We must hand
over our gruesome relic and free ourselves of all responsiblity.
But there you are—my wife had used two words which
belong to the stock in trade of one branch of the higher
education. And in any case, once our children were beyond
hearing I had groaned aloud.

Pam, I said, so long as we are at large in human society

responsibility is our fate. No, I added, our *doom*!

My wife's sharp look at me was familiar—also her decision.

All right, she said, I'll go. Jellyfish. She said too that I might try to make my conversation a shade more coherent —that sort of thing *could* be the sign of a mental breakdown.

I haven't mentioned that I met Pam during the time of our joint exposure to the higher education. She had begun with the fine arts, but changed to social studies— hence perhaps her flair (very evident during the time of our first encounters), for reconciling general theory and particular instance. Born myself to fumble any practical job in hand when it is unfamiliar, I was quick to admire and be grateful.

While I'm gone, she went on, I will trust you to be responsible for our children.

I was not in the mood for arguing. When the children showed signs of disquiet over the sound of the car I shouted that Daddy would be with them soon, and to dispose of the jellyfish allegation I joined them by way of a circuitous route past the rock pool. There were no human remains so far as I could observe—as I told myself of course there wouldn't be. Despite what *actually* turns up, it's always the bits and pieces I *expect* to come in my direction.

When we were through with the police sergeant and his offsider, who turned up after the youngsters were in bed (being Pam, Pam had arranged for our children to be 'spared'), we had a row—the kind of rumpus which I foresee will be an annual event guaranteed to coincide with our annual holiday. And although there was no mistaking what grim finger had reached for the push button on this occasion, that is not to say *any* couple wanting a thorough-going occasion will ever lack a watertight excuse. Nevertheless, common stuff—I mean when the pair of us could be in no doubt what we were up to, yet found ourselves compulsively impelled to demonstrate how damnably ordinary we are. Pam is my own age exactly—which means she has

come on right to the top of her form according to Kinsey.
As for me, well, according to the same authority senility
of that kind begins in males after sixteen. Not that I'm not
the man to meet his marriage account as often as the wife
likes to send in her bill—it's just that I am not always
bright enough to conceal my surprise that pay-time has
come round again so soon. (I owe to my historical reading
the discovery that according to Roman law a husband
might discharge or withhold payment of the debt according
to inclination. An Athenian husband on the contrary was
by Solon's law required to make three payments a month.
It was the Jewish people however, who had rules for
special cases: a daily settlement of the debt was required
from an idle but vigorous young husband, but twice a
week from an ordinary citizen sufficed; once a week from
a peasant, once in thirty days from a camel-driver, and
once in six months from a seaman. But a student or doctor
might resist all demands; and *no* wife who was in receipt of
a weekly sustenance could sue for a divorce. I believe too
that among the Jewish people polygamy would divide,
without multiplying, the duties of the husband—and
polygamy regulated in that way is something of which
I could thoroughly approve. After all, it is not unreason-
able for any man to wish for a number of wives sufficient
to ensure there remains always one on duty.)

From my general reading I have gathered that back at
the beginning of the century a wife would sometimes rebel
against a husband to whom she was, according to her own
view, 'just a plaything'. But from my experience I would
think that modern times have tended to reverse that
situation. Also, I will admit to irritating my wife by my
failure to adopt what she considers the right attitude to
our annual holiday—for her an extension of the child's
experience of a beach holiday; that is to say golden days
of sun sand and sea, in more exact words a daily round of
fun and games but with the lid taken right off. And no
regrets, and no guilty conscience. And of course she's
right in the pattern—you have only to check up on the

statistics for spring births ('plum duff babies' is I believe the description bestowed by the nursing-home sisterhood).

But perhaps I can put the matter on a somewhat more refined level, if I say that for Pam our annual holiday is what the whole of life could be if we never aged (I mean beyond our maturity), and could always reckon on a large credit account at the Bank with never a moment's worry about its maintenance. There is something very pro-American about my wife, but money and consumer-goods are not what I mean. What you buy with money is the happiness which you never for a moment doubt is what you deserve, and may expect without any argument to the contrary. If you are disappointed in your expectations, then some two-legged scapegoat must be sought for immediately and made to take the blame. Tonight, before my wife slammed the bedroom door (leaving me to write this kind of last will and testament), I bitched back at her with the declaration that a more accurate view of our situation on this planet was held by the Greeks, for whom life was damned awful apart from a few happy moments for which they were no doubt profoundly grateful. And apart from her retort (Ancient Greeks! I'd give the whole damn lot for one decent American any day), she remarked that she hoped I had considered the status of women and practices such as the exposure of infants—and that wasn't to mention slavery and what went on at stag parties. What did *I* think I knew about the ancient Greeks anyhow? Ha ha!

Now I expect I might have tried to patch matters up by making some kind of jest—perhaps by referring her to Kinsey, and Nature's cruel jest in throwing us into each other's arms at identical ages, when it would have been more satisfactory if her thirty years had been complemented by a mere sixteen years on my part (and ha ha to you). And no matter how vehement my wife's verbal reactions might have been, she would nonetheless have understood. But for me, to say any such thing would be merely to conceal the truth. To catch the interest of the parlour psychiatrist in her, encouraged by her social studies, I might perhaps have said that I could not rid myself of my first impression that it was some poor devil's severed member our youngsters had come up the beach to present us with. But what in the name of all that's sub specie aeternitatis would she have made of me if I had confessed the simple shocking truth—that even from her and my closest friends I conceal the melancholy which is induced in me by the afternoon slope of the summer sun? And that sex, Kinsey, and what have you are all the easiest kind of stuff to take compared to that horror?

Well, that's it. If these pages ever have a reader I would expect them either to ring a bell, or not to. It occurs to me that what our kids found on the beach might well represent somebody's drastic attempt at a solution (and it would make me very very angry to be reminded that what was found was a finger). Each man to his taste and his solution —and Pam by the sound of things behind the bedroom door has reached the limits of her patience. For that matter, so have I.

BEAU

It was during the war years that he began the practice of writing letters to himself. Postage in those days was trifling—a small investment which was guaranteed to bring the postman on up the hill to his bach quite two hundred yards beyond the last of the houses. The offer of tea and a biscuit was never refused—which assured for Beau ten minutes company while the man recovered his breath and talked about the kind of life he would live after the war, when he retired on the superannuation which was already overdue.

It's a great life you have away up here all on your own, Mr Ughtrey, he would say (pronouncing the name to chime with *ugly* instead of *Hugh*). It would do him, my oath it would!—but of course there was the wife, who always decided for the pair of them.

The penury of Beau's war years was a simple extension of his situation during the thirties, when he found himself obliged in his middle years to register as unemployed after his services as a commercial agent had been dispensed with. But until the war his life of unfinancial leisure (apart that is to say from house-keeping chores, which were always with him once he had moved from the private hotel he could no longer afford) had not been accompanied by any strong sense of isolation. There were many among the workless whose social background was not unlike his own: a round of visits on his bicycle would usually discover friends at their leisure—apart from perhaps digging for subsistence in their vegetable gardens. Then too, although

292

he had never to anyone's knowledge been married, he had long been known about the suburb as a man greatly devoted to the ladies—who greatly appreciated his line of old-style gallantry no matter what their age or marital condition might be. They would speak of his inclusion among the unemployed as 'unfortunate', and 'temporary'; and there were those whose purpose in accompanying him to the door after a call for afternoon tea was to slip a ten shilling note into his breast pocket, while they murmured, Now, now, not a word.

But then, as the decade approached the disgraceful catastrophe of its conclusion, his friends were returned into business circulation (until, somewhat later, they were called upon for war service unless they offered themselves voluntarily). Beau was the exception. His years were persistently adding up, and apart from his withered arm there was the question of his short-sight—which it was his habit to conceal by never wearing his spectacles except when solitary. Nor could his 'superior pommy bastard' accent (which he never at any time endeavoured to conceal), be reckoned in his favour. Though none of these disadvantages was at first sight evident in any degree at all. His stance, as he waited at the post office counter to collect his unemployed benefit, was that of a lofty guardsman stiffened by a corset—except that written into his features (his years were softening them into a kind of parody of the quality which had formerly prompted his friends to describe them as 'chiselled'), was the winning and imperturbable good nature which was his most distinguishing character. For any such formal occasion he would wear his out-of-fashion but good quality clothes preserved over many years: no stranger was at first sight likely to notice his arm: nobody upon acquaintance, apart from people of the crudest sort, ever mentioned it—nobody that was to say, apart from those who might be responsible for refusing him the jobs he tried to secure. His presentation to the world as the blue-eyed, tow-haired west of Englander, well-bred and sound in wind and limb (it was frequently said that he would have looked splendid as a naval officer), could not at first sight be questioned: his nick-name, Beau (he signed himself Leonard Ughtrey), was more or less what might have been expected from the suburb—and more especially the ladies, who were in no doubt at all about his accent: it was the clear hallmark of a gentleman.

It was nevertheless the hard and seemingly irreducible core of the matter that he remained unemployed. And although he promptly queued up to offer himself for any kind of war service at home or abroad when volunteers were called for, he was rejected after compliments on the unusually splendid tone of a sound constitution had been accompanied by head-shakings over an unfortunate deformity in a man's better arm; not to mention surprised tongue-cluckings over the discovery of a myopia so extreme, it showed no signs of the gradual alleviation which his advanced years might have been expected to afford.

But then his luck turned, and the war years miraculously proved themselves a kind of Indian summer, a late and easy recapturing of his youth which he could never have anticipated. Written off by the regular services, he presently found himself sought after by a variety of voluntary organisations: he enjoyed the right of free entry into an exclusive social club where, as a kind of ornamental Englishman who had been far-flung to the boundaries of Empire, he was a distinguished part of the show put on for the Americans; and he spent many agreeable afternoons among the 'sheep-skin' ladies, assisting to comb and stitch the woolly pelts which would protect 'the boys' against wind and weather wherever they served on land or sea. As a show-case Englishman he was grateful for the savouries and sweets of the snack bar (and that was not to mention reasonable helpings of choice liquor)—but he appreciated more keenly the full wonder of his rejuvenation when he was at large among the ladies: for even the most respected citizeness (demoralized no doubt by the insidious threat of universal destruction), might prove herself not to be entirely subjugated by the kind of virtue which he would have described as 'insurmountable', if he had been in the habit of repeating his smoking-room stories from the days of his commercial travelling.

What it all added up to was that the perks of the war years were wonderful beyond anything he had for years dreamed of—but his finances were so consistently tight that there were occasions when, having had the misfortune to suffer a bad bicycle-tyre puncture, he would lack the busfare to take him within striking distance of some generous perk which would almost certainly be available. And it was upon one of these melancholy occasions that it first occurred to him to write a letter to himself—although at first he would inscribe an envelope with difficulty in his cramped left-handed style and fold inside any old piece of scrap paper: it was some time before it occurred to him that the blank anti-climax of the postman's departure might be diminished, if his letter enclosed a communication which he could look forward to reading at his leisure. At first he could think of little to inform himself about except the state of the weather, and yet a strange kind of excited interest would be kindled by the words that he read: it was an additional pleasure to know that nobody was aware of the source of his communication except himself.

And so, when the war's momentum was suddenly arrested by the use of a gadget which was of itself a thing of unimaginable momentum; when the voluntary services were extinguished overnight, and the sheep-skin ladies re-dedicated themselves to bridge, mah jong and their husbands (with occasional guilty thoughts about how on earth they could have been deceived into supposing the end of the world was in sight, and nothing of that kind mattered any more), Beau's Indian summer was by no means immediately succeeded by a severe and indefinitely prolonged winter season from which all hope of spring could be permanently excluded. Some cosmic cat might have cuffed at a spinning planet, but that was not to say it would refuse to play a game with a planetary mouse. The pleasures of secret self-communication had been discovered—but in the meantime their full development must await the solution of a problem. The war's momentum was presently revved up again and directed into 'rehab'; and that among a number of things meant providing homes for returning heroes—for indeed almost anyone who had served in the regular forces. It was to be taken for granted that Beau was not to be provided for. On the contrary, the land occupied by his bach (in fact a decayed shack described by a visiting inspector as a 'sorry excrescence'), was required by the builders; and he received through the post, not one of his own delightful letters that day, but instead a notice to quit. He was not wholly dismayed: he was by now aware that quite apart from the official meaning of the word, his chances of rehabilitation within the framework of the suburb were very slender.

Nothing was the same any more. He was no longer 'poor dear Beau' to his friends and the ladies—who were themselves changed by the war, that many years older, tired, with troubles that ranged from inflated prices to the want of an adequate supply of breadline workers to dig their gardens. He had become 'oh dear, Beau Ughtrey'—not any more a friend so much as a problem, and one that would admit of no solution. As for the new young people grown up overnight, he could admire their energy and youthful good looks from a distance—until he was shortly aware that it would be as well if along with his isolation he included a sense of wariness: for anyone of his age young people could be dangerous. The postman (within a week of his retirement he had become a temporary celebrity by dying in the street under the burden of his wife's shopping parcels), had been replaced by a bouncing young woman whose short pants were so rudimentary that there was some question whether they could be said to exist at all, and the more especially when she was mounted on her bicycle. And she so strongly recalled for Beau a number of haystack adventures from his west country boyhood that he re-

membered with nostalgia a long-forgotten novel by
Thomas Hardy. Asked in for tea and a biscuit, the young
woman bounced a wad of hair from her eyes and replied
that she didn't mind if she did: and Beau was deceived by
the promise of her free-and-easy conversation into the
extravagance of writing himself a letter every day, while
his thoughts turned gratefully to the consolations life might
still provide for the old and solitary. But it was all an old
man's folly. It was while he explained that frank speech in
his day might be fairly interpreted as a firm invitation, that
he laid his hand for emphasis upon an area of bare leg.
And it was not so much the slap across the face he resented
(after all, according to his code any woman was entitled
to her defences against an advance pressed too far), it was
an expletive which no young woman who wished to remain
virtuous would in any circumstances at all ever employ.
Nor was it evident that this young woman was committed
to any code of her own which might command his respect:
it was beyond all doubt her failure to refrain from speaking
freely about what had been a private matter between them,
that he rapidly acquired about the neighbourhood a
reputation for having degenerated into a thoroughly dirty
old man.

It was clear to him that his eviction must be followed by
his voluntary withdrawal from the suburb. Many of his
friends spoke sincerely of their regret: several of the ladies
were so much overcome by accompanying feelings of guilt
(not to mention a sense of impending loss which they had
by no means bargained for), that they were unable to hold
back their tears. After all . . . But it was impossible to be
sure whether Beau was himself moved or not. Nor can it be
supposed that anybody was aware of the secret pleasure to
which he was by now committed, with the confidence that
it would lend itself to developments surpassingly rich and
varied. His replies to those who dared to raise the question
of his whereabouts for the future were evasive.

He transported his belongings on the night which pre-
ceded the morning when a young man would arrive on a

bulldozer, and in five minutes make matchwood of the place which had been his home for many years—piling them on a decayed two-wheeled motor-trailer (a useful kind of handcart except for the inconvenience of its long and heavy shaft), which had long been abandoned on the nearby roadside. Harnessed to the shaft with rope and detouring to avoid the hills, he covered the five miles to the inner rim of the city by daylight. It was with as fine a satisfaction as he had ever known that he at last unloaded, and shut himself within the four close walls where he could reasonably expect to remain private so long as he paid rent for what the advertisement had described as an outdoor flat; but which was in fact a converted toolshed, situated in the backyard of a large house that had surprisingly remained in an area now given over to industry. It was an additional satisfaction to suppose that his whereabouts were unknown to anybody with whom he had been previously acquainted.

He made himself a pot of tea and rested for half an hour —then he laid out paper pen and ink and began to write himself a letter.

It was more than a decade later, when he had slumped across his table and died with a pen remaining in his hand, that he was discovered to have been engaged upon what was virtually the same letter.

He was much commended by his landlady—a gentleman who had never been any trouble, minded his own business and always been punctual with his rent: she had never known him to receive any visitors.

Nobody who survived from his suburban years connected him with the short paragraph which reported the inquest. By some mischance he was named as Leonard Guthrey.

No personal papers were discovered, apart from huge stacks of pad paper closely written in the minimal style which is sometimes characteristic of the short-sighted; and these were delivered to the public library just in case they might prove to be of some literary value. Only a few odd pages had not been cross-written, and a very great number had been written over again on the diagonal. They were pronounced not to be decipherable. It did however appear to be established that Beau had come of a line of empire-builders: one of his grandfathers had been an admiral; the other a major-general; his father a captain in the navy. But that was all according to his own account: he had left blanks for all place-names, and names of persons.

CHARITY BEGINS AT HOME

Mrs Hinchinghorn's preference was for lodgers of the male sex: gentlemen were not as a rule so demanding, nor so apt to complain.

The gentleman at her door was a gentleman in the true sense of the word. Barr-Major? Was he an army gentleman? It became understood that he was Major Barr-Major; retired. With intervals while he waited to get his breath he told his anecdote: he had known a Doctor Doctor—but that wasn't the jest of the matter. Not at all. Doctor's wife, a fine big handsome figure of a woman. Well, take it or leave it, she had been a nurse. Nurse Nurse!

The landlady told herself she should have known: an army gentleman without a doubt, the very cut of an officer and a gentleman. She thought of India, soldiers in fancy dress, sun and dust, hot things to eat, sepoys, a story-writer called Rudyard Kipling—nowadays it was all James Bond. She too belonged to the early years of the century, marrying her Jimmy when he came home from his soldiering in the Far East. Jimmy hadn't been an officer—but what about Nature's gentlemen? Jimmy was a long time dead, but he had been one of that kind.

It surprised her when the Major said the room was what he had been looking for. It was very small, a flimsy kind of oblong box made from patent wallboard, and tucked away in a corner of the backyard beyond the wash-house. You might say it was a place to live, that was all; but it was detached and private. True, there was a steep flight of steps to the kitchen which he would have to share with the indoor tenants. Mrs Hinchinghorn was quick to mention that if he was a leisured gentleman he could pick his own convenient time for his cooking. She mentioned a Mr Ughtrey, who had occupied the room for many years: Mr U had been a thorough gentleman, nobody could have wished for a better.

From behind her curtain that afternoon, she watched the taxi-man carry suitcases into the Major's room after he had driven round to the backyard. While he groped in his pocket the Major very slowly eased himself out; nor did he appear in any hurry to enter his lodging after the taxi had been driven away. Mrs Hinchinghorn was not surprised. She understood the ways of gentlemen: a gentleman always took his time. (The thought crossed her mind that quite apart from being a gentleman, unless you were either very rich or very poor you could never be properly at your leisure.) It was always a pleasure to deal with a gentleman. She remembered Mr Ughtrey, minding his own business, never encouraging visitors who might be the worse for drink—and always right on the dot with his rent. It was her only complaint about Mr U that she had never seen enough of him. He had not been military—a writing gentleman, as it had been a surprise to discover when he was taken with his stroke. The Major was not quite so tall, more of the cock-sparrow build, puffed out up above and down below. And you'd say, florid. From the look of Mr Ughtrey you would never have thought he might die of his heart. It was the Major's colour that made her thoughts run on Jimmy.

But with infinite leisure, leaning on his cane as though he had the whole of time until doomsday at his disposal, the Major disappeared into his room. Mrs Hinchinghorn remained where she was, her thoughts now for her own person—which she had only to turn her head to see reflected in her long glass with a stain in it. She began with a short look. It was a kind of joke to think of the jokes Jimmy might have made if he had lived to see her grow a moustache.

It troubled her that nobody had seen the Major put a foot in the backyard for a week. And yet he was inside for sure, his curtain sometimes hooked aside, and sometimes not; his light on and off at night. It had also been Mr Ughtrey's habit to shut himself away. But there was always Nature—that was never one to excuse you from answering a call. And it made no difference if you were the highest gentleman in the land. Mr U had been just as regular with his shopping and his cooking. But in any case it was time now to collect another week's rent; and for the handling of a situation which called for courtesy combined with firmness, nobody could compare with Mrs Hinchinghorn's most trusted lodger, Lionel.

It was Lionel's oddity to compensate for the very lightest of legs by being monstrously muscle-bound in the arms and chest. Also, his years had incised upon his flattened face a network of lines so curious, that you could suppose he had in some way been chosen to bear to the world a message —although unfortunately inscribed in mysterious characters not yet deciphered. It was Mrs Hinchinghorn's anomaly to be reluctant to concede that Lionel was a gentleman of any kind, while at the same time thinking generously of him as class: that was to say, as coming of good English family. By his failure to add up to the full pound Lionel had unfortunately proved himself a throw-back: that he was only two or three shillings short was admitted. His landlady was nonetheless perennially impressed, and even humbled (it was a mark of her humanity), that no matter what the provocation might be, she had never known Lionel say an unkind word or do an injurious action. She sympathised with him in his severest disadvantage, the defect of a quality: his handwriting was copperplate, nor was his syntax and choice of words to be resisted. But Lionel had no pen friends, and wrote letters only to apply for situations vacant. Many who advertised were charmed to meet him on paper; upon interview only a few rare philanthropists had ever agreed to a trial.

For some years now a pensioner, Lionel inhabited a

narrow roughly walled-in cellar area with a doorway
concealed behind the kitchen steps. And it was because he
was her somewhat special lodger, one moreover who paid a
somewhat nominal rent, that Mrs Hinchinghorn entered
his room without knocking—to discover him lying on his
bed with his boots off, as was these days his frequent
custom. Lionel shifted his feet over so that his landlady
might ease for a moment the burden of her over-weight;
but he appeared not to remove his attention from his pin-
ups. Mrs Hinchinghorn thought their pattern on the wall
had not changed since she saw them last—but she recalled
that once on a visit and not finding Lionel at home, she had
found instead a pin-up lying beside the dent in the pillow
which his head had made. And she had immediately
understood—remembering with nods of her head army
stories confided to her by Jimmy during the intimacies of
their married years. Without any exception the little girls
pictured on Lionel's wall (cut from newspapers and
magazines, they would be somewhere about the tender
age of eight nine or ten), were of a forlorn and waif-like
character—that was to say, a character that resembled his
own. At her own level, in her own terms, Mrs Hinchinghorn could understand that it was not complement, much
more instead the image of identity, that Lionel looked to
for the easing of his heart's affections.

There was little habit of verbal communication between
Lionel and his landlady. He well knew that a service was
required of him; and she put in his hand the saucer she
had brought with the hot buttered scone.

There's an outdoor gentleman, Lionel, she said. He owes
me thirty shillings.

That was all, there could be no misunderstanding; but at
the door she made sure:

Major Barr-Major, Lionel. Get it? Remember he's a
gentleman. When you come up afterwards I'll make you a
cup.

While he ate the scone Lionel removed his attention
from the pin-ups to focus upon his garden shears. Their

sharpened blades were bright and shining with oil; and surrounded by child-waifs, they hung against the wall half-open in the shape of a St Andrew's cross. Until he precariously retired on the pension, Lionels' survival capital had consisted of his efficient effective relations with this handy garden tool: at suburban homes where he called on the off-chance, appraising glances would sometimes be quick to perceive a happy relation between the object in his hand and the surprising sinews that his rolled-up sleeve revealed.

Lionel greatly valued his shears as a pleasing reminder of times when he had been wanted.

It was not an exhaustive account of his adventures of the day that Mrs Hinchinghorn required from Lionel that evening. There had been much for her to observe from behind her curtain. Also, she was in some matters squeamish; and when she had seen him emerge from the Major's doorway, holding gingerly a chamber-pot that brimmed with the mixed abominations of a week, she had doubted neither the job he was in for nor its duration. When she had seen him light up a bundle of old newspapers underneath the wash-house copper, it was with a sense of gratitude that she had reminded herself of his thoroughness. But there were gaps in the day to be filled. Lionel explained that his reason for having gone out shopping was to purchase a rubber bed-sheet. It appeared that the Major's person had also been much in need of a wash—and that service had been rendered him without any disadvantage to blankets and mattress. Mrs Hinchinghorn demanded to know whether the Major had paid him for the price of the sheet, but Lionel was evasive: it was nonetheless satisfactory that he had had no difficulty in securing her thirty shillings. And she went off to bed with mixed feelings. She could picture the Major lying comfortably propped to read Lionel's evening paper (having eaten the light meal of bread and butter and a boiled egg which Lionel had provided): his body was clean, and his cheeks

would be fresh and smooth after his safety-razor shave
(Lionel had also mentioned trimming his moustache, and
putting a good parting into his snow-white hair). Mrs
Hinchinghorn thought too of his washed floor (Lionel had
scrubbed his mat with disinfectant, and it still hung on the
line), of sheets pillowslips shirts and other items that had
dried and waited now in the wash-house to be ironed. And
who by? Mrs Hinchinghorn reminded herself that her
establishment was a *lodging* house: lodgers were not to
expect that any board or special services would be provided. Always she had resolutely handled any such mis-
understandings exactly as they deserved. Lionel had
assuredly had a very busy day, but tomorrow she would
speak to the Major. And there would have been little to
puzzle her if it had not been for Lionel's look of satisfaction.
She would never deny the occasions when she had herself
benefited from his good-nature, but what had happened
today was an *imposition*. Why then did the odd creature
look as contented as the cat that swallowed the bowl of
cream?

And having slept a little uneasily on her question, Mrs
Hinchinghorn discovered that Lionel was up before her in
the morning. It was his frugal habit to eat only a slice of
bread and butter with his sweet cup of tea, so the breakfast
he was making must certainly be for the Major. She
noted its extravagance—eggs bacon and a large fried
tomato.

Lionel, she said, tell the Major I'm coming to speak to
him when he's finished breakfast.

She could not readily find her words when Lionel
returned with the Major's compliments, and he would
receive his landlady at eleven o'clock sharp—but Lionel
had no trouble with his own. He explained that it would
be eleven o'clock before he could be tidied up and have
the Major ready for the appointment.

And filling in the time, Mrs Hinchinghorn decided that
fine morning to wash out a few things of her own. But in
the wash-house she looked curiously at the items which

Lionel had washed for the Major. He was fussing in and out with a bucket for warm water dipped from the copper, but what he was up to in the Major's room did not interest Mrs Hinchinghorn. She set up the ironing board and plugged in the iron. It was a joy to iron for the Major. His shirts and things were somewhat worn, but of good expensive quality—and she noted carefully the places where mending was needed. It was not until afterwards, when she went with her own washed things to hang on the line, that she discovered how hopelessly her defences had crumbled. Every refinement of landladylike discretion was within her range, and to pass the Major's window was uncalled for. She had never for one second intended to look in—but she was noiseless in grubby rubber-soled slippers. With his head propped to read the morning paper the Major was lying naked and elongated for his wash. A woman now in her seventies, Mrs Hinchinghorn had never been loose or predatory; but she was nonetheless a woman, Jimmy had been long dead—and she looked greedily. It was her surprising discovery that it was not so much the Major who focused her attention. It was Lionel —though more strictly, Lionel's arms and hands. The power of those great sinews was being employed with the most careful delicacy, with all the tenderness and discretion of love.

What Mrs Hinchinghorn caught her breath on was a sudden stab of jealousy—its agony more torturing than anything she could remember in a long lifetime.

It proved not to be easy for Lionel and Mrs Hinchinghorn to arrive at a compromise. But it was at last tacitly accepted that the Major would be divided between them. With some regret Mrs Hinchinghorn resigned the grosser offices on his behalf to Lionel, consoling herself with the responsibility for his meals, and the refinements of them necessary on account of his being an invalid and immobile.

The Major was very regular with his thirty shillings, and one day not long before he died he exclaimed, God bless my soul!—and then waited for his breath to express his regret to Mrs Hinchinghorn for having somewhat deceived her. He wanted to say that when he had called at her door he should not have said that he was looking for a place to live.

And when it was all over neither Mrs Hinchinghorn nor Lionel was quite so much desolate as might have been supposed. Like many among the world's inhabitants, neither was in need of being informed in so many words about the mutual identity of love and hate. Over a cup, while they met and avoided each other's glances, neither could be in doubt there was much in life still to live for.

A FINAL CURE

When he had at last put his name to the separation agreement his wife refused to help him find suitable lodgings. It was her excuse that she was exhausted by the worry of his irresponsible behaviour, and the more especially his bad influence upon the younger children.

It was fortunate for him that he had the affection of his eldest son Roger, who rang up advertised numbers and went looking for likely rooms. The boy wished when he had finished school to follow his father and become a doctor. Stubbornly sure of himself, determined about what he wanted, he in most other matters resembled his mother: he resembled what she had once been in being fond of his father.

When he was confident that he had found the right room Roger assured his father a preliminary inspection wasn't necessary.

We've only got to pack up your things dad, he said, then I can run you over.

There was nothing to be done. There were no patients to speak of any more, he had signed the document and must get off his wife's premises. And they were indeed hers—she had married him with property and money of her own. It was fortunate for the boy and his career, and for the younger children—upon whose account she had pressed for the separation. Since he would be living in lodgings paid for by a wife-in-name it was also his own good fortune.

And he agreed with Roger that the room would serve. Ground-floor, a large front room with wide windows, with a couch, a table and an easy chair, all was run-down and faded though not yet frayed and torn; and the sheets on the bed were clean. And he was reassured about having to prepare his own meals when he inspected the kitchen—also run-down, but spacious, with a row of gas stoves to suggest that any serious jockeying for position among lodgers must surely be unlikely.

I'll manage, my boy, he said. In any case, people. I want to keep in touch.

His approval of Roger's judgment was clinched by an air of spaciousness about the entire double-storeyed run-down house, an elaborate wooden structure which dated from beyond the beginning of the century. It was miraculous that a house with a balcony of wooden fretwork and a slate roof nicely pitched had survived among all the factories and warehouses. And he decided that the best of its indoor attractions was the staircase, which descended in a progressively widening, pleasing curve.

Dignity, my boy; he said. Most attractive.

Roger mentioned that he had inquired, and actually (he hoped dad wouldn't mind if he said so), the house had been in the old days the home of a doctor. There was what remained of a stable at the end of the backyard.

Ah! his father said. Style! In those days a professional man would never be a moment in doubt how he stood.

According to his self-diagnosis, it was his recognition of the human need to know exactly how one stood that had been at the bottom of his domestic trouble. He could recognise this unsatisfied need in his patients—people who suffered (he remembered his Latin): they were diseased (and it should always be stressed that the word was more properly dis-eased) by their isolation. 'Patients' was just another word for humanity.

Long years ago he had begun to practise as a conventional bottle-doctor—and moved with the times until the writing of a prescription began to prompt him to pause over some curious thoughts. Shouldn't he by rights recommend a chemist who was certified to be neither colour-blind nor unable to count? And before very long he had begun to exhibit the unusual characteristic of moving according to his own time. Disease—it was isolation—being out of touch, with all the uncertainty of not knowing how one stood. Why prescribe when the physician was himself, or should be, the cure?—*not* the modern substance, sometimes unstable, and probably always poisonous, which was concealed in the pretty technicoloured capsule. The time he devoted to his consultations was much increased. People who suffered were not to be rapidly got rid of with the pseudo-magic formula illegibly scribbled. And once he had decided that time was of no importance in matters of such urgency (he repeated to himself the illuminating words and relished the contradiction), nobody saw much of him any more except his patients. Some of these unfortunate people might well deserve from him an entire day. And when not closely engaged with his consultations many hours were consumed by a footling correspondence with the Department. The subsidy was most inadequate —he was providing what amounted to a specialist service and should be subsidized accordingly. No? But surely the sum he saved the Department in chemists' bills should be taken into account? No? Very well then, was it the Department's policy to coerce him into again becoming a bottle-cum-capsule doctor?

But a doctor who never wrote a prescription! It was talked about around the suburb. Apart from a handful of eccentrics (and that included prolonged daily visits from a deaf old lady), nobody could be bothered with him any more. And the crisis came soon after his wife had decided that since he had ceased to earn enough to keep the house in cats' meat he must certainly be mad. She was not comforted when he begged for understanding *please*!

My dear, it's a truism—the more we *have* the less we can *be*.

A Final Cure

His wife also suspected some kind of impropriety, and irritated him by her sudden and frequent incursions to suggest a cup of tea—including one for the patient (usually the old lady), with whom he had been secluded for so many hours. She was inclined to be convinced that he was being as bad as he was mad when she discovered the disturbing nature and number of the doodles daily discarded in his wastepaper basket.

To be alone in his lodgings was at first a delight, the kind of quiet holiday he had never enjoyed over so many overworked years. Disengaged from every demand of daily obligation, and free to occupy his mind as he wished he read no newspapers—time was now much too precious to waste on appearances that were so absurdly contingent; and he vowed that he would not be deflected from his purpose of dedicating himself wholly to what was permanent. It was a surprise to apply himself so readily to the books he had put off reading for a lifetime—and he relaxed by relishing his opportunity for an attempt at recapturing a little of his thirty-year-old and now somewhat rusty promise for playing the 'cello. He avoided too the mistake of rushing headlong and heedlessly at establishing his contacts. In the kitchen he spoke the greetings appropriate for the time of day and left it at that. If the response came he would respond. The core of it all was his sure conviction that the permanent stuff of human nature was something neither he nor anyone else could ever get past. In one of his books he discovered the forgotten formula: nothing human is to me alien—and he began to believe that all government in the world had so far failed because human nature had never been properly discovered and understood. It was without question what you started off with—wonderful things might follow, but they must be surely grounded on the permanent truths of human necessity. All had changed in worldly affairs since Galileo had put his eye to that fatal telescope: it was not a man-centred universe—on the contrary, humanity was right out on a limb. And that was why all things human would always demand every scrap of humble reverence which every sane man would always and naturally want to muster.

But in the kitchen signs of response were not encouraging. He was smiling and benign, but when he one morning inquired, And what might your name be? from the tired and taciturn hotel night-porter (a part-time worker crippled by age and arthritis, he occupied the outdoor room in the backyard beyond the wash-house), he was answered by a look that surprised by being as contemptuous as it was sour. His landlady was polite and mentioned the weather—but she also remarked about that fiddle he played. What a pity it didn't sound a bit more cheerful! He would understand she was speaking in the interests of her lodgers in asking him not to play of an evening later than eight o'clock. But he failed to register her request since he had already begun to say:

How very right you are, Mrs Hinchinghorn! A sombre instrument indeed!

It touched him that in her room off the kitchen she that same day began to compete with him by thumping out tunes on her untuned piano.

A tall Dutchman spoke only (although frequently) to say he intended to see the landlady and lodge a complaint; and there were the two Miss Cooneys, not young, red-haired and perhaps twins (that was to say, if they were sisters at all), who occupied a room together and smiled but never spoke (he did not know that they had lately retired from the telephone exchange—and after forty years of listening without any right of participation were not much interested in participating now). His one cheerful and promising kitchen companion was a freezing-works chain slaughter-man (with appropriate gestures he explained about his job as a brisket-puncher), who watched the clock while he scurried about the kitchen, and belched over the food he bolted standing immediately it was removed from the stove.

And then, late one evening when the doctor was making

himself toast, the kitchen door was booted open by a very
large Maori in a torn jersey and bursting trousers, his
arms enclosing two large and bursting bags of mussels:
the ukulele slung around his neck was made to look like a
child's toy by the size of the vast old iron pot which was
likewise suspended. He politely greeted the doctor, and
made his excuses as he departed for his room upstairs
after putting mussels and water to heat. The sound and
thought of gumboots stamping up the stairway made the
doctor smile—but soon after he had taken the toast to
his room he was frowning instead. The chords strummed
overhead and the voice that accompanied them were
interrupted by the rumpus which had developed in the
kitchen. It was no doubt the persuasive odour of cooking
mussels which had brought there the landlady and the
Misses Cooney. Unpleasant words were loudly and un-
pleasantly repeated. A Miss Cooney was heard to threaten,
If you don't get rid of him this instant! . . .

The doctor never saw the Maori again.

But although troubled, he was not all that much discouraged by these unfavourable manifestations of human
nature. People were to be taken as you found them. It
was all genuine and valuable experience—and he reminded himself that it had for many years been his habit to
evade much experience taken for granted in his student
days: a busy doctor could rely too much on the laboratory
to handle many a raw and disagreeable task. One day
entering the bathroom, he was sharply reminded how
seriously he had slipped. Answering the phone, his
landlady had apparently been interrupted while her false
teeth were removed—and the sight of two unpalatable-
looking plates would not normally have disturbed him,
but the occasion had unfortunately been improved upon
by a bluebottle and a gang of houseflies. It surprised him
to be affected by nausea; and he was afterwards tempted
to suppose that he had only to announce himself a qualified practitioner, and his chances of being distressed over
encountering any such human contact would immediately

be reduced. He resisted the temptation, which succumbed to would have branded him a cheat. Contacts between individuals were two-way working: he hoped he might be accepted upon his naked merits as a human being even as he hoped to accept.

But there were many bad days when he was so much troubled by his doubts that he would emerge from his room only very briefly to satisfy animal necessities: feeling keenly his own isolation, he consumed the hours by relaxing over his doodles, drawing cornucopias which proliferated over sheet after sheet of scrap paper—integrated satisfying patterns of unimaginable yet meticulously detailed fruits, all of them tumbling out from curling goats' horns in a various and bewildering profusion: some, and some of the horns too, were so oddly shaped (what his wife had thought of as so 'suggestive'), that others too might have had their doubts about his sanity and moral health.

It was Roger who called one afternoon when his father was out buying his provisions, and without thinking inquired the whereabouts of Doctor Dudley. Soon after he had returned there came the first knock on his door; it was the night-porter, introducing himself as Clarrie.

Rheumatism! Well Clarrie, we know next to nothing about that one—in fact you could say nothing at all. He laid his hand on the man's shoulder. I think it helps, Clarrie, if each man will learn to live with his mortality —it's a shame we don't make that the first lesson we teach our schoolchildren.

Clarrie would have again mentioned his pain, but the doctor continued.

Yes, yes, I know—but we're all of us nagged by our aches and pains, Clarrie. Here! He took the man's hand and pressed it against his own side. Feel! There—that's it. Where I've had a pain for the last eighteen months. I wake up in the night—in a father of a fright, Clarrie. I say to myself—Doctor Dudley, you've had it!

Clarrie looked worried. All was a mistake—a doctor who told you he had a pain!

What about bee stings, doctor? Do you reckon it's worth a try?

The doctor smiled and put his hand in his pocket.

Buy yourself a new hot-water bottle, Clarrie. I know something about you people—you make do with some old thing worn out and leaking.

Bewildered and suspicious Clarrie backed out. He had *meant* to leave ten shillings in silver on the doctor's table. He was not ungrateful, but he disapproved. It was no way for a doctor to behave.

There were other knockings on the doctor's door—although a Miss Cooney smiled on him in the kitchen and apologized: If you will excuse us, doctor—it has long been our custom to consult a lady physician.

But although he welcomed each visitor into his room he contrived to evade any admission that he was available for formal consultations. Mrs Hinchinghorn wanted a prescription for aspirin, and he could fortunately 'tide her over' from a supply discovered among the odds and ends that Roger had packed. And in the same way he obliged with alkaline tablets sought by the Dutchman and also the slaughter-man.

Samples, my friend. You're welcome—I don't imagine they can do you any great amount of harm.

There were however several lodgers never seen in the kitchen, who even more mysteriously appeared only very seldom to have any use for the house's other conveniences. Across from the doctor's room there lived a little old man who with his head down appeared to be greeting the ground with a smile of affection, whenever he might be seen getting off smartly along the street on short chubby legs and a pair of little round feet. It had become the doctor's practice never to lower his blind or hide behind his curtain (he had read about the humanists of the Renaissance who hoped for self-protection and a quiet life by consistently allowing their private lives to be publicly inspected), so he was in no doubt that his little neighbour's disregard for the kitchen was explained by the regular midday arrival of a lady social worker in a shining car loaded with meals on wheels. But this service was limited to five days a week. On Saturdays and Sundays the little man seemed never to emerge from behind his closed door—although it was clear from the sounds of a broom that he swept his floor: occasionally he would lean from his window to shake his square of carpet. It was therefore perhaps a little contradictory that during one entire weekend when the doctor could not afterwards recollect hearing any sounds at all, he should also fail to notice that his neighbour's door had remained consistently not quite shut. Afterwards too, it was a Miss Cooney who was quick to claim that *she* had noticed. Yes, several times! Nor had it escaped her that on the last occasion several large blowflies had been in one great buzzing hurry to enter through the doorway. It was nonetheless the social worker who discovered that the doctor's neighbour was dead when she delivered his Monday meal on wheels. Fully dressed and face down, he lay on his square of carpet with his hands clasped in advance of his head. It was as though the ground on which he had smiled for so long had at last consented to an embrace.

There was immediately a gathering—the two Miss Cooneys, Mrs Hinchinghorn, the slaughter-man who was on strike that day. The last to join in was the doctor, and it was upon him that all eyes focused. Could something marvellous be expected?— the newspapers were these days reporting many instances of 'the kiss of life'. But the doctor simply looked as they did, and had nothing to say except, He's dead, you must ring the police. There was silence. The simple functional words were somehow offensive. The slaughter-man withdrew—he was very familiar with death, but this was no occasion for brisket-punching. Nor did the doctor stay—after he had invited more disapproval. He did nothing, but it was judged from his use of his handkerchief that he was affected. A display of feeling was hardly the sort of thing anyone would expect from a man in his profession.

The news item included the usual announcement, 'no suspicious circumstances'. But that view of the matter did not wholly satisfy the plainclothes men who made some formal inquiries after taking over from the uniformed branch. What the devil was a properly qualified although it seemed non-practising doctor up to living in such a place? What was the story? But the answers were nothing unusual: some kind of emotional trauma—you could say a bit dopey: yes, a crank but quite probably harmless: no prosecutions: no history of drink, drugs or violence: abortions no, not thought to be likely: not a pervert: his wife had money—that could be the story.

The doctor was not required to appear at the inquest, but Mrs Hinchinghorn's mention of him as a lodger was reported—with the unfortunate result that several of his former patients were enabled to discover his whereabouts. And he was soon so much occupied with familiar re-visitings that it virtually escaped his attention there were no more knockings on his door from his landlady and her lodgers. (His failure to notice his deceased neighbour's unclosed door over an entire weekend had been much discussed and held to be against him—after all, you would suppose a properly qualified doctor to be trained to notice things it might be important to notice; and in any case, what was one to think of a doctor who had for several days repeatedly passed up and down within a few yards of a dead body and never had an inkling! Who could have faith in a doctor without a nose for the very thing it was the whole aim and purpose of his profession to prevent?) A regular arrival each morning was the deaf old lady, and she would remain until he sent her home in the taxi he paid for; but it was one of his elderly eccentrics who arrived with a disturbing story. The man insisted that his health was much improved now that he had begun the practice of smoking reefer cigarettes, and he wished for the doctor's co-operation in buying up a large supply which was in danger of failing as police suspicions were thought to be growing uncomfortably warm.

Now the doctor was aware that the use of this drug was in itself agreeable and harmless: it could however prompt one into becoming addicted to the really dangerous drugs and was in any case forbidden by the law. He was shocked by his patient's cynicism and his indifference to the chances of corruption—and the more so as he was a man with a background of education who had at one time been prominent as a Church of England clergyman. It became his long and delicate task to induce his patient to admit the light of reason, and one that was successfully completed at last only by the use of a stratagem. Yes, he would assist in buying up the supply of cigarettes (by an ancillary stratagem his wife was persuaded into financing the transaction), but only so long as it was clearly understood that he was aiming at bringing that particular supply of the drug under proper control: that was to say, the reefers would be surrendered to the doctor, and his patient would be rationed and reduced until he ceased to make any more use of the drug.

The plainclothes men had in the meantime decided after much chewing matters over that a try-out on abortion was as good a tack as any; and the doctor was one evening called upon by a handsome well-set-up and powerfully-built young woman, a member of the uniformed branch clad at the moment in off-duty clothes (which only by an abuse of language could have been described as plain). After a competent show of hesitation and embarrassment, together with a plea that her confidence would be respected, she explained the purpose of her visit, intimating that she could immediately put down a five pound note as a pledge of her good faith. And then she began to feel herself genuinely embarrassed, because despite his appearance of sympathetic interest the doctor made no move to lower his blinds (although the circumstance was in fact no disadvantage, ensuring as it did that all transactions could be readily viewed by her male colleagues stationed on the far side of the street with night-glasses). There were however no transactions of any kind, and the doctor although he remained sympathetic appeared rapidly to lose interest.

My dear young woman, he said, my advice to you is that you have your baby—and may it be your blessing and happiness to bring healthy new life into our sick and sorry world.

As he reached for the doorhandle he withdrew from his pocket a pound note which he pressed upon his caller.

It's nothing, he said, simply a little something to help you with your baby.

A handy Justice of the Peace was located after the two plainclothes men had received their colleague's report; and provided with their warrant they were soon at the doctor's door. Through the night-glasses they had seen the doctor provide their young woman with money —without much doubt intending to assist her to achieve an illegal aim. But there was a good deal more to it than that—the young policewoman, trained to notice what might be important, had informed them about the many rude drawings which lay about the doctor's table, yes, very rude, definitely! It was satisfactory to search a cupboard and discover stacks of pencilled filth—but a very great satisfaction indeed to uncover what they had all along more than half suspected, a large haul of reefers, all neatly packed in cigar-boxes.

The publicity was all very painful and bad for his innocent wife and children: poor Roger was obliged to begin his professional career under a cloud. But there *was* the compensation that his professional colleagues most generously rallied round. You could say, to a man: there were some very eminent names among those who testified. Doctor Dudley readily agreed to retire to an approved Rest Home—but after some years there is still no prospect that he would want to emerge out into the world again. It had all cost his wife a large slice out of her fortune.

On most days he prefers to remain in bed—and yet when his health is inquired about he consistently replies that he is confident of moving steadily towards a final cure.

AN INTERNATIONAL OCCASION

Now that Mrs Hinchinghorn's funeral had become a memory, nobody doubted that as a lodging house the place was close to being finished. You could ask yourself, look right alongside at the raincoat factory brand new in cement and coloured plaster, its doorway embellished by an emblem, a Maori warrior holding up a feathered cloak in one hand and a plastic mac in the other: and across the road at the poor decayed place of worship lately converted to storage uses, packed to its rusty roof and peeled doors with rolls of linoleum and drums of disinfectant.

Nobody doubted that if the property wasn't already up for sale it soon would be, that it would be good sense to look around for a change of lodgings—which was all too bad when the rooms had remained relatively cheap. Also, besides being handy to the city, the old house attracted by its air of presenting to dingy industrial surroundings a brave worn face of better-days dignity.

But then surely it was a promising omen when Miss Bloom shifted into the deceased's room off the kitchen, at the same time letting it be known that having been appointed the landlord's deputy, responsibility for rent-collecting was over to her. There was no tenant (except now perhaps, Miss Bloom), who could claim ever to have seen the nebulous landlord: it was said not even perennial Lionel who had occupied a soft spot in the heart of the late Mrs Hinchinghorn, and on that account was believed to have paid only nominal rent for his makeshift room in the cellar, literally a hole in the ground, which he had tenanted off and on during his countless years as a pensioner.

It was a promising omen; but then it was soon said that the landlord would be holding out for some fabulous price which the industrialists were at present unwilling to pay. It was remembered too there had been occasions when Mrs Hinchinghorn, worn down like the house and with her good sense of discretion a little upset by the doom of her illness, had appeared to predict the end of all things with her hints that times had changed and she had noticed a serious and disturbing decline in the quality of her lodgers. She recalled better days when she had housed a very superior and distinguished army gentleman; also a doctor, eccentric mind you true enough, but a gentleman properly qualified to practise if he had wanted to. And she named a writing gentleman, a Mr Ughtrey—but this mention was without enthusiam: it was a mark of the poor quality of her latter-day tenants that they were never much impressed when she spoke about her writing gentleman.

Certainly in the old days it would never have crossed Mrs Hinchinghorn's mind to reveal to anybody about the place, or likely to be, any slanderous thoughts about present-day lodgers. So it was an irony that she had died without suspecting she housed one whose views were quite as derogatory as her own, besides a good deal more pointed and precise. He was Karl, an aging besides irascible-appearing Swede who had spent a lifetime working about the world, and was now for the time being settled in the country.

It was Karl's anomaly that he had never returned home since the remote day when he had begun his travels by stowing away on a ship in Göteborg; from which he had contrived to disembark, starved but undetected, in Montreal. According to his story that was the beginning of his adventures forty years ago and more, and all that followed was much too long to tell. But who knew? The day might come at last when he was nowhere else to be

found except on a boat headed back home for Göteborg.
And certainly there was nothing in Karl's conversation to
make you suppose that distaste for his home country was
among his secret reasons for such a prolonged expatriation.
On the contrary. Sweden was the most forward-looking
country in the whole world—and who could know the
whole world so well as he did? Sweden was more modern
than the United States, without any of the ultra-capitalistic
extravagance and nonsense; and more socialistic than the
Soviet Union without any of the disadvantages of Marxist
doctrine slavishly followed. Also Sweden was unique
among western countries in permitting all the sexual
freedom that was good for men and women, with even
besides a generous allowance for variety of sexual taste.
And Karl knew all about these liberal achievements
from the Swedish newspapers and magazines which he
subscribed to, and which he claimed had never failed to
catch up with him no matter where about the world he
might be temporarily settled. For Karl the country of his
birth had become a handy kind of standard measure, a
device that enabled him to read off and decide about all
questions of modern progress wherever encountered; and
it was perhaps his sound judgment not to risk any close
inspection which might have destroyed his confidence in
such a convenient and reliable apparatus.

Among the lodgers there had at first been only Lionel to
know that Karl was not at all the irascible and aggressive
person his appearance suggested. It was curious that he
had like Lionel a weathered face mapped with incised
lines—as though he too had been inscribed with a mysterious message, which it was unfortunately the devil's
own job to decipher. Or it might have been supposed that
Nature had caught up with him in the South Seas to
revive upon his face the more or less discarded Maori
art of *moko*. Perhaps his age-and-weather tattooings were
to warn you off, like the protective designs of the animal
and vegetable world. It had been Lionel who had one day
chanced to be about the house, and assisted Karl to install

in his room some new and handsome furnishings deposited at the front door by a carrier. It was, Karl remarked, furniture in the Swedish style; and if Sweden had done nothing else to benefit New Zealand, at least it had encouraged some improvement in the style and comfort of its movables—which was probably as much as the country deserved anyway, stuck in its present state of stagnation. Who was there prepared to say there was any New Zealander good enough to deserve a Nobel prize?

It was a rhetorical question a good way beyond Lionel's depth; but ever practical and obliging, he smiled and offered to assist Karl stack his native furnishings, poor and grubby and now redundant, out of sight in the dark cave of the cellar beyond his own poor grubbily furnished room. Karl had been grateful. He had taken Lionel back upstairs to his room and seated him on Swedish furniture while he opened two bottles of beer (not Swedish, not Kiwi; a compromise, Danish), besides putting within his easy reach a packet of imported rye bread. And already frankly enjoying the luxury of being taken notice of, Lionel had only to drink his beer to begin to feel important. Prevented from becoming talkative by Karl's keeping always one step ahead of him, he emerged from the occasion happily convinced that everybody was wrong about Karl: he was a good friend for anyone to have if you knew the right way to take him. Also he had agreed to sound out the lodgers one by one about an idea that Karl had talked such a lot about, a plan for improving the quality of lodging house week-ends by bringing everybody together for their midday Sunday dinner.

For Lionel it proved to be a task prolonged far beyond the after-glow of one bottle of Danish beer.

The lodgers were suspicious and they resisted.

It was all very well for Lionel who was for the most part happy-go-lucky because he was short of the full pound—although by no means a total misfortune if you reflected that the missing two or three shillings might well have been reckoned so much counterfeit coinage anyway. In Lionel's view Karl had only wanted to be friendly, and who on earth would want to say a word against that? Instead of the lodgers waiting their turns at the gas stoves on a Sunday morning Karl had said they need only combine and buy the meat and he would be responsible, vegetables pudding the lot.

But WHY?

Somebody was out to confer a favour and somebody was going to be on the receiving end. For what? For nothing?

It didn't add up.

A few words muttered by Miss Bloom suggested hidden thoughts about madmen expert in poisoning.

Who did Karl think he was? What made him think he was such a cook? But Lionel had been informed about that one. He told about the jobs Karl had done all over the world, on land and on ships; and cooking had always earned him the most money of all. Money! Lionel was tempted, and nearly told about the expensive new furniture even though it was his secret and Karl's and nobody else's. Instead he told about Karl's good job as third cook at the big new Tourist Hotel. But an unlikely story! Scepticism remained rampant, and Lionel thought again of the Swedish furniture: it was close at hand, and with Karl's permission might have been checked up on just to prove that neither of them was in the habit of telling lies.

It was Chris, a pensioner, who was most mocking and scornful.

Old Sourface! Chris said that one way and another during his life he'd had a bellyful of Squareheads.

Compared to Lionel, Chris was a raw and innocent recruit to pensioner status. How did a man make ends meet? Affronted by facts of life he hadn't bargained for, Chris wanted to know the answers. He would have been much too often short of the price of a beer if it hadn't been for visits from his 'angel', a family man interested in social good works, who in days when they were soldiers together

had conceived for Chris a powerful emotional friendship
which had never abated. Also it was strange that Chris
should find Karl's face sour—it was as though he had never
looked at his own reflection But perhaps in a glass he saw
something quite different: in the lively years of his life a
carpenter, a good competent tradesman as he readily let
you know, he had been quick and agile on the scaffolding
of giant power-dams, and among the dizzy rafters of vast
timber plants; a man who had often declared himself
fighting fit, hitting the grog at week-ends, eating well on
workdays, yet always keeping his weight down with hard
work. In slippers, with buttons straining to enclose a slack
belly, in grubby shirt and braces, he did not have to say
that now it was all quite different. It was seldom that he
reminded even himself that during far too many working
years he had steadily sold himself a pup—that the work
and the life was nothing much in itself, more a kind of
curtain-raiser to the day when he turned sixty and could
draw the pension. Then with a handful of chips saved up
he would take it easy, live in town and have the pick of
the women that were offering: life would be a long summer
holiday, all that he deserved and had worked for, paying
for in the hard cash of social security tax.... On days when
the sun shone and it was neither cold nor raining he told
himself there was nothing he couldn't stand if it all hadn't
been so tedious: living costs, *Truth* on Tuesdays, *Best
Bets* and a fifty cent double, stews made from cats' meat,
two Sunday papers, lack of a suitable woman (*not* compen-
sated for by his 'angel's' affection)—*everything*!

He was sick with snarling bad temper, his boredom was
an insanity. He told himself he was a bit of old New
Zealand, the genuine thing thrown on the rubbish dump
that nobody cared about any more.

Lionel was nonetheless not discouraged, persisting with
his persuasions until at last all went into reverse when
Dick and Dorrie became suddenly the nucleus of a kind
of snowball—magic because it grew in size at such a speed.
Dick, a hospital orderly, appeared to the eye as nobody

much in particular, a mild little man in his late forties, slight and bald; but he was believed to have fathered in wedlock a dozen children he now wished to have nothing whatsoever to do with; nor with his wife of whom he had only to be reminded and it was a miserable day of migraine. Except for Dorrie there was for Dick no more any general world vouched for by his senses; only a place of shadows without one clearly visible and tangible inhabitant— except Dorrie. And marvellously, his feelings about it all were interchangeable with Dorrie's. She had changed her name by deed poll to coincide with his, and so a convenient and comforting gloss was put upon an irregular situation. They were Dick and Dorrie, a pair who never wished to interfere with anyone, nor ever to be interfered with. But after paying his wife's maintenance, Dick had very little money left over, barely sufficient for food: so to pay the rent Dorrie went out sweeping and cleaning —two vast office floors in a great new glass building, a job which she finished early in the evening. She bought beer on her way home where Dick would have their meal ready and by nine o'clock they would be in bed—and immensely pleased to be there if a surprising variety of noisy endearments was anything to judge by. Early in the morning Dick would be away to work, but Dorrie remained in bed for the day with her beer and cigarettes, and a pile of hot paperbacks which Dick either shoplifted or 'borrowed' from hospital patients. Or she dozed, until it was time for her cleaning again. She never made their bed or cleaned out the room, that was for Dick at week-ends. And Dorrie was a good deal older than Dick, in her late fifties, wrinkled and gaunt: in the night her smoker's cough was heard by all the lodgers, and besides their complaints it evoked throughout the house tremors from grubby furnishings and ancient timbers.

Okey doke, Dick said to Lionel. Why not?

After all, Dorrie continued in bed over the week-end so what they ate was his chore. And although dedicated to meeting her demands, there were times when he remembered he was male to Dorrie's female. If there was any serious question of his taking time off it was a fair general principle that *he* should be the one to decide.

Lionel was delighted to return to all his contacts in reverse order. Jerry, the barman who stayed in bed all day on his days off drinking said:

If lover-boy and doxy Dorrie are going to be in so am I.

Grubby in split and ragged pyjamas, and displeased over being interrupted when he was opening a fresh bottle, he slammed the door.

Shove off, Lionel! You can come again and collect for my share of the meat.

And Slim who was a mutilated war pensioner with an iron brace on his leg, and a drunk too although he drank only to make himself more good-tempered and smiling than it was his habit to be—Slim who when Jerry was idle between jobs would compassionately and for company take him on his rounds of the suburbs where housewives would be sorry about a disabled returned soldier and allow themselves to be persuaded to have their kitchen knives sharpened; thus enabling Slim to earn beer money for both, and even perhaps a little over to help with Jerry's overdue rent—Slim when he was told by Lionel that Jerry had agreed said with smiles that what was good enough for Jerry was good enough for him.

They were at last all willing, even the nondescript Mrs Dashing, the most retired and anonymous lodger of them all, and not appropriately named when believed to be a respectable widow (it was Dorrie who had said, Take a look at her and ask yourself—as though it had never occurred to her that appearances might have provoked the same comment much nearer home).

But then when Lionel reported back to Karl and inquired what meat to buy it was touch and go all over again. The carving on Karl's face remained immobile until he snapped back: *Any* kind of meat! He muttered. He was a cook only a remove or so away from chef. It was

up to them to order. What sort of an insult was it, asking
him to decide!

Lionel was patient. Did Karl mind if he asked how
much meat to buy, because it was something he had to
ask wasn't it? It was a fair question. Karl agreed, and an
amount surprisingly small for so many was mentioned.
'They' were again sceptical. But okay, it was up to a man
to try anything once, he could always tighten his belt,
there were plenty of times in a man's life when he cracked
hearty.

For compensation there was a focus on quality.

Okay, make it pork.

Karl was soon to demonstrate he could make it anything.

Nobody had supposed that Karl would invite his own
guest—and it turned out *two* guests; for Lottie whom he
hastened to answer the door to as his cooking began its
penultimate approach to perfection was accompanied by
her very tiny daughter Coral. Also Lottie and Coral were
allowed into the kitchen, which apart from Lionel nobody
else had been that morning(Whatever you want to do
please go away and do it elsewhere, in the bathroom or
perhaps the toilet would be a good convenient place); although Jerry who had required only a mug of hot water
for his shave had also been an exception. Unfortunately
he had trodden a trifle heavily near the oven in which a
cake was baking, and slow to get Karl's message he had
been astounded to discover himself run out of the room
by the seat of his pants and his pinioned arms. Meanwhile
Karl was twisting his lips over a mixture of Swedish and
Kiwi swearwords. My cake does not tolerate vibrations,
Anglo-Saxon donkey. You want to make it sad, pig? And
so far that day sober, Jerry was surprised to find himself
without a word in reply.

While Karl took time off to stand and chat with his
guests, it was time for one last extension to Lionel's job as
kitchen man. Very very happy that Sunday morning, he had
already been around the lodgers to collect plates for warm-

ing; now he must set places at the kitchen table—although
not until he had borrowed from anywhere anything that
might serve to enlarge it. He must also borrow chairs, and
also remind lodgers not to forget to bring their own knives
and forks, besides spoons for dessert. He must do all this
and that—and all to be climaxed by his grand moment
when he was directed by Karl to go with the iron lid of
a casserole and a large wooden spoon to stand by the old
house's grandly curving staircase, where he was to make
the sound of a gong, although from time to time pausing
while he called in loud and standard Kiwi manner, Come
and get it! And all was done so well, and he resembled so
strongly the brave boy in the verses who was resolved to
remain faithfully at his station no matter what the calamity,
whether the ship or the house might of a sudden burst
out into flames and burn down all around him, that
when with a rattle of cutlery the lodgers began to emerge
from their rooms even cold and stony Jerry was touched on
the nerve to see him so pleased and radiant. It was to
cover up that he said to Slim:

Take a bo-peep at old Lionel. If he's not careful we're all
going to hear him start crowing.

In the kitchen there was already Miss Bloom, who in
her room was only a step away anyhow; and as the landlord's deputy it was only proper for her to appear promptly
and behave as hostess. Old enough for the pension, she
was nonetheless slender and neat in a suit a deep shade of
vue rose: she had been generous with rouge and powder,
eye shadow and eyebrow pencil: her bleached and silky
hair showed itself in curls on top and at the sides, but
behind it hastened to disappear into a woollen bag of many
pastel colours. Miss Bloom's hair-wealth required support,
unchecked it was said to flow to her ankles; but nobody
could claim to speak from the privilege of a personal view.
As the lodgers entered she was in conversation with Lottie;
and was enabled to continue on account of Karl's having
presented to Coral a Japanese girl doll, one that had been
cleverly fashioned to cling wherever it touched and so

330

look very loving. The child was carrying the doll on her shoulder, and the lodgers clustered around to admire this wonder; and it was because Coral belied her name by being Maori-dark that Jerry said:

She knows if she don't hang on tight she gets shoved in a shawl to carry on your back.

Lottie was introduced and shook hands with all except Mrs Dashing, who had at once recognized the young woman as somebody she had previously known as Maureen Rafferty. It was when they had worked together in a factory stitching bras; and after being arrested and fined for being discovered without any lawful excuse in a sea-man's bed on board a ship tied up at the wharves, Maureen had been sacked when she resisted pressure from the staff officer at the bra factory that she would in the future devote herself exclusively to comforting *him*. As Lottie, if a good figure and a smart mini-skirt were to be relied upon, she appeared to be doing rather well for herself. She and Mrs Dashing found each other a mutual embarrassment: from a little distance they smiled a little, and a little nodded.

They were all there and all spruced up for the occasion, even Dorrie with her hair less scraggy after a thorough brushing, and her face behind deep powder looking a trifle obscure and misty like a clever photograph: and there was the additional surprise of some semi-transparent thing, a piece of fancy coloured gauze pinned about her throat and neck to hide the wrinkles. Even her cough seemed to have been temporarily abolished; and Jerry decided he would in the meantime withhold the offer of a packet of lozenges which it had been his forethought to put in his pocket. He also readily decided that since Dorrie had never before been on week-end show, the real purpose of the filmy thing around her neck would be to conceal love-bites inflicted by lover-boy during transports which had today been interrupted right at their peak: and that was for sure.

They were all there, and supervised by Lionel seating

331

themselves—when somebody noticed: Chris, poor old Chris, always grumbling and grizzling, a genuine moaner if ever there was one, *wasn't* there.

Karl was to the point.

I will manage while you fetch him Lionel. I will begin to serve without your services which I value. So hurry.

But instead of serving Karl took from a carton some bottles of dry red wine.

Or I have beer for those who prefer, he said.

He said that he had provided no proper *aperitif*, no. And for that matter no *hors d'oeuvres*, no *consommé*. But there always had to be a beginning. Next time. Today he was recommending the red wine to drink with the Spanish rice, which he would call by a Turkish name if they preferred. *Pilaff.* Although perhaps a word more Persian than Turkish. But a Mediterranean dish, that was what he had decided—nothing Scandinavian, oh no. And more, not anything Nordic—German, English, no. And nothing, not today, nothing New Zealand. No. But something in between, on the way there and back, something half way out and half way in, that meant something Mediterranean, European, the true essence of Europe—yet not altogether because of Africa and Asia which were also Mediterranean. Oil garlic pimento rice. Also tomato, and cheese and sausage. And of course wine. What there is to eat and drink where people are happy. But they must not think he was speaking to alarm them, that was nonsense. He would not for the world overdo it. He had not allowed his hand to slip. He had prepared his enchantment with the flavours of happiness—but with discretion. A taste, a whiff, a suggestion. A *soupçon*—and that last one was the word!

They listened, they were all polite: all except Jerry perhaps, who said:

Take no notice of me, mate. I don't want you to think I'm interrupting. But if you was to offer me a beer while you keep on talking I won't complain.

Karl understood. While he opened a bottle he said that

332

if he was not mistaken Jerry was a native of Australia. He had known a lot of Australians, he had learned to understand their way of straight-speaking, also their great confidence about knowing all the answers.

Slim agreed with Jerry about beer, also Dick and Dorrie. Lottie too. And Mrs Dashing if nobody minded preferring not to take any liquid, it was doctor's orders, there was only Miss Bloom to say yes, she would be glad to try the wine thank you kindly. She hadn't tasted wine since her youngest niece's twenty-first birthday party, that would be more than ten years ago now. And what a surprise! Instead of sweet with a cheerful bouquet it had tasted like something out of the cruet.

For a moment it could have been that Karl would explain about wines. He held it while he supplied Miss Bloom in an off-hand summary kind of manner. Lionel reappeared to announce that Chris was coming: from the sound of clumpings and mutterings there could be no doubt about it, and he entered shadow-boxing. It was possible to detect his one swift passing glance at the company, and immediately he stepped up his performance to give a lively and vigorous display: poor Lionel who waited by the door to see Chris to the table was savagely attacked in shadow-style, and although he escaped destruction from hooks and jabs, straight-lefts and upper-cuts, it was only by infinitesimal fractions: he was an immoblized rabbit, helplessly staring back into Chris's dreadful eyes as he loured and fixed him above his guarding hand. And it went on long enough to become an opportunity for Jerry, who got up to hold an imagined mike in his hand while he rattled off a ringside commentary. And among the company there was perhaps only the tiny Coral who did not understand that Chris's extravagant display was rooted in that one quick glance which had informed him that all the company had spruced itself up for a formal occasion. Nothing of the kind had occurred to poor Chris. Guilty in slippers and braces, he thought of his grubby shirt soaking

333

for the wash. His braces travelled up and over a grubby singlet—that was to say the little that was left of it around the moth holes.

It was unfortunate that while Jerry paused to recover his breath, Karl misjudged the time to be ripe for a sarcastic remark. He said that if Chris took care to eat better he would be in better shape for his boxing career. That was a thing he would say for the European Nordics—although not the English, he was thinking of Germany. The German working man was healthy, and that meant lively with energy in the mind besides the body, because of his wholesome liking for sour cabbage. You only had to compare the bad habits of British people, and he included the local population: soft white bread, it could be made of plastic, with butter from the factory machine: and it went down wallop and splash into a stomachful of sweet tea. It was no wonder about the ulcers. And after a moment of silence it became clear that he had triggered off a burst of self-assertion disguised as sympathetic feeling for Chris. Karl and his natter were all at once ignored while they clapped and shouted. Good for you, old Chris! As though they yearned after him he was begged to come on over, sit down and be in. And come on Jerry too!

Very grim, Karl curtly ordered Lionel to stand by and reach for the hot plates while he served *pilaff*—although only to be interrupted by Chris's plaintive:

Hey, what's wrong with me? Don't I get a beer? What about it? Or do I stink?

It could have been that Karl's mouth was pursed from the strain of not informing him.

And about the food they were polite. Miss Bloom's word was tasty, Dorrie's interesting (Dick agreed and inquired intelligently about culinary details). Mrs Dashing was reminded of the peppery foods her father had become so fond of when he was stationed in the army at Hong Kong: she thought Karl had been too generous with the condiments (but then she was under the doctor). Lottie and Lionel proved themselves hearty and appreciative eaters.

Jerry and Slim were silent while occupying themselves with matters of judgment, searching their plates for pieces of pork and afterwards exchanging their muttered comments. What do you reckon? It don't taste right if you ask me, not when it's pork, not like you'd expect. But they cleaned up their helpings, which had been generous. Only Chris behaved as though he would in no circumstances co-operate. He tried one mouthful and pushed his plate away, saying that if nobody minded he could do with another beer, a request that was ignored until Karl affected a sudden smile. Another beer? Certainly sir. But when he set the glass in front of Chris he remarked: With my compliments, soak.

If it hadn't been for the rapid scrape of Coral's spoon as she cleaned up the last of what Lottie had called her din-din, the silence would have been ominous. But nothing happened. Jerry and Slim pushed back their chairs to sprawl in a manner which suggested that since the meal was over they would now be taking off (although thanks a lot, and God bless you mate).

Karl was quick with a fresh light in his eyes.

My dessert! Another enchantment, which even the Kiwi bird will fall over for, like the ninepin.

While he was serving Jerry began to insist to Miss Bloom that neither toilet bathroom and wash-house conveniences were of a standard that would satisfy the health inspector. Let him come and have a look, and he'd say no landlord was entitled to collect his rent when he was sitting tight and pretty on what was such a bloody disgrace—although tight-arsed and ugly would be a damn sight better description. And he was making no excuses for language which wasn't nearly strong enough by half.

I'll be calling in at the Town Hall this coming week to see the inspector. Because I'm sick of complaining, that's why.

Stale old stuff, it focused so little attention that Jerry aimed at a sensation by indulging himself in a disgraceful license. Seated alongside Miss Bloom, he reached up to twitch her many-coloured pastel-bag, causing it to tilt sideways so that all the bagged-up wealth of hair was suddenly tumbled out. Reaction was limited to a quick collective gasp, although Coral was loudest with something that resembled a laugh. And Jerry even Jerry, so much put out by his own bad behaviour, swiftly created his further misfortune by a blundering attempt at compensation. When Miss Bloom stood up, stooping sideways to shake out and retrieve her hair (and although short of her ankles it fell past her knees), he reached to grasp the full wad in his two hands.

Lovely stuff, he said. A woman's hair is her crowning glory, so they say. And when it's a kind of silk and cream she deserves a better name than Maggie. Listen you people, it's an introduction. Meet our Miss Magnolia Bloom.

In a whispering trembling voice Miss Bloom said, Excuse me. And after she had stepped a little shakily into her own room she softly closed the door.

There was a sad and embarrassing lack of enthusiam for Karl's cherry sponge together with what he called his dessert of discovery, his description for a chocolate *mousse* hidden away inside a thick sweet coating of meringue.

Chris had sat morose and abstracted with his hands cupped about his half-drunk beer, but now that everyone was making excuses he noisily got up to resume his shadow-boxing. But besides his fists his mouth was working, and from time to time his words made sense.   There were people who had never learned how to behave in front of a lady. There were people who had never learned to recognize a lady when they saw one. There were things no man would say in front of a lady. There were things no New Zealander who also deserved the name of a man would stand for. There were people born in foreign countries who had to be taught not to abuse Kiwi hospitality. . . .

His movements about the room left off being aimless, were directed instead towards Karl and Jerry each in turn. But his words became more general, with their drift not so easy to decipher. When in Rome, everybody knew that motto. He had never been in Rome. Paris. The time of the Great War. *Great*, mind you. Not the one you had to call two or nobody would know. He joined up as a lad with the milk still wet on his lips under a false age. Paris. Them days. Paris. There was a bathroom with a biddy, red lamp district. Talk about conveniences. How many of these young Kiwis had ever seen a biddy? A biddy wasn't anything necessary, a convenience but it wasn't necessary.

Karl interrupted with a laugh.

Our friend means to say a *bidet*, he said. That is good. Not a necessary convenience, but very handy.

He explained that you shifted off the toilet and on to the *bidet*. To wash your bottom. Very convenient. Very sanitary and satisfying. A comfort. It was time this country—ah! Took a jerry to itself. Ha ha. Yes, took the hint.

Shadow-boxing, Chris approached him very close. He loured, his mouth worked overtime and his sentences came fluently. Foreigners were ignorant. The French were ignorant and couldn't read their own language. There was a town called Albert. It was written down plain, Albert. But the Froggy soldiers were ignorant. They could read Albert plain, and they said Alber. Ha ha.

In Karl's laugh there was the cruelty of exasperation. As though dismissing the company after having had quite enough he distributed the wine and beer left over.

Lottie Coral and Lionel were left, and Chris shadow-boxed.

The cook has finished, Lionel, Karl said. It is you for the wash-up, but no hurry. It will interest Lottie to see my furniture and sit on it, so please a favour. An eye on Coral if you please. Perhaps take her for a walk, and *there*—something for an ice-cream. And please remember, plenty of time.

There remained only Chris, with nobody to see as his shadow-gestures slowed to a standstill. He leaned with his hands on the table until he noticed that Karl had filled up his glass. While he slumped into his chair his hand reached out; but instead he swept a place clear on the table to fold his arms before lowering upon them his dejected and desolate head.

There was something not wholly certain about the Sunday afternoon torpor. It enveloped the house, yet was nothing that could be defined or measured; for the sound good reason that so much of it was subjective, an emanation from anyone who might happen to be aware of any such thing as Sunday afternoon torpor. You might be acute enough to think 'Sunday afternoon torpor', yet immediately knew there never could be any such generalized thing. Because if there was anything certain in the world it was that each person had his or her own particular and private thing to constitute a powerful and dominating reason why he or she had not long ago decided to quit living in a world, and most particularly upon a Sunday afternoon, where there existed absolutely nothing, publicly exhibited and approved, which could be positively reckoned worth living for.

About the house there were the vaguest sounds and signs, it might be the drone of conversation or the rhythm of furniture that gently rocked, sighs protests suppressed laughter, each and every thing combined and contributed. . . . Lottie nestled with closed eyes, with fingers knotted upon handfuls of Karl's hair. But so good, believe me I am honest, next after the Japanese you are the best. Yes yes, tiny men, not like you, tiny all over but they know like you how to please a girl. Karl said it was like using a paint brush, it might be a big or a little brush, it all depended on knowing how to do a good job with the brush you had. Lottie said how could she explain to the cops? When a girl wants it to be good it's her best chance to try on the ships. . . . Mrs Dashing had surrounded herself with photograph albums. And that, she said to her imagined visitor, is daddy. And I think, really and truly I do, it's daddy at his best. In every photograph there was daddy; daddy mounted among the hounds; daddy in the conservatory among the orchids; daddy strolling across a carpet of bluebells beneath the sumptuous elms. Ah, she said, we look out our window here in this country and see a *very* different scene. . . . Dick was insisting that Dorrie had had her ration for the week. No Dick no, you're being a meany? He pointed at the marked-off chart pinned up above the chest of drawers. It adds up to a dozen, and that's not counting one repeat I forgot to record. Give us a break for God's sake Dorrie, think of my years. For answer she drummed her fists on his chest—and then for five minutes while all her energy went into her cough he was granted a reprieve. Think of *my* years, Dick, the years when I won't be here. My boy you'll miss me then, *then* you'll wish— He pressed the palm of his hand firmly on her mouth. All right Dorrie, go ahead. But dry up for God's sake. And on one condition—you do all the work, it's your thing not mine, and I don't want to know a thing about it, and why should I when I'm in the middle of this story in *Truth*? . . . Miss Bloom nestled. Her immense wad of hair was bundled up and cuddled in her arms. You poor darling, she whispered, oh what an outrage, my darling can you ever forgive me? But you must, without you whatever would become of me, without one thing left in the world to live for. And it was all a little unpleasant since her bundle had become so uncomfortably wet, saturated with her tears. . . . Only Jerry and Slim were totally silent, each remote in the oblivion of beer. . . .

Immediately upon waking Chris was conscious of a demand. He had an obligation to meet. He remembered Karl had said—well, he had handed over that innocent child to an old man. Lionel! Lionel was to keep an eye on the child. *Keep her amused!* Nobody was going to fool him, not old Chris. He had seen the inside of Lionel's room, several times. He had seen the pin-ups. Nobody could fool him, Lionel's pin-ups were all over the wall of the hole he lived in, and they were all a lot of little girls, not a one that wasn't well under age. But what made his obligation so urgent was that he had wakened with a remembered squeal ringing in his ears. He listened, and the house couldn't have been more silent. But if required he would swear to the squeal. He tried to remember. A squeal? A scream? But it was a squeal. There were squeals and squeals. It was said sometimes, 'a squeal of delight'. But more often people squealed when they were frightened or threatened or hurt. ... And then he had no more need to remember. It was the same squeal, and it came from beneath the kitchen floor, from the hole that Lionel lived in. And it was the squeal of delight. Of fun. Somebody was pleased. The demand that he meet his obligation was desperately urgent.

Through a crack in Lionel's makeshift door hooked shut he looked and saw Lionel holding the little girl on his knee while he showed her his pin-ups. It seemed too that he was making up stories about them. This one lived on a farm and rode a horse, or sometimes she went with a basket to gather mushrooms, and sit for a rest on a toadstool. Once the fairies came out to play with her and she was introduced to the fairy queen. Chris saw the little girl, innocent little Coral, squirm. Again it was a squeal—and again she had squealed because she was pleased.

Chris was very silent on the stairs. He looked through Karl's keyhole but only to be disappointed: that emergency had been provided against. He applied his ear, holding his breath—and was marvellously gratified to identify a squeal that had been taken firmly in hand, damped down until it wore the disguise of a giggle. Fast and silent down the stairs, Chris lit all the gas jets in the kitchen before he loosely piled heaps of old newspapers on the stoves: over the newspapers he spread all the butter and fat he could find. For draught he opened the windows wide, and then he went silently out the front door of the house leaving it open. In the street, out in the middle of the empty roadway, he began again his shadow-boxing.

It wasn't until the smoke was beginning to billow that the house came to life; and Lionel was the first to appear, dragging a screaming and crying Coral by the hand. He never hesitated, disengaging from Coral to run clumsily but fast to the turn in the street, where he quickly removed his shoe to break the glass on the fire-alarm. From under the billowing smoke Karl appeared in his dressing-gown, with an arm protecting a clothed but dishevelled Lottie. Mrs Dashing emerged through her ground-floor window, looking a little flustered with her arms enclosing a bundle of photograph albums. Karl was addressing rapid questions to Chris who took no notice and continued to shadow-box. Somewhere in among all that smoke were Jerry and Slim, Dick and Dorrie, and Miss Bloom most terribly trapped in her room off the kitchen. Chris became more and more absorbed in his shadow-boxing—and then, just a few moments before the firemen, there arrived in a little car his 'angel'. A little man with sparse hair and thick-lensed glasses, he stood pigeon-toed, smiling while he opened his arms to his friend—as though the one thing about the calamity that mattered was Chris's survival. Chris shadow-boxed in his direction, moving steadily in until as the sirens screamed he landed a terrible upper-cut. Even the firemen were for a moment petrified to see Chris's 'angel' float horizontally in the air, briefly transformed into something which appeared to justify its name.

MAKING FATHER PAY

Strangers were sometimes in doubt which was the father and which the son. A slight figure cut off short, with snowy hair that went well with smooth red-apple cheeks, father would never see ninety again. He was Old Charlie. Twenty years behind him (and for that reason Young Charlie), his son was an astonishing copy, except that a mild look of worry replaced the repose of the older man's features. Or was it that *his* apples were wrinkled as though gathered from the grass instead of picked fresh from the tree.

Once upon a time there had been the old lady to keep an eye on the pair of them. But years ago she had as you might say left her son to carry the baby—and because of father's eccentric behaviour the expression is apt. Long retired from a business partnership, he was said to be very well-off, although in these long latter years there was nobody to say he had ever been seen to spend money —but that is to say apart from the single exception of a bout of paint-buying. The intention had been that Young Charlie, who in his day had been a painter and paperhanger, would do the house up. Nothing had ever come of it, but the paint remained stacked in many out of the way corners: and in any case all was forgotten when the old man became devoted to fishing.

It is, however, doubtful whether that last word is the right one—for despite his daily angling, this fisherman was never deterred by the absolute lack of any trace of stream lake pond or sea within at least a mile from where

Making Father Pay

he sat with rod line float and baited hook. Seated on his little wooden stool he fished the little front lawn. And since the suburb was seaside, and as such inhabited by a great variety of amateur fishermen, there were many citizens to stop and look in at the gateway through the thick high wall of hedge: there would be waggish comment besides good advice about how to catch the fish that appeared to be fished for. It was generally believed to be piper the old man must be after, the more especially as there was no mistaking the gentles he from time to time baited his hook with: wriggling and writhing, they made the oatmeal in the jam jar at his feet look very much alive.

It is not my purpose to suggest any rational explanation for the old man's eccentric behaviour: sufficient to say that besides appearing to spend his daylight hours in a most satisfying occupation, he enjoyed good health and ate and slept well: also he seemed never to hear the advice, the funny comments and questions so very often directed towards him from over the front gate.

But what began eventually to happen in the mind of his son is perhaps another matter.

For a good part of each day Young Charlie would sit on the verandah. Clearly he was keeping an eye on the old man, but it might also have been noted that the paperbacks he read would often concern themselves with the question of somebody's mysterious disappearance. And a sharp observer might have noticed it was the same thing with a good many newspaper items (and indeed, not so long after the events of my story there were those who remembered a tavern-occasion when the whereabouts of a certain Mr Turfnell-Turner were discussed: he was the missing inhabitant of a topcrust suburb, a very helpless, very aged man who had quite unaccountably disappeared: and when it was Young Charlie's turn to say what he thought about the mystery he hadn't hesitated: 'It's easy, his old lady ate him.' But this macabre

343

solution was too much: exclamations were followed by uneasy laughter, and then silence).

Also, there was afterwards almost nobody to dispute that about this time Young Charlie's look of worry seemed to be mysteriously erased from his features. It was as though he must have found a new interest in life —and yet, quiet surprising when he continued to complain to neighbours and tavern-cronies about the burden his aged parent could be. But there was sympathy. It was remembered that in the old man's much younger days, long before the era of over-population, he had owned a large empty block of land in what was now a busy crowded suburb: yet always it had been said his hand was tight upon the purse-strings: it was believed he had been reluctant to lend a hand to his bachelor son in the difficult times of that long-ago Slump when house-painting jobs were simply not to be had. And to descend to petty matters—it was no secret to near neighbours that harsh words were sometimes heard upon the subject of gentles: there had always to be a good-sized lump of rotten meat strung up in the lemon tree just outside the kitchen door—to be flyblown, and so ensure a good supply of gentles for regular transfer to the fattening oat-meal of the jam jar. There were times when the voice of Young Charlie could be heard several doors away: his curses were for smells flies maggots and old men.

But as a topic of conversation, what was soon to become even more interesting than the effacement of Young Charlie's look of worry, was father's own sudden trans-figured appearance. Nothing could be done about snow on his head, or cheeks like red apples, nor was anything called for (it would be to interfere with perfection), but the clothing he had worn on and on since the time of the old lady had become more and more a shabby disgrace. Sudden transformation was at first almost not to be believed; and since the old man never left the property, clearly had been up to Young Charlie. Overnight father had ceased to be a drab old man—had become instead a most enchanting garden gnome: animated however, and the fishing instead of being absurd was now absolutely right. And so were the colours. Nobody had supposed that Young Charlie could prove himself so signally yet secretly gifted with such splendid imagination. Red woollen cap with gold tassel, green pullover, dark-blue corduroy trousers which tucked into multi-coloured shining boots—the figure was one which might be fancifully thought to belong among the magic signs of the zodiac. And from the comments of appreciating citizens who looked in over the gate, you could readily infer there would be no disagreement.

But in the event there appeared to be no doubt it had been no part of Young Charlie's serious intentions to put his father on public view all dressed in his finery—not as a free show, and not just yet anyway. It had not, as it were, been opening day, and the preview was quickly put an end to.

Nor was it until some months had elapsed (and the front gateway was so effectively boarded up nobody could look in any more), that Young Charlie had completed his preparatory labours: and because of the great thick dividing hedges neighbours had not been able to see in either, nor for the most part had there been anything unusual to hear—and indeed, it had seemed that even harsh words about smells or whatever had for the time being ceased. But for all that there had been a fine and beautiful morning when a great lorry, with a huge slowly revolving bowl of certified concrete mixture, had pulled outside the back gate. It had afterwards gingerly backed on to the property: and before departing had also delivered a labour-saving machine for spraying liquid cement on appropriate surfaces.

But all was surmise until the day when two passing fishermen were astonished to see that a bell had been fixed to the boarded-up front gateway, with a notice attached which said, PLEASE RING TO SEE GARDEN ORNAMENT. ENTRANCE PRICE 5C.

Young Charlie answered the bell, and afterwards the two citizens agreed the charge was not excessive. Old Charlie was not of course on view, but the fishing gnome was magnificient, a work of art if ever there was one. Young Charlie's drinking friends had all many times been told about the paint stored in the house for so many years—and what marvellous use had now been made of it! There it all was, red cap and gold tassel, red cheeks, green torso, and the trunk lower down a dark-blue ... all solid shining fresh, yes, fresh as paint! And of course fishing! And what was so very marvellous, the final triumph so to speak, all (as every good work of art always should be) that little bit extra to life-size.

Who can doubt that someday the cops will catch up on the culprit?—and I have myself seen one of them rest his elbow on the top of the red cap while he inquires from Young Charlie when he expects his father to return from a protracted visit to a brother in Australia. But who can know exactly all that he had to put up with in the lifetime of the old man?—who of course had to go sometime anyhow. Sometimes I imagine a moment before the cement covered his eyes—a sudden look in them which said, 'Thank you, son—thank you for conferring upon me this Immortality.'

Meantime lots of people, visitors, tourists and the rest, find it worthwhile to pay the five cents.

BIBLIOGRAPHY OF FRANK SARGESON'S IMAGINATIVE WRITING

Previous Appearance of Stories in This Collection

(CU, *Conversation with My Uncle and Other Sketches*; MW, *A Man and His Wife*; TS, *That Summer and Other Stories*; L, *Landfall*. Final entries in square brackets give the source of the text used in this collection.)

A Final Cure. *Landfall*, June 1967; Vincent O'Sullivan (ed.): *New Zealand Short Stories*, third series (Wellington, 1975). [L]

A Good Boy. First titled 'Sketch from Life', *CU*; as 'A Good Boy', *MW*; A. Thompson, P. Jefferson, B. Derbyshire (eds): *English First 5* (London, 1971). [MW]

A Great Day. *Bulletin*, 17 November 1937; *MW; Penguin New Writing*, No. 5, April 1941; *TS*; John Lehmann (ed.): *English Stories from New Writing* (London), *Best Stories from New Writing* (New York) 1951. [MW]

A Hen and some Eggs. *New Directions in Prose and Poetry*, No. 4, 1938; *Lady Newall's New Zealand Gift Book* (Wellington, 1943); Roger Sharrock (ed.): *English Short Stories of Today*, fourth series (London, 1976); *TS*. [Typescript]

A Man and his Wife. *Tomorrow*, 20 December 1939; *MW; Folios of New Writing*, Spring 1941; *TS; Queen* (London), 7 April 1965; A. Rutherford and D. Hannah (eds): *Commonwealth Short Stories* (London, 1971). [MW]

A Man of Good Will. First titled 'A Man Among his Neighbours', *Bulletin*, 24 December 1941; as 'A Man of Good Will', *New Writing and Daylight*, No. 4, Winter, 1943–4; *TS*; Phoebe C. Meikle (ed.): *Short Stories by New Zealanders* (Auckland, 1970); W. H. New (ed.): *Four Hemispheres* (Toronto, 1971). [Typescript]

An Affair of the Heart. *Auckland Star*, 24 December 1936, second prize in a Christmas story competition; *New Writing*, n. s. No. 3, Christmas 1939; *MW; Penguin New Writing*, No. 8, July 1941; *TS*. [MW]

An Attempt at an Explanation. *Tomorrow*, 29 September 1937; *MW; The Listener* (London), 10 April 1941. [MW]

An Englishwoman Abroad. *Tomorrow*, 24 May 1939; *MW; TS*. [MW]

An International Occasion. *Landfall*, December 1969. [L]

A Pair of Socks. *Tomorrow*, 11 November 1936; *MW; TS; World Digest* (London), January 1947. [MW]

A Piece of Yellow Soap. *Tomorrow*, 28 August 1935; *CU*. [CU]

Beau. *Mate*, June 1965. [Typescript]

Big Ben. *N.Z. Listener*, 15 November 1940. [Typescript]

Boy. *Tomorrow*, 20 July 1938; *Time and Tide*, 11 February 1939; *MW; TS*; R. G. Wilson and J. C. Kellett, (eds): *What is English*, Book One (Auckland, 1970). [MW]

Cats by the Tail. *Tomorrow*, 31 July 1935; *CU; Time and Tide*, 22 May 1937. [CU]

Charity Begins at Home. *Landfall*, September 1966. [L]

Chaucerian. *Tomorrow*, 4 September 1935; *CU*. [CU]

City and Suburban. *Landfall*, March 1965; C. K. Stead (ed.): *New Zealand Short Stories*, second series (London, 1966). [L]

Conversation with my Uncle. *Tomorrow*, 24 July 1935; *CU; Time and Tide*, 16 January 1937; *MW; TS*. [MW]

Cow-pats. *Tomorrow*, 6 January 1937; *New Directions in Prose and Poetry*, No. 4, 1938; *MW*; Phoebe C. Meikle (ed.): *Short Stories by New Zealanders* (Auckland, 1970). [MW]

Bibliography

'Gods Live in Woods'. *N.Z. Listener*, 29 October 1943; *New Directions in Prose and Poetry*, No. 9, 1946; *TS.* [Typescript]

Good Samaritan. *Tomorrow*, 4 March 1936; *CU*; *Time and Tide*, 19 June 1937; *MW*; Phoebe C. Meikle (ed.): *Short Stories by New Zealanders* (Auckland, 1970). [MW]

In the Department. *Weekly News*, 9 June 1937; *MW*; *TS.* [MW]

In the Midst of Life. *Tomorrow*, 2 October 1935; *CU.* [CU]

I've Lost my Pal. *CU*; *Man* (Sydney), October 1938; MW. [MW]

Just Trespassing, Thanks. *Landfall*, June 1964. (Katherine Mansfield Memorial Award 1965); Phoebe C. Meikle (ed.): *Short Stories by New Zealanders* (Auckland, 1970). [L]

Last Adventure. First titled 'The Near and the Far', *Weekly News*, 8 December 1937; *N.Z. Herald*, 9 December 1937. As 'Last Adventure', *MW*; *TS*; D. M. Davin (ed.): *New Zealand Short Stories* (London, 1953). [MW]

Letter to a Friend. *N.Z. Listener*, 29 March 1944; Bill Manhire (ed.): *N.Z. Listener Short Stories*, Vol. 2 (Wellington, 1978). [Typescript]

Making Father Pay. *N.Z. Listener*, 7 June 1975; Bill Manhire (ed.): *N.Z. Listener Short Stories* (Wellington, 1977). [Typescript]

Miss Briggs. *Tommorow*, 2 February 1938; *MW*; *TS.* [MW]

Old Man's Story. *MW;* *Angry Penguins* (Adelaide), 1945; *TS;* filmed as *Old Man's Story* (Zero 16 Ltd, 197*). *TS.* [MW]

Park Seat. *Book* (Christchurch), No. 2, May 1941; Phoebe C. Meikle (ed.); *Short Stories by New Zealanders* (Auckland, 1970). [Typescript]

Sale Day. *New Directions in Prose and Poetry*, No. 4, 1939; *MW.* [MW]

Showers. First titled 'What Do You Think?' *N.Z. Listener*, 9 February 1945. [Typescript]

Bibliography

That Summer. Written 1938–41. *Penguin New Writing*, Nos 17–19, 1943–4; *TS*. [Typescript]

The Colonel's Daughter. *Landfall*, March 1955. [Typescript]

The Hole That Jack Dug. Frank Sargeson (ed.): *Speaking for Ourselves* (Christchurch and Melbourne), 1945; *TS*. [Typescript]

The Last War. *Tomorrow*, 11 September 1935; *CU*; *MW*; Phoebe C. Meikle (ed.): *Short Stories by New Zealanders* (Auckland, 1970). (MW)

The Making of a New Zealander. *Tomorrow*, 18 January 1939. Awarded first prize (equal) in the short story section of the Centennial Literary Competitions, 1940. *MW*; *Penguin New Writing*, No. 13, June 1942; *TS*; D. M Davin (ed.): *New Zealand Short Stories* (London, 1953). [MW]

The Undertaker's Story. *Landfall*, June 1954; Charles Brasch (ed.): *Landfall Country*, 1962; C. K. Stead (ed.): *New Zealand Short Stories*, second series (London, 1966). [Typescript]

They Gave her a Rise. *Tomorrow*, 14 October 1936; *MW*; *TS*; Phoebe C. Meikle (ed.): *Short Stories by New Zealanders* (Auckland, 1970). [MW]

Three Men. Originally sub-titled 'Variation of an old Theme', *Tomorrow*, 1 September 1937; *MW;* TS. [MW]

Tod. *Tomorrow*, 11 May 1938; *MW*; *Folios of New Writing*, Spring 1941. [MW]

Toothache. *Tomorrow*, 2 March 1938; *Time and Tide*, 6 August 1938; Arthur Sewell (ed.): *The Practice of Prose*, (Auckland, 1942); *MW*. [MW]

Two Worlds. *N.Z. Listener*, 7 November 1941; Beatrice Davis (ed.): *Coast to Coast 1942* (Sydney, 1943); *TS*; Phoebe C. Meikle (ed.): *Short Stories by New Zealanders* (Auckland, 1970). [Typescript]

White Man's Burden. *Tomorrow*, 8 January 1936; *CU*; *New Writing*, n.s. No. 1, Autumn 1938; *MW;* *TS*. [MW]

Translations of some of these stories have appeared in

periodicals or anthologies in Denmark, Holland, Italy, Poland and the Soviet Union.
See also under the heading: Published Volumes.

Other Imaginative Writing in Periodicals

Life is Like That. *Australian Woman's Mirror*, 17 October 1933. Re-titled 'Three Women', *Auckland Star*, 19 September 1936, winner of a monthly story competition. An earlier version, very different in style and treatment, of 'Three Men'.

Conversation with a Landlady. *Tomorrow*, 7 August 1935.

Alma Mater. *Tomorrow*, 9 October 1935.

Noblesse Oblige. *Tomorrow*, 6 November 1935.

Rising Above It. *Tomorrow*, 20 November 1935.

Boarding-house Notes. *Tomorrow*, 19 February 1936.

From a Lady Editor's Notebook. *Tomorrow*, 29 April 1936.

Bed-time Story. *Tomorrow*, 2 September 1936.

Radio Talk. *Tomorrow*, 17 March 1937.

The Town of Troyes. *Tomorrow*, 12 May 1937.

A New Zealand Anthology

  I Horse Lords. *Tomorrow*, 27 October 1937.

 II Spur of Moment. *Tomorrow*, 24 November 1937.

III The Teeny Land. *Tomorrow*, 8 December 1937.

IV Ticket to Heaven or
    Cling to your Cheque. *Tomorrow*, 5 January 1938.

 V (a) Hollyhocks and Hailstones.
      (b) Egbert the Blade. *Tomorrow*, 19 January 1938.
                 Parodies of contemporary prose-writers.

Two Sketches for a People's Theatre

  1. Crisis in Czecho-slovakia. *Tomorrow*, 14 September 1938.

  2. Women in Politics. *Tomorrow*, 28 September 1938.

Episode. *New Zealand New Writing*, No. 1, 1942. Extract from 'That Summer'.

Growing Up. *New Zealand New Writing*, No. 3, 1944.
    Re-titled 'Old Goat, Young Lamb', *Southern Stories*,

Bibliography

Poems and Paintings (Melbourne, 1945). Extract from *When the Wind Blows*.

It Shows That Sinatra Can Be a Good Influence. *N.Z. Listener*, 19 January 1945.

When the Wind Blows. *Penguin New Writing*, Nos 27–29, 1946–7.

Up onto the Roof and Down Again. *Landfall*, December 1950–December 1951. An autobiographical essay. Part II reprinted in C. Brasch (ed.): *Landfall Country*, 1962.

Aunt Emily's Eiderdown. *Arena*, March 1952.

I for One. *Landfall*, June 1952. A short novel.

The Problem of Pocket Money. *Landfall*, June 1958. Extract from a novel then in progress, *Memoirs of a Peon*.

A Ponsonby Wake. *Mate,* November 1958. Extract from *Memoirs of a Peon*.

Prologue to *The Taming of The Shrew, Landfall,* March 1961. Verse.

Beginnings. *Landfall*, June 1965. Reprinted in R. Dudding (ed.): *Beginnings: New Zealand Writers Tell How They Began Writing* (Wellington, 1980).

Summer Days. *Mate*, August 1966. Extract from *The Hangover*.

An Imaginary Conversation, William Yate and Samuel Butler. *Landfall*, December 1966.

Conversation in a Train. *Landfall*, December 1967.

Father, and a Friend. *Landfall*, March 1970. Extract from *A Game of Hide and Seek*.

The Power of Thought (An encouraging fable). 'R. M. Shaw'. *Landfall*, September 1972. 'The Power of Thought' also appeared in the *Melbourne Herald*.

Riding High. *N.Z. Listener*, 3 November 1973.

Romantic Agony. *N.Z. Listener*, 16 February 1974.

En Route. *Islands*, March 1978. Extract from *En Route*. This issue of *Islands* was published 'In Celebration, for Frank Sargeson at 75' and includes stories and prose extracts from his work, as well as tributes to and memoirs of the man and commentaries on and reviews of his work.

Bibliography

Published Volumes

(A more detailed bibliography to 1950 is in Helen Shaw
(ed.): *The Puritan and the Waif.*)

Conversation with My Uncle and Other Sketches. Auckland:
Unicorn Press, 1936. 29pp. Stapled, paper cover. Stories.

A Man and His Wife. Christchurch: Caxton Press, 1940.
113pp. Sewn, casebound. Stories.—Cheap edition,
1941. Stapled, fold-over cover.

—2nd revised edition. Wellington: Progressive Pub-
lishing Society, 1944. 96pp. Sewn, casebound.—Cheap
edition, 1944. Stapled, fold-over cover.

When the Wind Blows. Christchurch: Caxton Press, 1945.
92pp. Sewn, boards. A short novel, being the first section of *I Saw in My Dream.*

That Summer and Other Stories. London: John Lehmann,
1946. 192pp. Sewn, casebound. Stories.

—A French translation by Jeanne Fournier-Pargoire, *Cet
été-là,* published in Paris by Editions du Bateau-Ivre,
1946.

I Saw in My Dream. London: John Lehmann, 1949.
279pp. Sewn, casebound. A novel.

I for One. Christchurch: Caxton Press, dated 1954 but
actually published in 1956. 58pp. Sewn, fold-over cover. A short novel.

Wrestling with the Angel: Two Plays. A Time for Sowing and
The Cradle and the Egg. Christchurch: Caxton Press,
dated 1964 but published 1965. 120pp. Sewn, casebound.

Collected Stories, 1935–1963, with an introduction by Bill
Pearson. Bibliography, etc. New Zealand edition, Auck-
land: Blackwood & Janet Paul, 1964. Reprinted 1966;
Longman Paul, 1969. 304pp. Sewn, casebound.
Reprinted with additional stories as *The Stories of
Frank Sargeson,* 1973. 352pp. Sewn, casebound. Paper-
back edition of *The Stories of Frank Sargeson,* 1973.

353

Reprinted 1974, 1975, 1978, 1980. London: MacGibbon & Kee, 1965. 273pp. Sewn, casebound.

Memoirs of a Peon. London: MacGibbon & Kee, 1965. 288pp. Sewn, casebound. A novel.

—2nd edition. Auckland: Heinemann Educational Books, 1974.

The Hangover. London: MacGibbon & Kee, 1967. 160pp. Sewn, casebound. A novel.

Joy of the Worm. London: MacGibbon & Kee, 1969. 159pp. Sewn, casebound. A novel.

Man of England Now, with *I for One* and *A Game of Hide and Seek*. Three novellas. London: Martin Brian and O'Keeffe, 1972. 233pp. Sewn, casebound. New Zealand edition, Christchurch: Caxton Press, 1972.

Once Is Enough. A Memoir. London: Martin Brian and O'Keeffe, 1973. 133pp. Sewn, casebound. New Zealand edition, Wellington: A.H. and A.W. Reed, 1973.

Damals im Sommer. Collected stories: a German translation by Hermann and Margot Stiehl. Munich: Biederstein Verlag, 1968. 288pp. Sewn, casebound.

A Pair of Socks. Selected stories: a Bulgarian translation by Ana Kovacheva. The Library for Workers, Sofia: 'Profizdat', 1970. 151pp. Sewn, paper cover.

More than Enough. A Memoir. London: Martin Brian and O'Keeffe, 1975. 160pp. Sewn, casebound. New Zealand edition, Wellington: A.H. and A.W. Reed, 1975.

Sunset Village. London: Martin Brian and O'Keeffe, 1976. 92pp. Sewn, casebound. New Zealand edition, Wellington: A.H. and A.W. Reed, 1976. A short novel.

Never Enough! London: Martin Brian and O'Keeffe, 1977. 144pp. Sewn, casebound. New Zealand edition, Wellington: A.H. and A.W. Reed, 1976. A memoir.

Tandem (with Edith Campion—*The Chain*), *En Route*. Wellington: A.H. and A.W. Reed, 1979. 168pp. Sewn, casebound. A novella.

Sargeson. One-volume publication of *Once is Enough, More than Enough* and *Never Enough!* Auckland: Penguin Books (N.Z.) Ltd, 1981. 432pp. Paper cover.

Bibliography
Edited by Frank Sargeson

Speaking for Ourselves. Christchurch: Caxton Press, and Melbourne: Reed and Harris, 1945. Stapled, paper covers. A collection of stories by Australian and New Zealand writers.

Plays Performed

A Time for Sowing. A three-act play produced in the Auckland Art Gallery, May 1961, by Christopher Cathcart.
The Cradle and the Egg. A three-act comedy produced in the Auckland Art Gallery, June 1962, by Christopher Cathcart.

Unpublished Works

A number of stories, 1928–35.
A novel of 65,000 words, 1930.
A three-act play, 1934.

COMMENTARY

Mr Sargeson has contributed essays and articles mainly on literary subjects to *Tomorrow*, the *Auckland Star* (reprinted in the *Christchurch Star-Sun*), the Christchurch *Press* (reprinted in the *Southland Times*), the *N.Z. Listener*, *Landfall*, *Here and Now* and *Numbers*. Other articles have appeared in the *N.Z. School Journal* and the *People's Voice*. Reviews of books and plays have appeared mainly in *Tomorrow*, *N.Z. Listener*, *Parson's Packet*, *Landfall* and *Islands*. Items of light verse have appeared mainly in *Tomorrow*.

Some of the radio commentary which appeared over the name of Ben Bolt in the *Observer* (Auckland) was written by Frank Sargeson. Comment in *Tomorrow* appeared over his own name, the initial 'S.', and the pseudonyms 'Sarge' and 'A Radical Man About Town'.

SELECT LIST OF WRITING
ABOUT FRANK SARGESON

James K. Baxter: 'When the Wind Blows', *Canta* (Christ-church: Canterbury University College Students' Association), 7 July 1948.

Robert Chapman: Review of *That Summer and Other Stories*. *Landfall*, September 1947.

—'Fiction and the Social Pattern', *Landfall*, March 1953. Reprinted in Wystan Curnow (ed.): *Essays on New Zealand Literature*. Auckland: Heinemann Educational Books, 1973. A detailed study of New Zealand society in relation to the themes of Frank Sargeson and other writers of fiction.

R.A. Copland: 'The Goodly Roof: Some Comments on the Fiction of Frank Sargeson', in Wystan Curnow (ed.): *Essays on New Zealand Literature*. Auckland: Heinemann Educational Books, 1973.

—'Frank Sargeson: *Memoirs of a Peon*', in Cherry Hankin (ed.): *Critical Essays on the New Zealand Novel*. Auckland: Heinemann Educational Books, 1976.

—*Frank Sargeson*. Wellington: O.U.P. (New Zealand writers and their work series), 1976.

Dennis McEldowney: *Frank Sargeson in his Time*. Dunedin: McIndoe, 1977.

William Plomer: 'Some Books from New Zealand', *Penguin New Writing*, No. 17, 1943.

H. Winston Rhodes: 'The Stories of Frank Sargeson'. *N.Z. Libraries*, September 1947.

Select List of Writing about Frank Sargeson

—'The Moral Climate of Sargeson's Stories'. *Landfall*, March 1955. Reprinted in Charles Brasch (ed.): *Landfall Country*, 1962. A reprint of Professor Rhodes's contribution to *The Puritan and the Waif*.

—*Frank Sargeson*. New York: Twayne Publishers, Inc. (World Authors Series), 1969.

Helen Shaw (ed.): *The Puritan and the Waif*. Auckland, 50 copies cyclostyled by H.L. Hofmann, 1954. Second printing of 50 copies, 1955. Essays by D'Arcy Cresswell, James K. Baxter, Walter Allen, E.P. Dawson, H. Winston Rhodes, Erik Schwimmer, Helen Shaw and Dan Davin. Out of print.